PRAISE FOR
AN UNCOMMON EDUCATION

"Elizabeth Percer brings the clarity and sophistication of the short form into her affecting debut novel about a young woman with lessons to learn. . . . Percer's gift lies in making Naomi—and her family, friends, and lovers—utterly, absorbingly real. *An Uncommon Education* feels like the kind of all-night conversation that breaks your heart when it ends."   —Mia Lipman, Amazon Best Books of the Month

"[Naomi demonstrates] how to make the kinds of choices that eventually lead to an uncommon but joy-filled life."   —Oprah.com

"A fine novel and a young writer to watch."   *—Hudson Valley News*

"Bonds of love, family, and friendship, sometimes damaged or beyond repair, are nevertheless celebrated in an intense debut by a noted poet. . . . [A] thoughtful coming-of-age tale that hovers observantly on the edge of melancholia."   *—Kirkus Reviews*

"Eloquent, haunting, and exquisitely written, Percer's stunning debut finds surprising beauty in the broken places of our lives. Here, winning can't mute pain, but love endures despite the odds, and the education of a remarkable young woman is as uncommonly original as this novel itself."
—Caroline Leavitt, *New York Times* bestselling author of
Pictures of You

"A wistful debut novel by [a] noted Bay Area poet."
—San Jose Mercury News

"Poet Percer's fiction debut is an intimate portrait of an intelligent, tender girl with a deep wish to protect those she loves."
—Publishers Weekly

"Haunting and poignant, Elizabeth Percer's coming-of-age novel portrays a bright young woman confronting her limits as she watches those she loves deal with illness and betrayal. Each turn of this elegiac debut revealed stark truths that left me both moved and astonished." —Lauren Belfer, *New York Time* bestselling author of *A Fierce Radiance* and *City of Light*

"Percer's lyrical novel has much to offer." —*Booklist*

"It's impossible not to care about Naomi Feinstein, a smart, sometimes lonely girl searching for her own life and a way to keep the people she loves safe. *An Uncommon Education* beautifully answers these questions by bringing Naomi to the Bard (the play's the thing), but also gives the reader something much rarer—a world, and a life, that seem real." —Nicole Mones, author of *Lost in Translation* and *The Last Chinese Chef*

"Elizabeth Percer relates the life story of Naomi Feinstein with beautifully scripted, lush prose drawing in the reader and providing an unobstructed view deep into the hearts of her characters. . . . *An Uncommon Education* is rich in history, steeped in family tradition, and full of emotion—a lesson in practiced elegance." —*New York Journal of Books*

AN UNCOMMON EDUCATION

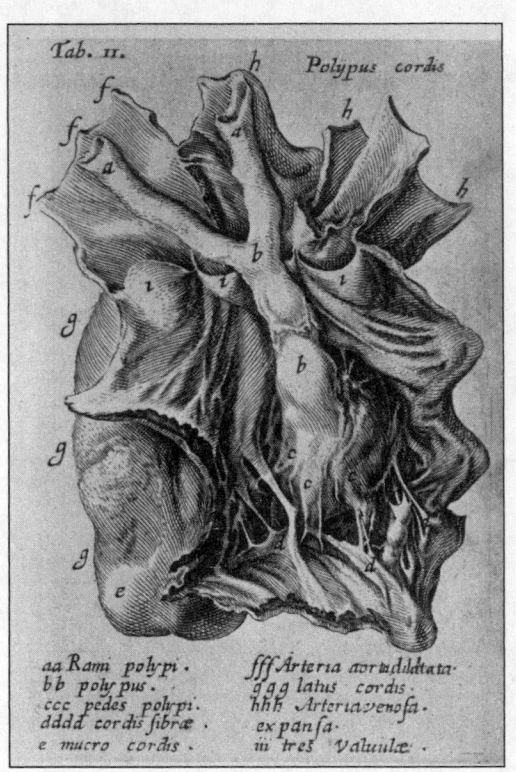

Tab. II.   Polypus cordis

aa Rami polypi.
bb polypus.
ccc pedes polypi.
dddd cordis fibræ
e mucro cordis.

fff Arteria aort dilatata
ggg latus cordis.
hhh Arteria venosa.
expansa.
iii tres Valuulæ.

AN

UNCOMMON

EDUCATION

A NOVEL

ELIZABETH PERCER

HARPER ✦ PERENNIAL

NEW YORK • LONDON • TORONTO • SYDNEY • NEW DELHI • AUCKLAND

HARPER ● PERENNIAL

FIRST HARPER PERENNIAL EDITION PUBLISHED 2013.

Designed by Fritz Metsch

Quotations from Albert Einstein's "The World As I See It" courtesy of the Philosophical Library.
Mrs. Kennedy's audio recording courtesy of the National Park Service, John Fitzgerald Kennedy National Historic Site.

Excerpt from *D'Aulaires' Book of Greek Myths* by Ingri & Edgar Parin D'Aulaire, copyright © 1962 by Ingri and Edgar Parin D'Aulaire. Used by permission of Doubleday, an imprint of Random House Children's Books, a division of Random House, Inc.

Library of Congress Cataloging-in-Publication Data has been applied for.

ISBN 978-0-06-211097-8 (pbk.)

13 14 15 16 17   OV/RRD   10 9 8 7 6 5 4 3 2 1

FOR MY GRANDMOTHER,

SHEINE SAKS,

who might have been a doctor

AUTHOR'S NOTE

Several places mentioned in this novel, such as the John Fitzgerald Kennedy National Historic Site and Wellesley College, have been intentionally fictionalized for the purposes of successful storytelling. Significant inaccuracies regarding the actual physical layout of these locations, for example, will be noted. Representations of actual locations and the cultures therein should be understood to be products of the author's imagination.

PART I

ONE

On the day after my mother's death, I returned to 83 Beals Street for the first time in fifteen years. I had stolen something from there when I was almost nine years old and kept it long after my reasons for holding on to it had lost their urgency. I suppose it was one of many talismans, real and imagined, I began collecting around that age to help me believe that what I told myself just might be true. Perhaps the strongest of these convictions, and the one it took the longest to let go of, was that believing that I needed to save those I loved from harm also meant that I could.

Until the afternoon of his heart attack, my father and I spent many afternoons at 83 Beals, otherwise known as the John F. Kennedy National Historic Site. The president had been born in the master bedroom of the modest blue-and-yellow structure in Brookline, Massachusetts, and had lived there as a very young boy. Just after Jack started school, the family moved to a larger, more impressive home nearby, and the Beals Street residence sat largely forgotten for several decades. But in 1967, four years after her presidential son had been assassinated, Rose Kennedy returned to the home, restoration on her mind.

In a completely unrelated set of circumstances, I grew up two streets over from Beals, on Fuller, in an older home that had once been beautiful but whose upkeep my parents could not afford. My mother had inherited it through some unclear chain of events, but she never fully claimed it as her own. I think this had as much to do with its derelict state as it did with the fact that we didn't have the financial resources to renovate. The paint was peeling on the outside of the house and the interior was deteriorating around the edges into warped wood floors and swaybacked ceilings. I loved it, as children will love anything that is softening into obsolescence, but I knew my parents did not. My mother spent most of her time confined to its master bedroom, and my father was mostly uninterested in housekeeping. He preferred to spend his time with me, developing impromptu lessons based on whatever books we could get our hands on, or developing local excursions for the two of us to take on foot.

The Greater Boston area may appear reserved and unwelcoming to some, but it readily reveals its intimate treasures to those willing to stroll through its meandering streets. There are small blue plaques on gates; diminutive, ancient townhouses with brightly painted doors; tilting cemeteries; hushed museums; gardens so small they only fit the statue they protect. But my father's favorite of these incidental treasures was the Kennedy house, not least because it had been restored by Rose Fitzgerald Kennedy herself, and by the time I could walk we were regular visitors there.

We always took the self-guided tour, mostly because I loved to push the red buttons that made Rose's smoothly nasal voice emerge from the speakers on the ceiling. At every room, we'd stop and peer in, each trying to be the first to bring the other's attention to a newly found favorite object. My father was a master at this game; when I won, it was usually because he'd let me. He never failed to be amazed by the home's pristine organization and charm, and it was easy to let his wonderment overtake us both. My father wasn't a simple man, but the reverence he held for the world around us was as striking as a child's.

I think this was mostly the result of his chaotic and tragic early life: born in Jerusalem in 1935 to parents acutely aware of the tensions in that region, he wandered from home one day when he was six, only to be found a few hours later and brought back safely to a nearly hysterical mother. "It wasn't only her nerves," he told me. "She was right to worry. Too many children were disappearing. Too many people. It was hard for anyone to stay calm, never mind a mother with just one child." Even though the murmurings of murder and great loss had been with them for some time, it was the personal shock of his brief disappearance that inspired his parents to book passage on the SS *Kawsar* from the Suez Port in Egypt to New York in October of 1941.

Because the Axis already controlled the Straits of Gibraltar, the trip took three months and involved sailing around the Cape of Good Hope. Decent conditions on the boat had to be bought, and his family had little money. Yet my father did not see his parents' deaths as the result of their poverty, as I did at first. Instead, he believed that they came as the result of small, natural choices. He spoke of these details evenly, like he would any matters of cause and effect: "The rats crawled over the bottom bunks; they put me on the top, even when my mother got sick. The food was bad; they let me have the best of it. Medicine was too expensive"—he stared at no one when he spoke of these things—"so they made choices any parent would have made." He paused. "I would have done the same," he added.

When I pressed him, as I often did, always hungry for more information than was offered me, he told me that he could hear the rats scampering across the floor all night, that he didn't sleep for worrying after his mother. "I was too young to argue with my father about who to protect, my mother or me, but I wasn't too young to be afraid."

By the time the ship docked in New York, my father's mother and twenty other passengers had died of dysentery. His father, also infected, died six weeks later. "Don't be sad, Naomi," he instructed me from the first telling, taking his thumb to smooth the creases on my forehead. "I was a child. I don't remember the worst of it. I just remember the good things, mostly. My mother's clothes carried the scent of the nasturtiums she grew in our backyard in Jerusalem. She always hung our laundry out there to dry. There wasn't much rain." He was frowning now; he hated it when I was sad. "And my father had a big beard and a funny face. Not handsome, but nice, with good eyes." I don't know if he was telling me the truth and I doubted it. It was far more likely that he would lie to protect me from his pain than that he had no memory of it himself.

The Lithuanian uncle who intended to shelter my grandparents and father temporarily upon their arrival became my father's grudging guardian. They didn't even speak the same language; my great uncle spoke Yiddish, Polish, and broken English, and my father had been raised to speak Hebrew. He knew a few Yiddish terms of endearment, but those did not come in handy. The only commonality he and his uncle shared was a desire to avoid my great aunt, Rifka, "a sour woman," my father said, his own face puckering. "Very sour. They had one book." He always raised a single finger when he told me this. "A photograph book of Boston Common and the Public Garden. I don't think they even knew they had it. It was beautiful." From that time on, my father spent most of his teen years in darkrooms, resurrecting images from pools of black water. By the time he was in his early twenties, he had moved to Boston and set up shop to make his way as a photographer.

He would tell me these stories when I begged to hear them, but they soon created echoes in my mind, bouncing off the much larger walls that guarded the stories he did not tell. In general, he was awkward about his struggles, not fluent in hardship. The only way he would speak of his childhood was to repeat a few, relevant anecdotes, like the fairy tales on the *Let's Pretend!* records we checked out of the library. I don't believe these summaries were devised solely to protect me. The first phase of his life was so marked by trauma he was able to detach it almost completely from his later realities; his pain a faulty limb that had been cleanly removed, only to be remembered as a phantom sensation. But he was also able to command the kind of joy that only those who have known deep unhappiness can summon.

Since I adored him, I was usually eager to share in his muted entertainments, to watch his face and marvel at how small, strange things caused it to fill with light.

Unfortunately, the Kennedy Birthplace was not reserved for us alone. It was also the place my father took the wealthy out-of-town clients who sought his services as a restorer of ancient photographs, a task that was done by hand until evolving technology made such craftsmanship obsolete. I have often wondered if this work was disappointing to him. He had wanted to bring fresh visions into the world, and had ended up restoring those that could barely be seen. I suppose the life of a struggling artist did not appeal to him. In the 1980s, however, when I was still a girl, my father's work was in high demand, particularly, and curiously, by elderly Muslim clients from New York and New Jersey. He didn't make much money in this line of work, but he made enough to support our family of three.

Because the travel time from Manhattan or Bridgewater to my father's studio was at least five hours, he usually made some attempt to socialize with the men who came to see him, as a way, he would explain, of "making their trip worthwhile." It seemed lost on him that they might not think of themselves as his guests. And, indeed, with their nervous faces and tight grips on those fuzzy, thin reflections, they were more like escorts than guests—interested only in nursing a tenuous attachment to the ancestors who were, literally, fading away in their hands.

Fortunately, my father was mostly oblivious in social situations and looked forward to a long-distance client visit as though an old friend were coming to town. He planned a handful of excursions for his visitor ahead of time, so that even if it rained he could share something of Boston's illustrious history with the company he so eagerly anticipated. Since it rains quite often in New England, and since most of his clients weren't particularly keen on sightseeing, they often chose the easily digestible and walkable Kennedy Birthplace over some of my father's more ambitious selections.

As much as he enjoyed sharing Boston's celebrated history with his clients, nothing made these excursions more appealing to him than bringing me along. From a fairly early age, I suspected that even if his clients had been nursing a faint interest in a National Historic Site, they would be extremely unlikely to find their restorer's daughter of any interest whatsoever, no matter how much her father fawned over her. But it made him happy to bring me, swelled him with pride, in fact, and I liked to see my father standing taller, his head thrown back almost imperceptibly, but to great effect.

Our last visit there took place on May 15th, 1983, an apparently normal, if not muggy, Sunday a month before my ninth birthday. My father had come home to eat lunch before meeting a new client later that afternoon. It was the third day of a heavy rainfall and I felt tired. He roused me enough to get dressed, out the door, and down the sidewalk, but by the time we were moving I knew I was not only tired, I was also sick. I wanted to tell him, but I couldn't bring myself to interrupt his indignant description of Mr. Saab's great-grandmother, a woman with a full black mustache and three chins, and my father was being asked to restore every line. Our walk was painstaking: he trying to convey a thorough description of that unfortunate woman, me focusing all my attention on keeping my lunch down. In retrospect, I'm glad it wasn't a sentimental occasion. There's nothing worse than ceremony when it comes to enjoying the last moments of something essential, like innocence or good health.

Mr. Saab had come, as many of my father's clients did, with a few other men who stood just behind him. To this day, I've never figured out if they were supposed to be guardians or relations or both. I trailed behind the group as my father started his tour. As he walked he held one arm out behind his client, guiding him, but also careful not to touch him, like an usher at a fine theater.

The Kennedy house always carried the faint smells of dust, mold, and old perfume. I usually took comfort in its musky odors, but on that day the minute they hit me I grabbed my father's jacket and pulled hard. He looked down at me and I motioned for him to come closer.

He smiled apologetically at his guests before leaning down. "I think I'm going to be sick," I told his ear, not touching it, afraid to move. He stood up slowly, his eyes fixed on me. I met his gaze, unrelenting.

He put one hand on my shoulder, "My daughter is feeling a bit tired," he said, "she'll wait for us while we take a look around."

"I can go home, Dad," I said.

"Of course you won't go home!" he said, as though I'd suggested an adventure not worth having. "Where's Mrs. Olsen!" he hollered, acting like we owned the place and he was summoning the help.

Mrs. Olsen was the government-appointed caretaker of the house. She appeared at the end of the hallway, coming forward cautiously and resentfully, her thick black hair a stark contrast to the paper-thin skin of her face. She must have been in her early sixties, but there wasn't a strand of gray on her head.

"Mrs. Olsen," my father said, continuing his performance, "Naomi is not herself. Would it be all right if she stayed here with you?" The question was a mere formality, a courtesy a rich man would display. To my astonishment, Mrs. Olsen nodded mutely. Maybe she, too, occasionally wanted to convince herself that this house was still someone's home. My father turned back to his client before the spell could be broken.

"Let's begin in the music room, to your right." The arm went out, the hand just behind Mr. Saab's back, blocking Mrs. Olsen and me, moving the men onward and out of the way. "If you'll be so kind as to stay on the hall carpet, it is a requirement here"—he frowned; this was a personal disappointment of his—"and press the red button to your right when you feel you have the best view. Mrs. Rose Kennedy herself, the president's mother, is the voice you will hear on the recording. I believe you will find her reflections amusing." This last word in his script was always improvised: sometimes it was "entertaining," sometimes it was "informative" or, if he was in an odd mood, "enlightening." I could tell he was nervous when he used "amusing"; he was encouraging them to be distracted.

As soon as they were done with the music room and had walked up the stairs and out of sight, Mrs. Olsen turned around smartly, leaving me standing just inside the front door.

If I had been feeling better, I would have enjoyed the thrill of being left alone in the house, the chance to pretend that I belonged there. I practiced leaning idly against the wall, pretending I were simply stopping here between lunch in the kitchen and my afternoon piano lesson. The front door hadn't been fully shut, so a breeze first carried in the smell of things growing outside, then picked up and blew the door open all the way, slamming it against the doorstop. I felt totally alone, as though my father and his clients upstairs and Mrs. Olsen in the back were just figments of my imagination.

With the door wide open I could see the rainwater dripping from the doorframe onto the welcome mat, already so saturated with water it was about to brim over. But it was getting brighter overhead, the sky beginning to dry. I walked outside and perched on the wet top step, listening to the distant sounds of people moving around upstairs. The wind died down and I smoothed my dress, one of my father's favorites, trying to talk myself out of feeling as sick as I did. In another minute my father's voice called down the stairs, "Naomi! You feeling better yet? Ready to join us?"

I stood up unsteadily and held on to the iron rail, leaned over it, and threw up into Mrs. Kennedy's dahlias. Afterward, I rested my cheek on the cool metal, wishing, not for the first time, that this perfectly staged home was mine. I pictured Mrs. Kennedy tending those flowers herself, or picking them out, holding up a bud to the blue paint on the shingles. I sat down until my stomach began to settle. As soon as it did I felt exhausted, desperate to sleep. I crawled through the front door and hooked a right, making my way under the velvet rope into the music room, the carpet burning my knees. I headed over to the piano bench, crawled up on top of it, and pulled Mrs. Kennedy's hand-stitched piano cover over me, so that I was lying on my back, my face to the ceiling, when I heard her voice coming through the floorboards above me, the words going in and out: "when the baby came she threw . . . many a tea party . . . disgruntled . . . John's particular pet . . ." They had reached Rosie and Kick's room at the top of the stairs.

The tour was almost over; Mrs. Kennedy was talking about the guests that the family loved to entertain. There were so many of her speeches I wanted to interrupt, wanted to ask her about. In the girls' room there was a rocking horse, a miniature sewing machine, and a tiny, glistening collection of ugly crystal dogs, probably Rosie's, my father would argue, because neither one of us knew for sure and we suspected no one did. I opened my eyes, grateful for the weak spring sunlight in the room.

When I turned my head I saw it immediately: a little bit of white, sticking out from the underside of the piano. I reached out to touch it, and realized it was thicker than it had first appeared. After a few seconds, I managed to worm free a small collection of papers from under the slats. They had been tied together with a string that was so frayed I had to be careful not to break it as I pulled the knot open.

I looked quickly to the door before examining my find: a photograph of Rose, my personal favorite (I'd seen it earlier that year in one of my father's books; it had been taken in 1954, and I loved to note the similarities between her young face and her younger son's); a letter; and another photograph, this one of Amelia Earhart in a dark blouse and belted trousers, her hand in her hair as she smiled at two men.

I read the letter first:

Many, many thanks for coming to see me on Friday. You were darling. I hope you liked every-thing here. . . . Mother says I am such a comfort to you. Never to leave you. Well, Daddy, I feel honour because you chose me to stay. And the others I suppose are wild.

It was not in its envelope, but I recognized it from a small collection of Kennedy letters my father had unearthed at the library and had begun reading to me earlier that spring. The Kennedys' first daughter,

Rosemary, had written it to her father in 1939, about a year before she underwent the lobotomy that took away her ability to speak, read, and write. After my father read it to me, I'd snatched the book from his hands, fascinated that such a thing could exist within the pages of such a serious, adult book.

I stared at the same words in my hand, now, in Rosemary's own writing. The sight of her uneven lettering brought the girl herself to life unexpectedly, and I closed my eyes, imagining her sitting with a pen and paper, searching for the elusive words that might have convinced her father to return. (She never found them; many biographies of the Kennedy family claim that he stopped visiting her after the lobotomy failed.) I wondered if she could have left anything behind that would have given a clue as to whether she had been born broken enough to deserve that surgery, or if it was somehow something she had earned along the way. I turned to the second photograph. I didn't remember any reference to Amelia Earhart in Rose's book, though the print had been signed: "To Rosemary. Amelia."

I turned that one over. On the back, at the very top, was written: "For my brave girl. Got this one special. Daddy." And, squarely in the middle, in careful printing of a different hand: "She could fly." Then, in the same writing, at the very bottom: "Rosemary." The letters were spaced widely apart and the ink was dark and thick. I imagined the author pressing the pen down deliberately.

My family had talked about Rosemary, or at least she'd come up over dinner not long ago. My father developed heroic crushes, as my mother called them, where he'd dwell on a person from history exhaustively, or for however long we'd listen to him. He took special care to nurse the one he had on Rosemary's mother, Rose, though I'm not sure if his adoration was pure or a front for talking about her as a role model for me. He never thought of my own mother as a role model, primarily because it was clear to all of us that she didn't want him to.

That night at dinner, I was only half listening to him, wondering how he could have a crush on a ninety-three-year-old woman. I imagined her crumbling at the slightest touch, becoming a pile of dust in my father's hands. "Now, *there* is an example of a woman with untold potential," my father was saying. He loved to imagine women as limitless creatures, thinking he complimented us all by doing so. "Not only was she the matriarch to a nation, but she was able to do so even after her own early dreams had been squelched! You know, she was never even given a proper education. If it hadn't been for her father," he continued, "Rose would have gone to Wellesley College. And then who knows what. Pass the potatoes, *ketzi*."

My mother intercepted me and passed the dish to my father. "She did go to the convent school, Sol. She did receive an education. And if Naomi is going to learn any of the manners you want so badly for her, you'll have to learn to say please."

"Thank you, my darling," my father said carefully, barely breaking his stride. My mother released the dish into his hand. "It was her father's political aspirations, you know," he went on. "She was devastated. But he couldn't have his Catholic daughter entering a progressive college during an election year." He put his fork down, deep in thought. "I don't think she ever forgave him. She always said it was her greatest regret." He looked significantly at me.

My mother was still watching him. Her fork lay neglected by her side. He was eating again, oblivious to her stare, but I was riveted, my eyes on my mother, waiting for her to formulate the words that would decipher her expression. Finally, she spoke: "For a woman who ostracized one daughter and killed the other, you certainly have a very high opinion of her."

My father looked up, his food halfway to his mouth. "She didn't kill Rosemary," he replied, the hurt and outrage in his voice making it sound thin and reedy, like a man who had just been pinched. "She might as well have killed her," my mother said quietly, looking down at her plate.

"It wasn't like that," my father insisted. "The poor child was born defective. Her mother did the best she could." "A lobotomy?" It was as much a question as an accusation. My father shook his head. "She did the best she could," he repeated. My mother's lips tightened. He had somehow made her angrier, but she said nothing more. I was already beginning to notice how, in my home at least, many conversations didn't end with the last words spoken.

Aside from the obvious fact of her beauty, I sometimes wonder if my father's early sadnesses had drawn him inexorably toward my mother. Maybe she felt familiar to him the moment they met; maybe, over time, he was able to soothe something raw in himself by tending to her so regularly. He certainly loved her. Though sometimes, when I watched as his energy and cheer emptied into her unchanging expression, I wasn't sure why. It was like watching a man throw pebbles into a pond, studying the surface and hoping for waves.

I know now that my mother was, most likely, a lifetime sufferer of clinical depression or one of its variants, but all of us were poorly educated on the subject, my mother not least of all. I suspect that's why so many of our behaviors around her pain were almost superstitious: the less we spoke about it, the less we acknowledged it outright, the less real it might become, like a demon that grows petulant when ignored and searches for a more attentive believer. But sometimes it was clear that her unhappiness had no desire, least of all to be acknowledged, and its very stagnation was part of what made it so penetrating. I'm sure my mother was aware that help was available to her in some way—occasionally she visited doctors, had "appointments," as my parents called them—but she never sought regular care, as though it were her sole responsibility to overcome what gripped her so tightly it seemed she sometimes couldn't quite breathe.

And so, as I lay on the piano bench, I found myself playing one of my favorite games: wondering what else my mother might have said during a conversation if she hadn't stopped talking. I wasn't even sure I knew what a lobotomy was. I was hardly alone in such ignorance, but at the time I simply thought I was too young, that this was one of the many things that adults understood and I did not.

The sound of heavy steps on the stairs startled me out of my reverie. I shoved the papers under my dress and made myself as still as possible, desperately hoping that they wouldn't notice me. Unfortunately, my father saw me the instant I was in eyesight, as though I had been glowing.

The hand went up, the men were down the stairs and guided out the door before they had a chance to look my way. I managed to tuck the papers into the waistband of my tights, smoothing them down just before my father turned around. I shut my eyes, trying to look sick enough to be near sleep.

I heard the front door close softly a few minutes later. Mrs. Kennedy's voice started again; my father must have pressed the button. "I shall try to point out to you some of the things as we go through the house that were important in our lives," Rose intoned. "Since the music room in the days before radio and television was the place for the family to be together, we shall start here." She paused. "We spent a lot of time in this room in the evening. Mr. Kennedy would sit in that red chair by the gateleg table. Usually I would sit in the wing chair there by the table opposite him." Words like "chair" betrayed her upper-class Boston accent, the vowels too long and set high in the mouth. She mentioned the piano but not the hours she had spent at it, the dreams she once had of becoming a concert pianist. "Life was so much simpler then," Rose's recording concluded.

The papers were growing warm against my skin. I wondered how to get them back where they belonged without my father seeing what I was up to. I wondered if what my mother had said about Rosemary Kennedy had been true, that her mother had all but killed her.

"Do you know"—I opened my eyes to see my father standing on the other side of the rope—"that Mrs. Kennedy also liked to take her children to historical sites in the Boston area"—he eyed me to see if I was listening—"as part of their schooling. She spent so much time teaching those children, it's no wonder she regretted the limits of her own education." I closed my eyes again.

"She always sounds happy to me," I remarked, affecting more nonchalance than I felt. I didn't fully believe what I'd just said. But at the very least she sounded content, and I was sure that was what she wanted us to hear. I opened one eye and forced myself to sit, and then stand. He opened his arms and I made my way across the room and under the rope and into them. He could still lift me then. My dress was a little too big, bunching between us and concealing, I hoped, what I'd hidden.

"I threw up in the bushes," I whispered, my head on his shoulder.

"Not so happy," my father continued, holding me close but staring off at something in the piano room, the aroma of whatever Mrs. Olsen had used to clean the wood floors lingering in the air. I could hear the house begin to settle; I was beginning to fall asleep on his shoulder. "Can you imagine the kind of political career she might have had if she'd been born just fifty years later?" He shook his head and said nothing else for a moment, and I started to drift off again. "Might have run for president herself, the old broad." I opened one eye again. "I'm not running for president," I muttered into his shoulder. "I'm going to be a doctor," I added, emphasizing the personal pronoun in case he needed to be reminded of what we both already knew. He patted me on the back, nodding to the empty music room.

I wonder now if he chose Mrs. Kennedy as a role model because she did share some commonalities with my mother: disappointment, an Irish Catholic upbringing, a natural grace, and the allure of an intelligent face. If he had chosen someone more confident, less likely to have hidden insecurities, I might never have made the transfer. Because, ultimately, although my mother had no interest in having me emulate her, I believed that she hadn't discarded me so much as left me to drift as close to her shores as I chose, watching constantly for an opportunity to come in. I think a child who watches like that has more than the usual tendency to latch on to her quarry with single-minded determination.

I decided to ask my father about Rosemary and her mother, so I looked up at him, trying to formulate a question to which I'd get the kind of answer I was looking for. There was a weak smile on his face as he stared into the room at Rose's picture on the piano. He was becoming more sentimental in his middle age, given to frequent reminiscing of what might have been or what could be. When I think of him in those moments, it makes the gap between our ages seem even broader: I, just discovering; he, summarizing already. I held him tighter, wanting his attention back on me.

And then suddenly we weren't standing. We were tilting forward, bending down, and my father was not just holding but gripping me. The tilt was very, very slow, and I remember waiting for him to say something, to explain as we listed toward the floor. Then his arms disagreed: the left clenched me to his chest and the right let me go entirely. I was able to brace my own fall as I sprung free, but my father fell heavily, on his back. I looked at him, at his eyes open in surprise, and then I was screaming as loud as I could; and I continued screaming; long, wordless cries for help, even after Mrs. Olsen was there and then people from the street outside and an ambulance had been called.

I sat and watched him, my throat quickly becoming raw and voiceless. All at once I could not understand what I saw, could not understand how this man on the floor was my father—a man who could not hold me, who could not stand. He was as still as a waxen doll, his chest all at once empty of air. As I stared at him I could hear the thumping of my pulse in my ears, the breath began to leave my own chest in a small, steady leak.

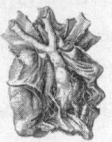

TWO

I scrambled back to him from where I'd fallen and lifted his head into my lap. The heavy weight of it frightened me almost as much as his collapse. Someone put a hand on my shoulder and tried to pull me away, but I couldn't hear what was being said to me. "Please," I begged him. "Please, please, please," I muttered out loud, while silently, fuming, like a train building speed, *not you, not you, not you*.

In the next instant I began to promise him everything I had to promise. I didn't believe in a God, but my pleas to a nameless *something* felt like the only way to shut out the total panic that wanted to take over. My mother's right wrist with its dark, thick scar floated in my vision, and I squeezed my eyes shut, holding my father's head and pressing my forehead to his.

I tried to think of what I could do to lure him back, of how badly he wanted to see me become something he had never been, of how I needed him to do that. I thought of Rose Kennedy, of the model he'd made for me of her, and wondered if I could promise to have no regrets, if such a promise was something someone could make. But

I could think of nothing else, so I did just that, whispering it into his ear, letting myself believe that the words themselves might carry within them the power of resurrection.

I realized, belatedly, that the paramedics had been on their way for some time, but they arrived out of nowhere at that very moment; a thousand capable hands descending in response to my critical oath, lifting him, pulling his clothes away, tying their lines, pressing the electric white blocks to his chest. I caught a glimpse of his pale, still face from between their shoulders and groped for his hand. They pushed me aside, working as one, and my father's body jumped and he took a breath. I heard myself cry out involuntarily, a useless protest escaping if only to be heard. A moment later I was told I would be checked for shock.

But as they shone a light into my pupils and walked me through my senses, a sort of clarity began to dawn, my mind careening toward the first thing it could latch on to as a counterpoint to panic. I took as deep a breath as I could, filling my lungs until they hurt, and then filling them some more, gathering myself back from some unknown place, inflating my body and straightening, taking in the instruments and techniques and formal curiosities, slowly forcing myself to drop anchor in the chaos, to understand rather than just watch, to make sense instead of wonder.

My father had known it all along—perhaps both my parents did— that an inescapable vulnerability wove through all our experiences and that it was better to focus elsewhere, preferably even further than the eye could see. But it took my own deep gulp of catastrophe for me to understand the power of such protection. And as I did, I felt a wondrous calm settle in as I watched the machines and the men and their instruments encourage my father's heart to start again. And as his pulse began its slow, mountainous march back on the machine at my feet, it seemed Rose and Jack and all their children were surrounding us, their hands on our shoulders as the paramedics began to lift and carry my father through the front door, all of the Kennedys gone and all still there, seeing what I saw and nodding their heads in understanding. And drifting on the outskirts of the crowd was Rosemary, her stare direct and intentional: *She could fly.*

Later in the hospital with my mother, I followed the doctors like a mute hound, transfixed as they achieved the miraculous shuffle of my father from death to life. My mother was beside herself, and in no state to look after me, so an intern was informally assigned to me, a kind young woman who handed me a paper cup of water by way of comfort. I drank the cold liquid down, staring at her and wondering what it took to earn a coat as clean as hers. "Do you want to ask me anything?" she offered quietly. I nodded, silent. She knelt down and put a hand on my shoulder. "Your father's doing great," she said. "You don't need to worry." I found my voice, blurting out my only question. "Did you have to cut open his chest to fix his heart?"

She blinked, then began to try to answer that question and the ones that followed. And so I entered a classroom of my own design, the hospital and our reasons for being there giving way to my curiosities. Before long, she managed to scrounge up a plastic model of the heart and use it as a shield between herself and my questions. She named everything on it and I was quiet, lingering on the most foreign words, *vena cava, atrium, aorta, ventricle, septum,* looking at the ugly red-and-purple thing and hoping it had no real business within my father. She noticed my frown and laughed a little. "It's not the most appealing thing in the world," she said, then leaned in close, "but the real thing is much worse. Nothing pretty about it." Almost instantly she pulled away, stealing a quick glance at me to see if I had registered the inappropriateness of what she'd just said. I loved when adults blurted things out to me. It was like getting away with something free and clear. I nodded, imagining a red, swelling, glistening thing.

My intern wore white, as they all did, with subtle drapings of metal over their shoulders and pockets. We talked of blood all night, but I never saw a drop of it on any of them.

I imagined a transitional room between where we stood and where the doctors worked, lined with countless replacement jackets and metals, all dutifully waiting for the next costume change. I wanted them to appear otherworldly, with powers to easily bring back the dead, and by the end of the night they did. It wasn't difficult to begin convincing myself that I, too, might be more than just an *I*, I might be a *someone*, a force in the world rather than a subject of it, vulnerable to the whims of my parents and other terrifying imbalances. These doctors, too, I reasoned, must have been children, once.

Reunited with my mother to receive my father's progress report, I fingered the surgeon's coat while he talked with her, imagining it on my shoulders. When he looked down at me, I smiled at him knowingly, producing my plastic heart from behind my back like a freak show magician. He recoiled, checked himself, then stared at me suspiciously. I sat back with satisfaction, my mother gazing at me, bleary-eyed and mystified, too tired even to ask.

The doctor gave a casually forced laugh, determined not to show any surprise or discomfort I might have brought him. "That's not what you should look at," he said, standing authoritatively. "Come with me." He raised an eyebrow at my mother to get her approval, but didn't wait for her reaction. I followed him down the white corridor to a massive door with a silver handle, something I would never have dared to touch. It was open with a flick of his wrist. "Over here," he said, striding toward his desk.

Above it hung a framed print. He pushed his chair out of the way and pointed to it. "That drawing was made five hundred years ago. Go," he nudged me forward, "look at it closely." I had to crane my neck back to see it well. "It's as accurate as any sketch you'd see today," he announced.

The paper was covered in scribblings, a sketch of a heart like an apparition emerging just left of center from the densely packed writing.

"It's da Vinci's." The surgeon interrupted my thoughts. "He studied pigs first, but their hearts are very similar to ours."

"So that's a pig's heart?" I asked.

He frowned, again squelching something less than polished. "No," he laughed, "not this one." He pulled his brows together, leaning into the drawing. "It doesn't really matter, anyway." He squatted down beside me, his voice suddenly reverent. "The first anatomically correct image of the heart known to Western man." He pointed up to it, over both our heads, "That," he said, "is what all of medicine is really about. Find a way to replicate that, you find a way to live forever." Who would want to live forever, I thought, thinking of my mother. But I didn't say anything.

"If it weren't for scientists like da Vinci," he was saying, "geniuses really, we might never have saved your father tonight."

"Wasn't da Vinci an artist?" I asked. "Why was he drawing pig hearts?" The surgeon stood up. "He was much more than an artist," he said, placing a hand on my head.

"What else do you have in here," I asked, looking around. He smiled and put his hand back on the door handle. "I think you've seen enough for now. Let's get you back to your mother."

I wasn't quite done. "But wouldn't someone else have drawn it eventually?" I asked, studying the print again.

Behind me the surgeon was silent for a beat. "Again, that's not what matters," he said more sternly. "It's the impulse to know, to draw, to demystify." He paused, unsure for a second. "He made the heart less mysterious. It was a courageous thing to do."

I thought of what the intern had said, about the organ being even uglier in person than it was as a purple-and-red plastic model. Maybe it was brave to look at something ugly and draw it anyway. "Has anyone tried to make a new one?" I asked, turning back to him. "So it could just be perfect, right from the start?"

This time his smile was real. "Not yet," he said. "Not exactly. You're young enough, though. You might just see that done in your lifetime."

I went back to my seat in the lobby and resumed staring at my mother. So far that evening, I had been able to stare at her for nine minutes and forty-three seconds without attracting her attention. She saw me settle in and returned to her magazine.

Sometime during that night, I discovered the package I had found under the piano in my backpack. I hadn't realized I had put it there, and a quick wave of fear passed through me when I realized I'd stolen it. I glanced toward my mother, but she was sleeping in her chair. Very gently, worrying that the papers themselves might even object to being taken from their rightful home, I pulled out just the photograph of Amelia Earhart, running my finger over Rosemary's name as though the ink might still be wet. I looked over at my mother dozing fitfully. *She could fly.* I watched my mother's expression shift in her sleep, wondering what sort of beliefs she might have held as a child, if she had always been unhappy or if unhappiness was something that she had learned. Maybe she, too, had written letters to someone she hoped would answer.

I opened my backpack and shoved Amelia back in, zipping it until it was as secure as I could make it, wanting, suddenly deciding, that the papers should be mine. Rosemary would never have wanted them to be hidden forever, I told myself. In fact, she must have just had them there for safekeeping, waiting for someone to find them who would see to and care about them. It didn't seem, all of a sudden, that Rosemary was so hard to understand after all.

I sat up straight in my chair, oddly comforted by the sight of my sleeping mother in front of me and the knowledge of my sleeping father near me. Around us the hospital still hummed, the doctors in their coats, with their models and confidence, rushing about, readying themselves to save even more lives. I was tired and overwhelmed and my mind began to drift again, my convictions growing unchecked and giddy. If they could save lives, I would, too, I thought. I wouldn't be just a doctor, I would be the very best of doctors—a cardiac surgeon—maybe even one who could design a replacement heart. I would keep my promise to my father and I would never let him fall again, and I would keep my mother from sinking too low to be found.

I, too, had been lost for a moment, and when I came back to my life it was in a form just slightly, but critically, different from the one I had left. I walked away from that hospital believing that I could one day learn to heal, that healing itself was something that could be hounded and captured, like a quarry that only needed to be chased to be won. It was a belief so strong that I would continue to build myself upon it, unable to let it go until I had tried and failed to save three of the people I most loved: two who, at very different times in my life and in very different ways, became the sort of friends we think we might never be able to live without, and then my mother, who in the end might have saved me.

THREE

My father was expected to come out of the bypass surgery by noon the following day. When it was done, the surgeon, heralded by a nurse in pastels, arrived busily within moments, his white coat flaring like a sail behind him.

"Mrs. Feinstein"—he held out his hand and my mother rose awkwardly to meet it. I stood with them. We'd already talked about my father's heart with him more than we ever had with anyone else, even each other, so it was strange to be so formal, as though the postoperative situation had reset our relationship and required us to meet again. "Your husband is resting comfortably," he told us after shaking my hand, too. "The surgery was successful."

And so we arrived home excited, with a tentative sense of enormous relief, but also with the understanding that complete recovery would happen only if my father took the time to rest.

It was shortly after that that we had one of our last formal Sabbath observations. We were never religious, but when I was a young girl my family still practiced a few collective Jewish rites that made us feel part of a whole. My mother had prepared an unusually nice dinner, taking the time for ceremony. The luxury of time spent so carefully would slip away from us as I grew older, as my mother would grow sicker, as my father and I poured every ounce of our weekend energies into my studies.

Before we ate, my father rested his hands on my head and said the blessing for daughters, something he had recently told me I was growing too old for. I felt the warmth of his palms, their weight on my scalp, and closed my eyes, letting his words surround me: *Y'Simech Elohim ke-Sara, Rivka, Rachel, v'Leah. May God make you like Sarah, Rebecca, Rachel, and Leah. Ye'varech'echa Adonoy ve-yish'merecha. May God bless you and watch over you. Ya'eir Adonoy panav eilecha viy-chuneka. May God shine His face toward you and show you favor.* When he was done I looked up at him, weak with the gratitude that he was there. He smiled back at me, thumping his chest harder than I thought he should or could.

In a few more months he would be so well that we could trick ourselves into shelving his illness away completely, eventually managing to deny even the thought of a repeat attack, though I know now that one would have been likely. But in that moment I let myself think of how lucky we were to have him back. *Abba-leh*, I whispered into his chest, a word I hadn't used since I was very small. I was thinking I would never let him go, even if it meant I would one day need to reach into his chest and place a heart there of my own design. He kissed me, pretending he didn't notice my sentimental lapse. "Enough, *Naomi-leh*. Stop worrying about me. You look like a little old *skeyneh*, with your eyebrows pulled together like that." He rubbed his thumb between them. "It's no good to look like you always have a question."

School let out a few weeks later. We weren't the type of family to make summer plans, even before my father's heart attack, so I was able to spend large parts of my day reading to him: the newspaper in the morning, mail in the afternoon, literature at night. He was worried about me, wanted me to get outside, but he was also tired, or liked to see the fight in me, and relented. I must have been overbearing, caring for him with my books and papers and unwavering attentions. But one of the greatest kindnesses about him was that he was pleased when I was pleased, not just because he enjoyed my pleasure, but because he willingly adopted it. He even let me help my mother dress his incisions in the beginning, then check them regularly, allowing me to believe they required my opinions to heal.

"I might have made some promises," I told my father as I sat with him on the afternoon of my birthday that June. "To make you better," I continued. I rubbed the edge of the sheet between my fingers, avoiding his gaze. "Promises," he said, a leading statement more than a question. I nodded. "To do well in school." "You already do well in school" he exclaimed. "To do better"—I was failing at this. "You couldn't possibly do better!"

I glared at him, frustrated. He took the hint and waited me out.

"To not have any regrets," I said finally, tense. I wondered if now would be the time when he would explain to me what that really meant, if there was a way to get him to tell me more about the idea of regret. "You know what I mean?"

He was on to me immediately. "Do *you* know what you mean?"

I sighed, blowing the hair on my forehead as I jutted out my jaw, affecting annoyance while I bought some time. I often pretended I completely understood the meaning of words or ideas I didn't fully understand. My father was constantly chiding me for this habit, leading me to the dictionary. But I didn't like how everything I read there stuck. I was afraid it was taking up space in my mind that might have been used for something I'd thought of myself. My father didn't know I could remember everything I read, and at that point I still wanted to keep it to myself.

"Yes," I said finally, feigning exasperation. "It means I will do everything I want to do."

"Good, but not exactly. It means you won't look back and wish you could have done certain things you didn't do."

I wasn't sure I understood the distinction, but I was busy acting smarter than I was. I kept my face fixed in the *And so?* expression that bugged him.

But he wasn't looking at me. "No regrets. We should be so lucky." He leaned back heavily on his pillow. I was surprised to see him so philosophical about the whole thing. He'd never expressed anything but full support for my enthusiasms, often translating them into ideas far greater than those I might have come up with on my own, like a magician taking a simple coin and changing the laws of the physical universe with it.

"I don't see why not," I said, imitating an adult's diction. He smiled a little. "Of course not, Naomi." He looked out wearily from his pillow. "You'll be the mother of a president and five other children and go to Wellesley and become a doctor. I have no doubt."

I frowned. The way he put it, anyone would have a doubt. "Not all those things," I said. "I don't think I want all those children." He laughed out loud, long and fully, bringing my mother to the room. She began smiling herself, as I was by that time. It was so good to hear him laugh like that. I let myself hope that, after the worst, things might be changing.

Among other things, I was excited that my mother had risen to the challenge of caring for my father. She usually spent most of her days in their bedroom, but when my father came home from the hospital we moved him into the guest bedroom at the top of the stairs, so he could be within shouting distance of anyone in the house. My mother drifted in along his wake, staying to tend to him. I saw her more around the house in those six weeks than I had during the previous six months. It was wonderful to run into her incidentally.

In general, she was someone whose life remained curiously undiscussed. Her past, as the daughter of second-generation Irish Catholic immigrants, was effectively erased the moment she converted to Judaism and married my father. It was like living with someone who had no script, whose life story was permanently sealed. It wasn't for lack of trying, on my part. I was forever trying to pull stories from both my parents about who we were and where we came from. Unfortunately, I quickly learned that trying to get more out of my mother than she wanted to tell only led her further into retreat, and the short but impassable distance she placed between us was prohibitive enough.

And so, instead, I learned to be mostly with my father and to keep my questioning to any subject that didn't have to do with my mother. That was how he preferred things, too; it was, I'm guessing, much easier to answer questions about the world at large than the microcosmos that existed within our household.

My father claims he first made headway with me as a scholar during potty training. "A captive audience for the first time in three years. What I read to you!" When I was four he began to buy me notebooks and pencils the Tuesday after Labor Day; by age seven he was slipping standardized tests into my homework pile. For entertainment I was given such things as *Infamous Women* coloring books; Shakespeare's plays in comic book form; my own miniature Torah, the scroll of which was covered in wavy black lines; historically correct figures of Clara Barton and Abigail Adams; math games made pretty with glass marbles; and a jump rope with a booklet of illustrated counting rhymes to accompany it. In addition to our regular visits to the Kennedy home, every April 19th we drove to Lexington before dawn to witness the reenactment of the Battle of Lexington and Concord; every July 4th we walked the Freedom Trail.

Because my father was an immigrant, he claimed, the great American promise was on the tip of his tongue. But because he had immigrated as such a young boy, and because my mother was uninterested in dreams, the language by which he translated this promise was not his own. He didn't exactly describe the streets as paved with gold, but he did everything short of this, so that I grew up with the most overtold stories in American history ringing in my ears, the ones whose melodies were easiest to follow. I loved those stories: Longfellow's Hiawatha, John Hancock's flamboyant signing of the Declaration of Independence, General Lee's surrender at Appomattox, the stories we told each other about that famous picture of a sailor kissing a nurse on V-J Day in Times Square. My father had a blow-up of it on the wall of his study, its clean black-and-white romance overwhelming the scattered prints carpeting the surfaces below it.

Not one to limit his daughter to American tales, my father branched out into the Western canon of knowledge and achievements. There was only one present for my birthday the year of his heart attack, a special edition of *D'Aulaires' Book of Greek Myths*. It was an expensive hardcover that was almost too heavy to lift. My mother must have had to order it, but it came in the mail in a heavy cardboard box addressed to him, so that after I trudged it up the stairs he was able to tell me it was mine. I was delighted, opening it in front of him.

I quickly singled out the Virtues as my favorites: Faith, Hope, and Charity, with their round shoulders draped in stone gowns. It was the closest I would ever come to a Barbie, though when my father saw me doodling them—Charity's hair short and spunky, Faith's hair modestly short, Hope's long and flowing—he warned me that the Greeks often thought of hope as evil. I wanted to know more.

"It's like this, Naomi," he said, settling down next to me. He was unshaven and wore a tattered sweatshirt. There was some chocolate smudged just outside his mouth, and his eyes were bright with excitement. "It can be dangerous to look forward too much, to think always of what should be instead of accepting what is."

"But isn't that what you want?" I asked. "For me to look ahead?"

"Not if it means you don't see today! Today will get you there, Naomi. Being a doctor, going to one of the best schools in the country, a girl needs much more than hope to make these things happen. They take work. They take the kind of student who, by the time she gets to a place like Wellesley, already knows who she is. She's already practiced in living."

I nodded wisely, picking up a blue crayon to fill in Hope's gown with my favorite color. I chose it for her skin, too, as well as her hair. My father watched me draw. "She's pretty," I told him. "You've made her pretty," he said carefully. "Pretty blue." He realized that I had mostly ignored his lesson about the dangers of only looking forward, and he was quieter now, considering.

I put down my crayon and riffled through the myths in front of me until I came to the Titans. "What about this one?" I asked, pointing. "Good or bad?"

"Mnemosyne," he said, picking her up and studying her. "It's rarely that simple, Naomi," he added, smiling at me over his glasses. "I suppose she's at the whim of each memory. We probably make her good or bad, depending on what we remember, or what we do with our memories."

My stomach clenched. My father closed the book and held my coloring of Hope up to the light. He looked like he might try to convince me again of her darker side, but after a moment he sighed and set my work down. "What should a child care about hope," he said to himself, "but that she's a girl who might want a nice dress?" He patted me on the head, satisfied.

After he left, I turned back to Mnemosyne—goddess of memory and mother to the Muses *who gathered her nine daughters around her and told them wondrous tales.* Maybe if she'd spoken directly to me, instead of muttering constantly in my ear, I might have liked her better. Maybe if she didn't help me do things that made others hate me, I wouldn't have torn her image to shreds later that night. I wish I could have known that it would take much more than that to make peace with my memory, to realize that just because I remembered something, I didn't have to hold on to it.

FOUR

Shortly after my father was up and walking, Teddy moved in next door. Our home, at 42 Fuller, backed up to the Rosenthals', at 54 Coolidge—Chava and Avraham Rosenthal and their son, Theodore Yehuda. A terrible name for a boy, my father would often say, and I had to agree with him. His very name was unsuited to him, an amalgamation of parts that didn't quite fit.

Teddy had spent the first six years of his life happily ensconced in a Hasidic enclave of Ashfield, a rural area of western Massachusetts. My father told me the Rosenthals moved next door because they wanted to be close to the Boston hospitals, as Mr. Rosenthal's health was failing. Teddy's parents had waited forever to have a child, until Chava was well into her forties and Avraham even older. Perhaps they fancied themselves the first Avraham and Sarah, able to earn a pregnancy with enough patience and divine approval. But her womb provided no such grace. And so they accepted a stranger's child, rather than the Orthodox-born Jew they had hoped for, and loved him well enough.

Because the Rosenthals moved to our neighborhood in the wake of my father's heart attack, one would imagine that Mr. Rosenthal's own cardiac problems would have created a bond between our two families immediately. But our parents guarded their particular troubles as privately as ever, as if embarrassed by the improbability of having so much darkness in common. Pain, I gathered, was not something to be shared with neighbors.

That summer was also an exceptionally rainy one, prompting my father to read and discuss the story of Noah and the ark. "For forty days and nights it rained, Naomi. But after, everything was better. Things grew that hadn't grown before, and the old things stretched and grew bigger, knowing that they would never live through such hardship again." We also took to watching *M*A*S*H* reruns because, my father claimed, Alan Alda looked like a good Jewish doctor. When we found out he was an Irish Italian, my father shook his head, "What does he know? He's just an actor. Plenty of people are Jewish and don't even know it. Can you imagine!" Once he was back to his old routines, he helped me scrub up before dinner just like Hawkeye and Hunnicut did before surgery: he held the clean towel as I soaped my hands until my wrists ached. I would then stand back, my arms bent up at the elbows as he handed me the towel and turned off the faucets. "Good," he would say, inspecting my fingernails. "A surgeon must first learn the art of sterile hands."

In the midst of one of the worst of those summer storms, a three-day deluge, my mother walked into my room smiling. Her face was flushed from laughing at something my father had said and it took my breath away—for a moment I was looking at a girl, a young woman, not my mother. "A new family's moved into the house next door," she told me. She'd come to deliver this news. "Daddy thinks there's a boy about your age."

She walked through my room and lifted the window shade, revealing the landscape, gray in the rain, that separated our house from the neighbors behind us. "Maybe he can be a friend." We peered out together, even though there was nothing to see. "Well," she said, looking down at me, "when the weather improves we're sure to see him."

She stroked my hair. "Maybe he'll be nice. Wouldn't it be nice for you to have a friend right next door?" She kissed me lightly on the top of the head before leaving her scent behind her.

I agreed with her. It would be nice to have a friend next door. Neither one of us liked to acknowledge the fact that I had none elsewhere. Even if I had been the sort of child who easily made friends at school, I would have hesitated to bring them home. My mother didn't like having visitors, children or otherwise. She never told me I couldn't have someone over, but the way she lied to her few acquaintances on the phone made me know not to ask. It didn't bother me too much, since I had never enjoyed any kind of popularity. I "knew too much," as Anna Kim, a popular girl in my class, was fond of telling everyone else. She had also told everyone who would listen to her, which was just about the whole school, that I was a liar and a cheat. Though I didn't agree with her interpretation of the incident that had led her to first form this opinion—a disastrous spelling bee—to be honest, I wasn't sure she was too far off the mark. I didn't like what I knew, either, and sometimes it did feel like cheating, the way I would remember things that other people could just let slip through their fingers. In some ways I think I might have been looking for an Anna when she asserted herself into my life as she did, someone to confirm my worst suspicions about my stranger capabilities. Someone to help me turn doubt into certainty.

Anna and I had been in school together since kindergarten, but she was as outgoing and well liked as I was shy and ignored. Our paths hadn't really crossed until earlier that year in school, when we both had Miss Rouselle for third grade. Miss Rouselle was pretty and smooth-skinned with brown wavy hair, and she smelled like pink erasers and Jean Naté (in her purse she kept a small yellow bottle of the fragrance, and took it out every afternoon after the bell rang to deliver one spritz, just above the collarbone). It was a pleasure to do as she asked, and I often did, busying myself contentedly around her classroom, putting my markers away, keeping my cubby tidy, looking up right away when she asked for our attention.

Miss Rouselle believed in children and their abilities. She told us this frequently, and liked to back up the statement with activities like the spelling bee she had scheduled for that afternoon. She had given us a list of thirty words, but she had also attached a spelling list of twenty words for fourth-graders, twenty for fifth-graders, and so on, ending with a few eighth-grade words. My father had told me not to worry about those, that she wouldn't get to them. But I was curious, and looked at them anyway, mouthing them as I did: "separate," "descendant," "digestion," "thicken," and, at the bottom of the last page, at the end of the list, beyond even eighth grade: "oxymoron," "torque," and "tintinnabulation," like a beautiful, mysterious finale, a triangle to close the symphony with its fine, bell-like call.

By the end of the bee, there were only three of us left standing: Michael Mauzy, a blue-eyed, wild-haired boy who never spoke to me; Anna Kim; and me. The three of us were frequently at the top of the class—I had begun to realize what I could remember and, with the nameless instincts of self-preservation, had already taught myself to show that I remembered just enough—and it was a familiar and pleasant place to be. I looked at the two of them with a sort of benevolent solidarity in mind, though we were not friends. In fact, I was feeling a little bit high from the excitement around me, a little bit reckless. Miss Rouselle was rummaging through her desk drawer, talking to us with a smile on her face; I assumed she was searching for two more first-prize blue ribbons to match the one she had already on her desk. But instead she pulled out more papers.

"Now," she said, "since you all have done so very well, I'm forced to go into a tie-breaker." She looked up at the class, beaming. "I'm so proud of all of you! You have gone far beyond my expectations. What a special group." She walked around to the front of her desk and perched on the edge of it, lifting her reading glasses, which she wore on a chain of rainbow beads around her neck, and placing them back on her lightly freckled nose.

"Fourth-grade words," she announced, with no preamble or further explanation. The effect was as dramatic as she'd hoped. Anna

Kim fixed her with a steely glare, and Michael Mauzy stopped fidgeting.

"Naomi," she said. "Let's start with you. 'Playground.' *I played kickball with my friends on the playground.* 'Playground.'"

The room was filled with the scent of close air, warm milk, wilting orange peels. "'Playground,'" I repeated, the word and its letters appearing immediately in my mind, waiting for me there. "P-l-a-y-g-r-o-u-n-d."

"Very good." She smiled confidently at me. I felt, not for the first time, that I had pleased her unexpectedly. "Michael"—she scanned the page—"'spelling.' *I did very well at my school spelling bee.*" A ripple of benevolent laughter scattered through the class. "'Spelling.'"

Michael spelled the word.

"Anna," Miss Rouselle said after we'd finished the fourth-grade words, her face growing serious to match the girl's. "'Mistaken.' *I thought my pencil was lost, but when I found it in my backpack, I realized I had been mistaken.*" Anna stood straighter, the only sign she ever gave of strain. Then she tapped out the word like a typewriter, a rattle of correct letters.

Michael had to sit once we got to the sixth-grade words and "honorable." He had ended the word by reversing the final "l" and "e." Already, Anna looked triumphant. She spelled right into the beginning of seventh grade, with "mileage" and "flammable." It was "embarrassed" that got her in the end, a spelling even adults found difficult, Miss Rouselle told us. It was her way to remind us that the things we struggled with were even poorly understood by those whose age lent them an otherwise rightful superiority.

"Naomi," she said gamely, "you want to try one more?" I nodded. "Okay. Let's see."

"Give her a hard one," Anna muttered, though Miss Rouselle heard her. She put a finger to her lips in response. "'Intermediate,'" she announced. She smiled the sentence to me: "*I was an intermediate swimmer, only able to hold my breath underwater for twenty seconds.* 'Intermediate.'"

I tried to take my time but rushed ahead, the letters spilling from my mouth like unwanted laughter. There was a murmur of appreciation from my peers. Anna frowned.

Miss Rouselle had taken off her glasses and made a show of putting them back on, her face in an impressed frown. "Excellent, Naomi," she said, "let's give you another. 'Situation.' *A competitive spelling bee can be a tough situation.*" She was winging it, I could tell. "'Situation.'"

I responded correctly. There was a hush in the classroom now. "Told you she was a genius," Justin Little whispered to Micah Higginbotham. I flushed with pride. Justin had a secret crush on me, and he was getting bolder as the year went on. "Okay, Naomi"—Miss Rouselle was standing now. "'Professor.' *My uncle is a professor of mathematics at Boston College.* 'Professor.'"

"Professor" was followed by "invitation," which was followed by "merchandise," which was followed by "symphony," which was followed by "dialogue." I was looking at the back of Anna Kim's head. Her hair was as straight as mine, but glossy, as black as a ripple of movement in the dark. Sensing my stare, she turned around, her face stony with anger.

"'Tintinnabulation,' Naomi." Miss Rouselle's voice came in from far away. "*I heard the tintinnabulation of the bells from the Custom House Tower.* 'Tintinnabulation.'"

I looked away from Anna Kim, into the middle distance, seeing the word. "T-i-n-t-i-n-n"—I loved that second, silent "n" in there, an anchor from which the bell could swing—"-a-b-u-l-a-t-i-o-n."

The first face that came back into view was Justin's, his forehead scrunched. I thought he might cry. We could tell from Miss Rouselle's silence that I had gotten it right.

"She's cheating." Anna Kim was at her feet, her shoulders set. "She"—she pointed her finger at me to make the distance between us clear—"cheated."

"Anna," Miss Rouselle said softly, but she was looking at me, not at her.

"She can see your paper from where she is," Anna announced. "Look at how tall she is." I was in the second row from the front, last chair on the right.

"I don't think she can, Anna," Miss Rouselle said softly.

Anna huffed her irritation. She marched over to my desk and stood next to me, ignoring me. "Tintinnabulation," she barked. Then she squinted, lifted herself onto her toes and leaned slightly forward, reading from the papers in Miss Rouselle's hands, "t-i-n-t-i-n-n-a-b-u-l-a-t-i-o-n."

Miss Rouselle pressed the papers to her chest as though a button had flown off her blouse. She blushed, as if we'd seen what she'd tried to cover too late. "Naomi?" she whispered, her voice as meek as a child's. I only shook my head. "C'mon"—Anna finally turned to me. "You couldn't have possibly known all those words." I stared at her blankly, my ears buzzing with the watchfulness in the room. And then, finally, the bell rang.

Michael stood up first, shoving his things into his backpack. The movement broke the spell, and the other kids stood, too, the tension suddenly diffused by the chaos of packing up. Anna left my side and walked calmly to her backpack, placing things inside it without hurry. She worked comfortably in the eye of the storm.

I felt a hand on my shoulder. "Naomi," Miss Rouselle said, squatting down to meet my eyes, "could you see my paper?" I shook my head. She frowned sadly; I thought she was waiting for me to say something else.

I took a stab at it. "I didn't see it," I said, trying to sound confident and not too much like I was pleading.

She looked up. "But Anna could," she stated. I looked at her blankly. "I can't quite let this pass," she confided in me, gently, taking my hand and squeezing it. Her eyes weren't completely brown; there were flakes of yellow in them. "I'll have to send a note home. You understand?" I nodded. Her hand felt cool and thin over mine. "You're better than that, Naomi," she whispered. "We both know you're better than this," she repeated as she stood up, reassuring us both.

She didn't send a note home. I thought she had changed her mind about telling my parents until the phone began to ring that night. It rang, was silent, then began to ring again. I looked up from my snack, guessing it was her. The ringing stopped. I wondered if my mother had finally answered it or if I had been granted some kind of miraculous, even if it had been desperately prayed for, reprieve. It was a Friday, and I stared at the unlit candles on the table in front of me, wondering if I could make them ignite with my mind. Somehow I had thought that sunset would bring not just the Sabbath but a sign that all had been forgiven.

My mother came into the kitchen a few minutes later. She didn't pretend to be there for any other reason than to sit down across from me and discuss the phone call she'd just had with my teacher. I felt outclassed and betrayed by them both.

My mother sighed, stretching her neck from side to side. "I know you didn't cheat," she said, surprising me. "Naomi. Do you hear me?" I nodded my head, strangely frightened. Her eyes were filling as she looked away, then stood up and turned to leave the room. At the door she put one hand on the frame and spoke over her shoulder, "This isn't the last time someone's going to think you're dishonest, for remembering things." She became so quiet I didn't think she would say anything else. Then, "There's nothing you can do about it." She was quiet again for another long while. "Just try not to apologize for it." I stared at her back just before she moved away, knowing that the only way not to apologize for all that I remembered was to keep it to myself.

So for the rest of the year I did my best to fade back into anonymity at school. And then my father got sick and then Teddy arrived, and I disappeared into our friendship, never happier, despite the fact that both Anna Kim's reign and her disgust with me only swelled with time. It seemed life was terribly simple; one was either hated or loved, one either hid or was revealed. Even when Teddy left when we were both thirteen, he was gone in a single afternoon. And when he stopped writing, at fifteen, it was a deafening silence. The kind that rushes through the ears, blocking everything else out.

* * *

At first, Teddy looked to be so unlike the nice boy my mother had hoped would be my friend that I resented him for it; my annoyance fueling a fascination greater than admiration ever could. It's probably also true that when my father began to work from home and my mother's door began to close more frequently again, I had nothing better to do than watch this strange boy wander around in his backyard, which is exactly what he did for hours at a time, always out in that constant, drizzling rain.

The only division between our yards was a drooping metal fence. The area between our two properties was overgrown and neglected, so that instead of two privately owned lots, it was easy to pretend that we lived at either ends of a long, dilapidated park. The longer the poor weather showed its persistence, the more genuinely interested I became in watching him from the back windows of our house, as if he were setting a record for being outdoors in a suburb during inclement weather.

I formed ideas about him as I watched. At first I guessed the adoption was a ruse and that he was actually both parentless and friendless; he was never with anyone else and he went inside only to eat. He even relieved himself outside, using an enormous rhododendron between the fence and one side of his house to do so. Only someone very slender could fit in there, and the plant flowered prematurely. Then, after seeing Mrs. Rosenthal come out and yell at him between a few breaks in the rain, I imagined he was a naturalist, collecting data; then he was half boy, half wild dog; and then, finally, he had simply been forgotten. Sometimes it was raining so hard I would lose sight of him; other days I could watch him through a light shower, like watching someone through a cloud. He always had something in his hands and I eventually concluded, out of frustration at watching and not meeting him, that he was able to spend so many hours outside alone and entertained, using a bush as his toilet, because he was not all that smart.

Sometime toward the end of the summer, the sun broke through for a few days, but I kept to my posts, more curious than ever before to see what the little *shtumie*, as my father had affably named him, would do on a sunny day. Sure enough, and as usual, he came outside and began to play. After a few minutes he stood and looked up at me in my bedroom window. I suspect he knew I would be there. He caught my eye immediately, then smiled and waved. I frowned, feeling suddenly exposed. For the first time since my father fell ill, I felt like a child again.

He raised his arm higher, just in case I hadn't seen him, and I lifted my hand in response. He dropped his arm and grinned. Then he began to wave me over. I slid off my seat with a put-upon groan and went to join him, pretending we did this all the time and there was no fuss to be made. By the end of the week we were playing doctor.

It wasn't a covert, behind-some-couch activity. Neither one of us knew a great deal about subversion. We just dragged an old picnic bench from the side of his house into the middle of his backyard and I lay down on it. We hadn't thought about costumes until the last minute, so Teddy had to run back inside to get one of his father's white shirts, but he took a while, and I spent the time staring up and studying the small, thin clouds, wondering how it could have been so gray for so many days before.

When Teddy eventually came back he was wearing a blue one.

"No white," he said, worried he had disappointed me.

I shrugged, touched that he'd wanted it to be just right, that he'd taken our game so seriously.

"So, lady," he began, "what hurts?"

I looked at him quizzically.

"What is it?"

"I'm not a lady," I said.

"What should I call you, then? 'Girl'?"

I didn't particularly like that, either.

"How about 'miss'?"

"Fine," I said. "Or just call me kid. Miss sounds like sis, or sissy." What I really wanted was for it to be my turn to be the doctor, but we'd agreed he could go first. I got the sense he was looking to play a different game than the one I had imagined. He probably wasn't expecting me to check his pulse for irregularities and listen to his heart for signs of a murmur. And I wasn't thinking that he would think to take off any clothes.

He had a string wrapped around his neck with a plastic ring around it. "Let's have a listen to your heart, first," he began, tugging the bottom of my shirt up past my waist.

I pulled it back down instantly. "My heart's up here, Teddy," I interrupted, glaring at him and pointing to my chest. He looked surprised, and then hurt.

"Mr. Rosenthal," he corrected me. "Dr. Rosenthal."

"Sorry. Dr. Rosenthal."

He moved his stethoscope up to my chest, sliding it against my thin, yellow T-shirt, the most intimate thing anyone had ever done to me. The game had started with me being in control—it was my idea, my obsession—but then it changed on us both, became something more shared and less defined. I realized I'd been holding my breath and let it out in a whumpf.

"Does that hurt?" he asked, Teddy again. I shook my head.

He re-fixed his face into Dr. Rosenthal's. I gave my eyes a break and turned them toward the shade of the tree that spread itself over the back of his house. The sky filtered through the leaves so that everything was blue and green and white like a blurred, joyous painting of summer.

"I think it's your appendix, ma'am," he said. I squinted up at him again. "Kid," he added solemnly.

"I don't think my appendix is in my neck," I said, pulling the chest piece from his hand. "I think it's here." I moved it down lower, back down to my hip.

"You said I couldn't listen there," he protested.

"Well, you can't hear my heart down here, and you can only hear my heart with that thing."

The plastic ring swung loose. He put his hand on my belly, as though listening with it. I barely felt the weight of his palm. "I don't know what to look for," he admitted after a moment. His voice sounded far away.

"I think you can only tell with an operation," I said, sounding more informed than I was.

Teddy took the string and pulled it over his head. "Maybe you should be the doctor," he said, handing it to me. His expression was grave, unreadable. I sat up, feeling dizzy, and we switched places.

Lying down, Teddy looked even thinner and taller than he did standing up. He folded his hands across his middle, like the submissive or the dead. I put the ring to his heart.

"My dad's sick," he whispered, sending the words by me and into the tree above. Everything around us was suddenly quiet, holding a collective breath. I had known his father was sick. The ambulance had come for him a week earlier, during the rain. And now there was a nurse who came every day.

"What seems to be the trouble?" I asked, not meeting his eye.

It was his turn to squint up at me. I took his hand to feel for his pulse, then held it, my fingers interlacing with his.

"I don't know," he said. He sat up, looking at me. "My mom won't say."

I reached forward and touched the lock on the left side of his face, the *peyes* he hadn't yet learned to tuck behind his ears. It was soft and insubstantial, the round curl it formed empty inside. "I'm so sorry," I said, meaning it as deeply as I knew how to mean anything.

"Can I show you something?" His eyes were flat and dark, the question urgent.

I nodded. Of course.

He ran back to the house, stopping at the bottom of the steps to turn around and say, "If I don't come back, my mom found me and I got in trouble. Go home. Don't let her find you." He frowned, then turned and ran back into the house, determination propelling his body through the door. It slammed behind him.

He was by my side again in ten minutes. "Got it," he said, breathing heavily as he sat down. "Here."

"Where did you get this?" I asked. He shook his head, riffling through the papers he'd thrust into my hands until he came to what he wanted me to see. The very top of the page was stamped with his name and the name of his parents. Just below, an ADOPTION DATE: July 3, 1974. "What is this?" I asked him, afraid to make sense of it on my own. He shook his head, frowning, his eyes and finger on the spot he wanted me to read.

> Discharge Summary. Unknown 34 y/o female adm. 3/22/74. Escorted by police re: c/o public disturbance. On admission to ED patient found to be mildly obtunded and in early labor. Initial examination revealed track marks BUE, BAC of 0.18%, and 3rd trimester pregnancy est. 34 wks. gestational age.

My heart dropped into my stomach. "Teddy, I don't know . . ." "Keep reading," he insisted, frowning at the paper.

> Admitted to ICU. Treatment initiated for substance abuse and withdrawal. 3/28/74 PROM. 3/31/74 delivered of 4 lb 2 oz (SFA) boy. 4/6/74 further obtunded. 4/7/74 manifested right hemiplegia. Expired 4/9/74. PM revealed ruptured left cerebral aneurysm in the distribution of the left middle cerebral artery. Massive intracranial hemorrhage. Also fibrosis of the liver; portal hypertension; mild early ascites.

"It's about my real mom, isn't it?"

I looked up at him, his eyes were open, so wide they made mine ache. "I don't know," I said, "I wish I did but I don't," wanting desperately to touch him instead of speaking. "When's your birthday?" I asked, looking away.

"End of March." Then, "What does it mean?" more insistently this time.

I looked back at him, desperately wanting to understand more than either of us could. "I just don't know," I whispered. I didn't tell him I would remember the words on the page anyway, that I would gladly store them until I could make sense of their meaning. I didn't realize that to give shape to the broken woman he had come from might reveal the soon-to-be-altered curve of his life, too.

None of us said anything for a while, both of us staring down at the impenetrable letters. "Hold on," I said. This time it was me who stood up and ran into my house. I was in my bedroom and emptying my desk a moment later, then back out to him after clattering down the stairs, afraid he might not wait long for me to return.

When I dropped down beside him I took his papers in my hand and put them on top of Rosemary's letters. I didn't give him a chance to see what I had added to the collection, I just pointed to the top, where his records were. "These are yours," I told him, stabbing the paper again with my finger as I had seen teachers do. "They're yours and not your mom's." I looked up to see if he was with me. His eyes were still wide, processing the information he needed to judge both what I was doing and me.

"Come," I said, standing up and walking over to the corner of our yard. I could hear him a moment later, running to catch up with me. I squatted down, digging out the dirt in what I felt was the most hidden place we had available to us.

"We're burying them?" Teddy asked, incredulously, though he was right beside me, watching my progress.

"We have to bury them," I said, "it's the only way to be sure they'll be safe."

"You're adopted, too?" he asked.

"No, Teddy! I just have some things I need to keep safe." He looked duly impressed and left it at that.

It was his idea to get a box. I nodded my approval and he jumped to his feet, disappearing once more behind his house. I could hear him shuffling through the junk his parents kept there and willed him, silently, to make less noise. I tried not to look at what was still in my hands. I wholeheartedly believed that Teddy's papers belonged to him, but I knew that Rosemary's weren't really mine. I knew I had stolen something that did not belong to me. *But*, I thought to myself, as I had in the hospital, *they aren't anybody's anymore.* She'd wanted them hidden, hadn't she? That was the important thing to remember.

I traced the printing of her name, the back of the Earhart photograph now in my lap and facing up at me. *She could fly.* I knew I should pity Rosemary for believing in such a thing, for believing in other women who could fly, for believing things could get so much better for her that maybe one day she herself would, but the pity never came. Every time I thought of those words I thought of something awful and wonderful and terribly wise.

To our mutual surprise, Teddy came back with a beautiful cedar box, a small medicine cabinet his father had built for their old house. "He won't miss it," Teddy told me. "He was just going to cut it up so we could build something else with it." The lid closed with a magnet, and the hinges were attached to slender chains. When we opened it, a waft of something fermented and sweet floated up to us. We gently placed the papers inside, as carefully as we might a living being.

After we buried the box we filled the dirt into the hole and patted it down. Teddy was so close to me that his breath was on my face, sour and soft. When we were done we sat down and looked at our work, Teddy lingering longer than I did. His hand in mine was gritty and warm, and I found myself leaning forward to kiss him on the mouth as lightly as I could, thinking of Hope in her stone dresses.

In an instant, something heavy and soft hit me in the head.

"Shiksa!"

I looked down. It was a bedroom slipper. I looked up to see that Chava was shouting at me in Yiddish, pulling Teddy, first by the hair, and then, when she got a better grip, by the ear.

"She's not a *shiksa*, Mom!" Teddy was shouting too, but this only made his mother stop and slap him.

"You talk back to your mother! I know a *shiksa* when I see one. Kissing! Not even in school almost." She turned back to me with one more burst of foreign invective, then pushed her son ahead of her into their house.

I ran in the opposite direction, tears making it difficult to see. I flew through the front door and into my father, who had been brought there by the shouting and the noise. I looked up at him, but he was staring out the door at the Rosenthals' house. I calmed down and wiped my face. We looked together while I caught my breath.

"What's a *shiksa*?" I asked.

My father's voice was low and angry. "What does she know about you," he said. "What does she know. Nothing. A Saks, no less, on my mother's side. Her son should be so lucky." He slammed the door.

FIVE

My father was tight-lipped and silent through lunch. He still needed to sleep in the afternoon, and after we ate he left me alone in the kitchen. His long naps made me nervous, and after having something hit my head unexpectedly I was rattled and suddenly couldn't bear to have him disappear from me, even if it was just to go upstairs. I tried to stall him but he grew annoyed, and by the time he left the kitchen I was even more rattled, worried now about my father and what I might have done by keeping him up an extra half hour when he'd just had surgery. It was still occasionally hard to think of him as being as healed as he was.

A few moments later I crept upstairs myself, past my father in the guest room, on to the end of the hall. Outside my parents' bedroom I lay on my back, my hands under my head as I listened to nothing on the other side, the presence of my mother drifting away. I wasn't allowed to go into their bedroom when the door was closed. I always wondered what was beyond that threshold, even when it was open. But that day it had been closed since the morning, signaling her complete resubmergence. I had known she wouldn't stay as active as she had been while caring for my father for very long, but I had not wanted to think of what would come after. And now, suddenly, I missed her terribly. I reached up and turned the knob above me, as though this was something I did every day and not some catastrophic breaking of our family code.

It was dark inside, and it took me a while to adjust to the light. My mother was sitting up in bed, leaning on her elbows, her body tense with surprise. I looked at her, knowing I should apologize.

"What's a *shiksa*?" I asked instead.

"A what?"

"*Shiksa*, I think. That's what it sounded like."

"Who called you a *shiksa*?"

I didn't answer her. "What's a *shiksa*?" I persisted.

She sighed and fell back into her pillows. For a minute I was afraid she wouldn't answer me. "It's a woman. A gentile," she said finally. "A non-Jew. Usually a temptress. Sometimes a seductress." My mother's disconnect from the outside world seemed to make her brave in matters of telling me certain mature truths, ones that might have made a more lighthearted mother blush.

"A seductress?"

"Naomi," she sat up again, leaning again on her elbows. "Did someone call you a *shiksa*?"

I nodded.

She looked down at me. "Come here."

I crawled across the floor, too eager to stand up and walk, and was in bed beside her a moment later. I rested on my father's pillow, looking up at her like we were going to tell one another stories.

She frowned. "It's a Yiddish word. Meant to insult women who aren't Jews." She studied me. "It's probably because you look like me. It's a shame, but some people believe in a Jewish look. And we don't have it." She touched my hair. She took a deep breath, letting it out slowly between tight lips before she spoke again. "You, in particular, look like my father's mother."

My own breath felt trapped in my chest. "I never knew that," I exhaled.

She sighed. "I suppose you wouldn't." Neither one of us mentioned that she was the keeper of a great deal of information I'd like to have but didn't. "I've only seen a picture, but that bow in your upper lip is hers. And her eyes must have been green like yours, too. My father's were."

This was more than she had spoken to me, ever, about her family. I wanted to know how to make it last, to capture her interest and keep it.

"I wish I'd known her," I ventured.

"My grandmother?"—my mother looked surprised. "I never knew her myself," she said quietly. "But this house is hers," she added casually, as if attributing a meaningless object to a distant acquaintance. I sat up on my elbow, amazed. "Well, it's mine, ours, now, but it was hers." She closed her eyes again at the shock in my face. "It's one of the reasons why Grandmother Carol doesn't come around that much. It was left to my father first, and he left it to me. She thought it should have been hers."

It was an unprecedented offering of information, so much so that I didn't think to make any real sense of what she was telling me. The fact that she was telling me anything at all was all-consuming. In all of my nine years I had managed to collect only a few key facts about her life: first, she had grown distrustful of the nuns who taught her. Then, when she was seven, her father died. Finally, when my mother was sixteen, my grandmother had kicked her out of the house because, as my mother explained so thoroughly, they "didn't see eye to eye." Still, she couldn't hide our shared genetics, and I had known that both she and I resembled the Irish who'd first sailed to Maine and then Massachusetts long before us: a certain blue and rose transparency to the skin, a straightness to the hair, a blush on the cheeks at even the slightest touch of wind. I thought of my mother's mother, Grandmother Carol, who looked as polished and stern as my father did messy and penetrable. I wondered if I resembled her at all, hoping I didn't. I wondered if there was anything about me that resembled him.

"Does Grandmother Carol also not come because we're Jewish?" I asked.

Her eyes were still closed, "Grandmother Carol and I went our separate ways long before I converted." She turned her head slightly my way. "She does make her visits to you, though."

She did, but it felt like we never really saw her. Once or twice a year she pulled into our driveway in her huge silver Cadillac and stepped outside, stopping just after she slammed the car door to check her hair, which was remarkable in two ways. One, it never moved. A stiff breeze would take it on with confidence and dissipate in the process. Two, it was the exact same hue as her car. She stayed for a cocktail, poured by my father, and for an unconcealed visual assessment of me before going on her way. It was like being visited by a cardboard version of someone I might otherwise have loved.

Beside me on the bed, my mother hadn't opened her eyes again. I couldn't think of any more good questions. She turned away from me, onto her side. I lay back on my father's pillow and put my hands behind my head, contemplating the ceiling. I was trying not to cry. Mostly because I didn't want to acknowledge that my mother was wanting to disappear just at the moment when she'd shown me some of what I so desperately wanted to see, but also because of the way Teddy's mother had stood watching him at the door, fiercely protective of a son she had made her own. I felt I was upsetting to them both: a child for my mother to comfort when she could not even comfort herself; the sort of newly minted, tainted Jew that Mrs. Rosenthal saw as no different than anyone else who didn't belong. But instead of crying I choked out a question. She asked me to repeat myself.

"Convert," I blurted, my words running out from under me, unsettling us both. I felt I couldn't stop. "Why did you become a Jew?"

She stared at me, her eyes emptying of thought. I'm not sure either one of us could quite believe I had asked such a personal question. I could see her trying to tell me the least complicated, least informative story. I shut my eyes to her expression, willing her to change it. It was silent between us for a long while.

"Judaism would have me," she said softly after several long minutes, answering me. My eyes flew open in surprise, and my mouth must have, too, because she smiled and shut it for me by placing a finger on my chin. "Also, it's a religion for people who have questions," she added. "Or at least for people who are more comfortable with questions than answers. It gave me your father. And you, too," she added, so softly that I wasn't sure if she had spoken or if I had imagined she did. "And it let me keep my doubts."

But with each question she answered, I thought of countless more to ask. They spilled into my mouth, silenced once there by habit, the room around me a familiar reminder of how things would be after this strange blip in time and space where my mother let me in: the cheerless decorations, the hollows under her eyes, the slit of light coming in from the nearly closed shade on the window.

"You know," my mother said, interrupting my thoughts. "There's something I've been wanting to give you for a while. I think you're old enough now." She gestured toward her dresser. "Bring me my jewelry box." I stood up and did what she said, not thinking immediately of the significance of a mother dispensing her jewelry to her daughter. The scar on her right wrist where she had tried, once, to take her life was always in the back of my mind. I hated it for being there, for being a permanent mark on her skin, a lifelong symbol of her ubiquitous desperation. I think my father was surprised when I asked him about the scar the year before; perhaps he thought by ignoring it himself I might never notice, might never make sense of it on my own. But I'd intuited as much after skimming a graphic novel version of *Antony and Cleopatra*—something about the blood pouring from the asp bites onto her pale white skin—then tricked my father into confirming what I'd feared.

"Yes," he admitted after he was done beating around the bush. "But it was before you were born." He paused, and I felt momentarily comforted. It felt right that my birth should have ended that line of thinking. "Also," he added, "she promised me she wouldn't try again, once we had you." I know this additional information was meant to comfort me, but it only served to make me wonder if I was enough to keep her alive.

I stood before her as she opened the box, looking over its edge into what was inside. I had always wanted to know its contents, and I was eagerly trying to make a complete study of them when she lifted the top tray and pulled a green velvet bag from the very bottom before closing the lid once more. She pulled a thin, silver cuff from within the bag, its mottled surface evidence of how long it had been neglected.

She rubbed its surface once with a finger. "I should have polished it first," she said, more to herself than to me. Then she reached over and took my arm, fitting the bracelet over it. I was a tall girl, but it threatened to slip down my wrist and off my hand. I clutched it, examining it as I did. My mother removed the bracelet with her cool fingers, turning it over and tracing the writing underneath to bring my attention to it. *God is nearest to those with a broken heart.* "It's from Psalm 34. Both your father and I learned this when we were children."

I was at once thrilled to know that they had this in common, and disappointed that it did not include me. I had no religious education to speak of. Both my parents had hated their Sunday schools and felt that if I were ever to become religious, it would have to be a matter of personal choice. And so I chose my religion to be whatever my father would answer questions about: science, history, my future.

My mother broke into my thoughts. "Remember, Naomi, as you learn to fix all those hearts. Remember where they've been before they got to you. Medical science will tell you that a life ends when the brain has died. But the Halacha insists that as long as a person's heart is beating, she is alive. Sometimes, the doctors aren't always right." She reached over and held my wrist, covering the bracelet, closing her eyes at the same time. After a while I asked her if she was awake and she didn't answer. I slipped my hand out from under hers, got up, and walked quietly toward the door.

"Naomi," she said to the wall, "close the door on your way out."

I can recognize now that not only was that the most she had ever spoken about herself since I had known her, it was the most she would ever tell me. I wonder if something about my father's illness had brought out something different in her, too, but if it did, it soon retreated. And at the time I don't remember wondering over anything she had told me, despite the fact that in one brief conversation she had managed to mention her family, God, and medicine. I just drank her in, always optimistic there might one day be more, confident the future would have what the present couldn't hold.

The next day I went back to my window. The wind picked up, but it stayed sunny, the trees light-filled and bent. I felt a huge sense of possibility about the day, and it wasn't just the unexpected glimpse my mother had given me into what I most wanted to see. I think I already sensed how important Teddy could be to me, though we hadn't known each other long. I dozed, on and off, waiting.

Teddy was back in the yard before dinner. I jumped off the seat at my window and ran downstairs, fearing he would disappear if I didn't get there fast enough. The wind slammed the door hard behind me and I knew my father would have come out to yell at me if he'd heard it, that my mother wouldn't have heard, or would let it go. We met in the middle of the yard. He looked tired and frantic.

"Listen," he said, looking over his shoulder, "I definitely think we should get married." He looked behind him again. The day had been scrubbed clean from his face. "But my mother doesn't like you."

"Why?" I asked, biting my nails. My teeth worked the fine pieces of dirt, giving them something to do. The back of his house looked back at us, a jumble of indiscernible shades of gray, the eyes of occlusion.

"You're not Jewish," he explained patiently.

"But I am!" I nearly hollered.

"But your mom isn't," he countered. The wind was lifting the hair off my head and his; it seemed we might fly away.

"She is!" I exclaimed. My mother, who never asked for a place in things, had wanted this place. It made me furious beyond all reason to think anyone would take it from her.

"But she wasn't born that way, right?"

I glared at him. "Doesn't matter."

He shook his head, dismissing my objection as irrelevant. "My mom doesn't really understand," he admitted, or lied, leaning forward. His breath was fragrant, like peanut butter, and a little sour, like milk. When he looked at me his eyes were the liquid amber they became when he was excited or angry. When he was furious, they were flat, almost gray, like cement. He had the coloring of a redhead, with long, light-brown lashes and freckles, though his hair was a dull, ashy blond. It almost always looked dingy, and it smelled wonderful. "We need to do something to make her like you," he said. The wind flew up my shirt, as cold as the sun was bright. I shivered. He grabbed my hand.

"I saw this a few months ago," he began. "She likes this TV show where grown-ups fight and kiss a lot. She usually yells at them in Yiddish, but this one guy, who I think was supposed to marry someone else, kept kissing this other lady and my mom got so mad she spat and said something awful, I don't know what, but I could tell it was horrible." He looked hastily over his shoulder. "She was muttering and so worked up she had me worried." He glanced over his shoulder once more. "But I heard her—'*Ayin hora,*' she says, like it's a done deal, like she knows something." I looked blank. "The evil eye," he explained, his teeth clenched. "Next week, the guy dies, and my mom's just sitting there in front of the screen, smiling."

I thought the wind might be filling my head, making the skin on my forehead stretch out and thin. I shivered again. "She killed him?" I croaked.

Teddy didn't answer me right away, but his eyes were watching me closely. "I'm worried," he whispered back.

My hand flew up to my chest. "What should we do?" I asked.

He leaned forward and whispered into my ear, his cheek on mine, "We need a plan." Then he squeezed my hand, turned around, and ran back inside. "Tomorrow," he mouthed at the door.

*   *   *

I hid myself in my room, staring at the walls in a desperate attempt at inspiration. I would need to do something definitive, something that would indebt his mother to me for life. Somehow it had become about her as much as it had become about Teddy; somehow I knew they were, on some level, one and the same, that I couldn't love one without having the love of the other. She would not let me take him away from her. I understood this, already, about his mother.

I thought about my own mother and her clean beauty, wondered if a child could be readopted, if we could steal Teddy and keep him. I thought about what she'd said about Grandmother Carol, wondering if, on her rare visits, she brought me candy as a way to try to quickly fix something that was broken. Adults assumed it was kids who loved candy, but they were the ones always presenting it to us like a cure-all.

I dug the plastic, jellybean-filled Easter bunny she'd brought with her that spring out from the bottom of my closet where I had buried it after my father had pitched a fit. I stared at it after retrieving it, everything about it perfectly intact, the pastel colors looking back at me opaquely. There was something both unsettling and miraculous about the fact that even though it had been buried for three months, it still looked as untouched as the day my grandmother gave it to me. Perhaps this was not just a miracle of plastic and corn syrup; perhaps there was more to this mythical creature than met the eye. The fact that some of the candies were the exact same color as my father's antacids gave me further courage. I clutched the rabbit in my hand and snuck down the hall to my parents' bathroom.

His father's heart. That was where the miracle needed to happen. What does a heart need? I tried to think. I thought of that night in the hospital, of the ugly mold of the heart and the meticulously drawn one with all its lettering. I thought of the orange bottles they'd sent my father home with, how he took them so carefully, each pill its own distinctive and mysterious color.

My parents' medicine cabinet was full of its usual mysteries. Cough syrup I recognized. My mother's hairbrush. Shaving cream. Many other bottles, the titles of which I could read but did not understand. There were three of the type I was searching for: the orange with the white safety cap, a device my father had already shown me how to unlock. I was hoping for one that didn't have many pills left. The second one I tried had only two, and my heart leapt when I opened it. I dumped them into the toilet, worrying that it was too loud, that the sound would wake my mother, praying as I flushed that the two pills wouldn't be missed. Then I replaced the contents with half the jellybeans, saving the other half just in case Mr. Rosenthal needed more.

Back in my room I tried to scrape the paper off the front but it wouldn't budge. I was sweating. I pulled off my sweatshirt and draped it on my bed, setting the bottle beside me to study it. I could make my own label, tell Teddy how to get it to his dad without either one of his parents' seeing where it had come from. But how? How to make sure that these oddly beautiful gems would work as I needed them to?

I screwed my eyes shut and stuck the bottle under my shirt, pushing it up first to the left side of my chest, then farther up to the spot on my neck where I could feel my pulse beat against it. I said the Shema, the only prayer I had ever said on my own, the one my father had told me to say when someone died, the one I now whispered to myself whenever we passed roadkill: *Hear, O Israel, the Lord is God, the Lord is One.* Da Vinci and his pigs' hearts swam before my eyes.

I studied the effect on the bottle. It was impressively unchanged, but warm. I went to my desk and cut a rectangle from a piece of white paper, wrote "Heart Medicine" in bold print across it, then "*vena cava, atrium, aorta, ventricle, septum,*" in small, careful letters underneath before taping it over the printed pharmaceutical label. At that point it looked completely different; the only thing it had in common with what it had been was orange and white plastic.

I tucked the bottle under my pillow that night and slept with it, bringing it down to breakfast in the morning. I always ate early, with my father. I saw him glance at my creation, but he didn't mention it until after he'd prepared my cereal and juice and set them down before me.

"What's this?" he asked, gesturing toward the bottle as though he had just noticed it.

"Medicine," I said, shoving food into my mouth.

He nodded. He picked it up and looked at the label, then set it back down. He studied it, trying to form another question.

"Teddy's father is sick," I explained, helping him out. "Mr. Rosenthal. I think it's his heart."

My father opened the bottle and looked in. "Are these jellybeans?" he asked.

"They were," I said. "I made them into heart pills."

My father nodded, swallowing, trying to take it all in. I felt vaguely sorry for him. "Heart pills," he repeated, still nodding. He looked me in the eye. "You know, Naomi, people go to school for many years to make such things. You can't just create such things overnight, *ketzi*." He was looking at me like there was something very important I needed to learn, something he thought I wouldn't want to know. His expression only made me more determined.

I stood up. "They'll work," I said, taking my bowl and glass to the sink and dumping the whole meal down, the milk and cereal and juice mixing in the sink and making me feel vaguely sick. I was sweating again. I turned around. "You'll just have to trust me, Dad." He still looked like he had something to explain to me.

I grabbed the bottle and ran out the door, though the sun was only just rising. When I reached Teddy's back steps he was standing there in short pajamas, his knees standing out and looking at me. "Here," I said, opening the screen and shoving the pills in his hand, "give these to your dad." I ran back down the stairs before remembering. "Two in the morning, two at night," I called over my shoulder. He nodded, his face a blur behind the screen.

That night I dreamt of my mother's last visit to the doctor: over two years earlier, the winter before the summer I turned seven. My father had brought her from her room and helped her into her coat after the babysitter had been called. They were trying to pretend that they were going to dinner instead of to the hospital, but I saw the number they left for the babysitter by the phone. I wish my hunger for information had known better boundaries, but I was too young to make the connection between nosing outside my business and learning things I might one day want to forget. The nightmare brought back every detail.

When they came home later that night, I pretended to be asleep in my room as I heard my father shuffle the sitter out and my mother go, too slowly, up the stairs. The quiet that came after was only more frightening, and I lay awake, listening to it. I knew something was wrong, and was all the more upset by not knowing what it was.

I lay in the dark for a while, my vigilance finally paying off when I heard a soft thump in the hallway outside my room. I opened my eyes wide, trying to make sense of the muted noises now just at the top of the stairs. I pulled the blankets off and went to the door. There was no one there, just the normal shadows of our upstairs hall at night. I studied them, wondering if one of the shadows might shift and frighten me. I remember one taller than me that might have been a coat rack or a man. I was more curious at that point than frightened, but I shivered as I stood in the doorway of my room.

I went down the hall to my parents' room. Their door was slightly ajar, and as my eyes adjusted to the dim light from their window I could see only one shape asleep in the bed. I walked back down the hall and down the stairs and looked idly through the living rooms, working up the courage to find my mother in whatever state I found her, suddenly afraid again. Once in the kitchen, I heard the front door shut softly.

I made my way toward the sound. On tiptoe, I could look through the windowpane in the front door, a kaleidoscope of frost patterns. I put on my coat, hat, mittens, and boots as quietly as I could, afraid of waking my father. I knew he'd tell me to go back to bed, and I knew I didn't want to. The thought didn't occur to me that if he had known she was gone, he would have gone after her himself.

The world outside was shockingly cold and completely silent. The trees were strangely immobile, holding themselves stiff in the cold. It was a windless night, but the freezing temperature charged the air with its own invisible errands. It had snowed lightly, enough so that I could see footprints leading from our door down our front path. I had never gone beyond that by myself. I hesitated for a minute before following the tracks that turned right and disappeared down the street. As I walked I felt nervous, like I always did when I disobeyed my parents, but all bets were off when one of them had broken the rules, too.

The cold stung the tip of my nose and made my eyes water. Within minutes the dampness on my lashes had turned to frozen beads I had to wipe away with my arm. I could not remember ever being so cold, and I wanted, suddenly, to turn back. The neighborhood was too quiet, scary, like an imitation of the houses and streets I knew, not the real thing. I was suddenly terrified that I would get lost, too, because I sensed that although my mother had left willingly she was also without direction. The only explanation I wanted for her leaving the house in the middle of the night was that she had somehow lost her way.

It wasn't long before I was no longer looking for her but needed to find her and have her bring me back home. Every new footprint I found filled me with hope and anxiety; I was closer to her, but we were that much farther away. I followed her tracks down another block and into the small park near our house, really just a field with a swing set and a sandbox. At night, empty and dark, it seemed much larger than it was. I spotted her standing near the swings, looking out toward the trees that fringed the edges of the small expanse. Her back was to me, and her figure in a light robe didn't look quite substantial, quite human. I shivered, afraid again, not because I thought she might be a ghost, but because I knew she was real.

"Do you see it?" she asked, pointing to the trees as I crept up behind her. I looked out at the empty, white-crusted limbs. "Over there," she said, continuing to point. I looked at her, wondering if I could see what she was seeing, afraid I couldn't. She smiled. "Look,

Naomi," she said, pointing out, insisting. The sky was beginning to lighten, the moon to fade.

"Sit, sit," she said, pointing to the cold ground. I moved closer to her. "Over there," she whispered, pointing again as she dropped to her knees beside me and pulled me close with one arm. I strained and squinted, just able to make out the muted edges of trees. "Look!" she said, ordering me. I wanted to shout. I *was* looking. I was doing everything I could to see.

"There!" she cried, pointing up and out. A single cardinal, its red feathers just barely distinguishable in the newly pale sky, flew up from the edge of the park and into the air. I gasped, watching its sudden flight, as startled by its color and movement as by the fact that my mother had been looking at something that was actually there. She was smiling at me. She caressed my head with her hand. "Don't cover your hair," she said, frowning, "it's too pretty." She turned back to the trees, watching for the bird once more.

She pressed me closer to her. The pockets of her robe bulged with hidden items. The one nearest me was hard, resisting. I reached into it. Her stillness was expectant, like a wild mother allowing her child to take food from her mouth. I pulled out the bottle with its mysterious words. Only her name and the date were familiar. She'd been given whatever it was to take home with her from the hospital. I looked down, trying to understand the cryptic arrangement of letters and numbers on the bottle. I recognized them individually, but as a collection they became nonsense, and I was furious that I couldn't understand, so angry that the tears began to sting my eyes again, warm and unwelcome.

My mother was watching me, smiling. It was as if someone friendlier and infinitely more relaxed had taken up residence in my mother's body. In an instant, I decided that I didn't trust or like her. I grasped the pill bottle tightly in my fist, then raised my arm and threw it as far as I could, twisting my arm and shoulder in the process. When it landed, the quiet park began shuddering in response—a chorus of birds now took flight from their branches, each new set of wings encouraging the ones that came after. There couldn't have been more than a dozen, but I remember being amazed at seeing so many birds in winter, and then turning to see my mother crying.

I looked down and away from her, trying to swallow my own tears. I didn't know exactly what I had done to upset her. "Naomi," she said sternly, wiping her face with the sleeve of her robe, "you made them all fly away." She was staring at my face. Then I noticed her feet, which were in slippers. "Oh!" I said out loud, pointing down to them. "Your toes!" I dropped to my knees, afraid to touch what I saw. Her toes peeked out from her wet slippers, dark and swollen. I placed my hand on them, just covering the exposed skin. She cried out in pain and looked down at me, her expression accusatory.

"We have to go home," I said, suddenly understanding something I couldn't explain. "Now," I said and stood up.

She looked up at me, confused. "Why?" she asked. "We can wait a while. We'll wait for them to come back."

"They're not coming back," I told her. "They're afraid of us. They won't come back." She put a finger to her lips. I grabbed her wrist but she didn't move. I pulled at her.

"Stop it, Naomi," she argued with me. "Stop," she insisted, struggling and twisting.

My face was suddenly warm again with tears. I pulled her, finally, toward me, and as she stumbled forward in the snow she cried out in surprise. Her eyes flew open, wide and curious. "My feet," she said, "they feel too heavy."

We walked home, her gait stiff like a soldier's. As we moved through the front door, my father stood waiting with the phone receiver in his hand, his hair a shock of sleeplessness and guilt. He went to me first, but I yanked my arm away when he clutched it. "We need a hot water bottle," I told him, pointing to my mother's feet. It was something I had heard on television once, on a pioneer show where the man had lost his fingers. I frowned. "Not too hot." My father was staring at us, openmouthed. "Where is it?" I demanded, hearing the whine of my own voice echo in the hall. He began muttering, mumbling, and for a moment I worried I had lost them both. He wanted to know what and how this had happened. I went to the phone and placed it back on the receiver. My father found the hot water bottle and I fetched blankets and wrapped her feet as he filled it. As they warmed she began to cry out in pain. My father rocked her back and forth, talking to me as she cried, silently now.

"She took too much, or it wasn't what she should have taken," he said. "It's a damn shame, Naomi. A damn shame. You shouldn't hear me use that word, but the truth, for such a child, should be told. How can those doctors make such a mistake?" I had been wondering the same thing.

She insisted on being treated at home that night. I slept on the couch opposite her, my father too tired to persuade me to go upstairs. But in the morning he insisted that I go to school, and by the time I came home she was in their bedroom upstairs. "Fine," he told me. I knew better, but they wouldn't let me say I knew, wouldn't let me see her when she was recovering then, or anytime later when she was at her worst. I wanted to attack what was wrong, to storm it with affection, or knowledge, and the more they kept it from me the more I became like a pet challenging an unwanted barrier. I tried to get to her, but my father usually found me and sent me away, or she did. Leaving made me nervous and angry. I was cruel to him, reminding him that he had been sleeping and I was the one who saw her leaving and brought her back, but he met my cruelty with disproportionate generosity.

"You saved her life, Naomi," he agreed solemnly, shaking his head. "There's no doubt about that. *And* her toes." He rumpled my hair. "An incredible child." I nearly spat my frustration. Instead, I went outside, slamming an unremarkable blue ball again and again against the side of the house, my palms soon stinging and stinking of rubber. When I came back in, I told my father I had decided I wanted to be a doctor, that I wouldn't make those kinds of mistakes. I told him for his attention, and I got it. "A wonderful idea, my girl," he said, pulling me onto his knee so he could look me in the eye. "Those doctors could use someone like you." I had no idea then what he or I really meant, but I had, for the moment, what I came for: my father's undivided love.

I woke up suddenly, disoriented. I threw off the covers and ran to the window, peering into the dark at the Rosenthals' house. It was completely silent. I sat back against the glass, wondering if I should go back to sleep or wait up.

After the sun was fully risen I went outside. Teddy wasn't there. He wasn't there when my father came to call me in for breakfast, and didn't come out until the afternoon, after I'd been shopping with my father at the hardware store for the longest hour of my life. A new screwdriver, the right screws, some twist-ties; a relic of a cash register that had to be punched with a finger.

When we got back home Teddy was waiting for me. I walked outside casually, fearing I might disturb him if I ran too quickly, that he might startle like a bird. I wondered how his mother had learned to give the evil eye, if her mother had taught her. Teddy beckoned me to him with just the tips of his fingers. When I reached him his freckled face was red from another recent scrubbing, his hair flying away from a recent wash. I had to stop myself from leaning forward just to smell it. He smiled expansively, as though he'd been preparing for several days to tell me his news. "It's working," he whispered, taking my elbow in his palm.

"What?" I asked.

"Your medicine," he said.

For a moment I recalled how I'd first thought he was not so bright, how watching him he'd seemed too innocent and wild to understand anything of importance.

"Naomi," he brought me back. "He's getting better. He sat up yesterday and asked to go to the window. Then he sat outside in our front yard for, like, ten minutes. He laughed, Naomi." It was the first and second time he'd said my name. "How did you know it was his heart?"

"His heart?" I repeated. He took my hand, laughing at my startled face. My breath was leaving me in surprise. "They worked?" My hand went to my throat as if something had flown there.

He nodded eagerly. "They're working!" His hair stood tall on his head and his eyes were filled with a moving light.

I had no idea what to say. I sat down, hard, on the ground.

Teddy squatted down with me. "Are you okay?" he asked. His pupils up close were small and focused. I stared at them, thinking of the small bugs that get trapped in amber, that die and are preserved forever there. "Naomi?"

The back door of his house slammed. His mother was standing there, her arms across her chest. I braced myself for whatever was coming.

"Tee-o-door," she called, frowning. "Does your little friend want to join you for a snack?" I couldn't see his face as he nodded quickly. We stood up together, not daring to look at one another, and went inside and into her kitchen, which was fragrant with yeast and soup. She gave us wedges of canned oranges and cheese in a red casing to share. Her back was to us.

"Tee-o-door's father is looking better," she said to whatever she was preparing for dinner. She turned around and stared hard at me, fixing me to the chair. "He is glad the boy has a friend." She had a glass in each hand and placed them before us. "He want to take you to the park when he can walk." At this she nodded and frowned once more.

Later that week my father presented me with my very own copy of *Gray's Anatomy*. I think my heart pills and the shamanistic line of thinking they suggested had alarmed him. "It's time you began looking at the pictures, at least," he told me, handing the tall white book over to me and my waiting hands. "So you're a little more familiar maybe with what you'll need to know." There was a man on its front, his skin pulled back, the red muscles striated and exposed, the bones with their scribbled, scripted names in red, too. Fortunately, maybe having learned his lesson from *D'Aulaires' Myths*, my father also presented me with the corresponding coloring book, the cover of which showed the same drawing in entirely different shades: a rainbow of color at the top with white spaces underneath, as if to say, *This one can be pretty!*

"Get a head start," my father said, tapping the book. "Most of those girls at Wellesley will probably have their fancy private educations to help them. Luckily, you're a Jew, and we Jews have always done our best learning at home." I was clutching the book to me, trying not to look like it was too heavy for me.

He continued. "Did you know Einstein mostly taught himself physics?" I frowned skeptically but he wouldn't relent. "You think the Sagans had money for private school? And Freud. Do you think he figured all that out in a classroom? Geniuses, all of them. And they read their books at home." He tapped *Gray's* again. "Let's get started."

SIX

Teddy and I both started fourth grade that fall. He attended Maimonides, the Modern Orthodox private school a few minutes from our home that was bordered on all sides by a ten-foot stone wall. I returned to Robert Kennedy Elementary. We were both home by three, with plenty of time to play outside before homework and dinner. Teddy had to wear long pants, a white shirt, a vest, his *tzitzit*, his *keepah*, and a coat to school, but he would change out of these into dark jeans and a T-shirt, leaving only the *tzitzit* and the *keepah* on before coming outside to play. I had to wait on my back steps fussing and counting until he was ready.

Neither one of us had many toys. My parents believed in creativity, and Teddy's mother believed in austerity. So between the two of us we had some sidewalk chalk Teddy had found, scrap paper, a handful of dolls neither of us cared for, three horses only I cared for, some jacks, my historically significant coloring books, and marbles. Having so little we felt we needed nothing, and usually spent our days climbing trees or digging or, in the winter, making things from snow that would melt before a week passed. The only thing we used regularly was the sidewalk chalk, which Teddy carried in his front pockets. He could draw, as my father would say, like nobody's business. I came home from school one time and he'd sketched three huge horses on the sidewalk in front of our house—my horses, with me in different gear, riding each one. I cried when the rain washed them into a silvery mess early the next morning, standing outside to watch the colors running into the gutter like melted fish.

He was a terrific distraction from everything that felt full of holes: school, my mother, my father's heart. We had invented a world; the universe had turned upside down and given us mastery over our lives. We felt bold together, invincible, capable of doing anything and everything, and the more this feeling overcame us, the more time we spent together, so that almost every waking moment of our lives was either at school or in each other's company, both of us delighting in our imaginary worlds as we spun them out beneath us.

That fall, the Jewish Youth of New England sponsored a drawing contest for children in grades four through six. Five winners would be selected, and each would enjoy two days with his family at the Milnah Resort in southern New Hampshire after school let out. The contest guidelines stipulated only that the entrants draw a family tree; beyond that we were free to interpret as we wished. Everyone in Teddy's class at Maimonides was entering, and my father saw no reason for me not to enter, too.

The right side of my tree, my father's side, was a series of lines and names, many with question marks after them. The left side, my mother's, was a jumble of leaves and flowers and berries. I think the judges must have thought it was an abstract rendering, though to me it could not have been more literal. Teddy's was gorgeous, the veined bark six different shades of brown, each leaf carefully engraved with the Hebrew letters of an ancestor's name, a small picture beside each one to represent the individual: Elhanon Rosenthal with his white feather; his wife, Rifkah, with her lit candle; their child, Saul, b. 1875, d. 1877, with his miniature wood wagon.

We both won, and the local media made a huge deal of having two winners in the same district, never mind that we lived within shouting distance of each other. We had our picture taken for the *Brookline Times*, and it was written that, as winners of the contest, we would be treating our parents to a stay at Milnah. Even my mother experienced a rare infusion of delight at the prospect of staying at a resort for a few nights, and my parents packed that spring with unprecedented enthusiasm, "Shall I bring the pearls or the diamonds, Sol?" my mother called from their bedroom. "The EMERALDS!" my father called from the hallway closet, where he was extracting his swim fins.

Teddy's parents weren't as thrilled, though none of us would have expected otherwise. Milnah had a glatt kosher kitchen and a separate house for the Orthodox, but his parents, getting out of their car in front of it, looked like they might have been arriving at a funeral. At least his mother did. I think his father was probably a little excited when he took in the lake and the wide lawns, but he deferred to her misery.

Until we found the mushrooms, the time passed slowly, all of us tiptoeing around Mrs. Rosenthal, who would have been better off locked in her room, but who positioned herself in a folding chair on the front lawn. She could see all three of the residences on the property as well as the lake, so that when we ran from the water to the house, she could track us with her eyes.

Teddy and I went into the woods to avoid his mother, and to ignore the fact that mine was already inside with the shades drawn. We ended up wandering fairly deep into them, pretending we were stranded there, that we had survived an airplane crash and had to forage for our food. Because we never got in each other's way, Teddy's and my make-believe games seemed to know no bounds; the longer we played, the more invested we became in their details and how it might feel if everything we decreed became real. I found the mushrooms first, and was so sure they looked every bit like the ones my mother used that I feigned nonchalance, serving them up to both of us as rare delicacies.

Almost at once, Teddy became practical. "They could be poisonous," he said, not touching them.

I lifted my palm to his face so he could smell them. He still looked wary. "I've seen my mother *cook* with them, Teddy," I said impatiently, not wanting to be doubted. His mouth was screwed into a frown.

"Also," I said, "there's no way a Jewish summer camp would allow poisonous mushrooms in the woods." He looked at me doubtfully. I sighed. "They wouldn't be kosher, Teddy," I said, putting one in my mouth.

Here's what I remember about the next three days: stomach pains deep enough to scare us both out of the woods and to our parents. My father's face when I told him: the round "oh" of his mouth, with no sound coming from it. Then, later, my father arguing with a doctor. I only remember the doctor's voice, not his face. I was in a bed, I didn't know where, and I was awake long enough to see that Teddy was in another bed nearby with a doctor beside him. His eyeglasses were wire-rimmed and glaring, and he seemed tense with fury. The fact that he was even attempting to argue with my father made him seem like a god. *Dr. God,* I thought to myself. Of course.

"The boy's mother is having a fit," my father yelled.

"They become agitated when separated," the doctor hissed. He had a thick, Eastern European accent, and he brought to mind the Nazi doctor in a PBS special my father had watched earlier that fall that I wasn't supposed to see. I moaned softly. He paid me no mind. "I will keep them together; their fevers cannot escalate." As he turned to go, the sun flashed off his glasses in a brief, brilliant explosion.

"Treatment initiated for substance abuse and withdrawal," I heard myself mutter.

"What? Did she say something?"

Dr. God was angry, I thought. He needed more explanation. *"3/28/74 PROM,"* I said. *"3/28/74 PROM."* He was peering in on me and I had to close my eyes. *"3/31/74 delivered of 4 lb 2 oz (SFA) boy. 4/6/74 further obtunded. 4/7/74 manifested right hemiplegia. Expired 4/9/74. PM revealed ruptured left cerebral aneurysm in the distribution of the left middle cerebral artery."*

"Please—" The doctor tried to speak.

"Massive intracranial hemorrhage. Also fibrosis of the liver; portal hypertension; mild early ascites."

"She's delirious," my father said, his voice coming through a tunnel. Not delirious, I told myself, no longer able to speak. A nurse rushed in from the corner, her white skirt holding her back. I closed my eyes. When I opened them again she was pulling the curtain between my bed and where Teddy had lain. I thought he had died. I tried to die myself. When I opened them again, Teddy was no longer in the bed beside me. I sat up, ready to scream, when a hand grabbed my right arm. "Naomi?"

It was my mother. I looked at her, terrified.

"No, no, sweetheart," she said softly, hurriedly, "he's already left for home. He already went home." Her voice was shaking as she tried to finish whatever it was she meant to say. "Naomi"—she gathered me into her arms so that I was almost pulled from my bed—"I wasn't here," she said into my hair, "when you came in. Your father said—" She drew away from me, staring into my face. "Naomi," she said again, my name coming into her mouth instead of a flood of buried words. She was stroking my face, her hand both light and insistent, her eyes unusually bright. "I'm so, so sorry. They said you'd lost your mind." I wrapped my arms around her and, for the first time in my life, she grabbed me tighter than I could her, pulled me into her lap and held us there.

I think my mother had tried to say she was sorry she wasn't a better mother to me. I think she'd tried to say this many times in my life, though I couldn't be sure. I'm not sure I needed her to say such a thing. I would never have fooled myself into thinking that her constant sadness didn't make me feel incomplete, but that incompleteness was tied up with wondering who she could and might be, and with the ache of that wonder. I never thought for a moment that she didn't give me everything she could have given a daughter.

Yet I wonder if part of my fascination with Mrs. Rosenthal didn't have a little to do with the fact that I knew how deeply she loved her own child, how far she would go to protect him, and how deeply she disliked me.

To our collective surprise, Mrs. Rosenthal continued to allow me into her home after we had all returned from Milnah and settled back into the routines of life, but only for snacks, never a full meal. And she wouldn't serve me fresh food, only packaged or overripe, even though her kitchen frequently smelled of baking bread and homemade soup. I tried, with feigned offhandedness, to impress her. I'd chat with Teddy and reference my grades, or how I was the only kid without a tardy that year, or how my teacher had picked me to clap erasers after school because I was the only one who had understood the math lesson. Teddy would open his eyes wide and nod his amazement, but she didn't buy our show. She rarely even looked at me. I went so far as to bring *War and Peace* with me one afternoon, setting it casually on the table beside me. She took one look at it and started muttering in Yiddish, the only word I understood being *goy*, which she repeated several times. I put the book on the chair beside me and slid it under the table. No orange segments that day, only the red cheese.

Alone, I would wander the possibilities of covering my hair in a long, dark wig, throwing away my shorts and T-shirts, and finding heavy skirts and blouses to wear, becoming modest. I savored this fantasy the way other children imagine they are the secret offspring of royalty or aliens. I knew, and I suspect Teddy did also, though we never discussed it, that Mrs. Rosenthal was always looking for a reason to separate us, to explain to Teddy why he didn't need me.

I think that's why I began to look to see if I had within me the power to reveal some nugget of myself that would make her turn from the stove when she saw me, her face first blank with surprise then quickly open with recognition, her steps quick as she went to the cupboard and pulled out one of the five china bowls she kept there, filling it carefully and generously with hot, fragrant soup from her stove.

* * *

As it turned out, Teddy was the one who came up with the idea that we should go to the library. He was convinced that if I just carried the right book, she would be won over.

"My dad's really smart," he'd say, as we sat side by side on the Green Line to Copley Station to get to the Boston Public Library downtown, our hands intertwined between us. For my tenth birthday, my father had taken me to get my own library card, and now Teddy had one, too, which emboldened us to argue that if we were old enough to be responsible for books on our own, we were old enough to go to the library on our own.

Teddy always whispered on the subway, as though the people around us might be trying to listen in. "She loves to watch him read. She brings him his book every night and makes me be quiet. And when the paper comes, she wants to know if anyone has made the news for winning an award. A Nobel winner is more exciting to her than an Emmy winner," he confided. His lips almost touched my ear.

We went through Asimov, Aleichem, Amichai, Heyse, Pasternak, Bellow, and Singer: she recognized none of them, or at least she made no show of recognition. We had a dark moment with Kissinger, a brief flash in her eyes and a sneer; like Tolstoy, he was quickly removed from her sight. We were too young to know we needed to move beyond fiction and non-, to know that if we would just make our way into the sciences we'd find her beloved Ehrlich and Bohr, the Konrad Bloch whose achievements made her blush with pleasure. But we did know about Einstein. Everyone, even the *goyishe* kids, knew about Einstein.

Of course Teddy suggested him early on, but he had what I thought of as the ability to find the least appropriate passages. His favorite book was a book of Einstein's "life quotes," a little volume that opened with a rumination on relativity and love. He took deep pleasure in reading me the following when I felt frustrated and annoyed by him: "How on earth can you explain in terms of chemistry and physics so important a biological phenomenon as first love? Put your hand on a stove for a minute and it feels like an hour. Sit with that special girl for an hour and it seems like a minute. That's relativity." I'd roll my eyes and sigh, but it never stopped him.

I was probably right to guess that the very last thing his mother wanted was to be reminded of romance, especially if the reminder were to come from me. In fact, I was sure that the only chance I had with her was to harness her undeniable attraction to intellect. Anyway, I argued, who ever reads Einstein for love? Teddy frowned but didn't challenge me. He just waited, bringing Albert up every few weeks, and placing him gently back on the shelf when I shook my head.

The truth is, I was still working up the courage to admit even to myself what I was planning for Einstein, though I knew I was saving him. I guessed that Mrs. Rosenthal would have the same reverence for him that my father did: the Jew to define all Jewish success stories, the one who actually changed the world's perception of itself.

And despite my outburst in the hospital, thinking I needed to save Teddy's life, it had been more than two years since I'd convinced myself to be quiet about my memory. Perhaps in those years my fears had softened, but I knew I was losing my willingness to hold back. Anna Kim would never like me; I wasn't any closer to finding friends at school who could be brought back home; I was tired of feeling ashamed enough to hide something from my father. So the timing was right, that summer, for me to sit down deliberately in a chair at the Boston Public Library and scan the row of Einsteins, finally deciding that, above all, I needed to stop pretending. Teddy followed my gaze.

He walked over to the shelf cautiously and studied the spines. After trailing his finger lightly over them for a few minutes, he pulled out a thick yellow one, about two inches wide. It was a nice-enough-looking book, with its friendly color and simple print. Teddy opened it like a magic trick, looking down at where he'd landed. Then he brought it to me, the book still open in his hands.

I flipped through the first few pages, understanding nothing, looking for nothing in particular. The book's title was *Out of My Later*

Years, New York, 1950. A note at the beginning claimed that the piece we had stumbled upon originally appeared as a foreword to Philipp Frank's *Relativity—A Richer Truth*, Boston, 1950. Everything in the middle seemed opaque. And then I found what I was sure was a sign: a chapter on the laws of science and the laws of ethics. Surely such a connection could bring even Mrs. Rosenthal and me together, the female scholar and the female watchdog.

I looked for the final sentence in the chapter, the one my father told me was like the last passage in a symphony, all that the author had been working toward: *Truth is what stands the test of experience.* She'd like that, I assured myself, growing more confident; it sounded rabbinical. I backed up one, then two, then three paragraphs, finally settling on the middle of the previous page: long enough to make an impression, not so long (I hoped) that I'd lose her attention.

I could see that Teddy was disappointed when I returned the book to the shelf—he must have also been thinking that his mother would have loved it if I brought home Einstein—but he didn't question me. I pulled a volume of Bohr from the next shelf and marched to the entrance, checking it out unceremoniously, my pace increasing as I made my way down the front steps and onto the sidewalk. Teddy was half running behind me, but I didn't say a word to him. I couldn't. What I was planning had to be done quickly, or I'd lose my nerve.

Mrs. Rosenthal was at the stove, as usual, stirring something in a pot. The red-skinned cheese was on the wooden block that served as their table, two pieces of it this time. My heart leapt. The timing was good. Beside them, a hard peach had been cut into quarters, then eighths, so that the entire offering included four pieces of fruit and an entire miniature wheel of cheese. Perhaps I had misjudged her. Perhaps she was warming to me. Perhaps this wasn't a moment of desperation. But I had to keep going. I was too afraid to stop.

I sat down, picking up my napkin and unfolding it slowly before putting it on my lap. Teddy was looking at me so intently I felt like kicking him under the table. And Mrs. Rosenthal was humming. Humming! Why was she humming? I looked at Teddy and he only shook his head, bewildered. He could make no sense of either one of us. He looked terribly lost.

His mother turned around to face us. She was even smiling a little that day, which gave me courage.

"Did you know, Theodore," I said, just as he took his first bite, "that Albert Einstein was not the first Jew to win a Nobel Prize?" My plate was still in her hand, the white of it almost glaring against her dark, creviced fingers. She put it down in front of me and turned her back to us.

A moment later she had resumed her stirring. "It was Albert A. Michelson, in 1907," I went on. Teddy didn't move. His mother stirred. The only sounds were the *tuck tuck tuck, tuck tuck tuck* of the wooden spoon hitting the sides of the pot, the bubbling of the soup. I knew she was listening. "But Einstein was the most famous Jew to win it. And as we all know"—I coughed out a little conspiratorial laugh—"it was for his theory of relativity."

I made a show of shaking out my napkin and replacing it on my lap. My hands needed something to do or they'd tremble. "But the theory was still new. It matured and deepened throughout his lifetime." I reached for a piece of cheese as I'd once seen my mother reach for a bottle of wine, casually, elegantly. "As late as 1950 he posited"—I had learned that word from my father last Thursday during vocabulary night in the Feinstein household—"that *science searches for relations which are thought to exist independently of the searching individual.*" Teddy stopped eating. His mother didn't move.

I took a deep breath. "*This includes the case where man himself is the subject, or the subject of scientific statements may be concepts created by ourselves, as in mathematics. Such concepts are not necessarily supposed to correspond to any objects in the outside world. However, all scientific statements and laws have one characteristic in common: they are 'true or false' (adequate or inadequate). Roughly speaking, our reaction to them is 'yes' or 'no.'*" I took a sip of water, pretending not to notice that she had turned around, the wooden spoon still in her hand and dripping now on her floor.

I clasped my hands together before me, a move I felt sure was inspired: *"The scientific way of thinking has further characteristics."* I was sweating between my palms and they had begun to shake: there were no more false movements to be made. *"The concepts which it uses to build up its coherent systems are not expressing emotions. For the scientist, there is only 'being,' but no wishing, no valuing, no good, no evil; no goal. As long as we remain within the realm of science proper . . ."* Had their clock always ticked so loud? *"We can never meet with a sentence of the type: 'Thou shalt not lie.' There is something like a Puritan's restraint in the scientist who seeks truth: he keeps away from everything voluntaristic"*—I had had to practice this word several times on the T ride home—vol-un-tar-*is*-tic—while Teddy had wanted to chat—*"or emotional. Incidentally, this trait is the result of a slow development . . ."*

"Ssssshhhhh," she had begun to hiss, quietly at first, the sound increasing until she stopped herself short once she realized she'd silenced me.

She dropped the spoon on the table and walked out the front door, Teddy and I falling out of our chairs to trail her. She was in my kitchen a moment later. "Vat is wrong with this girl, your daughter?" she demanded of my mother, who had been sitting with a book, babysitting dinner. She stood up. "Is she possessed?" Mrs. Rosenthal demanded, her voice getting higher, her accent thick with emotion.

My father came in from the living room in response to the intrusion, though he stood at the door. "Mrs. Rosenthal!" he said, surprised, affecting the false joviality that suited him. "What a pleasant surprise. Have a seat! May we offer your something?"

"Pshhhh," she exhaled, incensed. "Keep her!" she cried, as if ridding herself of me completely.

"I'm sorry," my mother said, standing. "I don't understand." She locked eyes with Mrs. Rosenthal. "Has Naomi done something wrong?" It wasn't so much a question as a challenge.

Mrs. Rosenthal turned on me, the query in her eyes answered on my face. "They do not know." It wasn't a question. "Show them," she demanded.

"Show us what?" my father asked. He looked nervous, vulnerable.

"She is possessed! Show them!"

"I am not!" I hollered back. "And I *am* Jewish." I stuck my tongue out at her, then began to recite the speech again, quickly now, rushing through it, making it to the third paragraph before my mother stopped me.

"It's okay, sweetheart," she said softly. "You can stop." No one said a word. "Einstein, yes?" She spoke so softly I'm not sure anyone else could hear. I nodded.

Mrs. Rosenthal eyed her as she might a rat that had just walked into the kitchen. *"Meshugenah,"* she muttered, "the whole lot of you. *Meshugas.*" She gripped Teddy's hand as if by doing so she could save him from drowning.

"It seems Naomi has, unknowingly, offended you," my mother began conversationally, though she had paused for a monumental beat before she spoke. "I can assure you, however, that she is not possessed." She spoke in clipped, articulate tones. My mother had never finished college, but she had the ability to speak with an intelligence so sharp it could cut through a room of commentaries. Even her posture was lightly intimidating. Mrs. Rosenthal stared at her open mouthed. She pulled Teddy closer to her. My mother was getting angrier, color blossoming in her cheeks.

"Naomi," my father said, crouching down to me. *"Ketzi."* He got my attention. "How did you know all that?" He had his hands on my shoulders, as though I might fly up to the ceiling. My mother closed her mouth.

"I read it," I said, looking at Teddy's mother. "Where?" my father said, his excitement almost as great as his confusion. "The library," I answered. He looked puzzled. "Physics, section 112.65 Ba to 112.65 Dr." It felt, very briefly, wonderful to let it all out. He frowned.

"She memorized it," my mother explained so only he could hear.

His eyes opened wide, searching mine. "Can you tell us what the other sections are?" he asked cautiously.

I put both of my hands gently on his arms: "112.65 Ds to 112.65 Ga and 112.65 Ga to 112.65 Fl . . ." He stopped me after a few more, then hugged me, tightly, wanting to press something away—doubt, the quickening vertigo of disbelief. When he released me it was to speak to Teddy's mother. "If you recall, the great Talmudic scholars," he said from the floor, "more than one of them had just such a gift. Naomi, as you may know"—he puffed out his chest; Mrs. Rosenthal would almost certainly not know the zinger coming—"is descended from more than one great Eastern European rabbi."

She shook her head. "It is not good," she contradicted him. "A little girl with the mind of an old man." She spat on the floor, then began muttering again. It sounded like an incantation. She looked up and at my father, both eyes locking on his. "A girl is not meant to become a great Talmudic scholar," she pronounced. "A girl is meant to become a woman. With a woman's duties."

My father bristled visibly. "No. A girl becomes a woman who, if she wants, becomes a doctor." He put a hand on my shoulder.

Mrs. Rosenthal glared at me, disapproval on every corner of her face. "She should become a mother. Then she would learn something."

"Mom," Teddy said, pulling lightly on her wrist. She looked down at him. His face was pleading. "Stop," he said. "Please." Her gaze didn't waver off of him, but her face began to fall in on itself as she took in his expression. She must not have realized until that moment that he, like me, needed the care of another child more desperately than either of our parents wanted to admit. She took in a breath quickly. "Tee-o-dore," she said softly. And they exchanged a look of such intimacy I had to look away. With one arm she pulled him to her chest and held him there. "Come here, girl," she said after a moment. *"Aher,"* she repeated in Yiddish, gesturing to me.

I moved out from under my father's hands and went to her, trying to feel brave. She was not very tall, but she was infinitely wider than me; her body could have performed a full eclipse of mine. She laid a hand on my forehead. Her touch was dry and papery, like the wasp's wings Teddy and I had collected when burying the ones my father had killed along with a nest that summer. We pulled off the wings before covering the split bodies with dirt, the transparent clippings taking to the air like rice at a wedding. Mrs. Rosenthal shook her head, tsking. She lifted her other hand off Teddy and put it on the side of my face, chanting, shaking her head. I realized almost an instant too late that I had become an object of pity, and dropped my head just in time.

And then, suddenly, I can't explain why, I threw my arms around her, giving her the hug my father had given me, the one my mother would never have wanted, pressing myself into her so she would know me, bodily, squeezing sympathy from her as though she were an overripe fruit, full of sweet juices.

She made a small, soft sound and stopped muttering. I held her for a moment longer, at peace. Then, alarmed by her silence, I stood back and looked up at her. It's true I didn't trust her. She hadn't wanted me to. Her eyes were shining now, though her mouth was turned down. She put a hand on my head, then dropped it to my chest, pushing against me. I took a single step back.

She shook her head and turned her face. "My boy is lonely," she said. She took a moment, nodding to herself, before she addressed the room: "So now you know." Teddy's mother took his hand and walked out the door.

The next day at snack I had my own piece of fruit. In exchange, I stopped going with Teddy to the library.

SEVEN

In the years before his father died, Teddy grew long and strong, like Paul Bunyan in the tall tales, so beautiful that even the reality of him was difficult to grasp. If he hadn't been so thin, he would have seemed truly unreal. But his young bones stuck their way out of the sleeves of his T-shirts; his knees were doorknobs as he bent to examine something; the line of his jaw strained against the skin: it took effort for his skeleton not to burst through. I took all this in with the flush satisfaction of devotion. I had decided it was just fine that we would be a family together. We were equally eager to be in each other's company, and neither one of us alone was really complete. There was still the problem of his mother, who hadn't warmed to me since the Einstein incident, but I was sure she had at least grown used to me. I was a constant presence hovering just near her, and I allowed myself to hope that she was less categorically opposed to me than she had once been.

Just before his twelfth birthday, for reasons that weren't entirely clear to either one of us, Teddy's *peyes* disappeared and his clothes loosened, both in formality and fit. Together we concluded that, as Teddy put it, "they were chilling a little," and that, as my father put it, at least one of his parents might "be warming to the idea of greater assimilation." And I, understanding myself to be the product of the greatest of assimilations, began to perk up, hoping that one day Mrs. Rosenthal might release her son just enough to let him drift into that undefined, soupy mess in which cultures merge and individuals emerge, forming fierce pairs to substitute for the intense connections they'd fought so hard to diminish.

He was still bar mitzvahed the following March. I was not invited, but a shaky video recording was made of the party afterward. I tried to act interested, but I wasn't. I felt more and more confused by Judaism, more like a half-breed member of a tribe that demanded one's full attention, and I realized that as far as I could tell, my parents' actual faith might be either blind or nonexistent.

Still, our mutual transitions into adulthood were definitely taking place, and I was fascinated by the small, critically different ways our bodies were changing. Teddy's Adam's apple seemed to leap from his throat when he swallowed, and I had new breasts that hurt so much sometimes I lay awake, shirtless. We were not yet sexual, but our bodies were preparing us to be. His being close to me hinted at a new thrill, and I felt sometimes anxious in his presence, hungry and nervous.

One Sunday when we were thirteen, a tremendous windstorm whipped its way through New England. It was a wind from northern Canada, muscular and swift. Teddy and I were giddy with it. It was mid-March, and the winter was on its way out. We had gone to a local pond, Hammond Pond, to be outside and search for mallard nests, and Teddy's father had given us his camera to photograph whatever we thought might be the roofs of the nest—the dry peaks the females like to tent above their eggs—so he could then look at our film to tell us what we had found. But when we arrived by the water, giggling, everything imaginable was littered with twigs and brush and broken sticks, so that the whole area was nested, the wind the author of the mess, fussing over this or that twig or branch. I took a step back and, with an exaggerated flourish, attempted to position the camera to capture the entire scene. When I put the camera down, Teddy was motionless, staring.

"Shhh," he quieted me before I could ask what was wrong.

We stood still, both of us trying to listen for what he had heard. The wind whipped my hair across my face and flapped the hood of Teddy's jacket against the back of his neck. And then, suddenly, I heard it: the low sounds of a duck, not quite a quack, more of a throaty, continual muttering.

An instant later Teddy pointed out what my own eyes had just landed on: one of the manmade mallard nests, tilting dangerously off its support. There were several of these constructions lining the shores of Hammond Pond; each spring, amateur conservationists rolled chicken wire that had been covered with sod into thick cylinders, then placed the cylinders onto rudimentary metal stilts that could be set into the water. This one had been partially knocked off its base during the wind storm, though it lingered there, threatening to topple.

In his heavy boots, Teddy waded into the water toward it. I don't know why I thought immediately of disaster, but tears were already welling in my eyes as Teddy wrapped his long arms under and around the nest, lifted it with unbearable care, and brought it into the shore grasses where I stood. Then he bent his long body to the ground, set the nest to one side, and dug into a clutch of cattails, thinning them out to create an opening there. I joined him, wanting to look inside the nest to see if there were eggs there and if they were okay, but Teddy tugged on my sleeve, silently urging me to help him instead. I did, bending down to pull hard on the long stems, trying to keep myself from wondering what might have happened to the eggs.

We worked quickly, the urgency of our intrusion soon palpable. The owner of the nest had emerged from within the shrubs nearby, her black, opaque eyes unblinking as she watched us. She stood not ten feet away, rigidly attentive. The tears began to sting my eyes again. I fought against the pull of fear, forcing myself to focus on the task at hand.

When we'd dug a large enough space, Teddy settled the nest into the thinned cattails. The moment he was done we walked away quickly. After we'd covered a short distance, Teddy stopped abruptly, listening. He had put one arm across my chest to stop me as well. I looked back when he did.

The duck was sitting where she had been. But soon after we became still, she began to stir, shaking her legs out from under her, dipping her nose to the ground to investigate. A moment later she waddled over to the nest and hopped up to its edge. She bent her beak to the leaves, parting them, and a moment later disappeared within.

Teddy sat down with a thump, and immediately started laughing. I did, too, my chest releasing its fears in great breaths, my laugh ringing around and through his. I dropped to the ground, and we began tickling each other, unable to contain our joy, rolling in the mud and wind. Some of his hair caught in my mouth, and when I looked at his face there was a smudge of dirt on his forehead. These messes were intimacy to me; I would have tumbled with him forever just to acquire more. When we were tired, we lay still on our backs. He leaned over and whispered in my ear, "Do you think we saved them?" His eyes were pale amber and wide. "I think so," I said, stroking his cheek with my finger, experimenting with a caress my father favored. In the past few weeks, kisses had become our greatest pleasure, soft and careful, like promises, and never too many at a time.

And just when it seemed we were alone in the world we were startled apart by voices, a collection of brightly colored coats, a group making its way through the woods that surrounded the pond. They had emerged only about a hundred feet away, their voices concealed and then amplified by the wind. They were carrying many things: baskets, blankets, chairs, wine, and a small dog. As we watched them, the wind grew fiercer, more assertive. And then, to our collective disbelief, the dog was whipped out from an elderly lady's frail side, soaring out over the distance between us. We froze in stunned surprise, watching the small creature writhe in flight.

It did not seem that anything so fragile could land and not be broken. And just as I had this thought, I felt Teddy's body lift beside me. For an instant I thought he was being taken by the wind, too, but he was jumping, high and long, reaching for the dog. I didn't breathe, watching the space where they might just meet, though I feared it was impossible.

But a moment later the dog was in his hands, then against his chest, and then they had both fallen into the mud, a tangle of slender bones and dirty brown hues of skin and fur and hair. From the ground, Teddy looked at me, his expression unbelieving and joyful. For many years later, when I would recall all this I would remember the thrill of believing we could have saved anything that day.

I have often wondered if his father died at just that instant, just as the small impact of the dog punched into Teddy's round chest, extinguishing his father's heart. If the shock of the small body against Teddy's had been too much. I hadn't known Teddy's father well, but I recognized that he loved his son deeply. He had even been fond of me.

When we came home later that afternoon, Teddy caught my hand again when I went to drop it from his. We usually separated once we came to our block, careful to shield his mother from something she didn't want to see. But that afternoon we were wind-bitten and triumphant. A life had been saved. Perhaps more than one. Teddy gripped my hand tightly to communicate his confidence, and the sensation warmed and thrilled me, the sting on my cheeks spreading to heat my whole body. As we rounded the corner to his house, we saw the white-and-red back of the ambulance, all of its lights on but not flashing.

EIGHT

Within two weeks the house was packed and sold.

The night before they moved, Teddy walked into my bedroom. "The back door was open," he said. He crawled under the covers with me and we lay in the dark, staring at nothing. I began to cry, and Teddy found my hand. "I'll come back," he promised. I shook my head. "How can you?" I asked, choking on the tears and the words.

He had no answer for me, and I must have fallen asleep shortly after. Just before morning he crawled out as silently as he'd come in, almost as though he had never been there. I wanted to shout out, but I couldn't. I was already in the dreams I would have of this moment for years, watching him leave, unable to stop him, knowing he was going as surely as I knew the sun was rising in a few minutes, bringing a bright, empty day. I stood up and found a collection of drawings he'd made of me on my desk. I sorted through each one, thinking of the way he had of placing his hands on the back of my neck and sliding them into my hair, lifting it swiftly up and back, forcing my chin to lift, displaying me to the sky. "You remind me of lemons," he said one day a few months before they moved. He opened his book and sketched all of me in a painfully bright yellow. I did not like the effect and frowned at it. "I think I like it better when you use charcoal," I commented.

"No," he shook his head. "You're just not used to your own brightness." He scooted closer to me so that our hips were touching. "This is how I see you," he explained, staring down at the paper. "Your face isn't really beautiful," he once admitted, "but it is wonderful. More wonderful than beautiful." I remember staring down at that paper, seeing a girl with a big, uneven smile looking out at me. I had never considered that someone might see me that way—bursting with light and wonderful.

He had continued drawing as definitively as I had given it up after our week at Milnah, sketching illustrations of me sick, then himself sick, then his mother in her chair, then everything else that came into view that puzzled him. I think that by drawing life's mysteries he could study them uninterrupted, for however long it might take him to make some sense of them.

For several nights after they left I didn't sleep. My mother walked by my room once, a shadow by the time I looked, barely pausing at the sight of me lying there. It was too much misery for both of us. My father would come to check on me before he went to bed. Even though my light was off, he knew I was awake. He sat down beside me.

"A remarkable young man," he said. "A good friend to you." He had both of his hands on his knees, steadying himself. I knew my grief was overwhelming to him, already, and I turned from him, facing the wall. He got up a few minutes later. "Get some sleep, *ketzi*," he said. "You have school in the morning."

For a month I only slept fitfully. The feeling of loss grew like a stone in my chest, so that every night when I lay down, the pain became heavier, pressing into me. I taught myself to sleep with my back resting against the wall. If, one night, someone were to appear at my door, I would already be halfway up to greeting him. I was torn between the present and a dream: his father had not died, his mother had not taken him away; it was only a misunderstanding, he was home. I used these fantasies like a drug, knowing before I entered them that they were thin veils before reality, but I was too desperate to refuse them. I could make no sense of why Mrs. Rosenthal had snatched him away as she did, why she could not understand the need for friendship, especially her son's.

Mrs. Rosenthal had acknowledged my misery by conceding a few personal details. They had gone to a new Orthodox community a short distance outside the established enclave of Lakewood, New Jersey. They could not afford to live in Lakewood, but Freehold was a new development, even more observant than Lakewood, she claimed, her shoulders back, her chin lifted with pride. She felt that Mr. Rosenthal's death was a message to herself and to her son to increase their attention to God. He did not like a halfhearted Jew, she intoned significantly. If I were older, I would have been only mildly shocked by her implied accusations, perhaps even amused; as it was, I was sure they were leaving because I and everyone around me would never be able to measure up to the God she believed governed us all.

Both my mother and father absorbed these happenings as members of an audience at a somber play. I asked my father in the weeks after the move how we might figure a way to visit, to go see Teddy soon after they'd settled in a bit, get him back into my life before, I thought, it might be too late. Instead he told me, "Mrs. Rosenthal has made it clear she wants a clean break for the boy, Naomi," presenting that line of reasoning as unassailable. "I think we have to respect her wishes."

Maybe he was trying to protect me from further hurt. But a gathering fury wove its way through me, whispering that my parents just didn't care enough to speak up; that politeness and civility took precedence over all. I couldn't even look at my mother, who mentioned Teddy even less than my father. In my darkest thoughts I blamed her, blamed her for going to the window that day and telling me to look out, seeing Teddy as a possible friend even before I had.

My father, at least, had the grace to hesitate a little in his resolve.

Shortly before they left, he went through the motions of objecting to Mrs. Rosenthal's plans. "The boy has a good school here," he argued, "and attachments." Mrs. Rosenthal didn't even bother to shake her head. Teddy and I were like tin soldiers, unblinking, tense in view of what lay before us. "I know what is best for my boy," Mrs. Rosenthal kept insisting, right up to the moment they left. She was once again standing in our kitchen, but this time there was nothing else to say. "I have told Tee-o-dore he may send you a letter," she said to me by way of goodbye. Then they were out the door and on the street, where a taxi stood waiting to whisk them away impassively and efficiently, like an ongoing force that had always been there. One only had to step in its path to be swept away.

One morning I sat in my bed, clasping my knees, tired of watching the changes of light. The sun coming through the window was weak and barely warm, but the energy in my body suddenly began to respond disproportionately until it became acute, almost painful. I grabbed my wrists until they grew white. It might have been rage, it might have been the limits of misery, it might have been still more grief. But whatever it was bubbled to the surface, taking me along with it. I stood up, threw on some clothes, and took off.

I started to run before I even left the house, leaping down the stairs, passing my mother in the dark with her coffee, and letting the front door slam behind me. There was just enough daylight to see the sidewalk and the streetlights, but it was misting and my eyes blurred. My father must have followed me almost immediately, I heard him calling, but I was already far away.

I ran through our streets, farther and farther, my feet smacking the cold pavement. The pain shattered into my hips and spread upward until I was able to gulp it back down in breaths that filled my rib cage to its limits. The rhythm of my feet hitting the earth began to feel like a sort of grace, an acknowledgment of the hardness of being alive and growing, the harshness of it.

I was still running when I realized the car behind me was following me. I turned to look. My father. I dove into the tennis courts of the Roosevelt Academy, a private school about a mile from our house about which I knew nothing. I stood on the court in the darkness, listening as my father killed the motor and slammed his door.

He stood at the wire gates and spread his arms across them. He looked like a huge bear, soft and unwelcome. I ran to the corner farthest from him and hunkered down, pressing my cheek against the cool chain link of the fence. In a few more hours happy children would meet their friends here, calling and being answered. My father and I were in the company of the first birds, their occasional songs wafting through the half-light like experiments in being heard.

My father walked through them and along the side opposite to me, picking up a racket and a ball someone had left there. The increasing light showed him weighing the ball in his palm, then dribbling it first with his hand, then with the racket. His silhouette with these props was comical; a bushy gray muzzle for a beard, a potbelly that had begun to distinguish itself over the past year or so above his thin legs. After a while he pocketed the ball and picked up another racket that had been left, crossing the court casually and placing it before me.

"Stand up," he commanded before turning his back to me and returning to the opposite side.

I curled my hand around the handle, enjoying the heft of it, the vague way it felt like a weapon. I stood up. My father lobbed the ball to me and I slammed it back at him, first with aggression and then with more fluidity, more power, a gentleness seeping into me as the rally took on a rhythm. I could feel my body wanting this, reaching for the soft *pock* of the ball against the strings, again and again. When I was exhausted I let my arm drop by my side and looked to him. He extended only one arm this time.

I was across the court and sobbing into his shoulder. I dug my head into his chest and hugged him as hard as I could, searching for his heartbeat, the rough canvas of his jacket releasing a scent of dry leaves and wool and soap as I pressed myself into it. He lowered his chin as best he could to kiss me on the head, smoothing my hair with his hand in response to my uneven gulps for air.

"Hush," he said soothingly. Then I felt him hold his breath as he measured out his thoughts. "You must have other friends," he whispered. It might have been a hope, a demand, a question: it might have been all three. I could feel his body grow still with worry, waiting for me. How could I make him understand that I didn't? I wiped my nose wetly on his jacket.

He continued, "Friends at school. Other girls?" I stopped crying but didn't answer him. I thought of Anna Kim and her unforgiving, cold leadership, the way most of the other girls followed her so gamely, the way I'd accepted my role as outcast willingly, even as I imagined other ways of being. How I had indulged myself in ideas of drifting among them as one of them, wearing both a light-colored skirt of my own and the bright, confident smile I practiced sometimes in the mirror. Teddy had caught me doing this once and tried it himself, prompting me to shove him away. Most of the girls had forgotten why I was to be avoided at this point, and I'd forgotten why I was supposed to object. All at once my body deflated in my father's arms.

He waited a long time for an answer from me. "When I was a boy," he finally said, "when I first came to this country, I had no friends. The only English word I knew was 'doll,' because a girl on the boat had carried one. I was seven years old by the time the ship docked. Too late, already foreign. The other children at school had made most of their friends. And I was not the most outstanding of boys." He stopped, lost in thought. "But you," he bent to kiss my head, "you can learn, do, be whatever you want. And with your memory! You can know everything, if you want."

I pulled away and wiped my face with my sleeve, trying to see him better. How could I know everything? "How could anyone know everything?" I asked him.

My father looked surprised by the question and didn't answer me at first, just continued to stroke my face. "I sometimes wonder what goes on in that head of yours." He looked at me closely. "Do you still wish to be a doctor, Naomi?" I nodded. "A cardiologist, no?" Again I nodded. "The heart is not an easy thing to save. It can be broken. You know this, now. Yes?"

"My heart isn't broken," I said bitterly. If it were broken, I wouldn't feel so angry. I wouldn't have run so far just to feel it pump even harder.

"Of course," he said, looking both startled and satisfied. "You are too young, too strong." He took my face in his hands. "A great heart," he concluded, his eyes glittering with a crazy kind of hope. It upset me, but also drew me, like a gnat before light. The sun was already warm, drying the dirt and salt on my cheeks into a tight film. I wanted to be home, to have my mother rub my face in the dark of our house with a clean, wet cloth the way she had when I was younger and had skinned my knees trying to ride a bike with my eyes closed.

"We'll find a way out of this," my father murmured. "It won't hurt forever," he added, kissing my eyelids so that they stayed shut.

Something passed through me that morning and the grief began loosening its hold. I woke up the next day wanting to run again, but I came down to breakfast first.

My father knew what I wanted the minute he looked up at me. "Another game?" I nodded. "Good." He patted his belly. "Good for me, too."

Every day after that I woke up early for a run, then met my father on the Roosevelt courts before school began. At first it was the two of us; before long he was watching me take a lesson. I had a good instinct for the impassivity of competitive practice, having learned a stoic face from my mother, but it was my father's eyes that drove me. Keen, never missing a movement, proud.

And while I had once shunned my ability to memorize texts, after Teddy left I filled my mind with whatever I could get my hands on. When my father found me with Einstein's essays on relativity, I confessed that I could not understand what I'd read. But it didn't bother either one of us very much. The rhythms of a confident intellect were like a lullaby to me, constantly soothing the ache that, before long, began to dull.

I wrote to Teddy every week on Sunday, after the longer practice, but after a year or so the letters became more routine than heartfelt. But I'd still come home after practice on Sundays and take the stairs by two, sweating as I sat down with my pen and paper.

Teddy's replies arrived regularly, usually toward the end of the week. He told me nothing about where he now lived, or about his mother, but he did write about the woods nearby and the birds he was finding there. He was doing a special study on yellow birds. He would try to describe them, but frequently failed. The worse his description, the more beautiful the sketch he included. My favorites were the ones that were simply annotated, a black word, underlined, beside a detail of yellow feathers.

Before long he began sending sketches he'd done of people, though most of them were of me. His letters came more infrequently, and were more dramatic, less personal, seeming to steal lines from his mother's soap operas—"I miss you even more than I ever did," he would write. And much of it was disjointed, "My mother barely talks to me now. I don't think she ever wants to leave this house." There was a sketch of a brown-and-gold falcon with the head of a boy enclosed, a frowning girl lifting him on her arm to the sky.

NINE

The last letters came just as I started high school. The first of them was addressed to "Dr. Feinstein." For an instant I thought he was teasing, joking with me before I even opened the envelope. But the tone of the letter was bland: some notes about poor weather, a lost cat found with a disturbing tear in her left ear, a cold that lingered in both his mother and him. I found myself searching for a certain sly humor, like the assurance of a friend's face glimpsed in the crowd of a strange city. I read it through twice, then a third time.

The next letter was addressed simply to "Doctor." Again more mundane details. But the final one was different:

> *Doctor,*
> *The hospital is not far from my house. I will be going there on*
> *April 13th. Visiting hours are from twelve in the afternoon until*
> *twelve in the afternoon. I will not accept any medications when*
> *you come. My mother will pay your bill.*
>
> > *TR*

I stood at the front door, staring at the black lines. I dropped my arm to my side, pinching the paper between my fingers until they began to sting, then hurt. His words ran over me, chilly, their chattering like a foreign language, my mind straining to pull sense from them. And all the while I was realizing that I was about to come face-to-face with some terrible thing that would show itself, even if I wasn't ready to look. Somehow I knew that the letter in my hands had opened a portal, one that offered a new view of something I thought I had seen in every light; a view of Teddy and his openhearted, naïve love in a retreating light, the kind of light that creates shadows.

I sat down heavily where I was and, with the letter in my hands like a tether, summoned the memory I'd been fighting to keep fuzzy since the day it imprinted itself. It came at once, as though it had been waiting to step forward:

Unknown 34 y/o female adm. 3/22/74. Escorted by police re: c/o public disturbance. On admission to the ED patient found to be mildly obtunded and in early labor. Initial examination revealed track marks BUE, BAC of 0.18%, and 3rd trimester pregnancy est. 34 wks. gestational age. Admitted to ICU. Treatment initiated for substance abuse and withdrawal. 3/28/74 PROM. 3/31/74 delivered of 4 lb 2 oz (SFA) boy. 4/6/74 further obtunded. 4/7/74 manifested right hemiplegia. Expired 4/9/74. PM revealed ruptured left cerebral aneurysm in the distribution of the left middle cerebral artery. Massive intracranial hemorrhage. Also fibrosis of the liver; portal hypertension; mild early ascites.

It terrified me as much as it had when I was nine. Maybe more so now, when I could admit to myself that Teddy had brought it to me because he suspected it contained information that related to where he had come from and how it had shaped him, information that someone else should know. And I had buried it.

My mother was on the phone, trying to make sense of our heating bill, when I walked into the kitchen. My father was away for the weekend to consult with clients who were too old or infirm to travel. He usually waited until he had at least three such clients to visit before hurriedly booking a motel and scheduling them all within one weekend. He didn't like to leave his girls alone, he would say, but I knew which of us worried him.

I went to the spot where we kept the medical dictionary my father had bought to accompany the *Gray's Anatomy* he'd given me on my ninth birthday. Along with Einstein's *Relativity*, he kept the three tomes on the shelf next to the stove, right above the salt, pepper, and other everyday seasonings. It was his decision to put them there, so he could quiz me while he cooked, a duty he'd recently begun to share with my mother. She didn't look up as I pulled the dictionary down, flipping to the words that I'd read that first week I'd met Teddy: "obtunded": *made dull*; "hemiplegia": *total or partial paralysis of one side of the body that results from disease of or injury to the motor centers of the brain.* "Massive intracranial hemorrhage" carried enough description on its own. The fear began swimming through me, rushing to my head. It doesn't take a trained doctor to create a picture out of a little medical terminology, especially when we are desperate to understand how it might reveal something about someone we love.

And the words I already knew, like "disease" and "brain," knocked up against one another, threatening. Diseases could be genetic. Even a nine-year-old might have known that, but I hadn't. And then there was the mention of the track marks on her arm, which as a younger child I envisioned as lines of black marker for an imaginary train, not to be confused with the mark on my mother's wrist, but now understood them for what they actually were. I was also able to guess that BAC meant blood alcohol content, and that 0.18% would have pervaded everything in her system, that if a baby were born in such conditions he might be compromised in countless ways. Sometimes I wish I could go back to the times when I could remember but not understand, when my mind felt like a vessel rather than a stopping point.

I made for the drawer where we kept our maps and train schedules and pulled a schedule out for South Station, the railway hub of Boston. I also dug out the heavy book of maps for the Mid-Atlantic area. It didn't take me long to sketch out the journey in my mind. I looked at my watch. It was 2:30. The next train was in an hour and a half and would get me to Trenton, New Jersey, the closest city to Freehold, by 10:30. I pulled my jacket on at the door and walked out without my mother looking up. I should have gone to find him long ago. Now I might have waited too long. I walked to the T, filling my lungs with the icy air.

The Greater Boston area is served by a comprehensive system of trolley and subway lines, so that if you are within fifteen miles of the city in any direction, the chances are good that you can ride public transportation into its center. Thanks to the Green Line running through Brookline and the Red Line into Boston, I was at South Station in plenty of time to catch the train to Trenton and begin to wonder about what I was doing, the danger I was putting myself in, the worry I would create at home. I tried to shake my fears off, letting what was now my desperation to see Teddy guide me instead. When the train arrived, I was the first to stand and found a good seat right away in a nearly empty car. I tried to settle in and make myself comfortable. We were expecting snow, and the underground heat had been turned up so high that the train had great gusts of stuffy, hot air blowing through it.

As the train heaved and jerked along the freezing rails, doubt began to seep in. I knew I might not be headed for the reunion I so wanted. Something had changed in him. I didn't know what it was, I just knew that he was different, and the undefined shape of it terrified me. He had gone to live a new life since seeing me last, and somewhere along the way he seemed to have drifted completely out of reach. Tears blurred my vision by the time we were above ground and I could look out at the passing cities. People don't always want you to remember them so well, day in and day out. For all the joyful images I had of Teddy, there were ten more I might see now as off-kilter and disconnected, piling over the Teddy I had known like layers of clean, cold snow. I dozed for a while, dreaming of him as a bear, Mrs. Rosenthal the one who hunted for his food. The screeching of the brakes woke me, and when we emerged the snow was falling in the dark over a town I wouldn't have recognized anyway.

I nearly collided with a flushed and triumphant engineer as I stepped into the station.

He put out a hand to steady us both, but kept his forward momentum. "Hotels are booked, sweetheart, and no cabs will run in this weather. Hope you have someone to pick you up!" He looked elated by the storm, winking jovially at me before going on his way.

I blinked in the bright lights of the station, taking in the strong smells of urine and fuel exhaust. My stomach turned, briefly, roiling with the beginnings of panic. I willed myself to make a plan. The information kiosk was closed, but I had some loose change and a map I'd grabbed from a box on the wall to guide me. There was a Yellow Pages, too, tucked in under the phone.

But as I scanned the list of Rosenthals, I began to realize that I'd be calling not just Teddy but his mother. There were twenty-two C. Rosenthals in the Trenton area, but no Chavas. I started to warm up and pulled one of my gloves off with my teeth, the finger I now used to trace the numbers leaving a smear of damp on the page. I could feel the alarm rise in my chest, the inevitability of realizing that I had nowhere to go. I left the phone booth and found a bench that had only a few unidentifiable stains on it. I sat down, figuring I'd only lie down once I had to. The station was well lit, I told myself. No one would be out in this weather. But then I saw a figure coming toward me, hunkered down under a hood.

The suddenness of recognition first brought relief, then a new wave of worry. I felt my heart begin beating again as she got closer, wondering if she'd be angry and, on some level, disappointed in me for being reckless, or desperate. Or both. She didn't pull her hood off when she stood before me, and my irritation flared. I wanted to yank it off her head, angry that, even coming to my rescue in the middle of a nearly abandoned train station, she would still need to hide. She handed me a slip of paper. "You forgot this," she said, taking a seat beside me on the bench.

I saw Teddy's envelope, not the letter, puzzling over it only momentarily before I realized what she'd wanted me to see: The return address: *T. Rosenthal, 1600 Pennsylvania Avenue, Apartment 6G.* No town, no state, no country.

"How did you know I'd come here?"

My mother reached over and tucked my hair behind my ear to look at my face. "I always figured it was a matter of time before you'd go look for him. You just needed a little encouragement. And you left the South Station schedule and the map book open to Southern New Jersey on the kitchen table." She picked up the envelope and waved it a little, making an attempt at a smile. I looked down at the Yellow Pages and found my way back into the R's. She allowed me a moment of scanning before closing the book on my hand.

"It's time to go," she said, standing up. "The roads won't wait."

I didn't move. Instead I looked at her, knowing how hard it had been for her to find me missing, how hard it would have been for her to realize she had to go after me and get dressed for this cold night, what it must have taken out of her to drive alone all this way, and I hated her for it. I hated her for being there when, for once, I hadn't wanted her. There was a taste in my mouth like sand, like those dreams I had sometimes where I wanted to talk but found my tongue too heavy to lift.

"I could have slept here," I said. And then, more defiantly, "He needs help."

"You think you can help him, Naomi?" she asked tensely. The circles under her eyes were a deep gray, making the blue of her irises stand out as she took me in. I looked more closely at the way her eyes brimmed, the way her mouth stayed flat and drawn, then at the small spidery wrinkles that were beginning to crawl from her top lip, as if words had long been clenched there, the tension of restraining them creating crevices in her skin. For the first time, I saw some ugliness in her. I frowned.

"You can't do anything for him, Naomi." She shook her head definitively. "I don't think anyone can."

"You read the letter?"

"I read it."

"It was my letter."

She looked surprised at my insistence. "You left it on the table along with the maps and the train schedule."

"It was still mine. What's wrong with him?" I asked, struggling to keep my voice from breaking into a child's cry.

She took a moment to collect her thoughts before answering. "Any number of things, I suppose," she said vaguely.

"So we need to find out," I said, standing.

For a moment, I thought she was about to argue with me, but instead she became thoughtful. She stared at me for a while before she spoke.

"Did I ever tell you that your father wanted to name you Ruth? I wouldn't let him. I was sure there was an omen there, something about having to leave home to be with the people you loved. So we settled on Naomi. She got to bring the one she loved back home with her. It seemed she got to have it all."

She sighed. "It's terrible having to leave home. Especially when you know you can't go back." She reached over and pulled me by the wrist of the jacket, trying to get me to sit back down. I wouldn't.

"Teddy has his home now, Naomi, and it's not with you. You need to realize that no matter how much you may want to fix things, there are times, including now, when those things will be beyond your reach." She took a deep breath, pulling her hands into her lap. "Anyway, he has his mother," she added, trying to comfort me, though her face stiffened after she said it. She must have known it wasn't the right thing to say. "I'm tired," she concluded.

In the car on the way home, we didn't speak until we reached the Massachusetts border. The clouds were still heavy overhead, but the snow had stopped. The only other vehicles on the road were trucks, their dragging weights rocking our car every time they passed by.

"If it was so terrible to leave home," I finally said, "maybe you shouldn't have." I couldn't understand exactly why, but I was furious. I didn't want to look at her.

She shot me a quick glance. "It wasn't an option," she clipped. "And it's none of your business."

"Of course," I said. "Your life is none of my business. I almost forgot."

"Naomi, I know you're upset . . ."

I was boiling. "And is this," I took her right wrist forcefully with my hand, my thumb over her scar, "none of my business, too? Or do you just expect me to wait until it happens again?"

She pulled over. After a few minutes she whispered, "Jesus, Naomi." I pressed my head to the icy window, waiting for the car to start again. It was already getting so cold that I had to sit on my hands to keep them warm. She was so silent, as she always seemed to be in the face of my most urgent questions, my voice the antidote to hers. She must have remembered, too. She must have also remembered our last night together in the cold. How could she not? How could she not have guessed that it all started with her?

"We weren't married in '73," she said after several more minutes had passed. The color of her eyes was now watery, her expression once again empty. "It was '74. February of '74." She waited a beat, letting me figure it out. My birthday was in June of the same year. She continued to let it sink in before going on.

"We had been dating for a few years and were living together, but I had no intention of marrying your father. I had no intention of marrying anyone. Then I got pregnant with you. And I panicked. I, my own mother, she . . ." She lost her way momentarily. "I didn't know what to do with a baby. I was so scared. Paralyzed." She shook her head. "I could only think you'd be better off without me. We'd both be better off without each other." She leaned forward, resting her head on the steering wheel, her hands on either side of it. I had a sudden vision of her driving off without looking up. I wanted to say something, anything, but my throat was tight with emotion, so thick it was hard to swallow.

"So, I tried," she said, finally looking at me. "But I couldn't follow through with it. And then I wanted to stop. Oh, God," her voice broke, "It was the worst moment, my resolve, all my reasons, everything was washed away in something else, panic, or something else. Something more than grief." She took a shuddering breath. "I didn't really think there would be anything other than grief left."

I waited for her to say that she couldn't follow through with it because of me, but she said nothing more. I watched her go through the motions of collecting herself, like folding a toy back into its box.

"So you got married because you were pregnant. With me."

"I got married because I thought your father would be a great father. I married because I'd found a little faith because of your father's. I married because I thought we could make a home for you, that with him you could grow up and be well, do things with your life."

"Because having a daughter wasn't doing enough," I concluded, wanting a definitive pain more than a doubtful one.

"I wish it had been," she said. "I wish something was enough, Naomi." She sighed. "You might not think I wish for much, but I do wish for that."

I have often wondered what else she might have wished for. I missed the opportunity to ask her that night, but I have thought of it many times since.

My mother and I never spoke with my father about the night I went looking for Teddy, or one another. If she had been struck by how far I would go to get what I wanted, from her or from Teddy, she never let on. She was simply there to bring me home, like a messenger disinterested in the contents of the message.

So I had to let Teddy go. Neither one of my parents wanted to hear of him—especially, now, my mother—and it became too painful to think of him as constantly as I had. As my mother had learned, no grief can be sustained indefinitely. So from then on, when Teddy did come to mind, I shook myself free from the thought, like starting from the ache of a worrisome daydream.

TEN

I had enrolled at Adams High School that fall. With nearly two thousand students in four grades, it was huge when compared with Beacon Junior High and Kennedy Elementary, both of which had been small, neighborhood schools. Although its halls were narrow, the ceilings were so high that it seemed full of empty space even when crowded with students. Its demands were empty, too: the right clothes, a light attitude, a willingness to appear to be having fun. I was able to meet none of the qualifications.

I did well in my classes right away, but Anna Kim continued to do well, too, and pretty soon we both distinguished ourselves as top students. To get back at me for the threat I posed to her, she spread the rumor that I had my sights set on Wellesley because I was a lesbian. I wanted to go up to her and shake her hand out of gratitude: having people believe I didn't like boys was a much better way to stay away from them than admitting that I never wanted to become attached again. Occasionally, one of them would remind me of Teddy—George Mason was tall, and awkward; Joe Giangrasso had muddy-brown eyes—but I was safe admiring them at a distance, never allowing myself anything more than the most basic and improbable romantic fantasies.

The Adams college counselors made it their job to inform those of us who were going to apply to "selective colleges" that we needed to start creating our applications four years before they were going to be written. This, we were made to understand, involved far more than getting the best grades: we had an extracurricular résumé to build as well.

The fall of my sophomore year, I signed up to be a transport volunteer at the Brigham and Women's Hospital, a job that entailed sitting in their basement for four hours every Sunday morning, waiting on a folding chair with about thirty other people in a crowded, windowless room for my number to be called. Most of the other people working there were paid employees who eyed me with distrust. I took to reading terrible magazines while I waited so I wouldn't have to answer any questions. After a while I became a part of the scenery. Two imposingly voluptuous sisters began sitting on either side of me and having loud arguments with each other in Haitian French. I liked to think they were acting as noisy guardians, keeping anyone more intimidating away.

Like everyone else there, when my number was called I was given a slip of paper with a room number on it and a grading: green for nontoxic and nonhuman fluid transport; orange for patient transport from one floor to another via wheelchair; red for transport of plasma or blood. I was never given a chance with the toxic fluids, just the human. These were ensconced in thick, malleable plastic that obscured them just enough to allow us to walk throughout the hospital without alarming nonnatives. I was given a twenty-minute break I didn't need every shift, and spent my time in the gift shop, wondering what the well bought for the sick.

I was also busy ignoring my own developing body and its desires. As my hungers grew, I simply ran more, pounding them out beneath me as best I could. I ran almost every day, even when I had a practice or a game across town—our public school team wasn't too rigorous.

Sometimes it was dark when I ran, which my father hated. But I had to; it was part of the tacit agreement I'd made with my body to let my mind run my life. And as I ran my mostly thoughtless runs, I often chanted, soothing myself by reciting incantations that might lend me their calming powers: the periodic table; the Einstein I'd memorized years ago; snatches of the Hebrew prayers my father used to recite; the various geometric theorems; anything that could serve as proof that the spinning universe could, indeed, be mastered. On my worst days, though, I found myself on a loop with whatever text was in my head, trying to work it out of my head and into the pavement, woefully unable to reach thoughtlessness or anything near it.

The spring of my sophomore year, I had the unfortunate timing of being the second person to walk into the school auditorium where a beautiful, popular boy, Anton Bascilia, had hung himself from the rafters. I liked to use the auditorium as a shortcut, bypassing the crowded halls, but that morning I opened the door and walked right into Lilly Fawlke, her mouth open, her face white. Anton was swinging above us both, the tongue of a bell that had no sides. It took me a moment to recognize his face; he had smiled at me once and, had I allowed myself real crushes, he would have soared to the top of my list. I cried out, then began to scream.

Lilly turned around and put her hands on my shoulders but I couldn't stop. I was sent home that morning, but snuck back for my afternoon classes. I thought no one would have noticed me and my hysteria in the wake of discovering Anton, but Anna Kim, beautiful now as well as popular, and still vying with me for top ranking in the school, saw everything. From that day onward she would let out a little cry every time I passed near her. "Oh! I don't know if I can stop!" Her friends laughed, the boys turning her jeers into sexual jokes, the girls punching them playfully on the arms. I went back to taking a shortcut through the auditorium, careful never to look up, though in my mind's eye I frequently pictured a body swinging overhead: sometimes it was Anton's, sometimes it was my mother's, and sometimes it was mine. I hated to admit it, but the days when I imagined myself there were the worst. Whatever happened, I knew, furiously, that I wanted to live. Those days I went to the girls' room, splashed cold water on my face, and made myself run after school until I had to stop to breathe.

Junior year passed by in a whirl of even more intensive work and dogged training, and by the fall of senior year I had my early application to Wellesley prepared. When Mr. Rutledge began a dissection unit with the advanced biology class, beginning with the frog, he inspired many protests and refusals among my classmates. By then, I had adopted an impressively stoic exterior and made the first cut on the frog, almost expecting a gasp of air to emerge when I did. Instead, the creature's insides seemed too simple, the forms within too straightforward to be the alchemical heart, liver, stomach, and brain. I made notes on my sheet, holding my disappointment in, eager for the end of the semester, when we'd dissect a pig, a day I felt sure I'd been waiting eight years for.

It became easier and easier to bury my misery under my drive. And along the way, it became logical to believe that the more I saw those around me fall, the more I needed to lift myself up as compensation. Maybe it was because of that day all those years ago when I witnessed my father's heart attack and sidestepped the pain with a resolution. Maybe it was because my mother and Teddy persisted in slipping in and out of safety as I stood by. Or maybe it was just because I knew that I could never let any memory go and would have to learn to shut certain things out to keep my own balance in check. For all these reasons, and probably countless more I could not name, I nurtured the perfect juvenile solution to the pain of losing. I would win, all the time, at everything.

It was that simple.

PART II

ELEVEN

I had continued to volunteer at the Brigham and Women's Hospital throughout high school so that I could claim with some credibility that my plans to be a cardiologist were well researched. On a cool winter morning early during my junior year, a woman walked into Central Transport, identified herself as Dr. Sally Orchuk, explained that she'd like to take on a shadow in surgery, and then, later, on our way up to the top of the building in an elevator, told me she had gone to Wellesley (class of 1973), had heard from the hospital's volunteer office that I was interested in the college, and that I was a good student.

"Take off the bracelet," she told me on our first meeting. I had only recently taken to wearing the cuff my mother had given me, briefly trying on the idea that the work I would do would make her proud. I looked down at it, a question on my face. "A surgeon should never wear jewelry," she grinned challengingly. "Plus," she straightened up to her full six feet, "it's bad luck." I unlatched it and dropped it in my pocket.

That summer I was allowed to watch her surgeries; the next fall, in the middle of our dissection unit (mice and cats), my long-awaited acceptance letter to Wellesley and a hefty financial aid package were firmly in hand. My father claimed it was fate, that Rose Kennedy was smiling down on me, rewarding me for all those childhood visits to her home. For a moment I missed the girlhood I'd had there, before I'd known suffering to be anything other than the sad constant my mother wore regularly, easy to look beyond. I tried to argue that Rose was neither a deity nor a monitoring presence at 83 Beals, but my father dismissed my comments the way he would swat at a fly. "You have no idea what she's doing," he declared, as though I were unthinkably wrong.

Three weeks before orientation at Wellesley a tournament was held for the incoming students who wanted the one first-year spot available on the tennis team. I was surprised to see more than two dozen girls at the tournament, held at Longwood Cricket Club, an establishment only ten minutes from my home. We were all trying hard to seem uninterested in one another. But it didn't take me long to learn that there were three girls from New York, one from Indiana, and one from Japan. Her parents had flown in with her for the weekend to compete for the spot.

It was the first week in August, the beginning of the end of a summer that had been exceptionally warm and humid. The air was so thick and wet it was difficult to breathe, and by afternoon any breeze quieted players and spectators alike, the light winds not relieving us so much as bringing to our attention what little we had in our lungs. Almost everyone stayed to watch the final matches, though there were only four of us competing by then. I took the court for the last time against the girl from Japan, Jun Oko.

She was tall, taller than my five feet eight inches, and I guessed that she must be exceptionally tall for her native Tokyo. She wore a visor low over her eyes even though it was late in the day and I was playing shade-side, and I could see nothing of her expression except her mouth, firm and wide, set in a tight frown. It was the first set and my serve, and though I was ready to begin, I stalled for a moment to let the breeze cool my skin. Across the court, I thought I saw Jun stiffen, registering my hesitation. I didn't wait any longer; if she hadn't made note of my stall, my father would have. He had taken to watching my matches as closely as most men would watch for the outcome of a bet.

I followed through with my serve and Jun sent it directly back to me. A movement so swift and uncalculated it was nearly insulting. In that instant we both knew she could send me running, but she didn't bother. I slammed the ball in the opposite direction, at least ten feet from her and one inch from the outside line. This, too, she reacted to strangely. She lunged for it, but hadn't been nearly close enough to be in position. She was a better player than that. The thought crossed my mind that she had conceded the point intentionally, by way of apologizing for her initial condescension. I don't know why I thought this; I couldn't see her face to study her expression. I didn't know her. But there was something in her manner, the extreme care with which she stood waiting between sets, that made me think that a false effort was more likely than an accidentally bad play.

I renewed my focus on Jun's dark head, the visor still blocking much of her face. It was irking me, the way she concealed her expressions, like she was too good to fully acknowledge me, or maybe she was hiding something. She hit my next serve with a return so forceful I had no chance of hitting it, though I went for it. This was a bad trait of mine as a player; when rattled I tended to spring to action, like startled prey.

I knew my father would be hoping more than usual that I would win. Nothing thrilled him more than a win when I was clearly outclassed. His most recent heroic crushes had been on legendary tennis underdogs: Nate Winkles in '85 at the U.S. Open, Anna Treblenka at Wimbledon in '90. He loved to recount these matches with relish, and would do so for as long as I'd let him. I managed to return Jun's next hit when I heard the first vague rumble of thunder. I ignored it, but missed the ball after that.

The leaves on the chestnut trees lining the court began to whisper, and another rumble sounded, louder than the first. I didn't care about rain, but the match would be suspended if there was lightning.

I renewed my efforts, still wanting that rally, wanting even more to make her run, to make that visor slip off her head. She picked up on my renewed focus and upped her game. I wondered if she felt the match as acutely as I did, if she, too, was conscious that this was our first showing as Wellesley students. The assistant coach was watching from somewhere in the stands but had been so quiet all afternoon that we had almost forgotten about her.

A heavy, soaking rain came immediately behind the next break of thunder. The people in the stands stood in nearly one motion, some pulling the backs of their T-shirts over their heads, all running to get out of the weather. I stared at them from the court, the rain driving at an angle into my face and down the collar of my shirt. Jun was watching me. I picked up a ball and put it into play, though her racket was at her side. She was surprised, but returned it.

The ref ran out to the middle of the court: "Game over. Rematch," he hollered, then ran off again.

My father was still in the stands, holding the schedule over his head. The ref was talking to the coordinator, who had managed to produce an umbrella at the sidelines. There were two more people still watching, an Asian man and woman sitting together. Jun's parents, I guessed, sitting there as if they had been the only viewers all along, as if the rain had washed out everything incidental, everything but our parents in the stands. Seeing Jun's parents as a unit like that made them seem stronger than my father, made him seem like an old man, lingering, lost in the stands.

I can't tell you why my father or I stayed where we were, but I realized after watching them a moment longer that Jun and her mother were waiting for her father's direction. Her mother didn't look at her father, but sat beside him patiently, her practiced stillness reminding me at once of my mother's. Jun stood like someone reluctant to abandon a post. Finally, Jun's father raised his hand lightly and Jun walked off the court without another glance at me. It occurred to me that within the distance between her parents and her there was an invisible, unbreakable line.

My father was suddenly standing before me. "*Ketzi*, it's cold, we're wet." His words were choppy, as if they, too, might get soaked if we didn't hurry. We made it inside the clubhouse, where he bustled about, putting his things down and getting me something to dry off with: a towel appeared, amazingly white and dry. "Oko Industries," he whispered, blotting my hair and staring at the Okos, who had appeared on the other side of the room as I tried to blot my face. He leaned in, "Probably the richest man in Tokyo, and he leaves his daughter to stand in the rain just because he thinks she's got an easy win." He shook his head.

Jun's father turned around. He looked my father, then me, in the eye. Jun and her mother stood side by side behind him. We regarded each other for another long moment until Mr. Oko finally bowed in our direction, the gesture at once formal, slight, and notable for its elegance. My father and I returned the bow awkwardly. Mr. Oko turned to leave, his small family following close behind. I saw him open an umbrella for the three of them under the awning before they made their way out of sight. I didn't see Jun again until a year and a half later, after we had been at school together for nearly as long.

TWELVE

Three weeks after the matches at Longwood—orientation weekend at Wellesley—the rain had still not let up. In four years, most of us would graduate in another downpour, and I suspect that many of us held both storms as a point of pride, acts of nature that seemed to punctuate our collective power, though it was not in vogue to refer to the heavens, to refer to anything but our own abilities, as commanding events into existence.

As we drove under the banner that marked our welcome and the entrance to the college, I produced a map from the depths of a thick packet and directed my father to the Stone-Davis dorm, an older structure near the outskirts of campus with views of the lake from its southern windows. We could see nothing but the brake lights of the car in front of us as we made our way onto the campus. The incoming line of cars snaked along the main road, our backseats and trunks full of the things we thought we might need to establish our existences away from home, as though we expected to forge individual armors made of our belongings.

By the time we arrived at the front entrance to the dorm, my parents and I had been in the damp, hot car for nearly an hour. I opened my door as the others ahead of me had, trying to hurry even though myself, my parents, and my things were quickly drenched, making the trip up the front stairs even more laborious and awkward than it would otherwise have been. After we'd managed to get everything into the main hall of the building, my father elected to return to the car and park it as my mother and I began to drag the first load of my belongings up the staircase, down three hallways, and into a room that measured, optimistically, at ten feet by seven. I knew it had taken extra effort for her to come with me that day, that she'd been planning to for weeks. I thought that keeping her busy might demonstrate a kindness I wasn't sure how else to show.

My roommate, Amy Wade, was already there, or so I guessed that the petite, blond girl standing in the middle of the room and looking at me with a mixture of open condescension and interest must be she. I smiled, as did my mother; we must have looked identical in our efforts to appear pleased to meet her. Amy smiled back, richly amused, before barking at her father, who was about to unload her books into the top shelf of the two-shelved bookcase we were meant to share.

"Dad, Jesus, she's going to think I'm taking over in here. She should have the top shelf; can't you see how tall she is? Christ." She looked back at me, grinning wide. "I took the bottom bunk, hope that's okay. And I hung the Matisse"—she gestured toward a large print of flowers and fish—"he goes well there." She looked at me to see if I would challenge her. I stared at the print, which took up most of the only wall big enough for it. "Amy Wade," she finally said, looking up at me as she squatted by a box, not bothering to hold out her hand, either because we were both girls or because she knew she needed no formal introduction. "From Wisconsin." Her look implied that she knew I had never been to Wisconsin.

"Naomi Feinstein," I said. "From down the street," my father, now at the door, concluded for me. He chuckled at his own joke, taking in the scene before him as he stood in the doorway. "Solomon Feinstein," he said, taking a step into the room toward Amy's father, who looked embarrassed, as he had since Amy had reprimanded him earlier. "Sol," my dad said, holding out his hand. "And this is my wife, Theresa."

"John Wade," he said, shaking my father's hand before grimacing a smile at my mother. "Feinstein. Is that a Jewish name?"

Amy elbowed him. "It's no big *deal*, Dad. All the good schools are multicultural now." He nodded, chastised, and returned to the task of stacking books.

"My mom's back home," Amy explained, studying mine. "She works fifteen-hour days, just couldn't make it. She's senior vice president at Procter and Gamble."

My mother paused before responding, as if trying to assess if she should act impressed by this information, something I guessed she would have done on my behalf. She looked over at me. I gave her no indication of my own reaction and she seemed relieved by this. She was trying, I could tell, to make me feel at ease, to let me set the tone for the day. "That's nice," she said to Amy. "That must make you proud," she added.

And then to me, "Do you want me to make up your bed for you?" She checked herself. "I mean, why don't I just leave your bed stuff there and your dad and I can bring the box home." She turned to Mr. Wade. "Do you have boxes you'd like us to take away for you?"

"Hey, that'd be great," Amy said. "We already started a pile in the hall. I don't know how they're going to get all this stuff out of here." My mother had moved over to my father. Her hand was resting lightly on his arm. "I think we should probably let the girls get settled," she said to him.

He looked up with the expression of someone who had expected to stay much longer. "She'll need help," he said, his voice rising. He looked over at me. "You need help, Naomi, right? Here"—he opened my own box of books—"let me put *Gray's* on the shelf for you, at least. You'll want it in easy reach." He turned to John Wade, who'd studiously ignored us after our formal greeting. "Naomi's going to be a doctor," he announced. "It's okay, Dad," I said, watching him. "I'll be fine, I can unpack once you've left. The weather's bad and you should get back before it gets dark." I was watching his face fall as I said all this. "Here, I'll walk you out." "It's not too bad," he said dejectedly. He shoved one hand, fisted, into the pocket of his cardigan. It was an ancient sweater, grayish blue, with large faux-bronze buttons. "Well, I'll still walk you downstairs," I said.

"You'll have to," Amy's father said solemnly. "They have rules about that here."

"Oh, Dad, not during initiation weekend, with all the dads around," Amy sang. Just then, a tall, muscular boy walked by our door carrying a full cardboard box. "Or brothers, or whatever"—a significant grin in my direction. "They have rules about fathers?" my father asked.

"No men over the age of twelve past the front desk without an escort," Amy recited from memory a section in the back of the Wellesley Guidebook we'd received a month earlier. *"No men over the age of twelve in the halls without a Wellesley student as escort. No male guests allowed to travel vertically between floors without a Wellesley student as escort."* She looked up. "Mind like a steel trap," she said, tapping her temple. The gesture looked like it felt awkward even to her.

None of us said anything. Her father, in particular, was studiously occupied with the bookcase, surveying his work. Amy kneeled before the box of books he had opened, reached for the few books that remained, and leaned over him, disrupting, then rearranging what he had done.

"Let's go, Dad," I said, taking my father's arm. My mother's hand was now resting on his other shoulder.

"Do we have your phone number yet?" he asked as we walked out the door. "I probably won't have a phone for a few days," I replied. The hall was crowded with arriving students and I was eager to have us moving. I felt vulnerable standing still in the stream, but also fiercely protective; they were mine, not to be scrutinized by strangers whose nerves might encourage them to judge others too critically: my father as grossly tender, my mother as too stiff.

"It's going to be fine, Dad," I said after we'd made our way silently down the corridors and back to the front door. There was a brief break in the constant human traffic we'd been navigating. It seemed, suddenly, that there would be no way to say a real goodbye. "I love you," I told him, giving him a firm hug which I hoped conveyed much more. "I'll call you when I get a phone." I hugged him again, taking in the damp wool smell of his old sweater. "Love you, Mom," I hugged her tightly as well. She smiled at me, the overhead light making her pale skin look thin. I shifted slightly so I could see her expression better. My father's face was pulled into a weighty scowl. Maybe they thought of it too, sometimes, that we were all we had.

My father hugged me once more, then followed after her quickly. He is a man who has never understood goodbye; he is still baffled by the idea that I now live in my own home, that I have had experiences that are foreign to him. I watched from the window by the door as they retreated down the hilled driveway, their focus on not slipping as they walked, my mother thinner from behind than I remembered, my father's shirt underneath his cardigan untucked in the back. It felt awful and exhilarating to watch them leave.

The first week at Wellesley was chaotic and lonely, and once the up-perclasswomen joined us there seemed to be even more cause for loneliness—they settled into the regal, perfectly groomed campus in a myriad of ways, so many of them poised with a private business and confidence far beyond my reach. I looked around me, realizing that outside of Adams High School and Anna Kim's domain, the world of my peers might be changing for me. But as I looked, I caught no one looking back at me.

It seemed that hasty, desperate friendships were all that was available to the first-years who were more socially ambitious; the women who bonded immediately operated in a realm that was both frightening and inhospitable. They were aggressively, almost hilariously, enraptured, and they were in the minority. Amy and I quickly joined forces once we realized that neither one of us was quick to make friends, though it wasn't a bond based on mutual liking. We simply established an unspoken agreement to help each other survive. We tried to meet each other for lunch and dinner in the dining hall, but when we couldn't I pretended that I was in a rush and had somewhere to go. I ate too quickly, my insecurity developing into a literal lump in my stomach.

After Amy and I turned out our lights at night, I stared at the blank wall above me, noticing the sinking sensation I had, the feeling that not only had my loneliness followed me to Wellesley, it was threatening to grow there. I'm not sure exactly what I had expected would be different at that point, but the growing hollowness within me kept me from sleeping. I missed my parents, but my calls home were awkward and unsatisfying. My mother said hello and got off the phone, at which point my father got on and I hinted that I'd like to know how she was doing. She was always "just fine." I knew this wasn't true, but I also had to have faith that my father would tell me otherwise if I needed to know. I couldn't bear to go home and see her, for fear I wouldn't leave, so I invited my father to campus for lunches on the weekend. At first he came, then he noticed I was eating alone and greeting no one, and decided, as he said, "to give me my space. You can't make friends with your father around all the time."

So we depended on the phone, but we were not used to being apart, or having exchanges that involved only each other's voices. His advice became canned, overly optimistic. He told me that I just needed to meet the other Jewish girls, to try the Hillel on campus. Despite the fact that we had become practically nonobservant as I'd grown increasingly competitive and obsessed with schoolwork, he still liked to pretend that when I was done with school and the like, happily ensconced in a home across the street from him, we'd once again observe leisurely Shabbats and the High Holidays together. I loved and hated him for this.

Still, I had no ideas of my own, so I tried his on for size. The Hillel was lean and serviced by chaste, confidently Jewish women. I scanned the crowd there, wondering if anyone else might share a chronically depressed mother from an Irish Catholic upbringing or a father who was an orphaned sabra. Not that I would have been likely to discuss such things.

There was one woman from Newton (the town neighboring Brookline, both geographically and culturally) who was delighted to meet me; but she was as unaffected and warm in her headscarf and long skirt as I was suspicious and insecure in my stiff dress. It was as foreign to me as I imagined a church social would be. I felt lonesome, mostly within myself, as I often did in Jewish communities, feeling the tug of recognition, the sorrowful comfort of the songs I'd heard first from my father, the sense that I was not as perfectly suited to this mold as I felt I should have been. Hillel kept me on their mailing list for the next four years, though I spent the same amount of time wondering if I had any right or reason to revisit. Alone at night, I lay awake and thought about how I was betraying my father's ideals in almost every possible way.

So, as usual, I dove headfirst into my studies, which, oddly enough, began to make me feel that I was in good company. At the library or in common rooms there were always other women on their own, papers surrounding them. These women kept me going, for better or worse. Being in a single-sex community heightened every comparison, every inspiration. Even passing another woman on one of the countless walkways between buildings would rarely result in a greeting or even an acknowledgment. I began to coach myself in adopting the coolness around me, enjoying the strange excitement of an unfriendliness even I hadn't dared to entertain before. At first if I saw a woman nearing me on a path, I would brace myself for being ignored, but within a few months I began to stiffen my posture and anticipate the exhilaration of such a bald rudeness on both our parts. It was amazing to pass another woman my age, at my college, and pretend we had no reason to acknowledge one another. It was a great, powerful lie, and it was as cold as the winter we were heading into, though sometimes as invigorating. At the library, I took to my own table and never worried that someone would ask to sit with me. Studying was hushed, and the walks home peppered only with more impassive strangers. We were not ships in the night; we were missiles in the day. It was thrilling and unkind.

In the interest of keeping ourselves well-rounded, students were encouraged to join "groups," many of which seemed interested in defining themselves against the general population or, when in luck, directly against an antithetical group. After the first few weeks, Amy finally convinced me to audition with her for an a cappella group, the Wellesley Symphonettes. I was still ready to believe that I might discover a hidden talent or passion, that maybe this place had yet to reveal something about me I hadn't yet considered, so I joined her.

Perversely, of the three such groups on campus, the Symphonettes required both a song and a joke. When it came to the joke, I was at a loss, completely forgetting the one Amy had looked up for me earlier in the day. The Symphonettes running the auditions sat in a smiling row, watching me, like an affable firing squad. Had they frowned or cleared their throats or sent me from the room, it would have been far less intimidating than the smiles fixed on their faces.

"Did you know we require a joke?" Their second-in-command asked softly.

I nodded.

"You see," the leader asserted herself, "we like to be enter-*tain*-ing. A good performance is about more than just musicality, you see. The audience wants to have a good time." The lipstick she wore was the type I had never tried to wear, sure it would smear across my teeth. Hers was lined into submission, a frame of red around the perfect white of her smile, like the careful painting of a professional clown.

During the spring semester, I had a lecture at 8:15 and had to force myself to eat in the dining hall before leaving for class, trying to lift my head from the sand and find the friendships I felt might exist there, just beyond my grasp. On the first of one of these days I worked up the courage to sit at a table with two other women, both of whom were upperclasswomen I didn't know; I had memorized most of the faces in my dorm, but I couldn't place these two girls: one, tall with red hair, the other, of medium height with nearly black hair and a tiny, pear-shaped nose. They were frank but unintimidating, and the redhead, who introduced herself as Heather and her seatmate as Beth, was an English major eager to tell the most infamous stories about the professors in that department.

Just as Heather was getting warmed up, a woman walked past our table holding a paper above her head. She headed to a table across the room, but seemed to leave a ripple of something behind her, something that made the three of us, as well as several others, watch her. Within a few minutes, the ripple had made its way back to our side of the room. Jennifer Seton, a wealthy and glossy blonde in the senior class, appeared out of nowhere and took a seat at our table.

"Sarah Stroeber just got accepted to Yale Law. She's number two in our class this year—Mira got her letter this weekend. That means Ann Graber's out." She held a comfortable command over her audience.

"Morning, Jen"—Beth spoke first; she stabbed a piece of melon as she did. "Ann could still get in."

Jen cocked her head, deeply amused. I think she'd wanted this reaction. "They take two from Wellesley every year."

"Nineteen eighty-eight," Beth replied. "Four."

"Nineteen eighty, only one," Jen replied.

"It's not a fucking pattern equation, Jen"—she pushed her hair over her shoulder—"it's Yale Law. They do what they want."

"Bullshit," Jen spread her hands on the table. "When Essex was president, she got a call every November 1st from the dean. They had an arrangement."

"Yale Law isn't interested in making arrangements with progressive female administrators, Jen."

Jen smirked, refusing the bait, "She was the president of Wellesley for twelve years. Of course she had an in. The dean worshipped at her feet."

"Yeah, well, she's gone." This last statement sounded oddly cutting; the silence that followed it charged. We had just lost a well-loved president, Ann Peabody Essex, to a coed university with a fancy basketball team. It was as if she had broken up with us collectively. I felt the loss even though she left months before I had arrived. We had a promising interim president, but there was something somber and suspiciously paced about her initiation, the tone in the great halls and festivities somewhat like a high-wire act begun just after an acrobat has fallen.

"Well, I guess my application's out." Heather's voice was barely audible. Beth looked at her for the first time since Jen had sat down, her dark face drawn, frowning.

"You applied, too?" I squeaked. It was the wrong thing to say.

Heather shrugged. "It's just law school, I guess," she said.

"No one's heard from Harvard or Stanford," Beth said quickly, sharply. Her expression was tense, aggressive.

"I gotta go," Jen stood up. "Sorry, Heather. I didn't know you were in the pool." Heather grimaced, as though this was one of the worst things Jen could have said. Jen smoothed her skirt, the heavy fabric obeying her palms unlike anything I owned. "See you in econ, Beth." She walked off.

I felt I should say something, that had I known what was to happen I would never have sat down. Heather's face was flushed. She looked at me, wryly. "Just don't let them talk you into this shit," she said to me. "I never wanted law school in the first place, but apparently I've got potential."

"I probably won't major in English," I said. "I'm premed."

"You can do both," Beth said, not looking at me, still watching Heather. She pulled her mouth in until it puckered. "You do have potential," she told her friend. "You also have potential in academia."

"Yeah, but lawyers make money," Heather sighed. "Professors make less than forty a year. I know"—she held up her hand, preventing Beth from saying anything—"they're respected." She stood up. "I have to review my notes before class. Nice to meet you," she said to me. "Good luck."

Beth watched her go. "Yale was her first choice. It shouldn't have been, but . . ." she was still looking away, in the direction her friend had gone. "My last boyfriend went to Yale. He was a prick," she smiled at me. "Of course, most guys under forty are pricks, but he excelled at it."

"My dad did some work once for someone who went to Hastings," I offered. "In San Francisco," I chirped, my voice false even in my own ears. "He said it was really great."

"Wellesley girls don't go to Hastings, hon." The melon was almost gone. She had a cup of coffee beside it that she'd downed earlier in a few long sips. Now she toyed with the mug, its ugly stains. "If you're not in the top three, you don't talk about where you go. You just pray for a good internship the first year." She set her coffee cup firmly on her tray, then looked at me. "You going to be okay here alone?" she asked.

I was taken by surprise. What she said felt like a kindness I hadn't been expecting. I nodded, mutely, my throat closing. "First year's hard," she said. "Second will be better. Good luck." She stood up and walked off.

THIRTEEN

The rest of that first year at Wellesley passed as a montage of classes and work. I had been placed on a backup list for the tennis team but was never called. My self-imposed workload prevented me from running much, and the more I studied the more I began to feel like only an intellect, a mind so removed from the concerns of the body that it could only be bothered with the most basic of needs. I ran when I could, but the activity began to feel less like an outlet and more like a requirement.

I spent the summer at home but I volunteered at the Brigham for as many hours as they would have me. Frequently, taking the T home at dusk or later, I would sit and watch the sights outside pass and pass, forgetting what time it was, or that it was summer at all. My mother was doing no better, and my father did his best to let me escape from the house. Avoiding them felt much easier than sticking around to face my apparent inability to affect any change whatsoever at home. When I returned for my sophomore year in the fall, I wondered if I had ever really been away.

Amy had convinced me to sign up with her as a resident assistant so we could share one of the much larger doubles offered to residence staff. She seemed to take it as a given that we would room together again, despite the fact that our friendship hadn't grown much beyond an uneasy companionship. But I think she stuck with me because she didn't know how to make new friends, either. So many Wellesley students seemed to be lacking the ability to have an easygoing engagement with the world; I suspected that many of us had not fit in where other young women might have. It would take a while before most of us could see what we needed in the others.

I was sure that between my wariness and Amy's brusqueness we would never be invited to join the residence committee, but they must not have had many applicants that year. Our new room faced the lake again but was nearly twice the size of the earlier one, and on the second floor. That entire year we had all of three students come to seek our help, all concerned about their grades.

Most of my coursework was predetermined by my premed focus, but I was encouraged by my advisor to branch out in my remaining selections. Professor Sanders, my first-year writing instructor, had applauded my thorough dissection of texts and recommended me for Professor Pope's Shakespeare class; I signed up for it in the fall semester. The class was fast-paced and engaging, and for the first time in a while I began to love not just what I was being taught but also the pleasure of learning it. Professor Pope was contrary and opinionated, shunned contemporary literature, and seemed altogether to be genuinely himself. I warmed to him immediately and felt I produced my best paper yet for an assignment due late in the semester: an interpretation of *Measure for Measure* in which I suggested that the disguised Duke was not only subversive but also, because I was young and arrogant, that he was more culpable than the outwardly corrupt Angelo. Professor Pope disagreed. He gave my paper a grade of "B double minus." I was hurt and defensive, and sought out time during his office hours to review it with him.

He had a tattered poster of the Globe on one wall and a window that took up the entirety of the one facing it, so that someone looking in from the outside would immediately see the great theater. He was a very small man, and older than I realized when face-to-face with him. The stiff brown tweeds he wore were more like a kind of armor than professional dress; they seemed to literally support him, as if he might collapse at night when they were removed.

"It's an outlandish proposition," he declared with a grin, "one I've never encountered in all my years of teaching and scholarship. Not because it's brilliant"—he leaned against his desk, facing me, neither one of us sat—"but because it's unfounded, outrageous. Angelo is one of Shakespeare's worst. You simply cannot compare the Duke's mild weaknesses to a man who tries to blackmail a nun." He was holding my paper as he spoke but not looking at it.

"But the Duke lets Angelo threaten Isabel without interfering," I said. His office was overheated and I hadn't taken off my jacket. I wondered if he could see my discomfort. "He won't come out of disguise to chastise him. And he knows better. Isn't that nearly as bad, or even worse?"

"Oh, he's a shady character, all right"—Professor Pope seemed so delighted he nearly laughed. He was clearly fueled by disagreement, the opportunity to share more of the encyclopedic knowledge that saturated his thinking. "But you've got nothing to support your argument in this paper. The play does not indicate that the failure to intervene is worse than the threat of rape and the unwillingness to provide clemency for an innocent life. A scholar must always rely on the text, Ms. Feinstein. Otherwise she puts herself on a sinking ship."

"I thought I had," I said.

"You did not," he said. Still standing, he crossed his feet at the ankles. "Your examples are weak, your arguments poor." He was right. I had hoped to impress him with my creativity, but I knew in the back of my mind that I had probably reached too far. I felt a flush overtaking my face. "I should have given you a lower grade, but your attempt amused me." His smile softened into something more sympathetic. I wondered how many students cried in his office. I could think of nothing worse at that moment than being one of them.

"Don't feel bad about the double minus." I realized I had been quiet for some time when I heard his voice again. "I once gave a student a B with seventeen minuses." He was still smiling. I looked up and actually laughed, a small bark that rang through his office. He looked at me quizzically, and in an instant I was back to being terrified I might cry.

"Okay," I said. I began to pack my bag quickly.

"Don't worry about a rewrite," he said. "You can't salvage this." He tossed my paper onto the desk beside him. "Just focus on the text on the final exam, and we'll see what you come up with. If your comments in class are any indication, you can read well." He tried to give me an encouraging smile, but it came off more like a smirk. "Good luck, Ms. Feinstein."

"Thanks," I muttered. I stumbled out, holding my breath, willing the tears to stop. Something within me was unraveling, some security I needed, but I couldn't bring myself to face it and know what it was. Another woman was waiting outside his office, Jenna Lieberman, someone I'd eyed as a possible friend for a while; she seemed smart and unaffected. She smiled at me. I kept my head down and brushed past her, the tears coming as I rushed outside, the realization that I'd snubbed her bringing on a fresh wave of humiliation.

My bag was heavy but I dragged it past my dorm and down to the lake. It was forecasted to be the coldest winter in fourteen years. Early October had brought two frosts, and the lake had frozen over midway through the semester. The leaves had changed brilliantly and quickly, and only a few trees had anything on them but the brown and bare remnants of fall.

Lake Waban is an area attraction, a place known to many who live nearby and popular with walkers. But in the sudden cold it was nearly abandoned. I made my way through a grove, too upset to find a real trail, stomping through the trees until I came to the main path at the lake's edge. I dropped my bag, not caring if anyone found it, not thinking anyone would. I set out as quickly as I could, flattening the frozen and dead branches underneath my feet. I didn't look up as

I walked. Two women were ahead of me on the path. I wanted them out of the way, tried not to hear their voices. I walked behind them for nearly a quarter of a mile until the cold air began to hurt my ears and hands. It had been too long since I moved that quickly, and it felt good, like that night after Teddy left when I ran down the streets just to be running. I wished I had stopped to change my shoes.

I don't know what made me look up when I did, but this is what I saw: one of the women still on the path, the other about fifteen feet out onto the frozen surface of the lake. I stopped as if I'd walked into a stone wall, my mind suddenly refusing to make sense of what I was seeing. The woman still on the path had her mouth open; she looked fixed to the spot, as if afraid that the sound of her voice alone would break the ice beneath the other's feet. I shouted, the sound coming from me before I realized I had made it.

Both women turned their heads. The woman on the ice smiled at me, then turned back and took another step. The other woman finally yelled, a sound more like a wild cry than language. Her voice faded as the ice began to crack, a whip across the lake. The woman on the ice crouched down, trying to lower her center of gravity as the surface shifted under her feet. In an instant she was underwater.

I froze, I don't know for how long, but I couldn't move. Then I started running. I don't know how quickly I reached them.

The other girl was already tearing through the undergrowth beneath our feet. "Find a branch, a stick, something." We were both already looking, our hands frantic and fumbling. "Fuck, fuck, fuck, fuck, holy shit"—the other girl released a stream of profanity while we hunted, time moving in unbearable slowness and speed. I found a long, unwieldy branch buried beneath the wet leaves and began to pull at it. She was suddenly at my side, both of us yanking hard. The woman in the water had surfaced twice but hadn't made a sound. It was too terrible to look in her direction, like seeing the headlights on a train from the tracks.

"Let me," the other breathed as we freed the stick. She vaulted toward the ice, launching the branch out in front of her. "Get on your stomach," I called, running to catch up to her. "I'll hold your feet." "Grab it!" she called out to the girl in the ice, though there was no head above water.

A minute later the woman resurfaced and grabbed for the branch, but it was crooked at one end, and the angle at which it hovered over her head made me fear it could push her back down. Somehow she got a hold of it.

The instant she did we pulled as hard as we could.

I don't know what would have happened next if each of us hadn't been holding on to our ends as tightly as we were. Somehow we managed to pull her up. As soon as her torso was out of the water her friend threw the branch aside and grabbed her under the arms as I pulled with her back toward the shore. The ice underneath us there was mockingly opaque. We hoisted what felt like dead weight to the bank. The frozen woman scratched her way onto the dirt once we got her close but was unable to stand once there. "Get her up, get her up," her friend chanted. I tried to help, but her body felt heavy and cold; I told myself it was only ice and wet clothes and shock.

We lifted her to her feet and managed to make our way through the woods, puffing in the cold and the effort of moving her. We pulled her through the door of the nearest building, Tower Court, where we shouted at the girl on front-desk duty to call an ambulance. It took her a second to comprehend us and then another to move to help us, her sweater set carefully laid against her body. We were all so wet by then it must have looked like we had fallen in together.

After the ambulance arrived, I sat down in a chair in the common room in a daze, finally realizing that some time must have passed because I was nearly dry, the left side of my body where I had supported her already faintly damp, sticky now in the heat of the room. Only the wrist of my jacket was soaked. Her friend had sunk into the chair across from me and closed her eyes.

I watched her for a moment, the even part in her straight hair, the worn jeans, the muddy boots. I tried to imagine where she had come from before here, what state her home was in. I didn't feel like I could leave yet. I had seen something she hadn't chosen for me to see, and the awkwardness of that knowledge kept me pinned to my chair, not wanting to draw any attention to myself and the reason I was there.

"Are you all right?" I said, loud enough for only her to hear me.

"She's a fucking idiot," she replied, her eyes still closed.

I nodded. "I'm sorry," I said. "Maybe"—I knew what I was going to say next would be clumsy, no matter what—"maybe she'll get some help. Maybe after they release her from the hospital. I'm sure she'll be fine." I didn't believe myself, and the doubt bore into my stomach, making me wrap my arms around myself reflexively.

She opened her eyes, only to stare out the window. "She will be fine," she agreed quietly. I nodded. It would have been a good time to leave but I didn't.

She looked at me, a half-smile playing on her mouth. Her expression was direct now, friendly, as if she could erase everything that had come before if she simply wanted to. "Look," she stood suddenly, "I have to go. Come join us for coffee tomorrow night. She'll be out by then. My last name is Abrams. Julie Abrams." She grabbed a scrap of paper off of a small table and jotted down her number. "Give me a call, we'll treat you. I've got class in ten minutes." She thanked me. I shook my head to wave it off but she was already running out the door. She popped her head in a second later, "What's your name?" The woman at the front desk looked from her to me.

"Naomi," I called back.

"You're kidding," she said.

"No," I said. She just shook her head, dropped it with a wave, and was gone.

FOURTEEN

I don't think I spoke to another person until late the next afternoon, a Saturday. Amy, now officially a joint major in astronomy and economics, had night lab on Fridays, and I left for the library most mornings before she woke. On Saturdays she tutored at the lab. I spent that morning doing research for a paper due later that week, picked up lunch on my way back to the dorm, and worked on an outline for the next few hours, halfheartedly waiting for Amy to get back. I looked up from my work shortly after three, stretched my neck, and wondered how cold it was outside. The dorm was stuffy and quiet. I stared idly at the phone, as I had done several times since the evening before, when I was finally calm and warm and dry, wondering if the events I'd witnessed had taken place, or if they'd only been the result of an overactive imagination. I had seen a woman walk onto ice, smile, and fall. I had watched her friend retrieve her, had helped to bring her out of the lake. And just like that, it occurred to me that we had actually saved her life.

I looked from the phone to the window. The sky was gray. Amy would be back any minute. I heard myself sigh in the room, hating how stuck I felt, unsure of what to do. What was the big deal, Amy would have said. I hated to admit even to myself how shy and self-conscious I'd become.

The doorknob turned and Amy flounced into the room, scowling. "Colder than a witch's tit," she muttered. "And I have night lab again tonight. The fucking idiot I had to tutor couldn't even find *Cassiopeia* on a *star* map."

"Cassiopeia?" I asked. "Wasn't she the goddess of vanity or something? Is she easy to find?"

Amy was glaring at me. "Cassiopeia, Naomi? The Wellesley 'W'? God. Sometimes I wonder where your head is at."

Right. I hadn't realized that Wellesley had a constellatory presence, as well. I sighed. Amy paid no attention.

Her face was blotched on the cheeks, sallow under the eyes. "I'm ordering a pizza," she turned to me, belligerent. "Do you want some?" I knew if I said no I'd piss her off. She was in the sort of mood where she demanded any and all attention be given to her, primarily so that she could spit it back with sardonic jibes.

"I've got plans," I said, breaking her gaze and standing up as soon as I said it.

She didn't respond for a minute. "With a guy?" she barked. "I didn't think you knew any."

I stared at her, wondering if she knew how unpleasant she could be.

"No," I said. "Just coffee with friends." Amy took me in a moment longer, huffed, and began unwinding herself from her coat and scarf. I picked up the phone. The paper Julie had given me had gotten smudged so I had to look in the directory for the number. Amy watched me as I held the receiver to my chest. She was conspicuously silent. The call was picked up after two rings.

"Julie speaking." The voice on the other end was very formal, perhaps mockingly so. I told her who I was, feeling instantly like an awkward prepubescent girl calling her crush.

"Naomi!" she exclaimed. I could hear her rustling something in the background. I forced myself to drop the phone cord I was twisting in my hands, and then she was speaking before I had a chance to get even more tongue-tied. "Meet us at the Hoop in a half hour," she said, more of a command than a request.

I had never been to the Hoop, the student-run coffeehouse in the basement of the Schneider Student Center; it was a place for artists and upperclasswomen, people who seemed, in general, to be living an entirely different reality from mine. Julie hung up just as I was forming another question. I already had an impression of her as someone who exited conversations a moment before they ended.

I threw my coat and hat on and walked out the door with my scarf still in my hand, refusing to meet Amy's look. "Bye," I said, slamming the door and walking quickly down the hallway.

The afternoon was unexpectedly chilly. I knew I wouldn't get warm between my dorm and Schneider so I hurried as fast as I could, pulling my jacket around me. I was surprised to notice that the left wrist of the jacket was still completely soaked; I shook it as I walked, then shrunk my fists further up the sleeves, drawing myself into the driest parts.

The entrance to the Hoop was at the bottom of a short flight of steps. There was only one door in, and the ordering counter—a high, stone semicircle—monopolized it, the days' offerings written on a board in colored chalk. Various semisophisticated sweets were on display in large covered glass jars: biscotti, chocolate-covered espresso beans. I thought I should order something just in case I was early, or in case they never showed up, but I didn't like coffee. I chose hot chocolate before I had time to think of something more suave, a drink that might have offered a more stylish defense.

There was nowhere to leave my jacket, and when I took my drink from the hip woman behind the counter who never made eye contact, it was hot, almost burning in my hands. The air in the basement was overly warm, too. My wrist felt only vaguely wet now. The Hoop was comprised of four connecting rooms, each room separation created by an arch rather than a doorway, so that its structure echoed that of an underground cave. I wondered what it had been before it was a café.

I found Julie already seated in the room directly to the left, the most immediately accessible but also the most deeply interior; it would have been directly underneath the center of the building. It was the quietest area in the Hoop, the women there studying in hushed conversations. Julie's half-drowned friend was with her, her back to me. I hadn't realized how tall she was until she turned around to greet me, walking halfway across the room and shaking my hand as a man would before hugging me vigorously.

"Sorry to scare you so bad," she said, pulling back. "But I'm all right, see? Strong as an ox." Somehow we were standing by their table. Her greeting had taken me by surprise. I couldn't think of the last time someone had spontaneously grabbed me.

Julie stayed seated, smiling at me. "Hey, Naomi. Meet Ruth," she gestured upward, to her friend. "Ruth, Naomi." "Seriously?" Ruth said, still standing, grinning. "I thought Julie made it up." "I'm pretty sure," I said. Ruth laughed in a way that made me think she would have laughed at anything I had said. I sat down on the last chair at their table and Ruth sat, too, so that she was between Julie and me, her back again to the doorway. I had the feeling after I sat down that Ruth had pulled the chair out for me, though I think it was my imagination working through her warm greeting.

"You know, I always loved Ruth's speech to Naomi," she said, sitting down beside me, "but I never thought I'd find a Naomi to say it to." She took my hand in hers. I was so surprised I thought I'd have to pull away, but I managed just to blush and keep my hand where it was.

"'For whither thou goest, I will go,'" she began to recite from the Book of Ruth. "'And where thou lodgest, I will lodge: thy people shall be my people, and thy God my God.'" She dropped my hand. "Except I can't believe in any God, even if you handed me yours on a silver platter." She winked at me and sat back in her chair, her expression one of total satisfaction.

"She's not an anti-Semite," Julie said, watching my face. "She's just a card-carrying atheist."

"It's true," Ruth nodded. "I hate all religions. Are you Jewish?"

she asked me, now examining my face as well. I wondered what I had revealed there. I nodded. "Good. Most Jews I know have serious God issues, too. Understandably, of course! They tend to get atheism better than most atheists."

She reached forward to lift a huge, steaming mug to her lips. "You know, it's my third time falling through the ice since freshman year," she went on, failing to acknowledge what I was pretty sure was a complete change in topic.

Julie's expression quickly soured and she looked up, interrupting Ruth. "Are you a first-year?" she asked.

"No," I said, "sophomore." I felt suddenly embarrassed. As far as they could tell, I must have appeared out of nowhere.

"Strange that we've never seen you," Ruth went on. I was grateful to her for thinking this odd, or at least pretending to. "Where do you live?"

"Stone-Davis," I said.

"We know someone who lives in Stone-Davis, don't we?" As soon as Ruth said this, I knew that it was as uncool as I'd been afraid it was.

Julie shook her head. She was wearing a brown fitted sweater with a light-blue scarf and no jewelry. Her hair shone even in the half-light of the room, the way my mother's did. Ruth was as ungainly as Julie was polished: her sweater strained around her middle, her pants too short at the ankles.

"No, wait." Julie corrected herself, inverting her wrist and pointing one finger toward Ruth. "Linda lives there." "Oh, yeah!" Ruth said. "Do you know Linda McDade?" I shook my head. "She's art history," Ruth said encouragingly. I shook my head again. "Don't think we've met," I said. I wondered under what circumstances they would grow tired of me and ask me to leave. "I think Hillary Clinton might have roomed there all four years," I tried. "I think you're right!" Ruth confirmed. Julie sighed loudly, blowing the few stray hairs on her forehead upward. "This paper's due tomorrow and it's just not happening." She leaned toward me, crossing her arms over her notebook. "So," she said, "how's it going?"

I had no idea how to answer her, there were so many things going, so few going well. "Good," I shrugged, "I guess."

"So, it's all good?" Julie was sniffing me out. I shrugged again. "I guess." I forced myself to release my shoulders, stopping just short of an old habit of cracking my neck. She smirked a little. "Right," she said. "How's the whole Wellesley thing working out for you?"

I wasn't sure if I knew the answer to that question, or maybe I just hadn't admitted it to myself. "It's been pretty hard," I said. I felt immediately exposed, unsure. "I mean . . ." What did I mean? I attempted to collect myself, sound less cagey, more confident. "It's a great place, just lonely." It was hard to believe that the words had come out of my mouth. I wonder if social inactivity had left me too contained, susceptible to overflow. I stared down at the table. "I'm taking Shakespeare with Professor Pope this semester. It's not going that well."

"Oh, Christ," Ruth said, "are you a favorite?" She turned to Julie. "What do you think? Not a favorite?" She looked at me. "You're certainly not androgynous enough, but he does like a pretty face. You'll learn a lot from him, though. Are you thinking of joining Shakes?" I shook my head, confused. I knew very little about the Shakespeare Society. I'd heard of it, but it was something that was kept quiet on campus, a place other students seemed to both respect and hold in mild suspicion, though I couldn't remember anyone mentioning what went on there.

"I'm not doing that well in Pope's class," I repeated.

"I'm thinking he's given her more than one minus on the midterm." Julie was looking directly at me, squinting.

"B double minus," I blurted. "But that's not important." I tried to summon control of the conversation. "Is everything okay with you?" I asked Ruth.

It took a moment for either of them to respond. It seemed I'd startled them. Maybe they hadn't expected me to assert myself so much as to redirect the conversation. But I was an expert, by that point, at deflecting. So much so that I sometimes wondered if taking attention away from myself had become the most noticeable thing about me.

"Sure," Ruth said. "I just need to learn how to dress better for the occasion. Last year I had silk undies on, and they weren't warm enough. I went with wool yesterday, but it gets too heavy. Even a light wool." She grinned. "It's a study."

"Jesus, Ruth," Julie frowned. "Please. She doesn't want to hear all about it."

"Sure she does," Ruth said cheerfully, sitting back. "Wait, your jacket is soaked!" She had glanced down and now leaned forward, grabbing my left arm. "What the hell? Is that from the lake?" Her face fell, her lower jaw jutting out.

"Of course it is," Julie interrupted. "Here, you can't wear that outside again. It's going to snow." She reached back to pull her coat from the back of her chair. "Take mine."

"No," Ruth said. "It's too small." She pulled her own jacket off and thrust it on my lap. I left mine on and held hers to me, the down warm, too warm by far for the heated room. It gave off the subtle, sweetly unfamiliar scent of Ruth's soap or shampoo or perfume; I felt like I was holding an exotic cloth, unsure of what to make of it.

"I'm fine," I said. "Really."

"You're wearing that home," Ruth said. "Now listen." She sat back again. "So you won't worry," she winked. "It's an annual ritual, much to Abrams' disappointment." She waved Julie off, not looking at her. "Have you ever heard of Frederick Wiefern?" she asked, leaning forward.

Julie rolled her eyes. "Of course she hasn't," she said to neither of us.

Ruth wouldn't look at her. "Wiefern," she began. Julie looked down at her notebook, pretending to work. Ruth was leaning back into her chair again, one elbow on its top rung, the hand suspended in air, "was a German immigrant. Had a dairy farm up near the Canadian border. Anyway, he was an intellectual back in Germany but couldn't afford to continue his studies out here. Would have been a professor, a great professor, I'm sure." I settled my hands around my hot chocolate. I felt comfortable, like a child not caring about the story, only caring that it is being read to her.

"Undeniably," Julie said without looking up.

"Anyway, Wiefern's theory was, *is*, that the human body evolved into its present form of, shall we say, buoyancy, because"—she rubbed her hands together like a fly before a meal—"now get this—it needed to establish an emotional equilibrium." Her hands stopped. She was looking directly at me, waiting for something. "Can you guess what that means?" she prompted.

I had a feeling that I didn't need to say or do much of anything for Ruth to be satisfied. I shook my head. Julie was tapping her pencil on her notebook. Ruth pressed her palms together, as if readying for silent prayer, though her eyes were wide and full of light. "Emotional equilibrium is obvious, but this idea of physical buoyancy is intertwined with emotional buoyancy; the two go hand in hand." She clasped hers together again, completing her point.

"Wiefern knew that the body and the mind needed padding, both of them," she continued. "That they worked together and didn't function at their best unless both, *both*"—she leaned forward, delighted—"had extra reserves." She sat back. "The whole body needs to be flush, otherwise it struggles, it fights itself and ultimately," her voice dropped, "ultimately, it saps the mind."

"In other words"—Julie held the pencil tip she'd been tapping to the page in front of her—"Chris Farley should be the halest man alive."

Ruth was still looking at me, smiling, waiting for my reaction. "Don't mind her. She just refuses to get the subtleties of the theory. If a preexisting self-loathing exists, as is the case with our poor Mr. Farley, any theoretical models will be compromised. Also"—she studied Julie amiably—"she's just bitter because she's got no reserves. She's built like her mother."

"Who was fat, may I say, until after she had kids. Watch out. You could have her genes." Julie looked weary, unable to resist the argument.

"Maybe." Ruth had her arms folded over her chest, looking smug, as if I'd stood up and cheered for her theory. "We're cousins, on the

German side. Our mothers are sisters." She leaned in. "My mother kept her name."

Julie jumped in. "They hate each other," she remarked.

Ruth shook her head pleasantly, as she might at a beloved pet. "Anyway"—she reached out and touched her fingers to my wrist, confidential—"I walk out onto the lake every year. It's a familial celebration. I know I won't drown; never have. Julie won't do it because she says it's crazy, but she's only afraid because she's so skinny." Ruth sat up straight. "I'm the Wiefern model: plump and sharp. I don't fear the water or the cold. And I haven't been depressed a day in my life, have I, Jules?"

"Not a day." Julie was reading her notes.

"Wiefern was our great-grandfather," Ruth went on. "I'm writing my thesis on him." She smiled at me warmly. I wondered if she thought we shared something. She had a way of reengaging as she spoke, each time making me feel anew that she was glad to see me.

"Wow," I said, wondering which professor, which department, which unknown corner of the college she came from, "is this a psych thesis?"

She waved her hand away at me. "Psych doesn't have enough imagination. Milton Fried," she announced, "in philosophy, is sponsoring me." I had heard of Fried. Incisive, adored, near retirement. "Does he know you throw yourself into the lake?"

Julie looked up suddenly, a smile beginning to creep through her exhaustion. Ruth didn't answer my question. She leaned forward and pulled the top off my cup. "Hot chocolate," she grinned, setting it back. "Bad day, right? I rest my case." I was beginning to enjoy the rhythm of being asked questions that needed no answer. Still looking at me in a satisfied way, she said again, "You like Shakespeare? I mean, if Pope weren't involved?"

I had liked it well enough to throw my best effort into the essay. "I guess," I tried to look casual, to at least pretend I didn't care as much as I did that someone was showing such interest in me. "He's a great teacher. I thought I'd written a good paper."

"Then come tea."

"Tea?"

"Oh, it means nothing. Nonsense. We put out tea for new recruits and call it tea-ing. Brilliant, right? It's one of those ridiculous college verbs. Like we need our own private language. God, the tea-ers are boring this semester." She looked at me wryly, as though about to make a joke. "They all think it's a sorority. I've never seen so many buttons and pearls in one place. And I doubt one of them has read a play outside of class. How many things do you own that have buttons?" she asked Julie. Julie shrugged.

All of a sudden I remembered how much I'd enjoyed the end of *The Winter's Tale*, which I'd skipped ahead to read earlier that week, how unexpectedly surreal and hypnotic it was. I thought about how Hermione had been mistaken for a statue before she revealed herself. For some reason I thought of Teddy, too, the sod nest we'd helped repair for the ducks. "I'm not sure I'll be much more interesting," I said.

"Oh, you just have the Wellesley blues"—Julie looked up from the paper she'd reentered. "The best of us get them the worst. We'll cheer you up in no time."

Ruth nodded. She dropped her voice, her grin a broad echo of her cousin's slight smile, "We like to think of ourselves as part of the Wellesley underground. I think the college does, too. They leave us pretty much alone." She leaned in confidentially. "A lot of people leave you alone if you put Shakespeare on the letterhead."

FIFTEEN

The second tea for that semester was scheduled for the following week. Posters covered with the iconic Shakespeare mask and quill appeared all over campus a few days before: gray and white, imposing but familiar. There was a hint of something else in them too—a sarcastic wit, or subversiveness; or perhaps it was just that such free sarcasm on our otherwise earnest campus was itself subversive.

I fell asleep hard the night before but woke up a few hours later. I opened the window a crack to see if the storm the local meteorologist had threatened us with was picking up, the ambient light outside making it difficult to see. I put my hand out; it was raining, lightly. I suddenly wanted it to be spring even though winter was just starting. I had a lab report due and decided to get out of bed to work on it, but thought better of it once I turned on the small desk lamp and Amy stirred. I put on a jacket and scarf and packed my bag for the library. It was almost midnight and it would be open all night, a strange schedule demanded by the Wellesley constitution. Some wealthy founder had thought modern women should be liberated from everything, including conventions of time. The others had made only one concession to her: the library would never close.

Once downstairs I pushed the heavy door to the dorm open and stepped into the cold. A wind I hadn't expected hit me, but I wrapped myself tighter in my things and decided to take the long way there. After a while it didn't feel cold anymore, and the drizzling rain felt good on my face after the overheated dorm. It was not the first walk I'd taken at night. Before I had arrived on campus, I would see the name Wellesley and know, for a brief instant, that it was a place inextricably connected to my sense of who I could become; the intimacy with which I knew and had thought of it creating an association that felt personal. And yet it excited me, too, the name both intimate and unsettling—the essence of a sure-to-be-realized promise. I sometimes liked to walk the grounds when they were virtually deserted to dredge up the old excitement, to reflect on the fact that I was in a place and position that Rose Kennedy, the nearest thing to an American matriarch, had longed for. Sometimes, in the right lighting, the false comfort of achievement still worked for me. The Wellesley grounds are receptive to such wanderings. Its founders knew that a woman aware of her own intelligence will be given to the pathos of it all, the romantic and tragic qualities of being a female thinker.

Wellesley's gothic architecture is echoed perfectly by its layout: there are dozens of winding passageways just on the outskirts of buildings. Several of these are extensions of the buildings themselves, arched and covered walkways, a few of which have balconies or windows, so that those on foot may take fantastical breathers along their way. On any given day I could have taken one of several paths to the same destination. That night I chose to weave around and through the covered walkway near Founders Hall, the home of most of the humanities departments and Mr. Pope's office. It was slightly chilling to know it was entirely empty and dark as I walked beside it. As I emerged from the covered path onto the academic quad, I had my head down in anticipation of the rain before I lifted it, startled.

There was someone standing there.

She saw me almost as soon as I saw her. The hood over her head shadowed her face. There was a little light from the buildings but most of the space between them was dark.

"Hi," she said.

"Hi," I replied, catching my breath.

She nodded, almost as if she'd been expecting someone—not me, necessarily, but my presence didn't seem to jar her. "It's hard to find a private spot on this campus," she said eventually, staring into the middle distance.

"It seems there's nothing but privacy here, sometimes." I was surprised that I would admit this to a fellow student, particularly one I didn't know. She looked at me for a minute, taking me in. She didn't smile, but her face relaxed. "We must go to different schools. Do I know you?" she asked.

I shook my head. "Naomi," I said. I cleared my throat and tried to sound more confident. "Naomi Feinstein." She squinted. "Do you play tennis?" "No," I said quickly before correcting myself. "I used to." I decided to quit for good earlier that year, telling myself that a surgeon would need to protect her hands.

She looked away again. "We played together once," she stated matter-of-factly. "At Longwood." She looked back at me and pulled off her hood so I could see her face. "I'm Jun Oko. Do you remember?" she asked. I saw her face, and then the match, and the storm.

"Oh," I said.

She smiled a little. "Yeah. Nice to meet you again." She held out her hand.

I shook it, a little surprised by her formality. "What are you doing out here?" I asked, trying, unsuccessfully, to dispel the awkwardness between us.

She looked me in the eye but didn't answer. It struck me that she might suspect I was policing her. I remembered how she had waited for her father's signal that day before getting out of the rain. "What are *you* doing here?" she asked sharply. I thought I saw the hint of a mocking smile, but she was looking straight ahead, not at me.

"I'm on the way to the library," I said, my tone implying that I had nothing to hide. All at once I wished I hadn't stopped. Although our match was a distant memory, there was something about her that made me want to irk her, or, at the very least, not offer any concession.

"How studious of you," she said. I raised an eyebrow. If I gave her an answer, the least she could do was give one in return. "I'm standing here, staring at absolutely nothing," she announced, articulating every word for emphasis. But then she suddenly covered her face, and just when I thought she was about to cry, she began to laugh, haltingly at first, and then gratefully. Or maybe it was I who was grateful for the chance to laugh, grateful for the near-freezing clean air it forced into my lungs. I had the sense that we had each been still holding the tension of that match on our separate ends for some time, that she knew what it was like to hold tension for too long.

Her laugh was stilted and infectious, as if she were trying to stop herself from brimming over. "I'm sorry," she managed finally. "But you came through here so quietly, like a ghost. Jesus. You scared the hell out of me." She sobered up. "I'm working on *Hamlet*," she explained, shaking her head.

"Are you in it?" I asked.

"Yeah, I'm Hamlet." I took that in for a second. We both cracked a smile at the same time.

"I really was just standing out here, staring at nothing," she offered. "I thought I'd practice my lines, but I got stuck out here. Have you ever noticed how staring at something you thought you knew really well makes it start to change?" She was smiling like she knew I'd understand. "Let's get out of here. You still need to go to the library?" I shook my head. "Come with me. I've got a little errand to do. If it's still a good night for it." She looked up at the sky, starless and black with clouds.

She turned around and began to walk straight ahead, between

the two buildings. I jogged a few steps to catch up. She walked very quickly, even though the path was dark and slick with rain. She didn't stay on it for long. At the edge of the quad she hopped over the low stone fence that surrounded it and trotted across the street there. I followed her, slipping a bit on the wet grass. On the other side of the street we ended up looking up at the roof of a small building. In the dark it took me a minute to realize it was the odd little house that stood on a side road of the college: the replica of Anne Hathaway's Tudor cottage, the meeting place of the Shakespeare Society.

"Come on," Jun said. She trotted to the back of the house and fished out a ladder, steadying its base on the ground, the other end just fitting into the rain gutter on the roof. She began climbing it fearlessly, though it wobbled a bit. The fall wasn't far, at first, but as she climbed, it seemed worse. I followed her.

I squatted down once we were on the roof, holding on to the edge, but she began to move forward over the uneven surface, like a crab hunting. She was running her hands over the roof as she moved, as if whatever she was looking for was written in a clumsy, diffused Braille. She stopped. I looked over the edge of the roof to see if anyone had stopped and could see us.

Like a flash against a dark screen, all at once Rosemary's writing on the back of the Amelia Earhart photo came back to me: *She could fly.* I had a sudden wave of vertigo and put my hands out at my sides, trying to lower my center of gravity. It was the first time in years, since the loss of Teddy, that I had thought of Rosemary's hidden treasures, and I felt an unexpected wave of guilt as I did, as though something I was supposed to keep watch over had been misplaced.

It was so dark I could make out only the barest outline of Jun. She moved like a pianist; determined but fine, led by the hands. Suddenly she crouched down, just a few feet in front of me. A moment later she made a small sound, something like an exclamation, but hushed. I could hear her prying something loose; it was a shingle or some other piece of the roof. She wrenched it free and placed it beside her.

"It's here," she whispered, looking down.

She pulled out something I couldn't see. "A chunk of stage left," she announced, holding it up, trying to get a better look and show me at the same time. "Buried here circa 1952." She grinned. For a minute I was startled by how much her expression reminded me of my father's at 83 Beals, holding up a book he'd reached over the rope in front of the dining room to snag, explaining to Mrs. Olsen that she'd misplaced it, that the Folger belonged in the music room. He was right; it had always been on the round walnut table to the left of the door, open to the King's speech in act IV of *Henry V*: "If it be a sin to covet Honor, / I am the most offending soul alive." He had been delighted to be the one to correct the situation.

Jun sat back on her heels. "I'm secretary this semester, and I've been doing some research," she was explaining. She acted impatient, quick to get to the part when we could both marvel at the find. "Some alum had a letter in the archives saying she pulled this from the stage at the Globe and buried it on the north side of the roof."

She held it, turning it as if it might give off light. "Cool, huh?" She lifted it up a bit higher, but the lamppost below was too dim. After a moment of trying to see it better, she put it back carefully, smoothing the shingle after she was done. She pulled a small hammer and a nail from her jacket pocket. She leaned forward, still squatting, and awkwardly tapped the shingle back in.

"You're leaving it here?" I asked. She stopped her movements to look at me. "You're not taking it with you?" I elaborated, regretting my obvious disappointment.

She looked amused by what I'd said. "No," she replied. "It's been safe here for almost sixty years. Best not to mess with it." She smiled at me. "I just wanted to check if it was really here."

She stood up and I joined her. All at once I was afraid she was done with me, that she'd jump down from the roof and wave me off, back to Amy and our airless room. "Do you know what time it is?" I asked.

She was running her hands over her work, checking it. "Late," she answered distractedly. "I've got an econ exam in the morning," she added, then smiled at me crookedly again. "Maybe it's time to get off the roof and go in. You look soaked."

We both were. Even though the rain had been light, it had been steady, and we'd both been out long enough to let it seep its way in. "I'm thinking of tea-ing," I said. As I said it, we both smiled again. "Seriously"—I suddenly wanted us both to believe me. "Do you know Julie Abrams and Ruth Wiefern?"

"I know you're serious," she said. "Abrams and Ruthie. Yeah. How do you know them?" I shrugged. "You should. It's different. Nice. I'll put in a good word for you," she added after a pause. "Ready?" She was over the edge of the roof before I had a chance to respond.

At the east end of the quad she turned before heading off to her dorm. "I'm glad to see you again, Naomi," she said. I was struck again by the odd formality of how she spoke, but also by the kindness it seemed to contain.

At breakfast the next morning Amy ignored me boldly, concentrating all her attentions on Fleur Simons, a pale-haired, quiet junior who was rumored to be in line for a Rhodes scholarship and who had taken a seat at our table when all others were full.

Only when I began to reload my tray to get up did she stop, nearly interrupting Fleur, to ask, "So, Naomi, where were you last night? Don't tell me you had a secret tryst and didn't even tell your roommate." She smiled wryly, shooting a knowing look at Fleur.

I was late for class. "I guess it's none of your business," I replied as I picked up my tray and left.

Amy caught up with me when I was already halfway across campus. "You on the rag or something?" she asked. For all her naked abrasion, she reacted with surprising vulnerability on the few occasions when I bit back. Her face was pinched and frowning, as close as she came to revealing her self-doubt. "I'm allowed my bad moods, Amy," I said, picking up my pace. I felt too tired to call her on her own game. "You must be happy you got to meet Fleur."

She couldn't mask a quick, triumphant smile. "Yeah, I guess. Maybe she can get me on College Government. I'll have to keep after her. So, really, Noms," she rarely called me this, "Where were you last night?"

"Were you worried?" I teased.

"Yeah, actually," she frowned, ready to bristle again.

I shoved my hands deeper into my pockets. The sun had come out and created a glare on the ice on the sidewalk. By mid-afternoon it would melt, leaving a persistent sludgy mess. "I just took a walk. Couldn't sleep." Amy was persistent. "What about coffee the other night? Were you meeting with a tutor or something?" "No," I said. "I don't need tutoring, Amy." I didn't want to go into what had happened at the lake. I told her I was thinking of joining the Shakespeare Society, and that I had met Ruth, Julie, and Jun.

She sighed heavily, looking relieved. "Oh. Well, you're not the type, Naomi," she began. She was clutching her hands under her armpits, her face splotched with the effort of keeping up with my longer strides. "They're a bunch of renegades, or weirdos or something. I've heard the college would shut them down if they could. They do stuff they shouldn't be doing. You should join a better group, if you're looking for something, something that will really help you rise to the top," she was beginning to relax. "Debate. Wellesley in Washington. Law firms and medical schools aren't going to care about societies."

I had nothing to say. She was probably right. But for the first time in my life I felt hungry to belong to something that would let me be something other than defined, would welcome any floundering attempts I might have to offer at play. In otherwise healthy organisms, loneliness has a saturation point. And watching another woman's gleeful escape from drowning had begun to reveal mine. "I'm friends with the president of Wellesley Debate," Amy was saying. "Want me to talk to her?" It sounded more like an insistence than an offering.

"Maybe," I said.

"Just don't do Shakes. It's a waste of time." Her hat was low, covering her forehead. It made her eyes seem smaller and more protruding than they were. "Plus, they probably won't take you; you're not exactly the sorority type."

I stopped. "It's not a sorority. And I don't really care if they want me. I just want to check it out. You could come, too." I knew she was my only friend at the time, but I despised her anyway, probably because of that.

She coughed a laugh. "Naw. Not my scene. I've got to focus on the sure hits. Anyway, I've got enough on my plate, and you're the one who needs more friends. Good luck, though!" She thumped me on the upper arm. "Can't wait to hear all about it!" She took off down the hill, her backpack bouncing heavily from her shoulders.

Tea, of course, was at four o'clock.

Whenever I had passed it before, the house's Tudor exterior had always looked like a façade, an elfin hideaway on the grounds of gothic royalty, but when the door opened I knew in an instant that it was real. A strikingly beautiful Indian woman with a nose ring answered my knock. She was dressed in a floor-length green velvet gown embroidered with a braided gold cord on the high waist and had a drink in one hand. Red wine. "Hi!" she said, revealing the straightest teeth I'd ever seen up close, "Here for the tea?"

I nodded and held out my hand. "I'm Naomi," I said.

"Nice to meet you, Naomi," she said in a deep voice, her smile still warm, her hand small and strong. "Come in, have a glass of wine." She had the slight accent of those who have learned English perfectly and abroad.

As soon as the door closed the Wellesley I knew disappeared behind it. The house was loud, warm, and overwhelmed with moving bodies. The woman who'd let me in gestured toward a room immediately to my right. She said something I couldn't hear, her name, I think, and smiled. I smiled back, but she was already gone down the short hallway leading to what sounded like a kitchen in the back.

I turned into the entrance of the great room, which was so packed with people it was virtually impassable. A series of small windows lined the east and west walls, and there was another set of doors on the north side that were closed, but from the shape of the house I guessed they led to another, smaller room. The woman who had answered the door had circled back and was now just in front of me, talking to a girl in jeans and T-shirt, both of their faces animated but their voices drowned in the crowd. A sound rose to my right, near the west windows, and I was startled until I realized that it had been a shout of laughter.

The room was dressed in browns and reds, though almost everything was fraying. Short, cheap curtains framed each window, the glass divided into a diamond pattern with narrow bars of iron. A woman with three heavy rings on her right hand walked by me, gesticulating. There was something openly anachronistic about the scene before me, but even the women who were in costume displayed an easy, almost exotic style. Many students at Wellesley dressed as women who could easily be dropped into suburban Connecticut and fit in seamlessly. These women made me think I might have fallen through a rabbit hole into an avant-garde fashion spread: they wore old velvet and fine wool; corsets and heavy silver bangles on long arms; each interpretation was different, many were stunning. I pulled at my thick, blue sweater, self-conscious of its plainness. At least it was interesting enough to look its age.

I began to make my way deeper into the room. I shouldered past a group of six or more women, two of whom smiled at me to let me through. Behind them was the tallest woman I think I had ever seen. Someone was singing. It sounded like someone might also be crying. I had almost reached the other side of the room. I broke free of the crowd as though stepping from a river.

A woman introduced herself to me when I approached the food table placed against the back wall of the room. "I'm Amanda," she said, "Wilcox," she added.

"Naomi," I replied, shaking the hand she offered me. She was unusually pale and small, her white hair cut close to the scalp, her eyes a watery gray. I had had an albino teacher in high school, but even he seemed to have more color than she, the pinks and reds in his white skin fine and complex. Amanda's paleness was of a cooler cast, the skin on her face almost transparent.

"Are you a first-year?" she asked.

"Sophomore," I replied.

"Me, too," she said, "I've never seen you around." The statement was clipped, an assertion. "This is our former president and current director, Phyllis," she said, drawing the attention of another woman standing close by. "This is Naomi," she said. "What did you say your last name was?"

"Feinstein," I said, holding out my hand to Phyllis.

"Nice to meet you, Ms. Feinstein," she said. I thought I heard music beginning in another room. "Though I already know you from Pope's class," Phyllis continued. "I'm Ms. Tratelli"—she mimicked Mr. Pope's voice perfectly. She had long, straight, red hair and deep-set eyes in a narrow face. She looked me in the eye. "He likes you, you know. He likes the way you think." I recognized her as one of those upperclasswomen who spoke well and frequently, the sort who were never alone and never at a loss for words.

I scoffed, then checked myself. "I'm surprised to hear that," I said, picking up a wineglass to look relaxed, but I didn't know how to select something, never mind pour it correctly.

"He talk to you about your paper?" I nodded. I felt self-conscious that we were talking school at what I thought was a party. "He likes you, then." She affirmed, nodding. "And you say smart things in class. Damn those first-years." She squinted across the room, then back at me. "Do you want some wine?"

"Uh, sure," I said. She took my hesitancy as something else. "We have beer, too. Tiney, get her something to drink." She winked at me and turned away. Amanda acknowledged the nickname with something between a grimace and a smirk before reaching forward and selecting a bottle of wine.

"I'll take it," a voice to my right said. It was Jun. Tiney handed the bottle to her and turned away.

I was surprised to feel as happy to see Jun as I did. "Hi," I said, smiling. "Hey," she said, grinning back. She looked into the room, watching Tiney retreat. She put down the bottle. "Do you want some tea?"

I nodded. She handed me a mug and chose one for herself. "Don't let this intimidate you. It's always a zoo, and most of us hate the teas, so it gets a little tense here; sometimes a little out of control." A petite, mousy-haired woman was standing on my other side, pouring tea silently. "Hi," Jun said cheerfully. The other woman smiled hesitantly. "Have a cookie," Jun said. She picked up the entire platter and offered it in her direction. The girl took one, hesitantly.

"I'm Ellie," she said, holding the cookie in her hand awkwardly. Jun nodded. "You're in my econ class. Do you live in the new dorms? I think we're in the same house." Ellie nodded. I felt simultaneously included—Jun didn't feel I needed the extra attention—and jealous, having felt the first tug of friendship, as if something sleeping and hungry inside of me had been gently kicked awake.

I turned from them and walked over to a small cluster of women standing a few feet away. The one nearest me was dressed in a deep-blue embroidered gown, her costume less frayed than the other woman's and contrasting sharply with her freckled skin. She looked my way, grinning, her eyes a dark green, her kinky, almost black hair framing her face like a mane. Her smile was wide and sly and I liked her immediately. "Anush," she said, offering her hand. "And this is . . ."

"Ruth," I said.

Ruth was dressed in short black pants and a faded green cardigan, looking more out of place in her ill-fitting streetwear than she might have in one of the costumes. She grinned. "This is Naomi," she told Anush. "Naomi?" Anush asked, affecting astonishment at the match our names made. "Feinstein," I added. "Is it Feinstein or Naomi," she teased. "Both, I guess. You can call me whatever," I said. "I like Naomi," Ruth said. "She pulled me out of the lake," she told Anush triumphantly.

Anush nodded, nibbling on a carrot. "Want one?" she asked, offering me a carrot from her plate. I took it, which pleased her. "Call me A.J. No one can pronounce my name properly. So at school I'm A.J." "Anusheh Jahedi," Ruth said. "Well, Ruth can pronounce it because she's Persian. And she likes the sound of her own voice. But she's in the minority."

"Half-Persian," Ruth mumbled, her mouth half-full of cookie. "You've heard of my German grandfather," she added conspiratorially to me. "Actually, one of the Wiefern tenets is that the strength of interbreeding between countries with dissimilar climates can be truly extraordinary."

A.J. jabbed her sharply with her elbow. "Shut it, Wiefern."

"My grandparents were sabras," I said, probably too eagerly. "My father was born in Jerusalem."

"Really?" A.J. asked, looking suspiciously at my face. "When did they immigrate?"

"Nineteen forty-one," I replied dutifully. A.J. still looked doubtful. She studied my face, suspecting there might be answers there. "Actually, I don't know much about them. My father grew up here." I knew I was telling them these details to try to fit in, make them like me, but stating my vague family history out in the open only made me feel I was betraying myself, that I had just pulled my own anchor and was beginning to drift away. Sometimes that, more than anything, was what made me saddest about the little I knew about my family; it could be worked into almost any story, like a party trick.

A.J. nodded. "So, we're doing *Hamlet* next semester"—she had finished her food and was wiping her mouth. She raised her smallest finger to discreetly pick a tooth. "You know all new members have to be in the play?"

I nodded, trying to look casual. It was getting noisier. I raised my voice, "I mean, I've never done much acting. But," I felt boldness wash over me, "I'd join the play."

"Laertes," A.J. said to Ruth.

Ruth nodded. "Perfect."

"Haven't you cast him already?" It seemed like a role they might not want to give to a novice.

"No. Let me go find Phyllis." Ruth walked away. A.J. put another carrot on my plate and followed her.

"So, I forgot to ask you last night"—Jun was suddenly beside me. "How come you didn't try out for tennis again?" I sat down on the bench behind me.

"I'm premed," I began, not knowing if I needed to explain any further. Jun brought a wave of warm air as she sat beside me; the window was drafty and I hadn't realized I was getting cold. The interior of the room had been heated with bodies.

"You want more tea?" Jun asked. I shook my head. "You look cold."

"I am cold."

Jun looked at me for a moment and then said, "You know, I didn't like you when I first met you." Her head was down, her hands in her lap. I would come to recognize this as her at her most thoughtful, her kindest state. And in that moment, her confession, the implied retraction of her first opinion, felt like one of the first real gifts of kindness I'd received since coming to school. "I'm not sure why," she added.

"Me, neither," I said. I didn't say that I hadn't particularly liked her, either. "Maybe it was the tennis."

"No," Jun said, "something else." Yes. There had been something else. She looked up at me. "Want a cracker?"

I took the cracker she offered and bit into it. "It's a drain, anyway," I said.

"Tennis?" she asked. She ate quickly, popping one cracker in after the other.

"Yeah," I said. There was a very brief silence, long enough to make me notice the noise. "Truth is," I said, "I don't much like tennis." I realized this to be true the moment I said it.

Jun frowned, looking at her plate. "Truth is," she said, "neither do I." She looked up, but not at me.

I nodded. "Seems the team has done well, though."

Jun nodded briefly, wiping her hands on her jeans. "We're okay," she said. "Second in the division. Hey," she looked at me. "Do you want to practice? You know, keep your game up?"

I didn't. I wanted to run without worrying about being watched. "I don't know," I said. Jun looked away. "Okay," she nodded.

I had disappointed her. The silence that descended was stiff, unlike the first.

I told her I guessed I could meet her at the courts. She smiled broadly. Her face was so open, such a contrast to what I had seen at the match. What else had I missed about her when we'd played?

Ruth sat down breathlessly. "Done," she said, satisfied. With what, I wondered. "Did you get enough to eat?" she asked me. She leaned into the wooden bench as she would a comfortable chair. "Y'know, the Wiefern theory is more easily distilled than I explained previously . . ." I stole a quick look at Jun, but her face was a blank, apparently refocused on her food. Ruth gestured toward her, becoming in an instant the dramatization of her own point, like those videos we watched in the eighties that were made in the sixties—the light music, the smooth narrator, the dutiful subject—"People have evolved to eat more to protect themselves not from a literal cold but an emotional cold . . ."

"Ruth, shut the fuck up." A.J. was there. She took a gentle hold of Ruth's sleeve, "You'll scare her off," she explained to her friend, an unexpected tenderness in her voice. Somewhat to my surprise, Ruth looked hurt.

"It's okay," I protested, "Really, it's interesting."

Ruth beamed at me as A.J. let her go.

SIXTEEN

When the entire society arrived, en masse, to stamp and shriek their welcome in my hallway that evening, Phyllis told me that I wasn't the first future doctor they'd appropriated, nor would I be the last. I told her that I thought I'd appropriated them, not the other way around, and she nodded her approval. The truth was that I hadn't any idea, really, why I'd joined, and I wasn't sure I needed to know. I was beginning to feel that Ruth had extended the branch to me, and not the other way around.

The initiation to the Shakespeare Society was surreal and melodramatic, which relieved me from taking it too seriously. Each of the new recruits was led upstairs in the unlit house and left there for the better part of an hour. We sat there in the dark, only a little light coming in from the streetlights outside; I could make out only two of the other four new members. As my eyes adjusted to the weak light from the upstairs windows I realized that the woman nearest me was sitting underneath a framed portrait of Shakespeare; reactively I turned my head to look up and saw that I was, too, though it was a different rendering. The print was worn, casual.

There was something cool or sad about his eyes, I thought, but the expression of the mouth was almost coquettish, as though, despite all his sadness, the man sitting for it had held a great and private joke. The Shakespeare across the way was almost entirely different, with nearly a full head of hair and the expression and pose of someone who was worried he might be a philosopher. I tried to reconcile the two images to each other. Every photo I had seen of great men was categorically similar to the next: countless images of Einstein and his white hair, Kennedy in his suit and movie star smile. But Shakespeare remained enigmatic. I wondered if this was a reflection on the changing technology of capturing faces, or just of how we wished to see them. How many images of an unrecognizable Einstein or Kennedy lay tucked away in dark drawers? How much of what I knew of them, of what anyone knew of them, was a fabrication of perception? Could it be that genius was only an illusion, a hand-drawn portrait done by a myopic draftsman? I tried to shake off the thoughts that had begun to spiral in on me but instead I began to shiver, sitting there in the dark. How long had we been there? Twenty minutes, I guessed, not having a watch. I was almost ashamed of how relieved I was when the door to the next room opened.

A woman in a heavy, full-length dress gestured for us to come through. The entire society was there, fifty or more women on two benches. It was exactly like the great room beneath it, except for a stage at the far end. Phyllis stepped forward from a table in the center. She lit several candles that were waiting there.

I could only see a few of the members from where I stood, but each spoke in turn.

The first: " 'Let's consult together against this greasy night.' "

Another: " 'Th'attempt and not the deed, confounds us.' "

A third: " 'O, were it but my life, I'd throw it down for your deliverance as frankly as a pin.' "

" 'I see a woman may be made a fool if she had not a spirit to resist.' "

The voices came scattershot; they were impressions, a patchwork story:

"'O, a brave man!'" A few laughs after this one.

"'Perchance, my lord, I show more craft than love.'"

"'For to be wise in love exceeds man's might.'"

When the last voice had spoken her quotation, Phyllis stood again. I wondered if the candlelight from the room could be seen on the street below, if some future dignitary on her way to the library could guess that the lights illuminated a century-old ritual she had no idea existed. I myself had just learned that the society had been formed in 1877 by Wellesley's very founders and that, despite an 1898 scandal involving the exposure of knees that hit the national news and prompted the college to monitor its activities more closely, had been honoring its iconoclastic ceremonies in private for the past 117 years.

Phyllis began a canned speech: "From here on out, in the tradition of the oldest female Shakespeare Society in this country, you will speak only in the voice of his women to the public of this place." She was smirking, enjoying the terrible script. She continued: "We charge you to remember the words of one of our founding members, Alice Fae Childress, class of 1879: 'Think not of what you cannot say. Choose instead to relish the words that are your lucky inheritance. May we join our voices in the verse of Shakespeare and so learn our own worth.' Naomi Feinstein, please step forward."

Startled, I did. "Repeat after me"—Phyllis directed my hand to rest on a tattered *Collected Works*—"'It is to be all made of faith and service.'" I did as I was told.

I auditioned for Laertes the next week.

"That was great," Phyllis grinned. "Very stuffed shirt and virile. You're a natural for Laertes. The girls were right. Have you ever acted before?" she asked. I shook my head, studying her from my vantage point on stage. She had pulled her hair up into a bun at her neck, emphasizing the angularity of her face. She had wrapped herself in a heavy cardigan. Even with the heat at full blast the room was very cold. But Phyllis looked unflappable, chic, in fact, dressed for a day in exactly such a room.

"One more thing." She stood and walked toward the stage. "I want to see you read with someone else." She pulled a pencil from her ear and gnawed lightly on the eraser as she studied the script in front of her. "In act one, scene three, Laertes has to take that direction from his father, you know, the 'to thine own self be true' speech." She smirked as she said this, enjoying a joke I didn't get. "Ruth"—she beckoned to Ruth, who had been sitting with her in the back of the room before she'd jumped up. Aside from the three of us, the only other person in the room was Tiney, who was serving as the stage manager. Ruth was assistant director to Phyllis's director.

"Ruth will read Polonius's speech, and I want to watch you while she does. I want it to look like you're dutiful but condescending, too, like you think you know it all but wouldn't dare interrupt your father. Let's see it," she marched back to her seat in the rear of the room.

Ruth had made her way up onto the stage and winked at me before launching into a grandiose, patronizing Polonius. "Fantastic!" Phyllis crowed when we were done. "You managed to look both constipated and full of yourself, no pun intended. Well, maybe intended. It works, anyway. Thanks, Naomi. You'll be my Laertes." She smiled. Ruth, once again, was beaming. "We'll post the official cast list later tonight." She strode toward the doors and opened them. "Next!" she called out, in the midst of a performance of her own.

I met Jun for a tennis practice a few nights after *Hamlet* had been cast. It was nearly the end of the semester, but a brief break in the freezing weather made Jun suggest we try the outdoor courts. I had to dig my racket out of the back of my closet. I was cold and stiff, and I swung the racket lightly as I waited to warm up, self-conscious of the last time we'd played and how out of practice I would be.

I was there early, and Jun didn't arrive for several minutes. When she did, she told me that the gates would be locked and we'd have to sneak in, an idea I wasn't keen on. I'm not sure who I thought would care, I just didn't care to get caught. I was comfortable flying below the radar, or so used to it that I was sure everyone would notice me gasping for air if I came up any higher.

As I began to know Jun, I realized that she was one of those rare people who have the great gift of being able to do many things extraordinarily well. Among her less noble traits was the ability to break into just about anything, seamlessly. Freeman, her dorm, was erected mid-century, a bad time for its builder, John Evans II. Legend had it that he was going through a scandalous divorce and that his cigarettes were laced generously with cocaine. The floors were uneven and the doors slammed shut when left open, frequently triggering the lock. During Jun's time at Wellesley, no locksmith was needed. She was as poised as any well-trained royal, and when she wanted to disappear she turned her regality to a stillness I've never seen matched. I saw it for the first time when she had dug the relic from the roof, and then again when we arrived at the courts and I watched her pick the lock at the gate; she never slouched, just moved with the fluidity of a natural force, as easy to ignore as wind or its absence.

"What will we do for light?" I asked as she shut the gate behind us.

"Oko Rule Number One," she replied formally. "Learn to practice in the dark." She hit the lights.

"Feinstein Rule Number One," I muttered, fighting the desire to crouch down. "Lie low." I pointed to a lit window on a large house situated on a slight incline to the rear of the courts. I was disoriented; I wasn't familiar with this side of campus and wasn't sure what building that might be. Also, it was a freezing, cloudless night and I felt too chilled to think well. The week had been unusually dry, and I was regretting that the outdoor courts were playable.

"Oh, that's just Binky Silas, the dean's cousin. There's something wrong with him, but nobody knows what. He lives with her, and she looks the other way when he pulls out his binoculars." She waved. "Give a wave. If we let him watch, he won't tell the dean we're here." She dribbled her way over to the court.

"What are the other Oko rules," I asked after the first rally ended. Jun squinted. "Of tennis?" she asked.

"Yeah," I said.

She served to me. "Oko Rule Number Two: Learn to practice in silence."

I missed her serve. "Isn't tennis always silent?"

Jun shook her head. "No. It's unavoidably squeaky. Anyway, a good player needs to know everything about her opponent. Breath is important. Usually I can tell a lot about a player by listening to how she's breathing. You didn't breathe when we played at Longwood." She slammed the ball in my direction.

I hadn't? I supposed she was right. "And three?" I exhaled.

"What's Feinstein Rule Number Two?" Jun didn't need to stop to question me.

I thought for a minute. "Know your Jewish players," I said.

Jun laughed. "Oko Rule Number Three: Learn to practice without touch."

"Impossible," I said. The ball was in play again.

"Gloves," Jun huffed.

I was out of shape, thinking too much. "So, four: smell, nose plugs. Five: taste. Licking the ball will be grounds for automatic elimination."

Jun's laugh was startlingly loud in the clear night. "The Japanese have a different idea of sense. Anyway"—she served again—"you're not worthy of Oko Law. You're out of shape." We rallied for a moment longer until she finally missed. She was a gifted player, and it was distracting. I wanted to study her instead of beat her. I had been good because of sheer determination and overall athletic training; Jun was a true tennis player.

"Oko Rule Number Four: Learn to practice alone," she breathed, "no opponent, for as long as you can stand it. Five: Learn to practice with multiple balls. Move, girl. I've got to break a sweat."

"Are these your father's rules?" I asked after another rally. I thought there was a hesitation before she answered. "My grandfather's. Come get a drink." I dropped my racket and trotted to her side of the court. The wind bit through my damp shirt. I grabbed my sweatshirt and zipped up. Jun was drinking deeply from her water. So she had been a little winded. She handed me the bottle.

"So who throws the other balls?" I asked.

Jun looked at me blankly. "Oh"—she grinned—"I have two siblings, a sister and a brother. My brother, Hiroshi, can operate one machine, and my sister and I can do two, so whoever's hitting them has plenty to work with." Her grin broadened. "The idea is to focus on one ball when others are coming at you. You should see us in action."

"I'll bet," I said. Her straight black hair stuck to her cheeks in dark lines. I remember thinking that if even one piece was out of place it would show on her smooth face.

The breeze kicked up and Jun tossed a ball at my shoulder, her aim true. "C'mon. Don't let the grass grow on the court."

My father would say this very thing to me when I was young and wanted my coach to explain the reasoning behind every new rule of the game. I stared at Jun, wondering if there was something there to recognize.

"What?" she said.

"How did you know about the dean's cousin?"

"Everyone does. C'mon," she turned back on the court. We were sweating again in ten minutes. I was more tired than I had been in a while. It felt good, but I didn't think I had much left. Had it been forty minutes, or was it only twenty? Jun stopped the ball. "Didn't anyone ever tell you not to bite your lip when you play?" I immediately thrust it forward. "What if you bit it through? Who the hell trained you, anyway?"

I stalled, suddenly defensive. "My dad," I said finally, "in the beginning. And then coaches."

I could tell she didn't quite know how to apologize. "He shouldn't have let you bite your lip."

"He didn't know a thing about playing the game." I breathed. "He was just a fan."

"So where'd your talent come from?"

"My father claims my great-uncle Hershel was a whiz at handball."

I made her miss the ball. I couldn't tell if she was laughing at the handball or Hershel. I had been serious, but smiled when she laughed. "You have an Uncle Hershel?"

"Maybe. What's it to you?" I snapped the ball her way.

She hit it back. "My parents had one name picked out before I was born: Jun. I think I was meant to be a boy. It's really a boy's name. Naomi is also a Japanese name," she continued. We rallied for a while before she spoke again.

"My father started training me when I was three," she told me. "I had coaches at four, tennis camp at five, competitions at six. When I went to school in London we had tournaments twice a year."

I missed the ball and stopped. I was done. I didn't want to tell her about how I'd started to play, how it had been like survival, like learning to fight. Only my parents knew about Teddy, and I hoped never to have to mention him to anyone else. I used to think that just the idea of him might break some kind of spell, might make his disappearance more real, less likely to fade away, revealing him in some unexpected corner. *I've said nothing about any of this*, I'd call out. *We can begin at the end, we can make it into a beginning.*

"I just liked to run," I said, "and my dad liked to watch me play." Saying that made me miss him. "I didn't really compete until I was thirteen. It made him too nervous." He'd sit in the stands, yelling, until I forbade him.

"What about your mother?" Jun asked.

"She's not much of a fan," I said.

"Mine, neither. She's more of a shopping mom. And she's totally out of luck with me. In Japan my height makes me stand out like a giant." The game had loosened her tongue as it had her body. "My mother used to reserve time for us in Tokyo stores every summer, but she gave up after seventh grade. Nothing fit me. It was like a weird nightmare, like shopping with all the money in the world in a country for dolls. She special-ordered my clothes, tried to make them look just like the ones in the stores. She had no interest in my matches, but my dad made her come to every one. I might have been a girl, but my father designated me firstborn."

She had conceded my exhaustion and resheathed her racket. She walked over to hit the lights. It was dark. We both took a minute to adjust to it.

"What about you?" she asked.

"What do you mean?" I replied quickly.

"Are you the only child in your family?"

I nodded, knowing she probably couldn't see me in the dark.

"And your dad wanted you to play tennis?"

I nodded again. I stared out at the dean's house, the light in the window.

"You're pretty tight-lipped, aren't you?" she observed.

Her directness shocked me out of answering right away. "I guess I am," I said finally. "It's kind of a family trait." It was the first time I'd said aloud, maybe even realized, that my mother and I shared something so significant.

Jun nodded. I was grateful she didn't pry. This, I think, was one of the things I had feared most about friendship: the need to explain the many things about myself I didn't quite understand.

"I am an only child," I told her. "And my dad did want me to play tennis. He's always been really supportive," I added lamely.

"But possessive, too, right?"

"Yes," I admitted, too startled by her astuteness to lie. "I guess he is a little."

"You remember everything you read, is that right?" she went on. I wondered if she'd been keeping a mental catalogue of things to ask me.

"Who told you that?"

She didn't answer me directly. "Word gets around the house pretty quickly. You'll be pretty useful at rehearsals if it's true." She gave me that lopsided grin. It was the first time anyone had treated my memory as a sort of joke, and it made me feel suddenly free. I felt almost embarrassed by my own giddiness and found myself trying to tamp it down.

I smiled just a little in return. "Most of it," I admitted. "I remember most, not everything. I have to be paying attention to remember everything."

She let go a short, happy laugh. "Who wouldn't?" she asked. But then we both lost our way for a moment, in the conversation, in each other's company, as though simultaneously struck by the desire to nurse private concerns. When I think back on it, I wonder if that moment, allowing each other the intimacy of silence, was the true beginning of our friendship.

The noises our game aroused had faded: the lights had stopped plinking and the wind blew hard through the gate. "Did you ever notice how so many things just don't seem real at night?" Jun said. The light in Binky Silas's window winked as something passed before it. "Poor guy. Needs a blow-up doll, I suspect."

"Yes," I laughed, "that would make him feel nice and fulfilled."

"Well, at least it'd still be there when the lights went out," Jun said, the tension somehow met and broken. "Do you want to play after next rehearsal?"

I had studying to do, but I was feeling less tired now, energized even. "Sure. I'd like that."

She nodded. "I'd like that, too. I get tired of all this"—she gestured. But I had to guess at what she meant.

"Do you get to see your dad much?" I asked.

Her mouth tightened, but she answered me. "Sometimes in the summer." This way she had of delivering partial truths felt as real to me as my own.

"He won't want to see you play Hamlet?" I asked.

"Oko House Rule Number One-A: No Hamlet."

"Would Gertrude be any better?"

She laughed. "No. Maybe Claudius, though. At least he becomes king."

SEVENTEEN

The following Tuesday night there was a knock on my door. I opened it to Ruth, standing with a thick stack of papers pressed to her chest. She smiled and held her free hand out to me, which was clenched until she opened it into mine. I stared at the box of matches in my palm.

"Forensic burning," she whispered after looking comically from side to side down the empty hallway. "C'mon."

Outside we met the other new initiates and most of the already established members of the society. It was a cloudless night again, the stars a bright jumble overhead. It was too cold to say much, and Ruth and the others kept the pace brisk. We were walking south, toward the lake, after picking up Ellie Pendergast, the mousy-haired girl from the tea, at Freeman Hall. Jun joined us there, too.

We walked along the east end of the lake, into the woods behind the president's house and farther south still, keeping the water always to our right, even as we must have reached the lake's far end and begun walking west. A few people had produced lighters, which, after a while, made it only more difficult to see in the dark. I tried to shake off an unreasonable fright that took hold of me, the memory of a red bird flying out of nowhere into a similar sky.

"What are we doing?" Ellie's voice, high and tense, stood out in the near silence: "What's forensic burning? What does burning stuff have to do with Shakespeare?" She was a stream of questions bouncing along at Jun's side like an agitated puppy. Jun answered her with tones so hushed and soothing they were difficult to make out. I spoke to no one, only listened to one woman from Hawaii tell us how on nights of the new moon, the stars lit the way for spirits to walk down to the sea. Her companion didn't believe her, and her questions interspersed Ellie's. "Why would spirits need to walk to the sea? Or light, for that matter?" *How long have you guys been doing this?* "Can't they fly?" *Has anyone ever been caught?* "Are they going fishing?" *Someone brought warm stuff, right? It's pretty cold out here.* "How could I make that up?" the storyteller finally interrupted her friend. They both laughed, and I, listening, did too, a little.

We entered a copse in the woods. A.J. directed the beam of her flashlight onto someone I didn't know, a physically intimidating woman with blond cornrows and broad, freckled cheekbones, drop a pile of wood into a wide, shallow pit in the middle of the clearing. She began ordering people around, as did a few other seniors, including Phyllis, who grinned at me when she saw me standing there in my flannel pajamas and robe. "Nice slippers, Naomi," she added to her nod of approval before turning around to collect another stack of papers from another senior. I walked over to the fire pit, and Mara, the woman building the fire, introduced herself in a disinterested way.

"This pile of soot's as old as the college," she said ruminatively, "maybe older." She heaved logs and sandwiched them in on each other; an art of effort. "So," she said. "Want to know what's going on?" I nodded noncommittally, affecting a casual attitude I couldn't actually adopt. Mara wasn't looking at me. She reached forward and shoved a heavy log deeper into the pile. "Forensic burning is one of the college's oldest traditions. Officially, it's also a dead one." Her voice was low and resonant, and as the fire grew I had to strain to hear her. "I guess some of the Shakes alums from the twenties thought the burning should continue. They used to burn textbooks to symbolize the forensic, back in the day when the college was in on it. It was a game for the juniors and sophomores: the juniors hid their books, and the sophomores had to find them. The idea was to not let knowledge just sit around, you know?" She was looking intensely right at me. "Kill it before it suffers from old age." She laughed at my face, which must have reflected my shock. "The good stuff always gets resurrected, hon. Don't take it too seriously. The phoenix always becomes stronger with new feathers." She grinned, her teeth white in the light of the burgeoning fire. "Don't believe what anyone tells you about college traditions," she ordered me. "The best have been ruined or squirreled away by a few brave souls. Hoop rolling, for instance, is a load of shit."

"Not to everyone," Julie corrected. She'd been standing with her arms folded, looking into the first flames as Mara lectured me. "I imagine fires became less popular when most of the college burned down," she added matter-of-factly. Mara didn't react to Julie's statement. She seemed wholly absorbed in attending to the fire.

I thought of those images I'd seen, in a back corner of the library, of the 1906 fire brigade: the women in their uniformly heavy dresses, standing in an assembly line of water, battling the fire in the dark with buckets, the smoke rising overhead like a mocking, amorphous spirit. The college's main hall, a five-story collection of library, dormitory, and classroom, had burnt to the ground. I remembered the before-and-after pictures: the marble columns, the wet students at dawn, staring at the still smoking foundation.

"The power of fire is not something people grasp as quickly as they should." Mara finally spoke. "And it always develops ten times faster than you would expect." Hers was now burning lustfully, transfixing all three of us. Julie had squatted down and was sitting before the fire with her eyes closed. A casual observer might think she was sleeping or praying. The three of us stood together around it for a while longer, not speaking.

Once Phyllis's arms were full of the stacks of papers she'd been collecting, she came over and tapped Julie on the shoulder. Julie stood up, yawned, and cricked her neck. Then she began ordering everyone to sit in rows, to form a crowd facing Phyllis, who stood directly in front of the fire, her back to it. She cleared her throat as a few stragglers settled down.

I could see how Phyllis must have drawn audiences. She took to a stage well. Her voice managed to be both authoritative and self-mocking as she began the ritual; she was clearly playing a role.

"Who is in the woods?" she called out.

"None," a voice answered.

"What is in the lake?" she called again.

"None," another voice replied.

"And the hills and houses?" she concluded.

"None," a chorus of voices answered, followed by giggling, either because protocol hadn't been followed or more than a few people were nervous and rattled. I shivered, pulling my robe closer. Someone had thrown several heavy blankets down as protection from the cold ground, but they didn't do much to cut the cold that seemed packed into the hard soil underneath.

"Sentinels," Julie announced, stepping forward. Eight women stood up and went to the edge of the copse, standing at intervals around the perimeter with their backs to us. "Forensic burning," she continued. She wasn't as commanding as Phyllis, but no one looked away from her stern stoicism. "A tradition from the earlier days of Wellesley, thought to be lost, kept safe by the women of this society." She spoke as if she were delivering a lecture to a class, easily, confidently. "Knowledge needs to be purged. Live knowledge can grow static or too strong; it can be mistaken as more powerful than the human minds who seek it. Dominance is key." She paused dramatically, turning back to Phyllis, who was smirking at her.

"Director, which play is it you wish to redeem?" Julie's voice deepened a bit as she addressed Phyllis, whose poise and command of her audience was striking.

"*The Tragedy of Hamlet, Prince of Denmark*," Phyllis answered.

"And what do you offer in return?" Julie asked this as Phyllis squatted down, drawing the stacks of paper back up to her chest. "*The Tragedy of Cymbeline*," she said, her voice unexpectedly soft.

"Let the burning begin," Julie ordered her. Phyllis walked through the seated crowd, handing out the stacks as she did. When mine was in my hands I could see that it was a copy of the *Cymbeline* script, that each one of us was given the same play, some of them dog-eared and full of notes, others seemingly new and untouched.

" 'How bravely thou becomest thy bed, fresh lily!' " Phyllis exclaimed, tossing hers on the fire. The smoke thickened, rising into the glittering sky and beginning to cloud it. To my left, A.J. stirred nervously, and the tension spread through some of the crowd, a few people looking up, most still focused on Phyllis. Ruth was at the fire, tall and well lit, her voice strong: " 'Jupiter descends in thunder and lightning, sitting on an eagle.' " The fire sputtered and smoked more when it received her script, causing a few surprised exclamations from those nearest it.

"Damn it, Mara," Ruth scowled, "you know the wood isn't supposed to be wet." Mara, her shadow huge in the firelight, glowered back. "Dry as a bone, Wiefern. Check it yourself." "I think she'll want to take your word on that," someone teased. Mara grinned and Ruth blushed. Phyllis and a few others laughed out loud. My face felt hot from the heat, but the rest of me was cold.

"You," Phyllis said, extending her arm toward an already intimidated Ellie, "next." Ellie muttered something that sounded like a collapsed question. "Just find a line, toss the script. It'll do the burning on its own." Her smile was either warm or taunting, I couldn't tell.

Ellie stood up shakily. I glanced at Jun, who was frowning sternly at Phyllis. "Do I have to?" Ellie asked once on her feet.

"Of course not," Phyllis said with false generosity. "You can pass, if you want."

Ellie nodded and swallowed, receiving Phyllis's cutting response as penance. "Um," she began, riffling through the script awkwardly.

The pages bent and stuck to her hands, the collection of them in her care an impossibly awkward thing, "Here's one. Um, act three, scene three," she looked up, trying a smile, "'How, in this our pinching cave, shall we discourse the freezing hours away?'" A.J., directly in front of her, nodded her approval and encouragement. I saw Jun smile, egging her on as well.

"Toss it," Phyllis said, returning Ellie to the moment.

"Oh, sure, okay," Ellie said, walking toward the fire.

"Your skirt!" Mara yelled. "Watch it!" someone else called out. Ellie fell a little before she caught herself, the script landing just at the edge of the fire. One corner of it lit, then burned out as Ellie scrambled back to her feet, getting tangled in A.J.'s waiting arms. Tears were running down her face as she took her seat again.

"What's the point of this?" I asked Ruth as she sat down beside me after her own toss.

Ruth laughed out loud, her face too close to mine to be seen well in the dark, "There doesn't have to be a point to everything. Well, that's at least part of the point."

"No," A.J. disagreed, "that's the whole point."

"The point is," a voice on my left said steadily, "that there are some Wellesley traditions—student traditions, mainly—that the college wanted gone but never died. Forensic burning goes back to the teens. The powers that be thought it was too dangerous. They were probably right." A thin hand extended in the dim light. "Calbe Tharpe," its owner said by way of introduction, then continued: "You're Naomi." I nodded. "Feinstein," she added. She turned around as A.J. tapped her on the shoulder.

"Flask," A.J. whispered. "If you want it."

Calbe took a dutiful sip. "Swill," she announced.

A.J. took it back from her and took a long, experimental swallow. "God, Ruth," she exhaled, "where the hell did you get this?"

Ruth stood up, smiling, and walked over to the group that had begun dancing to thin music projected by an aging boombox, ignoring

A.J.'s question. A.J. leaned back on her elbows, watching the flames reach up and out as the fire absorbed the last of the scripts.

"God, I hope they don't streak," Calbe said, her posture an unwavering vertical line from the back of her head to her tailbone.

A.J. grinned at me. "Toss it," Mara said a few feet away. A.J. obeyed. She looked at me apologetically. "Not for initiates," she said sorrowfully. "Though if you'd like to start the streaking . . ."

"Don't joke," Calbe chastised us. "A couple of winters ago two of our members got frostbite from doing just that."

"Frostbite *where*?" A.J. blurted out.

"Shhh," Calbe insisted, pointing to my face. "You're scaring her."

A.J. threw her head back and laughed. "Naomi doesn't get scared!" she exclaimed incongruously. I smiled at her, unclasping my knees and wondering if she was drunk, grateful to her for denying the very real fear I had at any mention of frostbite. I forced myself to relax into what was becoming a blur of noise and movement; in the midst of it all, despite the winter cold, the prospect of people stripping naked and running through the woods seemed quite possible. A sound several feet away caught our attention, something like a scuffle. Ellie was trying to worm Ruth's flask, now in Mara's hand, into her own. I wondered if she were already drunk. Mara stood as still as stone, Ellie's efforts comical beside her. A flare rose from the fire. Ellie's coat sleeve, like a wing, was suddenly a sheet of flames.

Ellie was screaming and flapping her arms. I reached her in a few long seconds, dropping the heavy wool blanket that had been under me around her arm, other hands joining mine to suffocate the flames, which after an unbearable few moments, quieted beneath it. Mara stood by the now dark pile of smoldering wood, a fire extinguisher in her hands as she watched the smoke rising from her feet in plumes even blacker than the night. It was suddenly dark everywhere, commotion and fear muttering their way through.

"Water," I managed, clearing my throat and then shouting it just as Phyllis and another bucket of freezing lake water appeared at our feet. I plunged Ellie's arm to the elbow in the murky wet, her scream an intimate, painful hollow in my ear, the steam off her skin and the smell of it hushing us as the company around us suddenly, nearly as one, became quiet.

"Don't take her to the infirmary," Julie said, breaking the silence. "Jun, your car. Take her to Newton-Wellesley."

"My car's across campus," Jun said in a low voice, "it's over a mile away."

Julie turned and faced her, "Go get it."

Jun nodded after a blink of hesitation.

"The lake," I said to A.J., at my side. "Can you walk?" I asked Ellie. She stared at me blankly, throwing me back to another night in the freezing cold years ago. I shivered. "You're cold," she observed, and began to cry.

"You've gotten into quite the habit of saving people," Ruth proclaimed merrily at my side as we trouped back into the woods toward the lake. Instead of feeling proud, I felt strangely exposed. In front of us Ellie wept as A.J. walked with her, one long arm around her waist, the other across her shoulders: a fully mobile embrace. Ruth chucked me on the arm, sending me stumbling. "She'll be okay!" she announced.

"She'll be fine," Phyllis said quietly at my shoulder, wrapping an arm around my own waist, a half-embrace; it felt, by comparison, like an acknowledgment that I was able to stand on my own.

The blanket fell off Ellie's arm at the lake, which was blessedly unfrozen at the spot where we approached it. We laid her on her belly and extended her burnt arm into the water. Her eyes were open and wide. The skin and the sleeve merged, a dark color those of us close to her were grateful we couldn't see any better.

Somehow Jun found her way onto a side road with her car and we loaded Ellie into it. Julie slammed the door behind her. "What's wrong with the infirmary?" I asked her.

She kept her back to me for a moment, watching Jun drive away. "Newton-Wellesley has an emergency room."

"And no connection with the college," Ruth added. Julie shot her a look. Ruth shrugged. "Her parents will find out anyway."

Julie nodded, looking at me. I was thinking of burned skin, its distinct red ripples, Ellie's arm to the elbow. Julie was watching me closely. "She'll get better care at the hospital," she stated. A series of hollers interrupted us.

A group of four had undressed and made their way into the lake; three were running back, a fourth was wading bravely in up to her knees. "They're drunk," Julie announced. "Get them out of the water!" Phyllis called from somewhere. "Party's over," Ruth said, her face a mix of regret and deep amusement. "Glad you joined Shakes?" I didn't answer, thinking of Ellie's arm and the time between trauma and care—maybe not a golden hour, but close enough—when, an instant later, Ellie was suddenly running, fully naked, past us, toward the lake.

Jun was close behind her, splashing in, fully dressed, as Ellie ran, calling out to the streakers, "Wait up!" "She's completely shit-faced," Julie observed. Phyllis marched over to us. "Ruth?" Ruth looked only slightly apologetic. "I thought a little more would ease the pain," Ruth protested. "No more drinking, ever, at forensic burning," Phyllis scolded. We all nodded. "At least not underage."

We watched Jun wrap Ellie up again. She winked at us as she walked past. "No pain," Jun remarked. Ruth winked back. "Medicinal," she explained sheepishly as Phyllis stared her down. "Well, maybe medicinal drinking," Phyllis said, breaking the tension. "Sound right to you, Dr. Feinstein?"

I hadn't expected she'd registered me as part of the interaction. We could hear Ellie singing as Mara and Julie began to rouse the other sober members to start collecting our things. In groups of twos and threes we made our slow way back toward campus, tired and reeking of wood smoke and alcohol and the muddy lake.

"She's a type," Phyllis said, suddenly at my shoulder. I was surprised she'd sought me out again. She lifted her chin to refer to Ellie, whose singing could still be heard in the clear night. I wondered if

Phyllis was afraid I'd be scared off, or likely to blow their cover, or upset at what I'd seen. "If the stakes aren't high enough," she went on, explaining Ellie to us both, "she won't play the game. Don't spend a minute worrying about her," she added. "Believe me, she'll never be happier than she is when she's on the verge of hysteria."

A.J. began to sing an off-key, drunken, and diminishing version of "America the Beautiful." A few more joined her lustfully, but as soon as we were back on campus paths, the group sobered, splitting into pairs and singles, drifting off hurriedly. I wonder how many of them were thinking they could capture a few more hours of sleep on such a quiet, frigid night.

Back in my own room, there was a voice mail from Jun and the emergency technician at Newton-Wellesley, forwarded to the whole society, announcing that Ellie was fine, that, as Jun made the tech report herself, "polyester had probably saved her life."

"Yes, folks, that's right," Jun concluded the message, "the horrid flying purple people eater that Ellie was wearing saved her life. Let this be a lesson to us all."

That night, I dreamt for the first time in a while, more a dreamt memory than an imaginary image: my mother sitting with her feet wrapped, me trying to read to her from one of her books, my mispronunciations and earnestness making her laugh.

The next morning I dug out a photograph I'd stolen from home of her standing in sunlight, laughing into it instead of squinting, an image I treasured for being both completely strange and as close to perfect as I could imagine. I taped it to the wall beside my bed.

PART III

EIGHTEEN

After an unremarkable Thanksgiving break during which my parents made noises about how happy they were to have me home and I dutifully ignored my mother's unusually sallow coloring, I returned to campus, finished my final exams perfunctorily, and then took advantage of the elective winter session to stay on campus until the spring semester began.

It was typical to cast the spring play in the fall, so that we could begin rehearsals as soon as we returned for the new semester. And so it was that *Hamlet* practices were in full swing as soon as classes began again. Here are some of the things we practiced when we weren't onstage:

1. Fight rehearsal: Once or twice a week, overseen by a kendo master who visited us three times that semester. We were told that his wages came out of our annual fees, but it was clear to everyone that we didn't really have that kind of money. Jun was as wealthy as my father had hinted, but she was not interested in acknowledging that wealth in public. Her generosities simply surrounded her. It was rumored that Sensei Mutsoko was a

hachi-dan who had been exiled by his countrymen for killing a man, but he did not act like a man who had been so lost.

Although kendo sparring is categorically different than fencing, Phyllis claimed that she simply wanted us to use it to connect with our inner violent aggressors. And with Jun, it was terrific fun; it reminded me of our tennis practices, but the pretend intent to kill was glorious play. Why had I even started with tennis when I could have just picked up a sword? Phyllis insisted that mammals thrive on fighting as much as on food or love. Sensei wanted our spirits to soar, our breath to float when we spoke our lines, the language to become the wind to fuel the action, or something like that. Sometimes the act even quieted my tendency to record every moment, so that fighting brought with it a sensation of extraordinary fluidity; a thoughtless, almost transcendent experience I hadn't found outside of running. I couldn't help but wonder why women have so little occasion to fight.

2. Walking like a man: When our voices weren't convincing, when our addresses were too indirect, Phyllis had us grab whatever we could find that could be rolled into a man-sized wad and jam it down the front of our pants. When the play was on, our breasts would be bound with cheesecloth. There were rolls of it stashed in the basement dressing room, and we began to use them two weeks before we played to an audience. Binding the breasts was at least a two-person job. There was a binder, usually Ruth or Tracy Leeds, because they were the steadiest, and the bindee, whose job it was to hold the other end of the cheesecloth and turn into it as tightly as she could, creating layers until she reached the end and the binder, who helped her to pin the cloth to her chest: two pins on top, two on the bottom. Once bound, we had to walk around a bit before we could sit or catch our breath.

No one could remember how long this tradition had gone on, not even Calbe, the junior from the night of forensic burning, rumored to have been Pope's favorite since freshman year. She was an active member of the society, but was also a sort of ambassador for Pope, the one who explained his disappointments and delights. In general, he found little about Shakes delightful.

3. Imagining Shakespeare: In an idle moment, I asked Calbe to explain to me what it was that Pope didn't like. She pulled her hair back carefully, as if preparing a speech.

"The purist, the scholar, is always irked by the practitioner," she told me. "There are maybe five other scholars in this country who know more about Shakespeare than Pope does. It's his life's work. Let me ask you something." She walked over and opened the set of doors that led into the secondary greenroom, a space to the south of the great room downstairs with access to the stage up a small iron staircase. The room was long and narrow, with a fireplace just to the right of its entrance.

Calbe stood in front of it and turned to me. "When was Shakespeare born, and when did he die?" she asked me. I had to admit I didn't know. She gestured toward the fireplace. I went over to it and read the dates above. "Fifteen sixty-four to sixteen sixteen," she read out loud. "Can't blame him, can you?"

I couldn't. But I understood, too, the desire to give in to the amateur experience of the plays, the faulty, slow discovery of each masterpiece. I wanted to nurse a crush on Shakespeare, not devote myself to him, to take the glimpse I wanted and savor its pleasures.

And I was in good company. So many of us came for the sheer thrill of the plays, clumsy players that we were with his words. I suppose it was no wonder that the college dutifully looked the other way. We were at our least polished behind those walls: women playing men playing at anguish and betrayal and doubt in an archaic form of our language. We were probably the ones who would have crowded the stage at the Globe: too rough to sit, too enamored of the players to absorb the play without commentary. Phyllis was convinced that Shakespeare himself would have preferred this section, that it would have been a welcome relief from the scrutiny of the higher rows.

She made the best sense, too, out of why our invitations to the president and dean of Wellesley so often resulted in empty seats. "It would never do for Gertrude to acknowledge Yorick, hon," she said once. "Recognize, yes, but acknowledge? Yorick was both jester and surrogate parent. He was the first to show Hamlet the flaws in the patriarchal line. Gertrude would never have looked him in the eye."

4. Dressing like a man: To understand the fixations of 2 and 4, you must recognize how many roles in Shakespeare are written for men. Also, men are better at posing as women; it's primarily a matter of added roundness for them, and they enjoy inflating their bodies. Women, on the other hand, need to compress and straighten themselves, stand taller. And even the bravest among us are reluctant to be that flatly exposed and falsely bold. Costuming was a challenge, despite the wealth of dresses donated to us, sitting in a musty closet to the rear of the basement rooms. Though when one of us tried to act too untouched, Phyllis corrected us.

"Oh, honey," she told me once, "it's the *men* that are so romantic. Just look at Will himself. Drama, drama, drama, life or death, do or die. They're way more romantic than chicks."

We were working on the last of the foils, repairing them for the stage. She was immobilized for once, holding in place the handle she'd just glued to the sword, waiting for it to set. "Think about a woman's body," she continued. "It's so evolved. Both efficient and subtle. Men are clearly the lesser model. They might *be* stronger, but they charge through life with their weaknesses ignored. But they sense the denial; deep down they know those weaknesses are there and they can't get to them. I hate it when girls play men like they're stoic. Like they want to prove just how tough they can be. Men know their beloved mothers could squish them with just a flick of the wrist. And it terrifies them, makes them rage and muscle all the more. Oh God, just talking about it gets me hot." I laughed at her, but she just shook her head.

5. Negotiating Phyllis's temper: She had no patience with the following: missed lines, missed cues, disengaged actors, poor actors, shy actors, hammy actors, actors late for rehearsal. She'd taken a shine to me when she realized I could be a human prompter, and I took to the revelatory experience of being able to use my memory as a game. I even got a word wrong here and there, errors Ruth loved to crow about when they turned up. Phyllis cut her short. She had no patience for ribbing, either. We were frequently being chastened to "sober up."

"Do you realize what you've got here?" she'd shout at us. "Do you know what it means to have this kind of language on your *tongues*? And most of you don't even have to play the half-assed women." She tried, unsuccessfully, to rein herself in. "Sorry, A.J." (Gertrude), "and Tharine" (Ophelia). "But, Jesus, folks. You're Hamlet, Jun. Fucking Hamlet! I want to hear every single one of those words in the back row, and in that beautiful Wycombe Abbey accent you've got. Go on. You of all people should know what it means to honor thy father. Hamlet knows he *wants* to kill Claudius. He *wants* to be right. That play's his creation, his one chance to toy with his prey. Would it kill you to look a little vindicated? Have some presence, for god's sake! Fuck!" she concluded before storming out.

6. Dying: This was particularly challenging to those of us who were new, or those who were less athletic. The problem with dying is that a player has to fall, convincingly. In other words, she has to fall intentionally, giving up control long enough to achieve the desired effect. The best at this were those who could both let themselves fall and achieve a soft landing. Jun had particular trouble uttering the line "O, I die, Horatio," and doing just that.

"It's ridiculous, Phyl," she objected. "Who the hell says, 'O, I die,' when they die? That's just bad writing."

Phyllis glared at her. "Would you care to rewrite the scene?"

"No, but we could cut the line."

When Phyllis was angry she got red in the ears first. "I'm

not cutting, it, Jun Oko, you sacrilegious, wooden excuse for a Hamlet."

"I don't see why we have to narrate what's obvious," Jun objected.

"It's called verse, moron."

"The key," Ruth called out from her assistant director's chair across the room, "is to focus on the Horatio part of the line. What's important is *who* Hamlet signals out when he dies. He calls to his friend."

"That's because everyone else is fucking dead," Jun grumbled.

"I just don't believe the Japanese can perform Shakespeare to Western standards," Phyllis declared.

Jun glared at her. "You mean unimaginative and pretentious?"

"Phyl," Tiney objected, silently watching them all until that moment, "that's enough."

"Now you're where I want you," Phyllis said to Jun. "Kill Naomi." She sat down.

I was told that a rocky dress rehearsal always meant a smooth opening night. The house's full basement consisted of a large common dressing room and an unfinished, cluttered back room full of props and costumes. Photographs and programs from past performances covered the walls and it smelled of body odor, the furnace that heated it, the musky clay of cake makeup, and the sweetness of fake blood. It could be accessed from the rear or front of the house, both of which had narrow staircases leading down. It was well lit and warm, and most of us waited down there between scenes.

Ellie was crying in the corner, her gauzy dress shirt already coming undone in the back. She was going through a breakup. All of us were trying not to watch her, though I couldn't help but wonder how she could, ever again, wear such a loose fabric. The scars on her arm were open to the world as the sleeve fell back, making me look away. Jun sat down beside me at the bottom of the stairs.

Tiney was on the way down the stairs when Jun took her seat, so instead of stepping around us she sat down on the step just above. I knew she didn't like me, that she had settled in to be near Jun. She regularly pretended at an intimacy with Jun that seemed to make them both uncomfortable. Tiney leaned in between us, smirking. She lifted her chin in Ellie's direction as she addressed Jun: "Still weepy, huh?"

Jun didn't say anything, but Tiney nodded as if she had. "She'll get over it soon. Probably sleep with Lulu's roommate. I hear it's a long time coming." I knew nothing of Lulu or her roommate. Tiney went on: "'Hell hath no fury like a woman scorned.' Leave it to Will to know."

I studied her expression, the way she didn't attempt to hide the cruelty there. I had thought Tiney more confident than she was. Wellesley wasn't known for its shrinking violets, but there were a few notable standouts: the very wealthy, very well connected women who seemed to subsist entirely on beauty and grace, and the unusually brilliant. Tiney fell into the latter group. She had won a rare merit scholarship to the college and had been the only freshman to be invited to join the White House Internship program. By her sophomore year she was a TA for Roger F. Chang, dubbed "the most influential economist of our time" by the nickname-hungry media of the nineties. Jun was an economics major, too, with similar laurels, though I know now that she was focused on returning to her father and his business rather than on public recognition. Their friendship was never easy. Even with the people she liked the most, Tiney was standoffish, flippant, letting her wittiness stand in for affection. At times her paleness made her seem otherworldly, of an ethereal kind of presence or mind. She was truly one of the fairest people I had ever seen, her hair so light it was almost invisible, her eyes so nearly colorless that they were difficult to follow, even if she was looking right at you. At other times she could appear a thorny, conceited girl, as insecure as she was accomplished, latching on to whomever she thought had the most power at any given moment with the tenacity and loyalty of a wounded soldier.

"Will never said that"—A.J. breezed by en route to the makeup table, trying to hold a carefully balanced crown to her head and pin it there as she walked. Phyllis had asked for a rerun of a few scenes that had been uncomfortably slow. "At least not our Will. It was William Congreve, that weird playwright who lived, what, like a hundred years after Shakespeare? Wasn't he a total perv, Calbe?"

"Of course it wasn't," Tiney said, looking again at Jun.

"Congreve. I'm sure of it. Not the Will you meant, hon. Congreve said that thing about women scorned—right, Calbe?" Calbe was reapplying spirit glue to the back of a small piece of facial hair, her nose wrinkled at the smell. "Congreve," she said, "1697." She rolled her eyes at me in the mirror. Of our fifty-three members, Calbe had already chosen me as her first pick for Popeian disciple. I'd turned her down, but she couldn't get past the opportunity of using me as a human reliquary of accurate Shakespearean data. It would never work, I told her, I wasn't interested in using my memory for archival purposes, but she kept at it, knowing I was flattered.

"I know which Will it was," Tiney spat. She was woven that night even more tightly than usual. She turned and acknowledged me for the first time with another smirk, as if daring me to contradict her. "Everyone knows which Will said that."

"Tiney"—Ruth, as Guildenstern, was studying herself in the mirror, grooming her eyebrows into place—"you should play one of the three witches if we do *Macbeth* next. You look exactly like a fairy, and no one would expect someone so delicate to make such a great witch."

"I would make a great witch," Tiney said, her grin stretching into a leer. "But I want to be Macduff. Someone more noble. Or maybe we could do Lear. Then I could be Regan. She gets to do the eye-plucking scene." She stood and walked to A.J., pulling her thick, dark hair up at the neck. "You need to pin it back first so the crown will stick better," she said.

Phyllis breezed in, examining us. "God, you make a hot guy," she told me. "You're even hotter than my current boy, and he's something. Wow. I always felt Laertes should be super hot." She frowned at my chin. "But your facial hair looks pubic. It's been bothering me. Take it off." She handed me the rubbing alcohol as I leaned forward toward the mirror. "Jun, you're okay. Damn. I can't decide who's hotter,

Laertes or Hamlet. The audience is gonna go into heat when you guys kill each other."

"Jun, definitely," Tiney grinned. She intercepted the rubbing alcohol and fetched the cotton. She sat down beside me, working alcohol into my chin with a cotton ball in small, persistent circles. The careful attention made me feel like a very young child, tended to when asked to do something clearly beyond her capabilities.

"Jun's always the hottest," A.J. remarked, studying her.

"You think all the girls are hot," Phyllis told her.

"Some are hotter than others. I'm just waiting for Jun to come out of the closet so I can get in line," A.J. grinned.

Both Tiney and I looked quickly to Jun, in the mirror. Her face remained impassive.

"She's got a boyfriend, idiot," Tiney said. "George, right, Jun?" she asked. Jun gave her a look, put down her brush, and made a pretense of straightening her shirt as she walked across the room. "He's back in Japan," Tiney continued. "You should mind your own business, Anusheh."

A.J. laughed lightly, studying her reflection once again, and pulled gently at the pins underneath her crown so they wouldn't prick her.

Jun returned to the stairs and climbed them, leaving the room.

"Christ, Ellie"—Phyllis was on to the end of the row—"you need to be re-bound. Have you put on weight? Ruth, give me a hand here." Ruth stood as Ellie lifted her shirt, then grabbed the edge of cheesecloth and walked to the end of the room as Ellie slowly unwound, a doll on a spit with a tear-streaked face.

Phyllis and Ruth went back to the stage, and the room was silent until Ruth returned in a hurry, demanding that Tiney help her find Ophelia's missing weeds. The run-through was over and the hired photographer had arrived, a smirking graduate student from MIT. We had a half hour to get every photo Phyllis wanted, both for posterity and vanity's sake. Tiney didn't move even as Ruth and I dove into a pile of detritus—fake hair, broken masks, spirit glue, torn binding. It was the first time I began to wonder at exactly how cold she could be, and I stopped searching with Ruth long enough to make a picture of her face: calm, untouched, determined. The lights flashed, signaling Phyllis's impatience. Jun appeared at the top of the stairs a few minutes later, covered in blood. Tiney ran up to her, handing her a towel. Jun took it without looking at her, reminding me in a flash of the way her mother had stood at her father's command and followed him.

I had told my parents about *Hamlet* but took a while to call again to invite them to a performance. I hadn't been able to diminish my father's concerns about the time it would take to be involved in a non-medical procedure, as he tried to joke, so I had tried to avoid the subject in the few calls I'd had with him since. Our weekly phone calls had become more infrequent due to the constant rehearsals and the informal dinners a few of us would put together after a run-through of the final act. During the final weeks of rehearsals, I often didn't get back to my dorm room until the early morning.

I don't know why I even asked for my mother when I eventually did work up the courage to extend an invitation for them to come to the play. I suspect my excitement surged into an enthusiasm I thought might be contagious, it whispered possibilities I would never otherwise entertain: I could wheedle my mother into something more hopeful; hope itself could be doctored. I fiddled with the bracelet on my wrist, which I had begun wearing again, inspired by the more decorated members of the society, though I loved the hidden intimacy of the engraving against my skin. I'm not sure I believed that God was closest to those with a broken heart, but the beauty of that line and its connections to my mother helped me to pretend that I knew her better than I did. As I listened to my father make halfhearted excuses about why she couldn't come to the phone, I reassured myself that there was still the possibility that she might show up to see the play. Flipping through the pages of a partially finished lab report on my desk, I reminded myself that most biological organisms gravitate more toward joy than drudgery, but the reasoning felt empty.

I realized suddenly that my father had been quiet for several moments on the other end. I could hear him busying himself with something, the dishes he told me, and it was then that I knew.

Maybe I had known somehow before; maybe it had already been creeping up on me in the form of an added uneasiness that I was only too eager to distract myself from. Maybe I had known because of those years before I left home, when she had begun to be even more withdrawn, her increasingly quiet body the harbinger to a more permanent deterioration. Maybe I already sensed that certain diseases simply do not respond to the modern conventions of healing, or perhaps that the carrier of a disease is just as significant as its prognosis.

"It might not be cancerous, *ketzi*," my father was still speaking, soothing.

It was in a good place in the brain, he told me, behind the left ear. She was an optimal candidate for surgery, but she had lost some of her hearing, and her balance would be permanently compromised. There would be an operation in the next few weeks.

I would be home, I told him. I would be home that night.

"No." He stopped me, and it wasn't concern for me that made him do it. The rushing in my ears made it difficult for me to hear him. "You know your mother, Naomi." He cleared his throat. I could hear him playing with the neck of the phone cord. He always played with it, our phone cord at home was a mess, but the worse he felt, the nearer his hand came to his mouth. "She needs her privacy. That's why I held off from telling you."

"How long have you known?"

"Not more than a week," he assured me, but his quick soothing raised my suspicions. "Just let her be. She'll call you in a few days. She'll call you tomorrow. You can talk to her yourself." He was rushing me off the phone.

Even if I hadn't suspected that there was a break in his voice just then, I would have hung up the phone when I did. Though afterward I could see him standing in his stocking feet, the cord still in one hand, his eyes on something else.

I closed the text I was supposed to reference for the report,

Molecular Biology of the Cell. I had only retained the words, not really understood them. I had learned this was more than enough to pass most of the exams, had used it as a way to make exams more interesting, in fact: understanding as a rush, a last-minute game.

I stood up, went to the closet, pulled out my jacket, put it on, and walked out the door and down the hallway. I walked past the woman at the front desk, who looked up at me, bored, before returning to her reading. It was unseasonably warm, even for late March, but the sun was setting. I walked out the door, down the driveway and down the street. I was at Freeman before I'd thought of where I was going. I walked by the woman on bells duty chatting at the front desk, down a hallway, to Jun's room. She answered on the first knock.

"You have a car."

She looked at me blankly.

"Please," I said, trying to control my voice, "can I borrow your car?"

She didn't hesitate, only retreated into her room and pulled her keys from a pair of pants before bringing them to me. "What's going on?" she said quietly. I shook my head. She told me where the car was. "Do you want me to go with you?" I shook my head. "All right," she said, "I'll see you later." I nodded.

I found her car in the student lot, a mile from her dorm. It took a minute to warm. In another minute I was driving down Campus Road, it took me less than that to drive under the gates of the college, a little more and I was out of town, and then, finally, thankfully, I was on the highway.

My parents hadn't changed the front lawn since I was a kid, though the trim on the house had been repainted since Thanksgiving. It looked nice. The dogwood was blossoming, the maple trees beginning to fill out again. There was a light on the second floor, a few on the first. I parked the car across the street and cut the lights. I watched the house in the dark, trying to see them move through the windows.

I got out of the car. The street was completely silent. I stood on the sidewalk, thirty feet from the front door, and could see my mother in the living room, reading. She was wearing her glasses. I couldn't see my father. I heard something move to my right; a dog that trotted home at the sight of me. My father walked into the room where she was. They were speaking to each other. He left, and one by one I saw the lights go out in the other rooms as he turned them off. I checked my watch. It was a few minutes past nine.

I lost him for a moment, and then the front door opened. He had a trash bag in his right hand and was closing the door with the other. I crouched down quickly, behind a bush. He startled and then stood looking out toward the place where I'd been. I heard my mother call him. I stood up, but he didn't move. The porch lights were on. Maybe they were in his eyes. I had just learned that an actor must play into the light and trust that the audience is beyond it. I remained standing, watching him. He didn't move. Finally, he placed the garbage to the right of the door instead of walking it to the trash can in the garage and dragging it out to the curb. Had he been afraid of what he had heard? He turned around and closed the door behind him.

He returned to my mother, still reading, in the living room, and took her arm, helped her up. The tears came, as much as I didn't want them, and I stuffed my fists into my jacket pockets as though I might squelch them. It didn't help. They only came more quickly. The light went out in the living room, and then, a few minutes later, in their upstairs bedroom. It was like watching a play not yet meant to be seen. I returned to the car, then got out again. I walked as quietly as I could to the porch, picked up the trash, brought it to the can in the garage, and dragged it to the curb. I got back in the car and sat there until I fell asleep.

I was awakened by the garbage truck before dawn the next morning. I felt disoriented; for a moment it could have been any time and any place. I got out of the car to stretch, and was overwhelmed by a pleasant feeling brought on by the pale sky and the sight of the peaceful neighborhood. I walked carefully around the side of the house, ending up in our backyard. But I felt like I couldn't go in the back door, either, couldn't bring myself to knock. When had my parents made this privacy, had they always had this power at their hands, the power to unite and shut me out, wordlessly? The barrier around the house was theirs, as tangible as if it had been constructed with solid materials. I stood there, the tears threatening to fall again. And then I turned around, took in the yard that had been mine and the one that had been Teddy's, the long expanse that had joined them together.

I had thought the Steins, the current owners of 54 Coolidge, had changed everything that bore any trace of Teddy, but I hadn't thought about what we'd made together, on my side, what might still be there. My heart dropped, almost as though it had just recognized a betrayal. We had made the hiding place in the far right corner of the lawn. The area looked promisingly empty. My father's halfhearted gardening had not spread to it. I was there in a moment, scrabbling into the dirt, digging as though the appearance of any real daylight was sure to reveal me in the middle of a crime.

It was all still there. The cedar box with what we'd buried inside. I took out what was on top first, what we'd added when we dug everything up on Teddy's twelfth birthday: six of our collected baby teeth in a plastic bag. "So they can find us and match us if we're ever in an accident," Teddy had said. A hand-drawn map of our neighborhood, which made me laugh; a photograph of the two of us in our bathing suits; an old scarf of my mother's; a lock of hair taken from his mother's dresser. "Whose was it?" I'd whispered. "No idea," he'd replied with equal solemnity. When the map was fully unfolded, a hand-drawn picture of a yellow bird fluttered to the ground.

I picked it up and put it in my palm. It was so transparent I could see the skin of my hand through it. I placed it beside me as I reached for Rosemary's papers, looking first at the photographs of Amelia Earhart and the young Mrs. Kennedy, and then the letter,

I hope you liked every-thing here. . . . Mother says I am such a comfort to you. Never to leave you. Well, Daddy, I feel honour because you chose me to stay. And the others I suppose are wild.

After the lobotomy, which had clearly failed to help her daughter, Rose said she had given up playing piano. She still did play, but only for Rosemary, and only when they were alone. Perhaps they had achieved an uneasy intimacy by then, despite how little they could understand about each other. I wonder if my mother might allow intimacy if it were similarly imperfect, if there was such a thing as an argument for it.

I reburied everything but Rosemary's papers and the report on Teddy's mother, the scarf, and the paper bird. They might have been items needed for a long winter: some for much later, if at all; some that I wanted to keep close by.

On my way out, I drove past 83 Beals. I hadn't wanted to see it ever again; the images I retained of my father's fall were too vivid to bear. To my surprise, it looked completely unchanged. Even a home that had been made into a museum, I supposed, might have been affected by the years. But not this one. I stopped the car and got out, standing on the sidewalk across the street. The flag waved in the wind but there was no other sign of life there. I thought of Rose's voice on the recording in the piano room. *Things were so much simpler then.* It wasn't the first time I had doubted her.

When I got back to Wellesley I reparked the car in the lot, then walked the length of the campus back to Freeman. I pushed the keys under Jun's door before returning to my dorm, trying not to wake Amy as I unlocked our door. I would call my mother. I would make her speak to me. I quietly placed Teddy's drawing, my mother's scarf, the hospital report, and Rosemary's collection into a drawer, a compulsion drawing me to hide them away again, perhaps a fear that their long time underground would make them crumble in the light.

"Where the hell were you?" Amy was sitting up in bed.

"Out," I said, shutting the drawer firmly. I moved to the closet and hung up my jacket with care, my back and shoulders stiff from the night in the car.

She flung the covers off and marched to the door, flipping on the light. Her face and pajamas, an old pair with nubs on the cloth, were pink and puffy. "I nearly called the police. You can't leave a note?" I took off my shoes, then my socks. I would shower. I could get clean.

"I was just out, Amy. I'm sorry you were worried," I added dutifully.

She snorted her disdain, momentarily speechless. "What the hell is going on with you? You missed last week's RA meeting for your rehearsal, you disappear for a whole night, I haven't seen you study, and you look too thin. Do I need to stage an intervention?" She seemed smaller than she had been first year; her face did. "Stop staring at me. Are you on drugs?"

I smiled.

"You've been crying."

"I just need a shower."

"I thought we were friends," she said. "I thought we were really good friends." Another girl's voice might have cracked, but Amy just thrust her face in mine, her hair sticking out and tangled. The frame it made for her plain face was oddly leonine.

"I'm sorry, Amy," I said, hating myself for dodging her but too tired to really care. "I need a shower." I imagined myself already in there, the warm water on my back.

She was relentless. "I think you should find another roommate next year."

"Okay," I said. I began to open the door.

"You know, if your grades slip too much, they'll kick you out." I closed the door a bit. My grades had begun to slip. There was more than one lab report that was hurriedly finished after a late rehearsal and a snack at the Hoop when I wasn't the only one who'd missed the dining hall hours. There were more than a few classes I had dozed through. I'd been able to stay afloat, but I was losing my singular focus on all things academic. At the same time, though, as I walked through campus recently I sometimes found myself breathing deeply, the feeling of air in my lungs occurring like a novelty. It had made me want to run again and, when I did, I found that

Shakespeare's lines were more to the rhythm of the body than the facts of molecular biology.

"Of course," Amy went on, more to herself than to me, "you have a fucking photographic memory. Your grades will never slip *too* much. You can always *just get by*. God, what a waste." She stormed back to her bed, throwing the covers back over herself. I thought she might be done, but she was glaring at me from her nest. "Do you know what you could do with that? And no internship, no recent work experience; you belong to Shakes and that's it. You didn't even try out for tennis. Med school is just around the corner. No one will take you, Naomi, if you keep this up."

I still had my hand on the knob, listening. "You know, there's no such thing as a true photographic memory. I think it's just an idea. The mind can't operate like a camera. It's naturally flawed. I must have read that somewhere." I grinned, hoping she might, too. When she didn't, I opened the door to leave.

She leapt out of bed again as I walked away, raising her voice now that it would carry into the hallway. "You're a wreck, Naomi, and you're wasting your time here." She checked herself for a moment after she'd said this, the words and her volume harsher than either one of us had expected. "I can't believe you're just *wasting* your time here." She shook her head, incensed. I thought she might stamp her foot, like an angry child. "Fucking Wellesley education and look what you're doing with it!" She gestured to me, as though I were evidence of something. "Do you have any idea what you're letting just slip through your fingers? Is that what you really want?" Her voice rose on these last words, a shrill, tight whinny.

I wanted the warm water. I closed the door behind me. I stood under the stream for twenty minutes, giving Amy enough time to get dressed and leave. Then I leaned my forehead against the shower wall until I felt tired enough to sleep.

NINETEEN

When I woke there was a message on my voicemail. Jun. Looking for me, asking me if I wanted to talk about anything. I deleted it. The phone rang, but only twice. I picked up the receiver and dialed my parents. It was just past four in the afternoon and no one answered.

Opening night was in two days. I was due at the house for a six-o'clock call. I was there by five, stopping at the phone in the entry-way to check my messages, try my parents again. Still no answer. I slammed the receiver into its cradle and walked into the kitchen. Ruth and A.J. were at the stove.

"You looking to play the ghost tonight?" A.J. asked when she saw me. Ruth turned around. I shook my head. "Are you sick, love?" A.J.'s watchfulness made my eyes sting with tears. I couldn't risk talking.

"She's fine," Ruth said. "Try this, I'm teaching A.J. to make samosas." I stared down at the food. I took a bite. It was doughy and spicy and nearly impossible to swallow. I gulped down some water, choking on it, as though relearning how to eat.

The front door slammed. The house was filling. Two or more members were arguing. I heard Ellie insisting she'd heard it was

Macbeth. A hand was on my shoulder. Phyllis, looking down. "A.J. says you're sick." I shook my head. "She's fine," Ruth insisted, flipping pierogis. Phyllis scowled at Ruth's back. "Are you okay?" she asked me. I nodded. "Then go get dressed. I want to run Ophelia's postmortem again before the run-through." I stood up, but felt dizzy as soon as I did. How long had I slept? Jun was there before I saw her, her hand on my arm. As if sensing us, Phyllis whipped around. "Is she sick or not?" she demanded.

"No," Jun answered. Phyllis frowned and turned away. Jun walked me out of the room, down the hallway, then let me go at the door to the basement. More people walked in. I opened the door and went downstairs, sitting heavily on the first chair I found. Jun was behind me. There was no one else there. "I can't talk about it here," I told her. She said nothing. The door above us slammed. More people.

I made it through the run-through, pretending to study between acts. I snuck down shortly after Laertes' death to listen to the phone tell me again that I had no messages. I walked out without waiting for Phyllis's notes, walked back to my room alone. It was hot and stuffy there, the heat not yet scaled down for spring, and I knew I wouldn't sleep. Amy wasn't there. It was late, almost two in the morning. I pulled on my running shoes and sweats.

I walked around outside for a while then went to the track. There were no lights and I couldn't find the switch. I walked to the starting line and began to stretch.

As I coaxed myself into a run, I tried to picture the tumor in her brain. White, the size of a ball; it couldn't possibly be that perfectly round. And was it white in actuality or only in an X-ray? How did it grow? When would it first have been there? Did she feel it, did she feel a foreign object or just the deterioration it effected as it grew, forcing other things to shut down as it blossomed, unseen? Someone came up behind me. Jun. I didn't acknowledge her, just let her run beside me, wanting to be lost in my mind as it spun, in my body as it grew tired.

We took a few more laps before I increased my speed, Jun matching me easily. I listened to her breath, then mine, until I was exhausted and stopped. I had classes in a few hours and opening night in a day. I crouched down to stretch but sunk instead into my own arms.

"How did you know where I was?" I mumbled to Jun.

She spoke softly, steadying her breath. "You fidget when you're upset, like you need to take off. I figured you were too rattled to be anywhere that wasn't open space." I looked up. She was smiling a little.

"I went home last night. I should have returned your car sooner." Jun said nothing.

"I slept in it. I didn't go in. It's my mother." I looked away as I told her. She was crouching, too, mirroring me. It was so comforting, the first comfort I'd really wanted; she seemed to absorb something for me.

The night was heavy with quiet. "Has she been sick for a while?" she asked cautiously.

"Sort of." I wondered if, when I became a doctor, I'd be less overwhelmed by the complexity of weakness. "The tumor is new." I shrugged, too exhausted to find more words. I suddenly found myself wondering if the tumor could be related to the depression, if they were two symptoms of one problem, of a mind invading itself. I looked at Jun, questioningly. Could she have read my wonder and replied with an answer?

"Come." She stood up. "Stretch."

I stared at her. "My father used to call me that."

Jun smiled at me. Her smile was never even, as though she didn't want to commit to a grin until she was fully sure. She wasn't a pretty girl, I remember thinking, but she had a welcoming face. "I meant to stretch. You'll be stiff."

I stood up, then stopped myself. I trotted to the side of the track and was sick. The release left me sobbing. Jun was beside me again, her arm around my shoulder.

"She won't return my calls," I spoke when I could. "She doesn't want to talk about it."

"She will." I felt her shiver. "Let's get you home."

"I can't go back. My roommate hates me."

"She won't hate you any less if you're standing out here."

We made our way back to Stone-Davis. When Jun and I walked through the door, Amy was there, waiting. "Is she drunk?" she demanded. It would be morning soon. Neither one of us answered. Jun was carrying foils and books. Phyllis had asked us to try having them with us at all times. "A soldier has to learn an intimacy with his preferred weapon so that it can be like an extension, and appendage, whatever works for you." She had taken to wearing a pair of heavy wooden clogs that thunked when she walked. "It has to be authentic, ladies. The audience will get up and leave if it looks like a couple of girls playing fight."

She had been standing in the center of the room when she'd said this, facing the stage from the middle of where the audience would see us, arms akimbo. She filled that space better than an actor might, its emptiness and echoes suiting the cadences of her demands.

"I don't see why the hell you have to drag your stupid swords with you," Amy said, trying to balance a foil up against the wall.

Jun caught it just as it started to fall. "It's too flimsy for that," she said, laying it on the floor. She smiled up at Amy. "They're not real swords."

Amy huffed.

"I'm Jun," she told Amy as I was pulling off my socks.

"I know who you are," Amy shot back. "Economics, right?" Jun nodded. "Oko Industries, right?" Amy didn't sound as bold as she wanted to. Jun's nod was slighter. "See you tomorrow, Naomi," she said to me. "Nice to meet you," to Amy. She left.

"Do you know who her father is?" I pulled the covers over my head. "No, of course you wouldn't. They say she's gay. That her father would *kill* her if she came out. Anyway"—she got into bed and flipped off her light—"at least you're making some useful connections."

I called Jun to borrow her car again the next day. "Maybe you should give her a little time," Jun said when I got to her door. For what, I thought, and made my face say that, though I knew there were many reasons why she might want more time. Jun handed me the keys.

This time I turned into the driveway and killed the engine there. I slammed the car door behind me, wanting to make noise. My mother was standing just behind the open door, watching me as I walked up. A cat skittered past me, followed by two more. I walked up the steps, my fresh bafflement easy to read.

She smiled, put one hand behind my neck, and kissed me on the forehead. "They're strays we've found. They were under the house. We'll be giving them away soon." She was suddenly chatty about the creatures, chatty enough that I took a second to bend down and look at them: a scraggly mottled thing, and a sleek black one—a baby, she thought. I listened to her absentmindedly, watching the motions without bothering to guess very hard at their meaning, like someone waiting for the subtitles at a foreign film. It seemed a long time before she was quiet again. We had just sat down together in the living room.

"It might not be cancerous," she finally began, repeating my father's optimistic tone and delivery. It sounded just as empty in her voice as it had in his.

"It might be, though," I countered. "Can you possibly be more specific?" I went on. My tongue felt dry in my mouth; my voice clinical in my ears. She frowned, my bitterness hitting its mark. I wanted to grab her, squeeze her shoulders between my hands. "Where is it?" I asked.

She pointed to an area right above and behind her left eye.

"Have you seen it?" I asked.

She nodded.

"Dad says they'll do the operation soon." Another nod. I shifted in my seat. She offered to make some tea. "No," I said. She had been getting up and sat back down. "How did they find out?" I asked. She told me she had lost some hearing in her left ear—well, nearly all hearing in the left ear, and that her balance was off.

"And you were going to fix hot tea?" I asked, challenging.

She laughed outright. It startled me into smiling. She so rarely laughed like that; whenever it happened I froze, as I did then, but it was gone before I could form an impression of it.

"I'll get the tea," I said. She stood. "Don't get up," I said. She didn't listen to me, instead walked by me to the kitchen. We were playing different games.

There was a grove of tomato plants on her kitchen counter. The walls had been painted, too. A creamy white, almost yellow. They hadn't told me they were painting the porch or the kitchen. I wondered if my absence had finally prompted my father to tend to something other than me.

"It's a good color," I admitted as she filled the kettle. I took it from her just as she was about to place it on the stove and light the pilot, doing what she'd been about to do. I had the feeling she was as irritated by me as I wanted her to be. But if she was, she didn't let on. She took a seat, folding the napkin I had thrust in front of her.

"Listen, Naomi," she said, her voice quiet. "Sit for a minute and listen."

I shook my head. Then I moved quickly to her side and wrapped my arms around her, my chin over her shoulder pulling her in even closer. Her faint scent rose up as she warmed in my arms. For a short while she didn't pull back.

"Listen, Naomi," she finally said, again. I let her go. "Grandmother Carol is going to come stay with me for a little while"—she hesitated—"she's actually due today. Your father's getting her." Grandmother Carol. The last time I'd seen her had been five years ago. She had told me she'd guessed I was too old for candy. "I can't quite explain it," my mother continued, "but she asked to come when we told her, and I couldn't say no."

"She's going to be awful," I squatted down, putting my hands on her knees. "Let me stay instead," knowing as I said it she would never allow it.

"You're at school, Naomi. There's no way. Your father would have both our heads," she conceded. "You need to be there, Naomi. It's good for you. Not just because of this. It's good for you to be there." She half-smiled. I hated the falseness, the niceties in her concession.

She looked older, the skin under her eyes slack and gray. "You're not sleeping well," I said. "I'm actually sleeping just fine," she said. "More than I should!" She was brightly cheerful. The conversation was over. The back door off the kitchen was being unlocked. In another moment my father and grandmother were inside, my father's delight at seeing me working in to an effusiveness. My grandmother took me in and frowned, looking like she'd swallowed something bitter.

"Well, Naomi, it looks like you've grown as tall as your mother." I nodded. "And you're at Wellesley?" I nodded. "Good," she said, dropping her chin once.

I walked back out the door they'd come in and sat down on the top step. The Steins had added a patio set with an umbrella. What would happen to it when it rained?

"Go back, *ketzi*"—my father was beside me a moment later. I turned to him. "You have things to do there. I want to see my daughter play Hamlet."

I tossed a stick out into the yard. "I'm not playing Hamlet, Dad, my character's called Laertes; he's just a sitting duck." I looked back out at the rhododendrons lining the house with their thicket of black-green leaves and dense pink blossoms.

"Well, then you must be a really great actress!" he exclaimed. "My daughter is no sitting duck."

I wasn't really listening to him. I leaned my head on his shoulder.

He reached his hand up to my cheek, "Go back, Naomi. Get out before your grandmother starts in with the Hail Mistys. She brought incense." I didn't budge. "Listen, Naomi"—I didn't want to—"there's an appointment on Monday with the surgeon. If you'd like to come, you should." "She won't want me there." "It doesn't matter," he said.

He took his hand from my face and clenched his fingers together in his lap as he spoke, "Your mother doesn't know what she wants. You'll come."

I had been told that Mr. Pope would attend opening night, but not that he would prop his feet onto the flat we had built to extend the stage, the one on which Laertes first appears, when he asks for the king's permission to leave home.

Even though it was Claudius's question that went unanswered, Tiney, as Polonius, glared at me, her face a caricature of white under lights and with makeup. In the trick of that moment, the whole play was full of ghosts; I could stand and view it from a remove and nothing would change but the staring, from Tiney, from Mr. Pope, from the audience. I think I spoke the line a moment before the last person in the audience to realize I was late grew still.

My father embraced me afterward in his light-blue shirt, his one item of dress clothing, my pancake makeup smearing his shoulder and cheek. We were all trying to pretend it was normal that my mother had come to see the play, too. I wondered what her mother was doing, alone, at home, and the thought of her there made me feel like we had been invaded.

My mother looked horribly thin, wrapped in a pale-blue cardigan that made her eyes seem to start from her head. She pulled a handkerchief from her pocket as my father spoke, wiping the cloth over his face. She didn't look at me, and I didn't look at her, though together we smiled at my father as he continued his praise, flanking him like guardians.

I walked them to the door, through the crowd. "Are all these girls your friends?" my father asked as we wove through them. And then, at the door, "I'm glad, sweetheart. You should have good friends. They seem like good girls. Not so stuffy."

Suddenly my mother's hand was on my shoulder, her face at my cheek. The night was breezy, and the wind felt good once we were outside, but her skin against mine was like being quenched. She kissed me on the side of my head. "What's the next play?" she whispered, standing back to look in my eyes. "Don't know yet," I answered. "Maybe *Macbeth*. I might not do it." She nodded, her mouth pleased, like someone looking forward to any number of possible outcomes. "I've always liked *Macbeth*."

"You ladies built this house yourself?" my father was saying, craning his neck back and looking at the roof. He tried to shake a support beam on the small front porch, testing its stability. He spoke again quickly: "Women, I mean. Wellesley women. Of course they built the house," he grinned. "I'm not sure," I said, thinking about it. "Maybe."

My mother squeezed my hand and as quickly as it had begun the conversation was over. They were gone before I realized they were leaving. I watched them cross the street from the small porch, wondering if I might have said something different and kept them, wondering at how one small thing said can mean the difference between interest held or lost. My mother slipped her arm around my father's waist, an intimacy I had never seen before.

A few people burst out the front door, laughing. They were followed by a steady stream of partygoers making their way onto the lawn to enjoy the cool night air. Sister Sledge blared from the stereo—"A tradition we can't kick, from the seventies," Calbe explained regretfully—and the lights went down everywhere but in the kitchen, which was packed with light and food, like a hive.

I walked back into the house. Phyllis was at the door, handing out masks.

"They're optional," she said in response to my quizzical look. "It's tradition. Most of the people who come to these parties"—she gestured to the crowd, thick at the door—"they're not ready to be done with the play. Too worked up, poor things." She held up a Snow White and a Minnie Mouse. "Two dollars for the night." She studied me. "You should have stayed in costume. It would have been better for business."

"What do you think? Minnie Mouse?" She nodded to a small woman grabbing the hand of the man beside her, both trailing Tiney as she marched in through the front door. They ignored the masks and Phyllis, who muttered something under her breath as Tiney guided her parents to a corner to say goodbye. They were both as fair as she, though the father, in particular, wore a humorless expression, and the mother's was too full of false cheer. Tiney was still dressed in her ornate, bloodstained costume. Her makeup made her face look stiff and old. I wondered why she hadn't changed.

I made my way into the kitchen just as Jun came in through the front door half backward, banging it as she made her way through, laughing and talking to a tall boy behind her. She saw me. "Naomi, Keigo came—my cousin. He's at Harvard. I mean, he's visiting, but I didn't think—hey, Keigo, this is Naomi." She was overflowing with delight. I smiled and offered my hand and he smiled back and took it with both of his.

He was very tall, with Jun's strong jaw and small, warm eyes. I realized how long it had been since I'd felt that thump of attraction at the sight of a boy.

"No flirting, Keigo," Jun said sternly. But they both laughed as soon as she said it.

"Come," Keigo said, pulling a Yoda mask down over his face, "let's go dance. I want to dance with some lezzies." Jun punched him in the shoulder, and I went with them into the next room, the music so loud we could feel it through the floor. Keigo caught my eye and inched closer as we danced, and I shot a quick look at Jun, wondering if it was okay. It must have been getting colder, because just a few minutes later it was too crowded to move without bumping into someone. A group of men, or boys, all wearing masks, walked in, pushing me into Keigo. He grinned, holding up his hands. I smiled. "What's with the chain gang?" Phyllis was asking, standing beside the one in front. It looked like he whispered something in her ear, and she tossed her head back and laughed.

It was suddenly bliss to leave school at the door, to dance in a dark room full of other people who wanted to do just that. Keigo became more and more good-looking as the night wore on, but I lost track of him and grabbed my first drink in disappointment.

I backed up, stepping on the foot of someone very tall: Ronald Reagan. He bowed low to me as I stared at him. He smiled a little when he straightened, bringing up just the edges of his mouth. The lower half of his mask, just below the nose, had been torn away. I found myself staring at his lips. He reached out suddenly and took my hand, kissing it quickly.

I snatched it away. He felt too tall, and I was dizzy. I downed my drink and sat down in the nearest spot, hard. Phyllis saw me and forced her way over. "Get up, go home, sleep it off. Don't ruin my fucking play." I stood up and hugged her. She pulled my hair back, looked me in the eye, and repeated what she'd said. I nodded. She assessed me a moment longer and squeezed my hand, dismissing me.

Somehow I made it home and fell asleep, but I dreamt of my mother. I had lost her in the Kennedy house, and after looking everywhere found her at the bottom of the stairs, Rosemary's letters in hand, waiting for me.

The next night after the performance, I'd had two beers before I was out of costume, trying, literally, to drink away my thoughts as others seemed to be able to do so well. I felt immediately queasy, though, and kept myself to the kitchen, refilling drinks and food, not yet ready to plunge into the crowd again, still thinking of the dream I'd had the night before. As soon as my stomach settled I grabbed another drink and made my way into the great room, which was even more packed than before.

Almost immediately I got jostled to the side and stood there, watching. I wondered if Keigo and Jun would show up again, if I could really get away with anything with him, given Jun. I had no ideas about the rules of her family, if she would care about such a thing. I wondered what it would be like to be touched by someone, intentionally. I felt myself grow distracted, thinking about it.

"You know, Shakespeare himself loved to wear masks," a voice said beside me. "But you probably already knew that."

I turned to see Reagan staring back at me. "That's creepy," I breathed.

He smiled. Again, just the corners of the mouth. It was a nice smile, I thought, an inviting smile. I moved closer to it. He stopped smiling, leaned forward, and kissed me, fluidly, shocking me into kissing him back before I could think of anything else to do. I leaned into him, into the curves of his mouth, doubt only a distant voice. *Had he read my mind?* Fear rose in my stomach. The first person I was kissing since Teddy was probably a rapist disguised as Ronald Reagan.

I grabbed the back of his head and pulled him into me, surprising us both. Maybe it didn't matter if Keigo was there. Maybe I was just wanting a warm body, any warm body at all.

"Take off the mask," I whispered.

"No," he whispered back, his voice now a little hoarse. He broke away from me for just a second. "Meet me in the back," he said. He stood up suddenly and walked with surprising confidence through the crowd, opening the greenroom doors on the south end of the room and closing them behind him. I downed the rest of my drink and followed him.

It was cold in there, but I could just barely feel it with the alcohol rushing through me. I began to think I shouldn't have followed him in.

"You shouldn't follow strangers into a dark room," he muttered, taking my hand. All of a sudden he seemed shy, too.

I had to stand on my toes to reach his lips. "Who are you?" He kissed me, quieting me. I reached my hands into his shirt, but he pulled them back down.

"No," he said, his voice breaking, just above his whisper. "Just your mouth."

I wanted more. I was suddenly angry at his evenness and it felt so easy to get what I wanted and the ease was intoxicating. I forced my hands back up his shirt and he pressed them to him, a compromise. His skin was soft and he was narrower than I'd thought. I wondered if he were very thin. I took a step back, trying to see him better. He wouldn't let me, stepping with me as I tried to step away.

The door opened. "Oops, sorry!" Whoever had opened it giggled before slamming it shut. It opened again while we were still watching it.

"Naomi, you're drunk." It was Phyllis. "Go home."

I followed her orders, spending the rest of the night and most of the next morning in a dreamless sleep.

*   *   *

As my father had promised, I met the surgeon that Monday, between the two weekend runs of *Hamlet*. Dr. Stern acknowledged me when my father announced my connection to Dr. Orchuk at Brigham and Women's, then turned eagerly to my mother, studying her in a naked way that unsettled me, if not my father. He slid over to her, taking her head in his hands almost immediately, speaking his hushed explanations, all the while sketching lightly on her scalp with a pencil by parting the hair aside, not leaving a mark, only impressions, like an object being viewed from a distant height as it moves through tall grass. He offered several words to me—*acoustic neuroma, craniotomy*—and a handful of statistics to my father—the percentage of such tumors removed completely (65%), the percentage of such tumors removed completely under his hands (92%).

His information was multifaceted, almost colorful. Had he not delivered it with such impassivity, spinning on his backless chair as if he were at the center of some odd carousel—we the horses, each with our own rigid purpose: names for me, numbers for my father, promises for my mother—it would have been a speech worth remembering.

Over the course of the appointment he continued to dote on my mother in his uptight, clinical way. I began to have the irrational feeling that if I didn't watch him closely, he just might try to take her away. There had always been something about my mother that made people want to possess her; maybe it was because she was beautiful, maybe it was because she was so deeply contained. At the time, I couldn't have said why I found Dr. Stern so distasteful, especially given that he was so solicitous toward his patient, but now I acknowledge that it had something to do with my own lingering, childlike desires to own my mother, to command her, open her up as easily as he planned to.

"When will her hair grow back?" I asked, interrupting one of his closing lectures. My father looked at me quizzically.

"Her hair?" Dr. Stern asked hesitantly.

"You'll have to shave her hair, won't you? To make an incision?" Dr. Stern stared at me as though I had asked him if he planned to pull it out strand by strand.

"I think you could guess at that, Naomi," my father interjected, trying to save the moment for me, "a bright premedical student such as yourself." He leaned in to the surgeon. "We should've known we had a biology major on our hands the minute she pulled apart her first insect. Did *you* know what a thorax was when you were four years old?" He shook his head with stale admiration.

I glared at my father. "I'm actually thinking of majoring in English, Dad." I didn't have the heart to break his in one breath, so I amended: "English and biology."

"English?" he asked, incredulity lifting his voice into its highest register. "Isn't that the language you already speak?" Again, a tone closer to a primal objection than an utterance.

"English and biology," I reminded him.

"What are you going to do, *read* to your patients?" My father laughed nervously, trying unsuccessfully to gain Dr. Stern's sympathy by opening his eyes wide in disbelief in his direction.

"Her hair depends on whether or not she needs to go through chemo," Dr. Stern said. My mother looked blankly at me. Until that moment, no one had thought of it never growing back. In an instant, I saw my questions for what they were: ugly, false curiosities. I put one hand on her arm, and she let me leave it there.

Before we left, Dr. Stern took one more look into her eyes, her mouth, her ears, like a man at a horse he admired and wanted to run. I stood before the X-ray of the tumor, taking in the gray orbs as a psychologist might Rorschach patterns, studying the film as most would an oracle, not a simple black and white image. I turned my back to it, pulling my cold hands into my armpits. I glared at Dr. Stern, who seemed to find my stance amusing. My mother asked a few more questions; my father wrote everything down; I dropped my hands and stood taller. I told Dr. Stern I wanted to know what her recovery would be like, and Dr. Stern told my mother that she would be in the hospital for three days and then would be allowed to return home, provided that he was pleased with her progress and he was satisfied that she had adequate care there. Even he didn't want to mention how all this depended on the results of the postoperative biopsy. Or at least I thought he didn't want to mention it. All he said was, "Brain cancer is something none of us want to see, of course," like a salesman genteelly distracting potential clients from the weaker elements in his product. My grandmother was not at the appointment, but she was identified as the at-home caretaker, and Dr. Stern nodded his approval.

I envisioned Grandmother Carol in my mother's orange apron, a frown set on her face at the sight of food cooking on the stove, the crown of steel-gray hair groomed just so. I began to understand why she had come to my mother's side; it must be easier to care for the sick than for the well if you're not particularly good at caring for anyone. The sick have clear needs that can be addressed efficiently and at a distance. I wondered if my grandmother loved my mother. I didn't think my mother could ever have been as strange and vibrant a child as I had been, a child infused with imperfect and baffling affections, who could easily frustrate any mother. But there was something, clearly, about my mother that made my grandmother uncomfortable, and I knew the tension between them didn't grow out of the one note of discord my mother had ever specifically mentioned, a dispute over the house her father had left to her. And I think I began to realize then I would never know what was truly between them. Though I think, even now, that the origins of such a significant rift shouldn't have been so easy to disguise.

I didn't drink the next weekend. I began searching the masks as soon as I had dressed and come back upstairs, hungry again.

"He's Carter tonight"—Phyllis found me. "Thought I would liven things up for you two." She pointed to a far corner of the room. "Also, you should have your fun early. We have one more show. And don't drink; it insults us both. No need to pretend you want sex only when inebriated. This isn't the fifties—or the eighties, for that matter. It's better when you're not, anyway." She put a hand on my shoulder and looked at me clinically. "I think this is good for you." She patted me a few times in an affectionate, satisfied way before walking away.

It occurred to me then that she knew him, that I could ask her who he was. But then she was gone, and I was glad the opportunity had passed. She seemed to understand something about me that I had not admitted to myself. Sex. I suppose that was what I wanted. The thrill and keen pain of running had brought its own pleasure, but what about pleasures of the less complicated kind? I thought of the long kisses Teddy and I had exchanged like gifts. Was that when I had last wanted things for myself instead of just insisting upon them?

I found him.

"Are you going to tell me who you are?" I asked him once, and when he didn't answer, I didn't ask again.

The next night, the final night of *Hamlet*, I stood in the greenroom with him for the last time. When he was done letting me kiss him and not touch him, we sat together in the dark.

"This will have to end here," he said after a minute. If it weren't for his voice and the sound of his breath, I might not have known he was there.

"I could meet you somewhere else," I said. "You could take off that mask and let me see you." I barely saw him shake his head no in the dark.

"That's fine," I replied. The top of my head tingled in response to the disappointment in my body. Then the desire returned, and with it a need to feel something stronger than the anger that came along with it, something that could consume even the worst of emotions. I reached out to him in the dark and found his hand. My fingers intertwined in his, which were warmer than mine in the cold room. He moved my hand up to his neck, then his chin, nudging the mask with my knuckles.

"No," I said. He froze. "No." It was suddenly important that I not see him, that I not take in an image and remember it, play it over and over again. I pushed him down on the bench against the window and straddled him. "Like this." I let my desire free: a terrifying, almost hostile thing. I had never, suddenly, wanted anything more badly than to be with him just then, just as we were.

I touched his belt first, then his stomach, a soft gasp the only other sound he made until we were both partially undressed and I pressed his chest to mine. His body was long and warm and full of new lines for me: the sinewy length from his thigh to his knee, the shorter, tight ligament running from his hip to his groin, the thick trunk of muscle on his lower back. I began pushing down on his waistband so I could feel more of him, and then that wasn't enough, either. I stood up to take what was left of my clothes off and he stopped me, breathless, with one hand.

"What?" I whispered.

He shook his head. Then he leaned it back against the bench we were on, letting me take over. I climbed over him, finding my way in the dark. The anonymity drove me like a compulsion. I was hunting something just out of sight, the quick, unknown burst of sensation just out of reach. I pushed us harder, wanting to consume my defense-less need with a ferocity I didn't care to check, though he stopped me, just for a second, and kissed me on the shoulder. He might have been thanking me, or marking me, or giving me the chance to stop. He must have sensed it was my first time, but I ignored his tenderness. We moved quickly.

"I should go," I said when he was done, still wanting more.

I stood up and pulled everything back on. I was fully clothed before he'd moved. As I reached to tie my hair back he pulled me toward him, resting his head for a moment in the space between my ribs.

"I wish I could see you again," he said softly.

I turned around and walked quickly toward the door.

"Naomi," he whispered. My hand was already on the knob. I didn't turn around.

TWENTY

My mother's surgery was scheduled for a few weeks after *Hamlet* closed. I didn't want to officially notify the college, so I simply skipped classes to be with her. She let me come back to the house, so long as I slept in my old room and avoided The Carol (my father's name for her). She also let me stand by her when she walked. Her dizziness was worsening, and her balance was off.

My grandmother had been helping my mother for a while by then, but she was always slow to come around when my mother wanted to get up, and even then she'd grumble about how my mother should just stay seated, that she or I could get her anything she needed.

Finally, toward the end of one afternoon, she still hadn't come to help my mother move from her chair to the couch, and I stood to do it, though I had been asked not to interfere. My mother gave me a look, but at the same time my grandmother appeared at the door.

"I don't know why we don't just get you a walker, Theresa. It would be so much easier. And who knows if you'll even be able to get around after the surgery." She threw down the towel she'd been folding in her hands. "Naomi and I can't be running around for you all the time and then leading you wherever you want to go. Really, it's just selfish." She said all this calmly, but I could tell she wasn't. She made a noisy, disapproving exit a few seconds later, but despite her deliberateness I had the sense she was rushing, anxious to leave.

I felt like an intruder, standing in the wake of seeing my mother hurt by her own. I went over to her and took her hand, didn't lean down to support her whole body as I'd intended to, and told her, "It's no trouble at all. It'll be my job, something I can do for you." By just offering my hand I wanted to show her how easy it was to help her. And I realized as I said and did this why my grandmother had not. I thought about how nice it would be to have my mother's body leaning into mine. I thought of how each time my grandmother had come close to her, she had stopped just short of the reach. And suddenly I understood that my grandmother was afraid to touch her daughter, that it frightened her. And I knew just as suddenly that it wasn't a new fear. I searched my memory for the last time I'd seen Grandmother Carol touch my mother, but no memories came forward.

I saw it in my mother's face, too, that she knew this about her mother, saw the sadness, though she buried it quickly by dropping her head and taking my hand, saying, "She's probably afraid we'd both fall if I leaned on her." But I knew she was also saying that it was fine if I held her, that she wouldn't mind it, either, and for the first time in my life I allowed her the quiet that followed gladly.

She went into the hospital a few days before the surgery for pre-op. The Carol drove the Cadillac down the driveway to stay at her own home until my mother returned. I had a feeling that hospitals were repulsive to her, that their threat of intimacies would be intolerable. And I think I understood, I think we all did; maybe we were all a little grateful. Consistency held her together, and that was a kind of blessing at the time.

My father and I spent the day of the surgery in a waiting room just outside. He became quieter as the day wore on, so I spent the time scurrying back and forth to the cafeteria and vending machines to feed us and supply the coffee. I say scurrying, but I only made a pretense of going quickly. Once out of his sight, I took my time in the hallways, listening to my shoes on the hard, shiny floors, watching other patients being wheeled from place to place, looking at the visitors, admiring the universally white walls. Anything could hold my attention because I let it; I couldn't bear to see my father, of all people, at a loss for words.

She came through in stable condition. We were allowed to see her later that night, the left side of her head shaved, the tubes coming out her nose. Only her eyes were familiar. And her hands: the long fingers, the short nails.

Of course she couldn't speak, but my father henpecked the doctors and nurses, fussed near her. At one point, he picked up a red pen from her bedside table and held it up with a look of disgust, "What the hell is this?" he muttered to himself, though loudly enough so that I'd hear. The nurse in the corner looked up. He was already waiting to catch her eye, the offensive pen held out before him. "What the hell is she going to do with a red pen? What if she needs to write a letter?" The nurse stopped paying attention to him and finished her business of clearing trash from the corner table.

She did say, though, when her hand was on the door, "Would it be black or blue that you'd prefer?"

"Either one," my father nearly shouted, trying to bring her into his outrage by raising his voice, as if she'd shake her head and widen her eyes in shocked agreement. Instead she grimaced very slightly, a concession to a sympathetic smile, and left in one swift movement, the door not even clicking as it closed.

"Dad," I said, "are you sleeping here tonight?"

He gave me a look that seemed to say he hoped he didn't need to explain things to me, as well. I stood up and walked by him, pulling the cot closer to my mother and blocking his way, so he was in a sort of corner made by the two beds, the pen still in his hand, his hand now at his hip. I snapped the sheets out, making the bed with some show. "You'll need to get some sleep, Dad."

"It's only eight o'clock, Naomi," he said as he looked at the clock. And this quieted us both for a few moments, because it felt like it was nowhere near such an early hour.

He put the pen on the bedside table and looked down at my mother, watching her face in a private, exhausted way. I thought of the last time we'd been in the hospital as a family, the heart attack that had been the catalyst to so much that now defined me which now seemed so very far away. My father had only grown stronger as he aged, like a gnarled tree, while my mother seemed to be disappearing, just as those old photos he still repaired had faded from not being watched.

I went over to him and looked down on my mother, too. She'd had her eyes open only briefly, and was sleeping again.

"When you were a kid," he said, still looking at her, "you never slept." He dropped his voice. "Even before Teddy left. You were the worst sleeper. I used to stand and watch you when you finally did. Your lips were so relaxed." He reached out, but only touched the edge of my mother's shoulder. I sighed; the breath hurt. "You'd also forget to breathe," he said, now smiling at me. "When you ran, you'd forget to breathe. We used to marvel at how you'd get so far." Something that had been straining between us finally released itself, sagging like a quiet sail.

"I'm getting you dinner," I said. I think I was imitating her, to help, somehow, though it was poor acting. I actually don't remember much more of that night except the trip to the cafeteria, staring down at some anemic salad before choosing a grilled cheese sandwich, an apple, and juice: a child's meal, brought up to him on a tray.

Though somehow, by the time I got back home and into the empty house, I convinced myself I wasn't worried. I didn't want to be, and was still young enough for such purposeful disillusionments to hold their own promise. My father found no such peace. He experienced every moment of her pain and early recuperation. He tried to forbid me from going back to the hospital room, but I refused to listen and set up camp in a folding chair in the corner of her room each afternoon after class. I was out of the way and could see everything. Dr. Stern nearly beamed over her. He expected she'd be home right on time. She was. And the tumor, he thanked God, had not been cancerous.

But back at home, my mother was no longer able to climb the stairs to her bedroom, had to be seated properly to hear a conversation, and looked frequently overwhelmed in a vague, impenetrable way. She was with us more often, willing to be cared for, but it seemed she had also retreated more, somehow. Even though she had become less contained in our company, she was also more distracted and visibly nervous, as if perpetually waiting or listening for something just out of sight.

I managed to peg Phyllis in the crowd at graduation later that spring. She was wide-mouthed and happy, about to leave for several weeks in Italy. I told her how I'd wanted to see Rome as she kept her hands on my shoulders and stood back, looking at me, her grin spreading slowly across her face. "I'd like to escort you around Venice one day, Naomi. That's the Italy I can't get out of my mind."

"Truth is"—and she admitted something that would have made someone else lean in close, in confession, but she just opened her arms wide and raised her voice a bit, both of us smiling, the crowd wouldn't notice—"it's the whole reason I took this miserable job I've got in September. I can travel. Teachers travel. Remember that, Ms. Feinstein." She squeezed my hand.

I took in her smooth, sexy beauty. "Who was he?" I finally asked, finally acknowledging what had happened to someone other than Jun, whom I'd told only briefly. Phyllis's grin remained fixed. It took an instant for her to remember, then register my question.

"I can't tell you that," she said.

Before I could get angry, she pulled my hand into hers. "Trust me, Naomi. Some encounters are best left anonymous. You did each other no harm. You had a little fun. I told him you were a sure thing, he gave me the appropriate gentlemanly response. My advice," she paused, a wry expression the only hint that she knew I didn't want her advice, "is that you leave well enough alone. Sometimes that's best for everybody, isn't it?"

"You told him I was . . ." I stumbled on her words.

She cocked her head at me, affecting a deep amusement. "You weren't?"

My throat tightened. "It was a setup?" I didn't recognize my own voice.

Phyllis laughed. "Oh, Naomi," she said, sobering when she saw my expression. "What did you think when you saw the masks?"

"You told me . . ."

"That the audience doesn't like to let go of the play."

"So they wear masks."

"They wear masks and they do what they want under them. They always do. You think you're the first? There's a reason why people crave stages and props. Most of us who join Shakes understand that. Don't judge us or yourself quite so harshly."

She stepped away, lifting her arms up and out, dismissing the conversation as better left forgotten in the wake of the day. "Venice," she said loudly. "Someday. I think you could understand it, my poor, idealistic Laertes, its leaky beauty, the way it wants to pretend it's not noticing but cares desperately about everything its casual tourists think of it." She looked up, suddenly, all the way to the sun. When she did, I looked up, too, so that when I looked back down my sight burned white and I had trouble tracking her as she made her way back through the crowd.

It would be wrong to say that I had felt dismissed by Phyllis, though it wasn't until a few days later that I realized she had given me what I wanted: the invitation to let that encounter be an isolated one, easily buried within the rapidly developing past. I think that growing up in the shadow of my mother's containment meant that I felt pinned in by it, as though the slightest strong movement from me would cast us both, shattering, to the floor. It was almost liberating to think that it was possible to love and discard in the same, swift act. To leave nothing disturbed as a result.

In the wake of everything that had happened that spring my mediocre grades had not been improved upon, despite my initial intentions to do so. So between sophomore and junior years I was advised to diversify, to leave the Brigham and volunteer at Abiomed, Inc., of Danvers, Massachusetts, a company in the process of developing a completely independent, battery-powered, artificial heart. It was one of three sites nationwide that was expected to do so, and thanks, once again, to a strong recommendation from Dr. Orchuk at the Brigham, I secured a place in their summer internship program. My days there consisted primarily of watching and fetching.

The lab was littered with far too many things to include in an implantable device, and the researchers shifted through them with dogged patience, like archaeologists separating stones from integral fragments. Until that point, the most modern heart replacement technology was an enormous, clunky device, a descendant of the DeLaval Alpha Milking Machines. It stood to the side of the room as a reminder of what to surpass. I would stare at it when my father's heart attack became like a distant memory, when the loss of Teddy's father to the same disease was like something that had happened too long ago to remember.

"It's amazing," I said one day to the friendliest researcher there, "that in all the years of hearts failing, that's as far as we've come."

"Yeah," he said, "pretty pathetic." I thought it was actually a little noble, had a little presence, as I put it.

"It's a behemoth," he objected. "An artificial heart should be as seamless a replacement as possible. If we do our job right, even the patient won't be able to tell the difference."

I continued to live at home that summer. I was doing what was expected of me, but the days at the lab felt too long and oddly staged. I found myself wanting to laugh out loud sometimes at the detached ways in which the researchers talked about complications, inevitable failures, or, worse, partial successes. At home I helped my mother bathe when she let me and, most nights, cooked dinner for my father.

The Carol still checked in from time to time, glad to see me there, as she said each time, occasionally with a tuna casserole in hand. My father and I found them delicious: the potato chips and dense interior a virtual anesthetic after the hardest days.

A few weeks before my junior year was to begin, he came into my room and sat heavily on my bed. I had been reading on my stomach and turned over to face him. He put his hand on my back. "It's time to go, Naomi," he said.

"Where?" I asked. "Back to school," he said, and I was about to catch him on stating the obvious when I suddenly understood what he'd meant, so that when he added, "to living at Wellesley," he didn't need to.

"Oh," I said, looking down at my book, folding it over and studying its cover. It was the old copy of *Relativity* my father had kept on the kitchen shelf. I still didn't understand much of it, so that the process of reading it was more like a meditation than a learning experience of any kind. "I don't even have a room assignment, Dad," I said, and as soon as the words had left my mouth it felt like one of the worst things I could have said.

He wasn't kicking me out. He was gently pushing me toward the best place for me, the place that, years ago, had given me tuition, room and board. For my father, attending college wasn't just about completing a course of study. It was about immersing myself in the practice of having and knowing everything. I think he still believed that, even then.

"What time is it in Tokyo?" I asked him the instant I thought of it. His eyes frowned back at me. "I'll work it out," I said. He sat for a while more on my bed as I pretended I had other things to do in the room. He muttered something; it sounded a bit like he had said he loved me. For such a normally demonstrative man, the softness in his voice caught me by surprise. I stopped what I was doing but he had left the room before I had a chance to respond.

I had written to Jun once that summer after receiving a letter from her in Tokyo. She had included her phone number in it. I was digging around in my things when my father came back to my door. "Eight-thirty a.m. tomorrow morning," he said. "They're sixteen hours ahead."

I turned around. He was standing just at the threshold. He was wearing his rattiest cardigan and hadn't shaved well. I wanted to pull out some clean laundry for him and get him a new razor. "You need a shower," I said instead, not moving.

"If you need to call you should call now," he replied and left again.

"It's too early," I muttered to no one, but hurried myself into working up the courage and went to the phone soon after.

The exchange hummed through, a tone instead of a ring. I thought no one would pick up, and then someone did, a man. I was suddenly terrified it was Jun's father and he'd be annoyed by the early-morning call.

I tried to speak clearly, "This is Naomi Feinstein. From America," I added idiotically. "Is Jun Oko available?"

There was a small pause at the end of the line. "She is," the voice said. I held the line for what felt like too long before it was picked up again, "You said your name is Naomi?" I nodded, then answered yes. He had said my name carefully, pronouncing each vowel. I was sure it was her father. A second later Jun was on the line.

"Dad, hang up." The receiver was replaced.

"What is it, Naomi? Is your mother okay?"

"She's okay," I said, holding back. "The recovery went pretty well." I had to stop and collect myself. It was so good to hear her voice. "Jun, I don't have a room for next year." She knew this. She had told me, in the letter, that Ellie had decided to move into her much older girlfriend's apartment—*to see how things might go*—and that if I had decided not to commute from home I could room with her. I could hear the static in our connection as I told her I hoped the offer was still good. She didn't say anything. "I know it's probably too late."

"No," she said. "Actually, that would be great."

She started to tell me about the room assignment, but in my excitement I interrupted her; for the first time that summer something was being fixed. I leapt—"I'll just go over and figure it all out, fill out whatever forms they want." I was grinning. I didn't know what else to say. "How's your summer going?" I asked.

I could hear her smile for sure this time. "Good," she was saying. "I've spent tons of time with George Osaki, an old family friend. Can't talk now, I've got an audience."

"Right," I said.

"So I'll see you in a few weeks, I guess," she added, sounding genuinely happy.

"Yes, yes," I said. We hung up. I stood by the phone, smiling. I was suddenly struck by how much I had missed her. My father was at the door again. When I looked up he seemed surprised to see me grinning, but then his ragged mustache twitched up at one corner, as if jerked by an invisible string.

PART IV

TWENTY-ONE

My first impression of that fall was that it would be different from the ones before it. I was rooming in Freeman with Jun, Mara was to be our director for *Macbeth*, the auditions for which I had missed last spring to be with my mother, as had Jun. We were both preoccupied with other concerns, unable to play. But for the first time we had a class together: The Writer and Her Critic, taught by the latest celebrity visiting scholar, Jules Weingarten. I'd actually heard of him, which made me feel even more confident. For a short while it seemed the school and I were coming together again as the result of a natural progression.

Professor Weingarten had been wooed away from Yale to Wellesley for a short appointment, and it lent him a certain sexy, masculine cachet even before he arrived. I think we liked to entertain ourselves with the idea that he had left a bunch of scrawny boy geniuses for Wellesley's stiff beauties. I was still proud to call myself a student at the college, though most of my classmates had become, if anything, even more intimidating over the years. So many of them were self-actualized by that point, no longer needing to pretend at confidence.

It made them less hostile but more enigmatic. No one thought of the women at Yale: they appeared vague and undefined from our lookout.

A.J., Tiney, and Ruth had also signed up for Weingarten's class, and we ended up sitting together for most of the semester; or at least A.J., Tiney, Jun, and I did. Ruth found whatever seat she could when she arrived a few minutes late, or waved sheepishly at the door when it was simply too late for her to dare come in, holding her notebook up to the window to let us know she'd be asking for notes later. Usually A.J. or I nodded; she wouldn't leave until someone did. Julie was away for the semester, studying at Oxford.

Weingarten's appearance took some getting used to, and I wonder if it contributed to our initial fascination with him. His head was large and asymmetrical; his hair thin, kinky, and reddish and sprouting in two places: just above the temporal lobes and above either ear. His appearance was a study of arrogance: the eyes were small and hooded, the nose a waxy beak, the lips too expressive and slightly dry. His skin was the color of thinned honey and covered in small, dense constellations of acne scars. When excited, a long blue vein stood out from just below his hairline and ran the length of his skull to just above the back of his neck.

Most of his lectures were extraordinary, too, like a symphony wherein every movement seems too wonderful to be trumped by anything afterward, until it is. On the first day he started class, as we learned he always would, by taking a minute to leaf through a page or two of the texts in front of us all. He started to speak while still looking down: "Writers and critics," he cleared his throat. "A relationship many of us have wondered about. An uneasy relationship.

"What we'll begin exploring today, and what I'd ultimately like to have you write about in your term papers"—he still had not made eye contact with anyone in the class, though we were all watching him—"is the relationship, the epistemological, existential, political—what have you, and we'll get into this—relationship, between writers and their critics." He paused here, took a sip of coffee, turned toward the board, and studied it as if he were either not sure what would appear on it next or where to begin writing. "Let's take, for a moment"—he continued to stare at the board—"as our starting off point, the argument that posits that a fundamental difference between the writer and the critic, and the reason why literature soars and critique stings, is that the writer pursues what interests him while the critic pursues what bothers him." He had written "writer" and "critic" on either side of the board with the word "interest" under the one and "disturbs" under the other.

He walked back to the podium before looking back down at the text, but I didn't think he was drawing from it. Instead, he seemed to be taking courage from the sight of words on paper, maybe enjoying the reassurances of black on white.

"Because the critic pursues what disturbs him," he continued, still not looking up, "he is infinitely more knowledgeable. He must be"—head still down—"because when a mind chooses to seek out what disturbs it over what interests it, it will find far more material than the one in pursuit of its own joys." He had the habit of leaning on one fist as he stared down at the table. "Yet although he comes across as jaded by this knowledge, although his writing is frequently dispassionate and dismissive, it is the critic who is far more consumed with his own romanticism; he reads with the buried hope that someone will come along who is so without fault, so aesthetically or morally or perhaps epistemologically brilliant, that he might be forced to believe unequivocally that one other man, or woman, might exist who could make everything that disturbs him about the world, or his chosen world, the literary world, insignificant.

"And, curiously enough, in times past, when a critic has stumbled into such territory, it is indeed only one man or woman who captures his fancy, as if to be so bewitched by a text is to experience some bastardized form of monotheism." He looked up briefly, over his glasses, checking our reactions. Everyone was quiet, watching and listening to him. "And so the critic is the closet believer, though he is doomed, some might argue, to spend most of his life either deluded or miserably misanthropic, at least as far as the written word is concerned."

A small hint of a smile on his face now, a light laugh moving through the class. "Or perhaps I should say ideologically doomed," he added, nearly muttering this last bit directly into the book.

A moment hadn't passed before Sharon Minks—a woman I wasn't friendly with but knew well for her compulsion to discredit her professors the instant after the first tenet of the lecture had been introduced—jumped in. I tuned out what she said, but wasn't able to prevent the memory of her expression from forming: protruding, greedy eyes opening just a bit more the instant her mouth did.

Professor Weingarten listened to her and replied, shooting down what she'd said calmly and without effort, though it didn't stop her. She rose to the fight like a pack dog tethered too long; she couldn't help but pant her way through the first five minutes of discussion. Fortunately, she usually blew over before too much damage was done to the discussion as a whole; unfortunately, this was most often the result of some uncomfortable allusion the professor would have to make to her unfounded and irritating comments. We were in three classes together at Wellesley; apparently, I realized with concern, we had similar tastes. When she was in a class, it made me miss the quiet, staid lab, my fellow students and I hunched over our materials, not speaking, finding answers.

But then Jun raised her hand. It startled me to see her do this; most Wellesley students were pretty vocal in class, but Jun preferred to listen. She was saying something about how interest and disturbance could be one and the same thing, that many artists were disturbed and many critics easily delighted, a point Weingarten seemed to be on the verge of conceding, if she had stopped to let him speak. But she kept driving it home, and although he listened to her far longer than she deserved, you could tell from his face that he was just getting demoralized, probably wanting to keep his patience, at least on the first day; but between Sharon and Jun, I don't see how anyone could have.

All his tolerance did was make Jun more determined, though her logic began to lose its focus. And only once Weingarten's patience was visibly worn did Jun's argument begin to take on its final, relentless form. There was no way Jun would prevail, and I thought back to our tennis match almost three years ago, the way her calm had infuriated me, had made me fight for something I couldn't name.

He finally put his foot down, insisting we move on. But Jun still had to get in her parting shot: "Critics get excited, too, Professor. Especially between the sheets."

The statement broke the tension just enough. A few people laughed and Weingarten was able to redirect. But I couldn't. I had finally realized what Jun had been doing, and the shock of it shut everything else out. She'd been parroting Phyllis, it was a Phyllis argument she had been forwarding, the one Phyllis loved to make about how critics were never nearly as tight-lipped as they seemed, and her last statement was a repetition of Phyllis's words verbatim. And the look on her face when Jun spoke them—a very small, very perfect smile—made me realize something I should have seen long before.

Something had happened between her and Phyllis. Phyllis, who, according to Ruth and Calbe's insistence at a late night rehearsal last year, would sleep with anyone. The instant I remembered this, I regretted it. But there was truth behind the aversion I was fighting to squelch. Bold, indiscreet, unapologetic Phyllis.

It was all I could do to just keep my seat as the class erupted in a ripple of laughter and whispering at the next student's contribution to the discussion, which deteriorated into even more base humor. Even Weingarten smiled a little. But I sat there, paralyzed by what I wasn't supposed to know.

No one, I was sure even then, would have made the connection between what Jun just said and what might have happened with Phyllis, but it wasn't the knowledge that pounded in my chest. It was the realization that Jun had let it slip. I thought of how all those on campus who had taunted her for two years, who had assumed that she was disingenuous in her sexuality, who would not bother to realize that her carefully constructed remove was the sign of an integrity and a fear too private to explain to even her closest friends, who would probably pick up on the next slip or the next. And in the midst of all this, I was suddenly most afraid of what it might mean for her that she had never seen her own move coming.

TWENTY-TWO

When we left class it was pouring and no one had an umbrella. The five of us usually talked on our way out of class and the building, but instead we strategized out loud as to how we were going to make our next commitments in the weather. I was glad for the noise, the nonsense, and after a minute I ducked out of it and into the rain.

I didn't see Jun again until later that night. We had planned to meet for dinner at the dining hall, but I skipped out. I was trying to decide if I had something to say to her or not. As far as I knew, she didn't think I did. Again and again, this was what needled me most, what kept me away from her most of the day, consumed by a sort of guilt.

She was cheerful and unruffled when I returned to our room. I had picked up two umbrellas at the bookstore, and she was surprised and pleased when I gave her hers. She took it and held it in both hands, marveling at it, almost the way a parent does when a child brings home a project from school. I had the sense that she was rarely given gifts.

As she placed the umbrellas in our closet, I threw myself down on my bed. This would have earned at least a glare from Amy, but it didn't draw Jun's attention. She was humming, arranging the books she'd just bought for the semester.

I watched her for a while, until I could no longer stomach her contentedness, which seemed to grow larger the longer I allowed it. I sat up. "Jun," I said, "how long did it last?" She looked at me, her face an open question. "The thing with Phyllis."

She dropped her head immediately, my shot hitting its mark.

I needed to move in the silence, and did, to the other side of the room, pretending to busy myself there.

"Who told you?" she said, turning a book in her hands. It was one of mine, though she wasn't reading it; she was only focused on turning it carefully, smoothing its cover. "Did Phyllis tell you?" She looked up at me. I should have guessed she'd be bold, once the secrecy had been broken. She was too forthright to bury a raised hand.

I shook my head. I found, in my own hands, a book as well. I must have unconsciously mimicked her, wanting to be on her side even as I upset her more and more. I held it still, resisting the urge to turn it over, look down at it and smooth its cover.

"Today, in class"—I saw a flash of panic in her eyes—"you repeated her. Word for word." She frowned in doubt. "I just guessed," I lied.

"You just guessed?" she asked. Maybe she spoke to attack, but we both knew it didn't matter if it was a guess or not, that I wasn't accusing her, that I was just worried about whatever it was she had meant to keep hidden, that I knew what it was for someone to want desperately to hide something, that I just knew.

"I'm sorry," I said, frozen, afraid to move. I needed to make the moment hers, though I'd invaded her privacy so deeply I wasn't sure if she'd take it.

She laughed. It wasn't particularly convincing, but it wasn't false, either. "You know how Phyllis is," she said, grinning at me just barely.

I did know how Phyllis was. How she made every desire and dislike known, how unwilling she was to have anyone else's interests at heart. Suddenly, I was angry. "I do know how she is, Jun. Couldn't you have made a better choice, first time around?"

Her face darkened, closed. "How do you know it's my first time around?" she asked, her voice curt.

"Well, here, at least. Right?"

"So you've been keeping track of my conquests? This from the girl who hasn't had a date in two years, then goes and shags someone in a back room when she's drunk?"

"I wasn't drunk."

"Great. Even better. What gives you the right to say anything?" she persisted.

My stomach clenched. "I have as much right as anyone else. And I shouldn't have let all that happen. It was a mistake," I managed. But my insistence felt false. Had it been a mistake? Hadn't it been just as intentional as anything Jun might have done with Phyllis?

She threw the book down on the floor. There was nothing else there. "And I'm not supposed to make mistakes," she muttered. "Brilliant. That's just bloody fucking brilliant."

"I don't really care who you sleep with, Jun," I started in, not sure where I was going, "but what's the point of keeping it all a big secret?" She wouldn't nod or shake her head. I lowered my voice. "It didn't matter, did it?" I couldn't stop myself from asking for her affirmation, uneasy as I was. I suddenly understood Amy more profoundly than I had in the two years I'd lived with her. Of course it had mattered. I didn't know why, but looking at Jun's face, knowing how she hadn't wanted even me to know, I knew that it had mattered so much she could no longer contain it. I felt myself begin to cry out, but instead I started to laugh.

I laughed and laughed; Jun kept looking at me, so worried, so pissed, and I only laughed harder. "Bloody fucking brilliant?" I repeated. "Did you really just say bloody fucking brilliant?" And then she started to laugh, too, the way she had when I'd run into her staring out into the dark the year before. I came over to her when we were done, asking for forgiveness by sitting down beside her.

Jun nodded. She had softened. "You're right," she said. "I was wrong to let things happen with Phyllis. I guess I'm just tired of it all. This fucking campus is so fucking tightly wound, no one makes a step without everyone else knowing, and I'm just sick of people I don't even know coming up to me and asking me my business. It's just not right."

I nodded, then spoke while my nerves were still chasing me, though as gently as I could. "You probably could find a real girlfriend here, Jun. Someone who would be good for you." And then, just before I lost heart, "I'm sure you're not the only lesbian in Japan."

Her reaction was automatic. She didn't even look at me. She just stood up and walked away. I stayed where I was, wondering if she was done with me or readying us both for something more.

"My life is supposed to go a certain way," she said finally, her expression almost pitying. "This isn't the place where I get to define myself." Her face hardened. "Wellesley is just a stopping point. It's just one in a long line of decisions that were made for me before I was born. I'm not sure how to make you understand." She grabbed her arms behind her back, like a reverse defense. "Maybe you can understand this.

"My personal life is not the most important thing about me. I think you know what I mean. There's something about what's been going on with your mother, I don't know, it just looks to me like you're on hold, too." She grabbed a tennis ball off the floor in front of her and threw it above her, catching it as it fell. She threw it again. I caught it, keeping it out of play, working my thumb over its coarse, frayed surface.

"Maybe," I finally conceded.

She nodded, sitting down on my bed and folding her hands in her lap. "To be my father's daughter in Japan, the one he has acknowledged as his successor, it's like having something separate from me but inseparable. Something that grows every time someone new is born to the family, and their place in it sets, so that if my link of the chain were broken, miles of things around it would break, too. Not just my family, though that would be the worst of it, but all the people around the idea of my family, the people who take pride in Satoru Oko and his strong family and the potential his good children hold for the future of the company. And, by extension, for the country itself."

She stopped, collecting her thoughts. She stood up and started to pace. "It's a small country, Naomi, not like the U.S. Our shared histories define us. We depend on each other. And power is one of our drugs, particularly if it's the proud kind." The room darkened, the afternoon was old. "Do you know how many people know I'm here?" she asked. "Do you know how many people probably even know what dorm I'm in, that I'm rooming with a nice Jewish girl from Massachusetts, that I'm majoring in economics, what my ranking is on the tennis team?" She was hardly able to make the items on her list sound like questions, her tone rote, her face almost immobile.

"Well, you are first," I said. "It wouldn't be that hard to find that out."

She grinned widely, as though together we had made a joke. "I'll miss you, Naomi," she said, startling me. And then I thought of where we'd both be in a few short years, and I suddenly missed her, too, even though she was still standing there.

Over my desk in our room I had pasted an image of Orpheus and Eurydice from the d'Aulaires book my father had given me years ago, the one I'd kept over my desk at home after my father had tried to paste Mnemosyne together and I'd thrown her away. I thought it was a concession to my father to give at least one of the Greek myths a place of honor, but I also never got tired of looking at Orpheus: his instrument over his shoulder, his wife following him out of the underworld in her bare feet. She looked so real, with her thicket of black, curling hair under that veil and her careful steps. In my mind, it had always been clear that the image was of the moment before he looked back. I still sometimes dreamt of Teddy and me like that, me trying as hard as I could not to look back, hoping he'd drift my way if I only presented my best self. But, truth be told, I never understood how anyone could not look back, just to check. Who can believe that those who won't show their faces will return when we want them?

* * *

It was never quite as easy between Jun and me again, though, oddly, I think our friendship had deepened. I thought more seriously about learning from her studiousness and refocusing my energies on school-work, but I felt oddly distanced from the drive that had so easily propelled me before. I'd only show up to listen to the lectures, then let the work slip from my fingers as I walked out the classroom door, like letting jewels fall anywhere once unclasped and at home. Maybe that's why the letter from the dean didn't surprise me when it came.

When I opened it I thought I'd immediately be reading something from the dean, but the first page was handwritten by one Grayson Alexander, an alumna writing to me about her med school experience at Johns Hopkins and as a doctor, urging me to keep my grades up so that I might be able to secure some of the "indelible friendships" (medical school) and "incredible, life-altering experiences" (South African clinics; Harvard residency) she had had as a result of (not directly linked but liberally implied) her foundational training at Wellesley. Even compared with her peers, her accomplishments were outstanding. I could almost hear the voices of the committee that had selected and described her: *innovative, compassionate, creative.*

"Huh," Jun said noncommittally, looking over my shoulder. "I could see you doing something like that."

We both guessed what the other letter in the packet said, the one that bore the college seal. "Dear Ms. Feinstein," it began. "It has come to our attention . . ." Why is it that so many hide behind the protection of overused language to deliver bad news? Maybe it's to deaden the blow, but the emptiness of the words makes the news seem cold, without the possibility of the warmth and messiness of personality. And, indeed, it was only my GPA, a 3.4, which was two-tenths of a point below what was expected of me, that earned me the warning, that compelled them to tell me I would not be admitted to my medical school of choice if I did not keep my grades up, that compelled them to express concern that my diminished performance reflected a lack of enthusiasm. There was help available to me if I wanted it. But we all knew—me, Jun, Dr. Grayson Alexander, Dean Silas, and the pre-med faculty advisor, who, together, had signed the official letter—that it wasn't only a matter of what I wanted, what struck my fancy. It was a matter, primarily, of what I should have wanted.

"Did you ever request personal time?" Jun interrupted my thoughts. She was sorting through her mail.

"What?"

"When your mom got sick, Noms." She was looking directly at me, now. "You didn't request personal time then, did you?" I hadn't. "Did you talk to your advisor?"

I didn't answer her, just walked over to the bin to dump my junk mail. A credit card offer, probably, a few deals on spring break travel. "I don't know why they didn't send me the letter over the summer," I ruminated, pretending to be more thoughtful than I felt. "I might have been able to do something before I picked out my classes."

"Like what?" Jun asked.

"I don't know," I said. "Something." The truth was I knew I had been heading in this direction. So much of schoolwork is designed to please both the student and the teacher, a way for lovers whose shared passion is knowledge to exchange promises. But either party will grow nervous if the other is inattentive. And understanding is not enough; the understanding must be offered regularly and willingly. No lover likes to have to demand affection of his beloved. It didn't matter what I could memorize if I wasn't willing to perform, to demonstrate my knowledge willingly. I knew the hastily completed lab reports I'd submitted created echoing silences where a straightforward response had been expected to an equally straightforward call. What was I doing, I wondered.

"I'm not sure," I began again. Another woman burst through the front door, ignoring us as she got her mail, making noise about it, taking the time to toss her undesirables into the bin I was standing near before heading upstairs.

"It's not too late. You could work harder, Naomi, maybe not disappear into Shakes next semester. You only have to show up for the meetings to stay current. Lots of us bow out for a while when the work gets to be too much."

She was right. The mailboxes stood in their glass and bronze rows, hundreds of single handles in a shining square. I fingered one, knowing I couldn't open it.

"It's up to you, though," she said. "It's your choice."

She had gathered her own things, but stood waiting for my response. I folded the letters back into the envelope. "I'll call the dean tomorrow," I said, "see if she has any ideas."

"Okay," Jun agreed, and we made our way back to our room. As we walked, Jun began talking about something entirely unrelated, a distraction for which I remain grateful even to this day. By the time we had dropped our things and turned on the lights, I was relieved, even glad to have the opportunity to reach out to the dean, like a thief finally caught and offered fair justice.

TWENTY-THREE

Dean Silas had office hours every Tuesday afternoon, so I went to her office the next day, hoping she'd be booked as I made my way there. But there was no one scheduled during the time when I arrived, and only two other students had signed up for appointments later that afternoon.

Her office was at the end of a large, carpeted hallway, one of a handful of administrative rooms on that wing of Green Hall, and it was a hushed place, hushed, I imagined, even when busy. The carpets were a rich, dark color, the walls a dull, matte white. Sketches of various Wellesley buildings sat in ebony frames on the walls.

The dean must not have been expecting any walk-ins, so we surprised each other a bit when she came out to check the list. She ushered me through the door graciously, taking a minute to study the clipboard that had been hanging outside while I took a seat. "Ms. Feinstein," she said, offering her hand as she walked through the door, so that I had to stand again to take it, and nod my hello, tell her it was nice to meet her. The formalities made me want to leave all the more.

"I suppose you've come about your letter," she said as she walked toward her desk. She registered my look of surprise with a smile, "Believe it or not, I'm aware of every letter that goes out of my office to a student." Her smile relaxed. "Also, I've never met you before, and you look fit to be tied, so I assume you're here under duress. Premed, if I remember correctly?" I nodded. "Tough road," she said amiably, leaning back in her chair. She had a pencil or pen, something that she used to tap the desk from her relaxed position. I watched it, not responding to her observation. "How can we help you, Ms. Feinstein?" she asked when I continued to say nothing.

She must have been an older woman, but her energy and enthusiasm were immediately noticeable. She wore a corduroy skirt and a button-down shirt, tucked in. Her belt was plain, as were her shoes. Her face was lined but her eyes were bright, and she wore her shoulder-length gray hair back in a small, neat bun. She radiated what I can only think of as a characteristic New England confidence: tradition had raised her, and raised her well, and it would put her in a solid grave.

I had no idea what to say. I wasn't sure if I was there to argue my case or to be reassured, opt out of the program or announce my renewed commitment to it. "Honestly," I said, "I'm not sure."

She seemed to like my answer, and nodded sympathetically. "Not everyone is cut out for medical school," she said. "It's a glorified hazing, really, to prepare you for the rigors of tending to patients. Not unlike, I imagine, the rigors of tending to students." It was meant to be a joke, and I found myself wanting to laugh a little, to ingratiate myself to her.

"Though you can just get out of your seat and walk off"—she was talking, still, about students. "Your dependencies are much more subtle. My work really is a privilege. The way you all disappear after four years, no time really. And some of you I never even see, which makes a visit like this a cherished moment for me, sort of like when a bird lands on one's shoulder." She blinked. "You ever study ornithology?" I nodded. "A little," I said (I'd gone through bird books in high school when Teddy was still writing, trying to place some of his birds), which surprised her, and a small, pleased smile worked its way onto her face. "Great field. Girls today are too busy to indulge in just bird-watching, though. Have to make it a profession, you know." She sat forward suddenly in her chair, leaning forward on her outstretched arms. "That's the world we've given you, I'm afraid. Tell me, Ms. Feinstein, may I call you Naomi?" I nodded. "What is it that interests you?"

Again, I wasn't sure. "Cardiology," I answered confidently. "Particularly cardiac replacements." I was trying too hard and my voice was halting.

She smiled, though. "Well, that's just great. I hope Wellesley's not lacking in opportunities to help meet your goals. I understand you were able to take advantage of one of the best undergraduate cardiology internships in the nation. Abiomed. Is that right?" She waited for an affirmation. I nodded, smiling weakly. "Well, good."

She stood up, came around to my side of her desk and leaned on it. "Listen, Naomi, if you want to stay on this track, you've got to get those grades up. The rigors of the best medical schools begin with admissions. I'm not trying to push you into it, it really must be your decision, but if it's what you want, don't lag. There are ten more women who'll want your spot, twenty more men. Don't let it get out of your reach because you gave up the fight. You don't want to attend a second-tier school if you can get into a first-. Give me just a minute," she twisted around and riffled through a pile of folders behind her. "Ah, here you are," she said, turning to me again. She opened my folder, scanned the first page. "No, these grades won't get you into the schools you'll want to attend." She pushed the thin glasses she was wearing up on top of her head, as if to see me better. "If you were a lesser student, I'd direct you somewhere else. But your early grades show you have it in you, and you have claimed to want it." As she said this, she studied me. I wondered if she had just fed me a line she wasn't sure I'd digest. "It's your decision, though," she repeated herself. "Yours alone. You need to decide this for yourself." Each repetition felt more pregnant than the last. Perhaps we were both expecting me to respond with the same focus and determination she had directed my way.

I nodded, if only so she'd know I had heard her. "It never really occurred to me that I wouldn't be a doctor," I said.

She was willing to wait me out, but it was taking me a while. "Go on," she said.

I thought of the beauty of the body, the way that it strove toward healing despite the inevitable, the fascination with it I hadn't yet lost. I thought of how I had been frightened, at first, by that *Gray's Anatomy* cover, tracing the red lines with my finger to try to understand them better. I thought of those first explorations of Teddy's body. I thought of Mr. Rosenthal, how he'd shared his love of birds with his son. How his death swept Teddy away beneath the wings of his mother. I thought about how even that rigid doctor at the hospital near Milnah had known that Teddy and I should not be separated. How he had seemed as powerful and strange as a god. And then I thought of my most recent encounter, how touch could consume inhibition. "But somehow, something isn't as I expected it to be," the memory of Teddy trying to listen for my heart in my belly flashed through my mind. "I really can't explain it otherwise, there's just a block coming between my idea of what I wanted to be, who I'd be here, and what it's all like, where I am now." I knew I wasn't making much sense, and that my words were empty, words she'd probably heard a hundred times in that room. But she was listening, patiently.

"Some of our best students are lost here, Naomi," she said quietly. "You'd be surprised by who has sat in that chair. But don't miss out, my dear. You don't want to regret missing out on what you have just now; so many opportunities, right at your fingertips. I can't tell you how many alumnae wish they had just one more semester at the college, or could go back and revisit their best years. And it's they who make this college." She fixed me in her stare. "We're a fine institution, make no mistake about that, but there's something about a Wellesley woman, something that draws a certain kind of girl here when she's young. And meeting other girls like her makes her into a woman by the time she leaves, and then an alumna who sees, in the real world, what rare opportunities she had here, what she can make of what she learned and what she's capable of doing. Did you know that Rose Kennedy used to say that her greatest regret in life was that she didn't attend Wellesley when she could?" I was momentarily shocked by her choice of an example, a page from my past read aloud. But she took my surprise for true astonishment, and I knew there had been no real familiarity. She smiled conspiratorially at me. "Imagine what more she might have done. I'm sure she would have blown those sons of hers out of the water." This last bit she declared almost gleefully, then sobered at once. And what of her daughters, I wanted to ask, but didn't, wondering if there was anything about their lives that might have been different had their mother's ambitions been met.

The dean shook her head to rid us of the stalemate that threatened to introduce its way into the conversation. "Just remember, these opportunities are your inheritance as a modern woman of the world. Don't waste them, Ms. Feinstein." She dropped her gaze, walked back around her desk and scribbled something in my folder. "I'm going to recommend a tutor for you," she said. "Betty Warren, my secretary, will be giving you a call, but here's her number, for your reference. And here's mine, too. My direct line." She slid the paper across the desk to me.

"Thank you," I said. I looked down at it. I thought about the incongruity of healing again, the reverence I felt every time I thought about how inevitable demise was, how we fought against it so courageously, how that fight could bring a joy that perfection couldn't offer. "It takes a lot," I said, "to make a good doctor." I looked up at her. I thought I saw confusion flicker through her face, but she had corrected it before I could know for sure. She was a professional. "I mean, it's not just the schooling, you know?"

"I'm sure that's true," she replied.

And then, for some reason I could never have explained at the time, I stood up and put the paper gently back on her desk.

"Ms. Feinstein," she called as I got to her door. I turned around.

"Good luck," she said. For an instant she looked older and, even more briefly, very tired.

The weather was unexpectedly warm that afternoon, and I took my time walking home. The women I passed were acting friendlier than usual, but there was still that sense that we were all moving quickly toward important destinations. As I walked by Severance Green, a wide stretch of lawn that runs behind the south walls of the academic quad, I saw a tall man walking toward me.

I think if I had seen his face, I might not have recognized him; it was the way he carried his body that brought the shock of recognition. He was still several yards away when I put it all together.

He looked up as he got closer, and must have read the expression on my face. "Professor Weingarten," I said. He stopped in his tracks. My own heart was in my mouth, beating and filling it. "Oh," I said quietly, instinctively turning to walk away.

In a few steps he was next to me, passing me. "Follow me to my office," he said, then walked quickly on, leaving me to follow behind.

I felt sick as I trailed him. The smells of the warm, muddy lake hung heavy in the breeze. As I walked I thought again of that image of Orpheus and Eurydice, though this time it was Eurydice who came to mind, looking longingly at her husband's back, not trusting him to do the right thing.

When we got to his office he shut the door firmly behind me. Then he walked over to his desk and sat down, dropping his head immediately into his hands, deflated. I wanted to feel pity for him, but I didn't. I stared over his shoulder at the window, looking out, wondering why it faced his back.

"Did you know? When I registered for your class?"

He nodded, his face still in his hands.

I began walking around the perimeter of the room, running my hands over the books that lined the walls. I thought again of what my father once said, about how I could know everything. It was hard to imagine that in a few years' time I might be on my way to collecting just as many books, even those whose contents I already knew by heart. They could sit on my shelves, too, like so many tiers of calcified thought.

"It was my first time, you know," I said casually, still looking at the books. He made a small sound, like a moan. He sat back and looked at me. "What I want to know," I continued, "was if I was yours." He looked confused, momentarily. "Your first student," I added.

"Oh God, Naomi." He stood up suddenly. "Yes. Yes, of course. I'm not some kind of"—he stuttered—"predator, for God's sake."

"But you spoke with Phyllis." He looked momentarily lost. "She was handing out the masks." He nodded, just barely. "I spoke with Phyllis," he admitted.

And he had come to the house and put on a mask. Had he known or sensed what he was looking for? Had I? I fingered a slim volume of Mirabai's ecstatic poems. "Are you a religious man, Professor Weingarten?"

"Jules," he said, sitting back down. "At the very least you should feel free to call me Jules." He rubbed the back of his neck, roughly, making me want to grab his hand to stop him. "No. I'm not a religious man. Just mistaken."

"It was a mistake." I nodded, trying the idea on for myself once again.

"No, I didn't mean that. I didn't mean to say that you were any kind of mistake."

"Why wouldn't you?"

He thought for a minute, looking almost calm for the first time since I'd stopped him, "Well, to begin with, because it felt right, like it was supposed to happen."

"Like predestination? Are you sure you're not a religious man, Jules?"

He stared at me but did not speak.

"I think," I said, replacing the next book I'd taken off the shelf—a Harold Bloom, preaching to the choir—"that maybe it was just that you're lonely, too. As lonely as I am."

"You're right," he said simply. He had composed himself somewhat. "Naomi, it did mean something. It meant enough that, at least on that last night, I was willing to lose my job for you. I don't know why. I wish I could explain better. It was just how you wanted me to reach out to you, it felt like who you were didn't matter."

"I would never want you to lose your job for me." I continued to stare at his books, feigning interest in them. "I'm not planning to tell anyone about what happened." All at once I felt tired and deeply disappointed. In myself and him.

"I know that," he said, his admission tinged with impatience. "I said I knew what I was doing. It's not your responsibility to resolve this. On top of everything else, you don't need to hear me beg."

For what? I wondered. More or less of me? For his job? "For your job?"

"I wouldn't beg you for my job, Naomi. No—beg you to be quiet." At this my stomach turned in shame. His reassurances only drew more attention to his own deep anxieties. "Which I wouldn't do anyway," he added hurriedly. "I made my bed. I can lie in it."

"I'd rather you didn't," I said. I wondered why it was so difficult for either one of us to say that we just wanted this all to be over. I took in his odd, homely face and thought of how his body had felt so smooth against mine. I wondered if, when I did become a doctor, the body would ever appear so two-sided again. Or if every body would appear multidimensional, unwilling to be understood at first glance.

He nodded, apparently resigned to some unwanted fate, one that may or may not have involved the admission of our interlude. "I'm leaving soon," he said.

"Back to Yale. Yes, I know."

"No, I'm through with teaching." He grimaced at my look of surprise, trying to morph it into a smile. "You see, I don't like the students that much." I laughed at that. His smile relaxed into something more genuine and sad. "These past few years, it's all turned sour," he shifted and began fidgeting with nothing on his desk. "Students constantly trying to prove me wrong, prove themselves right, instead of just, well, proving something. And they're relentless, too hungry for my taste." He lifted his shoulders up, tensing his neck. "I'm so busy telling others what I know, I feel like I've been emptied of whatever I had of myself in the first place, not that I'm soulless, but sometimes . . ." He had been staring off and suddenly looked into my face. "Maybe I am more religious than I admit," he said, allowing a little delight to make its way across his face. "Naomi . . ."

I didn't want him to continue. "Good luck," I said, walking toward the door. I turned around right before I opened it. "I'll be dropping your class, of course." He nodded. I felt a new wave of shame and lust, seeing his head bent forward over his long body. I walked back and put my hands on his shoulders to kiss his cheek, gently inhaling the savory musk of his warmth, trying to memorize the sensation, wondering how long it would be until I felt something as sweet and immediate. I turned my face away, though, afraid of what it might show.

"Do you know," he said into my hair, "what it was about you?" I didn't answer, not sure I cared to hear what he wanted to say. "Every word," he went on, "every word was perfect. I knew you'd really taken the time to pay attention to what was written on the page, to savor it. Most actors, they're careless, showy. You were so faithful. It just charmed me, so completely." He pulled back, trying to see my face. I wouldn't look up at him. "I couldn't stop thinking about it, and you."

"You came looking for me, didn't you?" He had asked Phyllis about me. He had come to the door knowing what he wanted, or at least not denying it.

I heard his smile in his voice. "Don't sound so shocked."

I looked up. "I'm not," I said, though I was. The sense that I had cheated us both threatened to overwhelm me. "I didn't give my lines that much attention," I said. "I *was* being showy."

He gave me a wry grin. "There's no need to put me off," he said, tucking a piece of my hair behind my ear. "I'm prepared to do that on my own." He paused for a minute before speaking again. "I read once that men are the only ones who ever really fall in love. That women don't. That they only love to be loved."

I pulled back. "You're not in love with me," I said.

"No," he said, dropping his hands, "but that's why I would never dare to try."

"You think I can't fall in love?"

He looked weary again, as he had on that day in class when Jun's argument had become unreasonable. "I don't know you, Naomi. I only wish I did, and that circumstances were different. But I do know that you need to fall before you fall in love. And it doesn't look like you'll be doing that anytime soon, does it?" He laughed, long and low, at my look of skepticism. Then he sat down, resting his head in his hands as he did once before in the hollow between my ribs. His voice was suddenly hoarse. "Please go. Please. I'm afraid I'll ask you to stay." I did as he said. When I was outside again I found myself walking hurriedly, like someone being pursued, but before long I broke into a run, as though trying to catch something just out of sight.

TWENTY-FOUR

Jun finally asked me what happened a few days later. "You'll feel better if you tell me," she said, making us both laugh at what we weren't sure was true. Neither Jun nor I shared confidences easily. But I did tell her, about the dean, and then about Weingarten. "So it seems," she nodded sagely, "that I am not the only one given to sexual indiscretions." She perched the glasses she wore only for reading on the tip of her nose and looked down on me. "Have you anything to say for yourself?"

"Not really," I admitted. "Nothing at all, in fact." I nodded, testing the truth of it. "For once." She laughed, and I did, too, the shame and anxiety I'd been flirting with dissipating, if only momentarily.

It was the week before Thanksgiving break, and the school was beginning the process of slowing down for the long weekend. Josephine Miller, a member who had recently returned from a year abroad in Tel Aviv, had been elected director for the spring production. Julie would take over for Mara as president that semester, and with her at the helm, a staid, formal semester seemed to be on the horizon for the second half of our junior year. Adding to Julie's evenhanded leadership, Josephine made her announcement of the spring play just before we left: the classical and arguably dull play of the Trojan War, *Troilus and Cressida*. The beloved *Macbeth* was about to go up, and as was often the case when an obscure play was proposed to follow a sure hit, grumbling was heard throughout the society.

"Why the hell did she choose that?" Tiney wondered out loud after the meeting that brought her announcement.

"Because it's begging to be staged," Josephine answered sharply, just behind us. "It's a play about war, ladies. Wars aren't supposed to read well on the page." She scoffed, though we hadn't rebutted her. "I can't explain it if you can't imagine it. You'll just have to wait and see."

The idea of going home for Thanksgiving was an awkward one; my mother needed her rest and my father didn't want to leave her, even for a moment. He was frequently exhausted, eagerly enacting the few wishes she imparted, quick to return to her side. And she looked for him if he didn't come. Occasionally, when I visited them, I felt like an intruder. They had developed some secret, private intimacy over the course of the illness, one that made them reluctant to speak with me about anything that might be of the smallest importance until checking with the other. My father still doted on me when I was home, but I could tell he never stopped thinking of my mother.

Three days before the break, Jun looked up suddenly from her studies and stared at me. "What are your parents doing for Thanksgiving?" she asked. Her face was pale in the light from her desk, which brought out the blue circles under her eyes. She turned it off, stood up, stopped short of shaking herself free of her work. I didn't want to tell her I didn't think I had any. My father had made a halfhearted offer to make dinner, and I'd told him not to go to any trouble.

She threw herself onto my bed. "Come to New York. My uncle's there with my grandmother, but I've just heard from my dad and they'll all be there for the holiday. My whole family." She pounded the quilt with her fists, like a dog asking to play. "Come, Noms, your parents don't want to do Thanksgiving, do they?" I shook my head. "Oh perfect." She began hopping around the room. "You'll come, you'll come, you'll come." I was laughing too hard to stop her. "Don't be an idiot," she finally said, stopping herself in the middle of the room, the beginnings of disappointment threatening to overtake her expression before she stopped herself in that, too, and insisted, "You'll come, right?" I nodded. "And let my dad pay?" I shook my head. She picked up a pillow and whipped it at me. "Yes!" she said, then returned to her desk.

I got my own things out and tried to make sense of my notes for a test the next day. I looked up a minute later because she was grinning again. "Stop being so happy," I told her.

"Yes, Dr. Feinstein," she replied.

Jun's grandmother was very ill at the time, and I soon learned that Jun's uncle was in New York as her medical guardian, though it was unclear to me how long this situation had been in effect. Jun explained that her uncle was her father's younger brother, and I guessed that he had been appointed to his current role by some larger Oko-family dictum. She told me that the apartment in Manhattan was big enough for plenty, though I had a hard time envisioning anything grand or impressive, most likely because of Jun and her extensive wardrobe of jeans and flannel shirts.

As we were packing, though, she pulled a box down from the top of her closet. It had a skirt and sweater set in it. When she took it out we both stared at it a moment. I was the first to start laughing. She punched me in the arm. "My mother will take me shopping again if I don't wear it," she said, fingering the silk. She returned from the bathroom fully dressed in her mother's costume, and I was surprised to see that it suited her as well as her usual attire. I looked at my own jeans and sweater, and began to feel doubtful. "Don't worry," Jun said without looking at me, "she won't care what you're wearing." And I knew even before we'd left the room that it would be the first in a series of weak lies, a hopeless effort at trying to seam together who she was at college with what her parents would want to see. It was attentive and careful work, but it couldn't be woven into anything fine.

We flew from Logan to JFK, though when I commented on the

luxury Jun told me it was a compromise: she had wanted to take a bus and her father had wanted to send a private plane. "Really, it's amazing the things he thinks of to spend money on," she told me. We were standing in the queue to board, the crowd around us all having their hushed, last-minute conversations.

"When I'm seated, I wonder if we'll still fight over it," she added ruminatively. It took me a minute to guess that by "seated" she meant working at her father's company; I wondered if her choice of words was a reflection of how the British or Japanese spoke of business, or an unconscious reflection of how working with her father would be much like having a position of authority that extended beyond the business world, a way to come into inherited responsibilities.

We were picked up in a private car—I guess Jun lost that fight, too, or chose to avoid it. Once the doors closed she immediately dropped her things around her, the way I might have spread out in my bedroom at home.

"Keigo's going to be there," she reminded me when I commented on her slovenliness when clearly the driver had put some effort into keeping the car pristine.

"Don't try to distract me," I said, blushing so hard I had to crack open the window for some air to cool me down.

She laughed generously at me, making a big show of creating an even bigger mess in the car. We chatted, excited, for a while, but then I knew we were near our destination because Jun started to collect her things and get quiet and look out the window more frequently.

We finally stopped when we reached a particularly imposing highrise on the Upper East Side. The driver delivered our bags directly to a doorman, who carried them to the elevators and pressed the button for us. The driver followed us in, speaking to a second doorman at a reception desk who picked up the phone. Jun acknowledged none of this. She was grinning at me as I took it all in, though I think she was also nervous, hopping back and forth to make me laugh and jutting her thumbs through the straps in her backpack.

When the elevator arrived, the driver bent down to pick our bags up, but when the doors slid open, Keigo popped out, hugging first Jun, then, after a moment's hesitation, me, grabbing a bag from the driver, tangling us all up as we arranged ourselves inside. The driver had to reach over from the back corner to press the button.

Jun and Keigo talked busily, interrupting each other. I watched the dial as we ascended, wondering when we would stop. The top floor. I looked at Jun, as if to say I should have guessed, but she was still chatting with her cousin. He'd cut his hair since I'd last seen him, and it made the strong lines of his face stand out even more. He caught me looking at him and smiled. In spite of myself, I blushed again. Would everything have been different if I had gone for Keigo that first weekend, instead of Weingarten on the second? Would I still be navigating that underlying current of shame? Jun was looking at me now, and I forced a smile at both of them. When the elevator doors opened, we walked out onto the marble floor of a massive room with an unobstructed, wall-to-wall view of the Manhattan skyline.

"It's a rental," Jun said, qualifying the splendor; she seemed embarrassed by the impact it had on me. There were two older women at the door as soon as we walked in, chattering in Japanese with each other. Keigo dashed off, presumably to fetch someone. Jun introduced them as her aunties, never giving me their names, but they smiled and bowed and took my hand, more of a holding than a handshake, until a man and a woman appeared on the far side of the living room: Jun's father and mother. We all stopped as they approached, like actors interrupted in a scene. Jun's father led the way, her mother, just as I remembered, following behind him. He frowned, walked toward Jun, then stood before her, silent, appraising. He said something, ruffled her hair, then grinned. Jun threw her arms around him, and her mother broke into a smile too big, I thought, for her exceptionally small face.

There was a great deal of chaotic reunion and introduction from then on; that afternoon I met countless members of the Oko family, never fully clear on who was staying in the enormous penthouse and who was simply visiting, particularly since the door continued to open and close as people I was sure were staying for a while exited and others entered. The table setting alone must have taken hours, mostly done by Jun's aunties and other female relations, with the peripheral support of what I believe was a hired caterer and maid. Just before dinner, Jun's brother and sister arrived.

They had been on a cultural outing, Jun whispered to me, and I understood they had visited the Museum of Natural History and one wing of the Met, according to their father's directions. Jun's older brother, Hiroshi, was amiable and heavyset. It was difficult to tell his age, but he exuded warmth and ease. Jun hadn't mentioned he had Down's syndrome, and in the right light he looked like a placid deity, pleasantly satisfied with the mortals surrounding him.

Her younger sister, Ayame, was delicate and petite like their mother, and hung on every word Jun and Keigo spoke. They alternately teased and taught her, laughter the only constant. Ayame had applied to Wellesley that fall and studied me with a mix of shyness and lack of subtlety that made me think she was very young.

As Jun's guest, I was unable to walk from one spot to another without an affectionate pat on my shoulder or back and a stream of kind Japanese from whomever I passed. Keigo volunteered to be the one to give me the grand tour but Jun waved him off, effectively leaving us to our own devices. Keigo grinned, then took my hand in his, very briefly, before remembering where he was and dropping it. I found myself wishing he hadn't, a crush developing faster than I could stop it.

Jun's grandmother was being treated at the Memorial Sloan-Kettering Cancer Center. Although Jun did not speak to me of the details of her cancer, I was left with the impression that she would not recover from the state in which I saw her. She was a tiny woman, wrapped tightly in a blanket and seated in a wheelchair, her head perpetually leaning back on a cushion secured behind her neck, her eyes covered in large sunglasses placed, I guessed, over her eyes so that, in her immobility, she would not be blinded by the overhead lights. Jun's aunts attended to her at all times, cooing to her and laughing over her, leaning in to her to speak, pulling back to smile, patting her on her arms and legs enthusiastically, joking with one another as they did so. It was the sort of behavior I would have expected to see around a baby worth celebrating. Hiroshi preferred to sit by her, holding her arm in his hand. She responded to no one.

Keigo jabbed me in the shoulder. "Dinner," he said. And then Jun was there, directing me to sit next to her, showing me how to use all the utensils, draping the napkin over my lap with mock solemnity and making sure that I had a fork and spoon, should I need them.

I was glad that I didn't recognize anything on the table. I received constant attention from Keigo, who appointed himself my tutor. Ayame jumped in earnestly when she felt he was explaining something inadequately, or confusing me, her even brow deeply wrinkled, and Keigo only messed up all the more when she did. He was deeply witty, both in English and Japanese, but I missed most of it. I felt like a thief, pretending to listen while I studied the strong lines in his face, his quick smile. I hadn't spoken about Weingarten to anyone but Phyllis and Jun, and as far as I knew, they were the only ones who knew. Still, I felt like I wore my fleeting, first tryst with the wrong man on my face like a banner.

The meal was a kaleidoscope of structural and sensual details, rounded out by the natural, deep colors of raw foods beautifully displayed. At the end of the meal, though, several pies emerged with a flourish. The party clapped and laughed, and I was asked to make the first incision.

"Apple pear . . ." Jun's father's voice broke across the table, bearing a hush in its wake. I looked up, and he nodded at me. A contented, though significant, silence fell as I cut the first piece. I was suddenly nervous, my hand shaking just a little, enough so that I was afraid anyone near me might notice. I lifted the piece to the somber caterer standing beside me, bowing my head just slightly. Mr. Oko finished his sentence, ". . . in honor of our American guest," and smiled at me, echoing my own slight bow. Jun was pleased, too, and I felt flush with the attention.

We all stayed up late that night, and the next day I awoke to a silent apartment. I felt overheated and still tired. I dressed quickly and wandered from the bedroom, wondering how so much silence had fallen after yesterday's chaos. I imagined the entire Oko clan leaving in a line as I slept, chatting in low tones as they hurried out. I sat in the living room for a while with a Japanese magazine, then put it down and walked to the window. The view was even more expansive in the day and the light, and I knew I wouldn't be able to stare for long before having to look away. A headache had dawned and the sun felt hot. I turned around when I heard a small noise behind me.

Mr. Oko bowed his head just slightly in acknowledgment. "Good afternoon," he said, formally.

I returned the greeting.

"Jun-ko said you did not sleep well. She was worried. You should sit," he said, eyeing me closely. "Indeed you do not look well." He was wearing something very much like what my father would wear were he as well groomed: pressed khaki pants in a light color, a white button-down shirt with a blue sweater-vest over it, a pair of thin glasses. He was quite small, in person, though what was far more noticeable was the way his even expression spoke to a profound sense of self-command. "I am glad to see Jun bringing a friend home from Wellesley College," he began. He added, "I am sorry to hear that your mother's health has not been good." Each sentence he spoke was uncrowded by the next.

"Thank you," I said again. I wondered when Jun had told him this. I could recall few, if any, of her calls home from our room, and wondered if she waited until I left the room to speak to her parents. I looked at Mr. Oko, the straight way he stood in a small body. "She's doing much better now," I added, though it felt like a lie.

Mr. Oko nodded. "I am sorry that I must work this Thanksgiving," he attempted to use the word casually, though it sounded awkward in his mouth. "I am sorry that I work so often when our family comes together. Jun-ko must mention this to you."

I shook my head.

He nodded again. "She is a good girl. We are very proud of her." I thought he wanted to say something else, but he shook his head instead. When he spoke again, it nearly surprised me; I was growing accustomed to the silence that had settled. "You have met my son, Hiroshi," he said.

"Yes."

"He is our oldest child," he said. He stopped a moment and took a deep breath and held it, puffing his chest out.

"He is a good boy. When the doctors told us of his condition, my wife and I, we felt we had a great sorrow." He stared into the middle distance. "We had great hopes for a firstborn son. Sometimes hope is too great, becomes a curse.

"When Jun was born"—he hesitated just briefly—"we were so pleased to have such a healthy child, so strong and laughing so hard. Jun-ko has good lungs, right from the beginning. Maybe too good. She actually climbed the roof, one summer, in Okinawa. We were sure she would burn her hands. I had to climb up after her. She was standing there in a cape, well as could be, explaining to me why she thought she could fly. I found myself wanting to believe her." I wondered if Rosemary's father had wanted to believe her. Maybe wanting to believe was an act of love not many daughters received from their fathers, though Jun and I had both received it from ours. Mr. Oko brought his hands into his lap and looked at them there before continuing.

"And then, her mind, in school. She did not only bring home good marks. She burst through the door with them." He smiled as he looked back up, and I did, too. He took another deep breath, as though his speech winded him. "Sometimes the firstborn comes second, we say, my wife and I. Our daughter is a leader," he said, and although there was a hint of force in his voice, I felt he was confidently sealing something he was sure I knew rather than trying to convince me of something I might doubt. "And a leader needs friends. A leader needs a better friend than someone who is not a leader. Jun has always been busy, how do you say, high-strung maybe, though around you, she is quieter, perhaps softer. This is a good thing," he said and nodded. "Good," he said once more, apparently confirming something for himself.

"Do you know what?" he added. "I have never done what you just did, stand by the window to see what is in the view." He laughed, I believe at himself. "My wife has chosen where we will live in Japan, and here it is my brother's wife who chooses. Have men no eyes?" And he laughed again, just as the front door opened, just as I had begun to like him.

Jun was not the first through the door, but she was the first to notice us together, and it stopped her in her tracks like a caught animal, though it was us she wanted to capture, for study, without drawing attention to her curiosity. I smiled, trying to reassure her, but she seemed to be looking through me. By then many other people had filtered into the house.

The gentle sheen of fever took over shortly after that, softening my memory, so that the next thing I remember is staring at Keigo until he waved a hand in front of my face, and then standing outside with Jun, waiting for the car to come, our bags beside us, goodbyes being made. I was now quite comfortable being in the eye of the Oko storm, standing in the midst of them as they went to each other.

I noticed, though, that although Jun was hugging and talking, she seemed to be standing alone as well, as though she had already left. I studied her, so tall. I wondered why she was a leader, why this was the word her father had chosen for her. As if sensing my gaze, Jun turned and looked at me.

It was as if we were alone, when I spoke, because no one would listen but Jun, "Do you have any pictures of yourself when you were young?" I asked her. She looked at me quizzically, and I don't remember her answer. I do remember sitting, or maybe falling, down on the cement steps of the building a few moments later, noticing the quartz in the paving, a small hand on mine matched to a face that blurred when I looked up.

I was sick enough to be delivered to the Wellesley infirmary instead of my dorm when we returned. We had left a day early to try to avoid the forecasted storm, but it meant that we arrived to a cold, empty campus. I lay in bed, disappointed that I hadn't had more time to spend in the warm hub of Jun's family, wondering if I'd get to see Keigo again. It was a bad flu that year, and the newscasters were claiming that nearly half of the Northeast was down with it. I landed in the infirmary a few steps behind a nor'easter, which shut the roads down and stranded my parents at home.

My nurse was primarily lumpy and dressed in a Kelly green jumper. She dressed me in the kind of paper that hospitals barely render into cloth. When I was awake and she was in the room, I kept thinking of how comfortable she looked. On the second afternoon, she flipped on the television in front of my bed. She must have thought I was asleep or too groggy to notice, but instead the lights and sounds came spilling over me like an alarm. A woman in a spiderweb of a bob—twisted within, precisely outlined—told us exactly how much snow had fallen, and two men were interviewed with footage of their cars hemmed in on the Back Bay. Chet Curtis told us that a few rural schools in Maine and Vermont had closed due to flu. Someone had been clever with the images here, or the computers were down, and sketch drawings of ministrations during the 1918 flu were thrown up on the screen and lightly mocked by the news team. Their fake laughter comforted me. We were beyond catastrophe. I closed my eyes.

I opened them a moment later when the nurse emerged from the tiny bathroom with towels draped over her arm. I caught her eye when she came out, and she acted just shy of startled, maybe even offended, when I did. I had meant to ask her to turn off the television but she had actually looked at me, and now we had seen something of each other. She walked over to my bed, huffing down into the chair beside it and looking into my face.

"My nephew had it, too," she said, squinting, as if we were continuing a conversation. She sighed, her breath stale with a long-past cigarette break. "Poor kid looked almost as pathetic as you. I'm guessing you haven't been taking very good care of yourself at school." She frowned, then put a hand to my forehead. "So few of you do." I wondered if, with her hand on my forehead, she could read something of what was in there. "If this doesn't break, I'll sponge you," she said matter-of-factly. "Now rest." And I smiled, maybe even giggled a little.

She did end up having to sponge me. I woke up, thinking she was my mother, and grabbed her wrist. I had wanted to look in her face, to be sure, but she thought I was stopping her. "Shh," she demanded, "hold still."

Fortunately, the flu left almost as suddenly as it had come; I still felt sore and weak for a while, but enormously better, too, and a nice, lighthearted feeling set in, the giddiness we feel just after we've been very sick and everyday experience becomes saturated with the pleasures we usually overlook.

TWENTY-FIVE

I showed up for Josephine's *Troilus and Cressida* auditions instead of diving deeper into my studies when the spring semester began, ignoring the fact that my name wasn't on the list. I don't know what brought me there, other than that I had spent the morning buying more textbooks and filing my work from last semester while noting that spring was insinuating its way across campus, prompting me to open the windows wide, which led me to take a walk that brought me to the front steps of the society.

I scribbled my name on the list as I chatted with Ellie about a vision she was claiming to have had about the costumes. She was getting stranger and more likable the longer I knew her. She was one of those girls who used anachronisms studiously and with pride. She weeded contractions from her sentences so that every statement of being or having been was carefully, almost awkwardly, pronounced by her small lips, halting her conversation just slightly in a charming, offbeat way. Occasionally she tried to work in an "I shall" into her sentences, though she smiled right along with me when I noticed it.

Josephine granted me the role of Cressida, despite my subpar acting, she told me. She had a gift for capitalizing on the weaknesses in her players to enhance her play, and she claimed I was the perfect mix of coldness and vulnerability. Tiney was cast as the solipsistic, hungry Paris; A.J. an insistent Diomedes; Ruth a winning Ajax; and Julie, in her first play since her semester at Oxford, an earnest and arrogant Hector. Most everyone else got to romp around and play stupidly inflated soldiers; I felt left out. But Josephine had been right when she'd defended her choice of play, telling us that it was begging to be staged. All those Trojan warriors fell flat on the page, but as embodied characters they miraculously came to life. Despite this triumph, though, Josephine still didn't like me just as she didn't like the character of Cressida, and she made no effort to hide her distaste. It made for tense rehearsals.

"Your first monologue is a flop," she said frankly after we'd worked on it several times. "It's not a great speech, but it deserves a better performance." She took off her glasses. "You're Jewish, aren't you?" she asked bluntly. I told her I was. It was no secret that she was majoring in theology, had her eye on Harvard Divinity School and a rabbinical ordination shortly after that. I envied and resented her purposefulness. She acted as if she were better than most of us, and sometimes I wondered if she was.

"Your mother's a convert, though, right?" she went on. I confirmed this, also, too surprised at her invasive frankness to ask how she knew all of this. She nodded to herself, a prejudice satisfied. "So you know what it is not fully to belong, yes? To want to belong to something close to you? But to feel like you never will?" I barely had a moment to feel offended. "You just don't seem Jewish." She sighed, her dislike effectively expressed. "But then, you know isolation. Use it. It's the most interesting thing about the role. Otherwise she just comes across as a traitor."

Jun helped me with lines but kept her distance from the society. She attended meetings, but they were the only time she relaxed, oftentimes into that laugh leaking relief. But it was clear that her mind was elsewhere.

The choice role of Helen in *Troilus and Cressida* had fallen to Elena Page, a newcomer who landed the role because she promised Jo she was going to take some pole-dancing lessons to make her cheapness authentic. She also swore to share her newfound knowledge with the company.

Elena proved to be the consummate teacher, earnest and gracious. She taught with her hair pulled into a ponytail and green plastic glasses, making her seem like a child playing at school. Her soundtrack featured Shaggy and Marvin Gaye until Jo claimed that it was underrepresentative of women artists, so she switched to Björk, whose "Birthday" became, colloquially, "Birthday Suit," and could be heard at full blast upon opening the door every Tuesday and Thursday afternoon. A.J. appointed herself as her assistant and sat beside her, relaxed and receptive, taking notes on performances for Elena to refer to later and provide commentary accordingly. They might well have been judging the progress of lanyard weaving at summer camp. They drew many students; it wasn't just A.J.'s seductive ease, it was Elena's rare sweetness. Her clear laugh was easy to hear throughout the house.

Jun didn't join the play again that semester, but we saw more of her whenever Elena was around. Jun attempted to downplay the fact that they had started dating, but I could see from her newly adopted and frequently seen beatific expression that things were going well. I tried to stay out of it, tried to act as if it were the most natural thing in the world that Jun was now openly allowing herself to enjoy such rare happiness.

On stage, Tiney, as Paris, doted on Elena like a Napoleonic caricature: small, smarmy, insistent. Elena took all this in with a good-natured playfulness, and their scene together was as humorous as it was sensual, an effect I found particularly engaging. For all her serious intent, Jo liked a good drama, and Tiney and Elena made a campy, insightful show of what were, if they ever existed, a few weeks of great sex. Elena was under scrutiny for Jun's relative withdrawal from the society, and Tiney made it her job to tell people to leave Elena alone.

She had a way of seeking peripheral ownership of Jun that I can notice now: the way she defended Elena, the way she had always had Jun's *Hamlet* props ready when she needed them, the way she made sure that on one of her increasingly rare visits to the house Jun saw the copy of her photo op with Helena Bonham Carter pasted on the kitchen wall. It had been taken in London that summer, right in front of Wycombe Abbey, Jun's high school.

"Are you stalking me, Wilcox?" Jun laughingly asked. Tiney's grin was tight. "It was their Midsummer Shakespeare Festival, Jun! What tourist wouldn't go? I just ended up there!" Each exclamation came across as less sincere than the one before it. "Was Branagh there, too?" A.J. interrupted. "I hear he's been poking around with her. That it's over with Emma." "No," Tiney insisted, suddenly serious. "True," Jun said. "My sister saw it in the London *Times* last week." "Oh," Tiney said, "that explains it; I let my subscription lapse." Jun and A.J. roared with laughter. "I did!" Tiney insisted. "I'm serious." It seemed she was.

As the weeks went by, Jo became increasingly obsessed and high-strung. She seemed bent on some quarry just ahead but infuriatingly out of reach. She wanted to scour us for our deepest emotions and insecurities, mining them shamelessly for the play. A.J. was the only one not bothered by her, and I tried unsuccessfully to learn from her good-natured affability, though this rendered me even more in awe of it. She laughed at my worries. "I don't think Cressida's so full of turpitude as she says. Don't take her so seriously! Troilus totally just offers her up to the Greeks! She should have dumped his sorry ass. Fucker." She straightened her lapels cockily. "Should have stayed with Diomedes. Stable job. A little possessive, maybe. But, really, the perfect mate."

I laughed. "I'm not sure you'll find many people who'd share your interpretation," I said.

"Look at you!" A.J. exclaimed. "So serious again. Isn't that the beauty of all this? What we get to do here—make Shakespeare all about us?"

I suppose she was right. I believe I loved those plays as much as I did because they wouldn't allow me to stop and think, forced me to act, so that being onstage became like a dream that changes one's life: foggy, the details virtually lost, but the essence dragged into one's consciousness—essential, shocking, quick to spoil. I sometimes wished I had the mind of a true Shakespearean scholar, one that could sit before art and develop a profound appreciation for it, rather than run amok through it, trying to fill myself with whatever glittery thing that caught my attention.

Jo crumbled after the final performance. She stationed herself in one of the two ceremonial chairs arranged along the south wall of the great room. We had various folding tables and chairs as well, but they were cleared aside for cast parties, and only the large chairs stayed, bookending the fireplace. Jo sunk into the one on the far right, the vice president's chair, the one furthest from the front door and nearest the kitchen, so that no one coming in for the party could see her, but everyone who wanted or had taken food would. Her hair was frizzy with lack of care, looking like an oversized, poorly made wig that made for an exaggerated frame of her already overwhelmed expression. As the party went on, and more people came, she became as fixed and neglected as the piece of furniture she kept herself to.

Paradoxically, the play that should have tanked (according to the inside naysayers) had drawn bigger and more exuberant crowds than usual: family, friends, and friends of friends. My father had come to see me, but was out the door before I had the chance to go through the motions of wondering why my mother hadn't come. I couldn't tell if it was me or my mother or the play that had made him look so confused and out of place, but he dismissed my concern with a customary wave of the hand. Our brief, strained exchange made me want to walk out the door after him and back into my old life. But I shook it off, reasoning as I did that he was the one who had led me to where I was, believing that it was not my fault that he didn't know what to make of me now that I was there.

The after party only brought more people, people who'd never thought they'd like anything other than *Hamlet*, but who followed one another into the house to meet the soldiers until there wasn't any room to stand. I ended up making frequent, laborious trips outside to the front or back lawns. At one point I was standing on the grass, talking with Tiney, when Ann, the red-headed senior from Texas who'd played Troilus, reached up and clapped a firefly in her hands, then popped it in her mouth. Her perfect white teeth were showing before any of us had caught our breath.

"Southern fast food," she said, grinning, before breaking into a barking laugh. "Hell," Tiney said. Ann deepened her own smile at Tiney's frown, the white teeth making me think of the taste of the bitter insect in my own mouth. "C'mon, Wilcox," she chastised, "live a little." She stood up and grabbed Tiney by the hand, "Let's go find some fresh meat," she suggested, yanking Tiney back into the house.

Jun was there, though she stuck to the perimeter of the party. I watched her pass once, twice, then three times through the hall with Elena, then saw them sit together, and then didn't see them again. I kept trying to find my way to her, at least to see what she'd thought of the play, but there was too much going on.

She had also brought Keigo, or perhaps he'd come on his own. I tried to play down the pleasure I felt at seeing him. He had brought one of his roommates with him, a shorter boy with dirty-blond curly hair worn long. Keigo introduced him as Arthur, though Arthur immediately corrected him.

"Art"—he stuck his hand out toward me, bending just slightly as he did, effectively raising his hand up higher than it would have been. It was a very quick movement, but there was a graciousness to it that I'd seen in the type of boy who had been raised to respect women. "Do you guys do this all the time?" He didn't wait for an answer, so I just nodded as he continued talking. "This is just so totally cool! You guys are awesome! The whole play was just amazing! What's this?" He'd bounded over to the fireplace, was touching it with one hand.

"The fireplace?" I asked sarcastically.

He shook his head, grinning, "Yeah, I mean, but the stone. This is, like, really old stuff here. You don't get this kind of carving except in England. Was it imported?" I was amazed at how quickly he could create questions for which I had no answers. I tried to guess where Calbe might be. "I can find someone who'll know," I started, but Art was distracted again, eyeing A.J. "Can you introduce me?" he asked, leaning in and gesturing with his head.

"Sure," I said.

"Down, boy," Keigo said, grinning.

A.J. came over at my wave and put a hand on my shoulder. "Beautiful," she said, smiling. "And I am absolutely positive you should have stayed with Diomedes. I was much sexier than Ann."

"Hi," Art said, introducing his hand to her, "I'm Art Segal." He pumped her hand with both of his. "You were amazing."

"Thanks," A.J. said, matching the breadth of his smile.

"Can I have a tour?" Art asked her.

"Sure," A.J. said, her tone gently mocking. "Let's go."

"Wait, wait," Art said, turning back to me. "Umm," he said, stealing a glance at Keigo, "I'd like to give you my card," and he fished something out of his pocket and handed it to me. "You really were wonderful." He looked at Keigo again. "My favorite. We have a reading club of the plays at Harvard," he said, looking at me straight on now. "Will you come?" He opened his eyes wide, the way a child does when asking. I caught my breath, embarrassed for him.

"Maybe," I hesitated, not wanting to promise anything.

"I'd like to see you there," he said, maybe a little sadly.

"Okay." I took the card, warm and dog-eared, and put it in my pocket. A.J. led him away.

Keigo had put on a little weight, and it suited him. "Hi," he said, looking down at me. "You make a lovely traitor." He smiled.

I blushed, trying to stop by looking away. "Thanks," I said adding, "It's good to see you again." A shifting in the crowd pressed him into me, but he didn't move away. I was distracted by how close he was, and it was difficult to find something to say. He took my hand.

His was unexpectedly warm. We stood like that for a long moment, neither one of us saying a thing. I was trying not to analyze why these parties brought out the carnal side of me, wondering also if Jun had any idea what was going on between us. Maybe it was the metaphorical masks we wore on stage, and then the real ones we offered at the door. Maybe it was the spirit of play, or the effect that heavy door closing at the front of the house had on so many of us: a literal barrier between our private worlds and the world outside, the one in which many of us wore blinders and followed a worn path. "Give me a minute?" I asked Keigo, and he nodded. I darted through the room and down the back stairs. There was no one in the dressing room anymore, so I was able to change alone. I threw my costume on a hanger on my way out and ran back up the stairs. The crowd had begun to thin a little.

Ann and Art were now chatting beside Keigo. As I approached them, I heard Art suggest we all take a walk together; I had no idea what had happened to A.J. Outside it was warm but misting. I didn't have a jacket, so Keigo gave me his, instantly making me feel both gleeful and a little disappointed: his self-conscious chivalry a little canned. I held myself within the jacket, enjoying the shroud of dryness. Ann looked back at me, winked, and put an arm around Art.

"Have these boys seen Lake Waban?" she cooed back over her shoulder.

"I've heard of it," Art was saying. He and Ann were of the same size, and from behind they looked more like relatives than strangers.

"I'd like to see it," Keigo said, clearly. He had softened the wit I'd seen at Thanksgiving. Without it he seemed too thoughtful.

We let Art and Ann wander ahead of us as we made our way across the dark green. When we could no longer hear the house but could not yet see the lake, Keigo stopped me with one hand and leaned down to kiss me. I remember thinking it was a funny place to do such a thing, given that we were probably even more visible than we had been, standing as we were in an open field. But it was a nice kiss and I let myself enjoy it. He shivered a little without his jacket and I put my arms around his waist to keep him warm. After a while he pulled back. "They'll be wondering what happened to us," he said, lifting his chin in the direction of Ann and Art. I doubted that, but we set off to find them anyway.

They'd turned on to a curve on the path ahead of us, and we couldn't see them right away. Before long we could hear Ann, though; she was one of those people who actually said *Hah hah hah* when she laughed, and it carried. Just before we caught up to them, Keigo stopped. I turned to face him. "Come visit me next weekend," he said quickly. "Come to Harvard for the day."

"Okay," I said, charmed and made a little giddy by his impulsiveness. Art and Ann appeared a moment later, making their way quickly now toward us. Ann was grinning more broadly than I would have expected, making me wonder if something lecherous had happened during the few minutes they'd been out of sight.

"Do you know," Art said as soon as they were in hearing distance, "that there's a tradition about this lake? If you walk a Wellesley woman around it three times, you're supposed to ask her to marry you!"

"What if you walk more than one woman around it?" Ann blared.

"I don't know! Maybe whoever gets back to the starting point first gets asked?"

"Hah hah hah! Hah hah hah!"

Keigo grinned at Ann, then at me. "Sounds reasonable," he said.

"Really?" Ann said. "I think the whole thing sounds inane," and started to laugh again. I don't know how any of us could have resisted laughing with her. Art was watching her like he would swallow anything she might say whole and delightedly. We made our way back into the house.

Keigo ran ahead to see if he could find Jun, who had called a taxi for him. Art decided he'd try his luck with the buses later. He had his arm around Ann's waist. I didn't want to go back to the dorm. It would either be lonely or Jun would be hoping for some privacy with Elena. I thought I'd wait around to see if Jun would emerge. Half an hour later I was still sitting in the kitchen and had worked my way through two cups of Ruth's punch. I picked up a half-empty cup from the table and swallowed what was inside it, too. I was suddenly tired and couldn't remember when I had last eaten. And then, just as suddenly, I felt that if I didn't get some air I'd be sick. I stood up and walked myself over to the door. Ann caught me coming out and hugged me, kissing me on both cheeks. "So I think I'm going to sleep with Art," she said.

"Cool," I said, when I really wanted to ask her why. But she disappeared before I could and I was left standing alone outside. I would walk home, I finally realized. I could walk home. I heard the door slam behind me and someone grabbed me by the wrist. Tiney.

"Where's Jun?" she demanded. Her makeup was still on, the tan of the base paint making her horribly orange, like a poorly veneered puppet. But it wasn't just her skin; her features were strangely contorted. Was she drunk? Part of me hoped that she was.

"I don't know," I answered.

She dropped my wrist. Her eyes were nearly shut, narrow with disdain. I wanted to look away, could not understand what had made her so angry, or fearful, or something else. Maybe I was going to be sick after all.

"Ann said she was here with Elena," she hissed, under her breath, away from me.

"I don't think she was," I said, then felt suddenly I should be clear. "I don't know where she is, Tiney."

"My name is Amanda," she spat. "Applications for the LSE Summer School are due tomorrow, Monday. We're supposed to proof each others' . . ." She trailed off. "We're supposed to meet at ten in the morning tomorrow." She caught herself on this last statement, made it sound halfway normal, as though she was just worried about getting something done, about some deadline.

She turned to leave. "Tell Jun we're meeting tomorrow at ten," she said, over her shoulder. "Don't forget." She knew I was in no shape to be entrusted with her message. I tried to shake my head but she was intent on impressing her fury on me. "I'm not going to lose my spot at LSE because of her," she told me. "London School of Economics," she pronounced carefully, her enunciation patronizing. There was something about her manner that was sobering me up, and I remember thinking at the time that it must have been the sharpness of hate. Looking back, that's the funny thing. I remember thinking she just hated me. It didn't occur to me that such vitriol could have nothing at all to do with me, that such profound emotion must run far deeper than any single relationship ever could. At the time, though, I remember thinking about saying something else to her, if only because I wanted so badly to defend myself, but she had already turned away.

PART V

TWENTY-SIX

The following Monday I was glad the play was over. We were heading into the end of the semester, and final preparations around campus gave our world an unusual sense of order. I straightened my desk, did my laundry, fussed about our room until it looked cleaner and more together. Jun came in, nodded approvingly, told me she was glad she had a little woman to take care of things around the house, and checked the messages. Keigo had called for me. Jun made a show of gathering what she needed and walking from the room, gesturing theatrically toward the telephone on her way out.

Keigo and I made plans for me to come to Harvard. I was excited and preoccupied, wondering what might happen between us. I managed to push Weingarten from my mind and tell myself that I could start anew, and Keigo was all I could think of for one blissful day, before the phone rang again early the next morning, this time for Jun. It was her father.

"Naomi." She said to the phone after she hung up. "Grandmother Oko died." I told her I was sorry, but she kept speaking. It had been a fatal stroke, she explained. She and Keigo would have to be at the airport the next morning; of all the kin, they were the closest to New York. She observed that Keigo and I would have to make plans later. Her deep calm was unsettling.

She had finished packing before the sun came up, zipped her bag shut, and called a cab. I went out to wait with her. The cab was there quickly, one of the few cars on campus that early on a Tuesday morning. Keigo hopped out, making a fuss about how he would be in touch with me. I nodded, urging him to get going. I watched the cab take off unhurriedly.

Jun and Keigo were gone for only a few days, but it was during that time that most of the irreversible events of that semester transpired: an early round of auditions had been held for the next fall's production of *The Tempest*, to be directed by Ruth; Tiney had attended and I had not; she had been cast as the inconsequential Francisco—she really was never much of an actress, she could never surpass her steely exterior; she had been awarded the coveted Natalie Bolton Faculty Prize in Econometrics and attended a department party given in honor of exceptional students such as herself; and she had taken the time to carefully word an accusation of cheating and intellectual dishonesty against Jun.

Later I realized that the official letter incriminating Jun would have been sent in late April, made its way to the dean's desk that same day and, after an initial review, would have been formally dated April 27, 1995. It was handed to Jun the next afternoon, shortly after she had returned to campus.

I wasn't brought in until my own letter arrived through campus mail the following Monday. I think this explains why although I had breakfast with Jun the day she returned, and although she was bright with the details of everything but the funeral, I saw almost nothing of her for the next few days, only saw her sleeping at night in the bed across the room from mine. I received my letter on May 1st, which is also when Elena Page received hers, and the two of us were to meet with Jun, Tiney, the associate dean, and the dean, in an attempt to avoid trial, before the end of the week.

It's best to put it simply, though I still haven't come to terms with it well enough to think of it that way. There are papers I still have with dates, there are even college records, but it has never ceased to be an understanding I can only enter into slowly. Though in certain terms it was easy enough to follow; Tiney had been more ruthless than most of us could have imagined, and Jun had stood, unwittingly, in her way.

From a strategic standpoint, Tiney was wise to wait until long after midterms to make her accusation, though she claimed this was because she was so shocked to have discovered what she did, and so unwilling, at first, to believe this about someone she considered a friend and confidante. By waiting, she achieved two things: a general fuzziness about the chronology of the events she was claiming to have transpired, and an impression in the dean's mind of her own reluctance to rat her friend out. Both aided to build her hollow credibility, the way a skyscraper goes up at an astonishing speed, both because it is so tall and because it has no core.

The facts, as Tiney told them, were as follows: there had been a midterm examination for sophomores with which she, as TA of Professor Chang's class, had been entrusted. The exam had been given to her for proofreading a week before it was scheduled to be administered. Although she was not supposed to remove it from her office, Tiney claimed to have made the regrettable mistake of bringing it home with her to do the work—her room was far more comfortable, better lit, anyone might understand this—with the intention of returning it in the morning. Unfortunately, as she claimed, while studying together for their own examinations—Tiney had trusted Jun in every way—she had mentioned that they'd have to cut their studying short because she was eager to finish her proofreading work before morning, when she needed to get it back to Professor Chang's office. I laughed when I first heard the details, sure they would seem as ridiculous and staged to everyone else as they did to me.

In a calculated twist of events, Jun's lover happened to be preparing for said examination and, sure enough, the examination was not in Tiney's bag when she looked for it after Jun's departure later that night. Tiney claimed to have developed reluctant suspicions, forced herself to go to the professor and the dean, explained that the exam was missing, that only one other student knew she had removed it to her room, and that Elena Page, a struggling economics student, stood to benefit from Jun's theft. The Chief Justice (a student-held and -elected position) was asked to make a search of Jun's private study carrel at the library—a privilege afforded select juniors and seniors heading toward a thesis—and the exam turned its dutiful face up within a stack of papers, inanimate and undeniable.

I was asked to attend the upcoming meeting as a character witness for Jun. When I received my letter, I opened it in our room, sitting on my bed after I read the request and its accompanying details for hours, waiting for Jun to come back to our room. I watched the afternoon light sweep its slow way out and stood up only once, to turn on the lamp. I studied the ceiling, my hands, the sounds of the dorm. There was nothing to do with that awful time of waiting. I must have shut my eyes just before Jun came in, because I wasn't yet asleep, but the sound of the door opening startled me. I glanced at the clock and saw that it was just past midnight.

Jun froze when she saw the lights were on. She stood with the door half open for a minute, so I had to study her shadow, wondering if she'd back out. I knew she didn't want to talk to me. We both knew Tiney was lying, but the shame of having been targeted, the extra attention around her, had made her retreat into a shade of herself. It was an added cruelty, to force a public argument. I was suddenly embarrassed that I had waited for her as I did.

Neither of us spoke when she decided to walk in and close the door behind her. I made myself wait until she was ready to talk. I was holding my letter, and watched her glance at it before putting her things away.

"It's not all that bad," she said finally, sitting on her bed. Her hair had grown so long by then that she only ever wore it back, exposing her face more than the stylish bangs and cut she'd had for most of the time I'd known her. Her forehead was the most open part of her, wide and smooth.

"How can you say that?" I asked quietly. She frowned, shutting me out, pretending to be occupied with the mundane details of putting her things away and getting ready for bed. I repeated my question, but she wouldn't look at me. It began to dawn on me that she fully intended for it to be her affair, not mine, and it angered me, that she wouldn't ask for help, that she intended to face it alone, to be noble, to sink right in front of me without uttering a word.

"It's a complete lie," I reminded her.

"That's not what matters," she said, finally. She leaned against her desk, avoiding eye contact with me. "There is more than any one given truth at a time, and some are less important than others."

I threw my covers off. "You sound like a fucking ascetic, Jun." I was suddenly so angry that my hand was shaking as I picked up the envelope the letter had come in. I tore it, then tore it again. Jun reached over and put her hand on mine. I understood why she favored silence, but her stoicism was unbearable. The void of feeling was too great, it echoed the truth she spoke of: that there was nothing she could say that would erase what was already done, the stain that was already upon her. She'd have to work with or against it, but it was already there.

She walked to the window, the furthest spot from me in the room. "The exam was where she said it was," she said.

"The college will weigh your denial, Jun. It's why they've called me in, and Elena, too. They've heard of framing before."

Jun turned to me, a broad smile on her face. "The college is not what matters, Naomi." She stood, staring me down with her smile. "My parents will hear of it." Her smile collapsed. "My father will know."

"That you're innocent," I tried to complete the statement I wanted her to make. But she was always the stronger player.

"That I was dating Elena." Only her lips moved. "Even if he knows

I'm innocent, that is what will be most damning for him, and the news will arrive in an underhanded way."

"Your father is a man of the world."

"The private rules of a family are more important than that."

"Are those your family's rules, or your father's?" She just looked at me. "What does Keigo think of this?"

"Do you actually think I would tell him?" Jun asked, her face holding the mild frown of genuine amazement. "Does anyone in this country have a sense of how a family works? Or are you just self-important enough to think that your personal opinions really matter?" She didn't say this to be cruel. The cruelty was in what I didn't want to believe. My parents and I listened overmuch to one another because there was no one else around. Everything Jun said or did seemed to be sculpted by the generations before her. I hated their careful work, and her for folding herself into it so completely. I'm sure she hated me just as much then, too. We were each trying to convince the other that what she held on to was not secure.

"The college seems to think so," I said, indicating the paper she held. "They expect someone to speak in your defense."

She tossed the paper on my bed. She looked me in the eye. "There's nothing left to be said."

It took a few days for the slow descent of whatever it was that blanketed the accusation in confidentiality to create the paralyzing silence that Jun had wanted. The college asked me not to mention anything to anyone. Keigo called a few times, for me, but I couldn't talk to him, Jun's silence clamping my own volition into place as well. I saw nothing of Elena, and Tiney only in passing. The whole situation was so surreal to me that when I did see Tiney, it was like seeing an effigy of someone; her practical existence almost hard to believe. She had a blue scarf that spring and she wore it everywhere. If I caught a dot of blue from away I wondered at what seemed like puppeting, if she was now everywhere near but quick to vanish.

* * *

The meeting between Elena, Jun, Tiney, and me was set for May 5th, a Friday. The campus was still decorated with poles and bright ribbons for the annual May Day celebration, another residual tradition at the college. I always felt baffled by the strips of color that hung from the trees, having only seen pictures of the celebration in a book on old holidays for children before coming to Wellesley. But there were no longer any dancers around the maypole at the college, just a campus picnic and the wide swaths of ribbon carried up into the breeze every now and then, the poles themselves grounded prettily near major entrances on campus. The ice on the lake had melted and a few wild blossoms were emerging in the afternoons and wilting overnight. For the rest of that day and the one after it, Jun continued to avoid me. But I woke her up early that Wednesday morning. I shook her just after the sun came up and she rolled over. I don't think she had been sleeping.

"Let's run," I said. She studied me for a moment, and I thought she might turn from me to go back to sleep. But then she got up, and as I watched her walk silently to the closet, pull on a sweatshirt, then sit to tie her shoes, I could let myself pretend that we had been freed of everything between us, as though being released into a regular, unaffected action that could let us resume where we should have been.

Just as we walked out the door, Jun stopped. She put a hand on my back and one on my arm, stopping me before holding up one finger to ask me to wait. She had forgotten her keys. It was an unmistakable simulation of her father's gestures; I had seen him act out the very same movements at Thanksgiving. Jun had gone ahead of me into the dining room and he had stopped her: one hand on the back, another on the arm, then a finger, signaling for her to wait. It struck me when she mirrored it; and the extent of the shift she had enacted within herself was all at once apparent. She did not only fear her father's reaction; she was inviting him into the situation. I am convinced she wanted him to be there with her.

During the winter we had run only occasionally and had stuck to the indoor track, but that morning we took to the lake. The path was almost dry for the first time in months, and there were long stretches of light dirt. We ran for over an hour, until we were both exhausted. We made our way to the lake's only beach, a small, rocky clearing that always surprised me with its waves. Spring in Massachusetts usually surprised me, arriving so definitively after such a long wait. In a few short months it would be summer, hot and humid, and I would be home, probably for the last time.

When I next looked at Jun there were tears on her face. It startled me to see them, but she didn't react to my surprise. I felt I'd stumbled upon one of the deer that sometimes lost their way onto campus, that if I moved too suddenly she might take off. I felt often that way about Jun, come to think of it, that her friendship was a rare and delicate thing. I wanted to reach out to her, but it would have been a commentary on her tears, and she wouldn't want that. I waited beside her. It was probably only a few minutes until she spoke.

"How is your mother?" she asked.

I began to say something else but she waved me off. "She's better." I lied. I hadn't been home since my father's birthday, in March, which he hadn't wanted to celebrate. "Jun," I said, struggling.

"There's nothing you can do."

"But you've done nothing wrong," I insisted. I felt I were speaking off topic, but I couldn't understand yet why. "Isn't that significant? I mean, your parents will know it's all nonsense. They'll be outraged on your behalf." I felt so naïve, but also so stubbornly sure that her innocence deserved someone's idealism, some assertion of its rights.

"I've done nothing wrong," she repeated.

"So," I said, still trying to win the argument, "you need to say that. I can help you say that. I know you did nothing wrong. They want us both to say just that."

She didn't respond to what I just said. She picked up a handful of stones and began tossing them idly at the shore of the lake. "Did you know that Tiney and I joined the society together?" she asked me after a while. "We were roommates first year, and we joined together."

She smiled. "God, it was a great year. The society was at its best. Incredible actors in the senior class. You should have been there." She turned her smile to me. "We both took to it like fish to water. For a while, Tiney and I really were friends." She paused. "Have you met her parents?" she asked me. I nodded. I had only seen them once, but I remembered.

"I thought they were snobs at first, too aloof to be welcoming. But it's more than that. Her father is a cold man," Jun said. "That's all I can say definitively about him, though his coldness runs deep. It runs through Tiney, too. Toward the end of first year I saw it in her. She wore it, subtly, like an extra skin, but once you saw it, it was hard to ignore."

"What happened?" I asked, afraid she would stop.

She sighed, summoning energy she didn't seem to have. "There was a girl on our hall who was failing, who came to Tiney for help. Tiney would tutor her, but after the girl left, she'd be smirking over her shortcomings. Triumphant. She even laughed outright a few times, maybe she thought we were sharing a good joke." Jun wrapped her arms around herself. "She helped a few other girls that way. Couldn't have been more gracious or careful with them; then they'd leave and she'd cut them down." She looked at me, to be sure I was listening. "She took such pleasure in it.

"Once, a girl had lost something, a journal, and came to all our doors, tearfully, asking if we'd found it. She was kind of a sad sort; it wasn't the first time we'd seen her in tears. But a few days later, Tiney showed up with it, told me she'd found it on a bookshelf in the common room, and was snickering like someone who'd won a prize.

"It was still on her desk the next day. She caught me looking at it, she must have known what was on my mind, and she made a big show out of having forgotten to return it, marched it over to the girl's room straightaway. It was almost like she could read me well enough to know just how uncomfortable I could get before turning away from her, and then she'd do the right thing. I think that bothered me most of all; she knew how others reacted to her, but sympathy never stopped her. Only the fear of losing something herself. I know she feared losing me as her friend, but I started to think that she liked me only because I did so well at school, because I was in some way as untouchable as she was academically, in the same league. You know, keep your friends close, your enemies closer?" Jun sighed. "Tiney wants the Marshall, Naomi."

I told her I didn't understand.

"It's very rare that they give it to more than one Wellesley student in any given year. Tiney and I are both planning to apply for it senior year. She didn't know until this year that I had citizenship and could apply."

Jun looked at me. "She knows who I am, Naomi." She paused as if wondering how much more she needed to explain. "She knows this is not a fight I'd choose."

I was incredulous. "You mean that you won't speak out against her? That you'll let her win?" I heard my nine-year-old voice in the emergency room, studying the plastic heart and marveling at how different it was than I had imagined.

"No," Jun said. "That I'm fighting a bigger battle. Listen"—she turned to face me, the sun throwing half her face in shadow. I remember wanting to turn her so that the whole of her face would be shown, wanting to make her squint in the light. "This isn't something you need to fix," she told me. "It's between Tiney and me. You should never have been involved."

TWENTY-SEVEN

Jun's father arrived on campus that night, her mother in tow.

I came home from afternoon classes to find our door open but blocked, Mr. Oko standing in it, watching Jun move slowly around the room and her mother fuss, packing a small bag. Jun saw me first, and Mr. Oko turned around when she looked up. He bowed slightly, and I used my bow to duck into the room and drop off my things. I meant to dash back out, but I would have had to rush by him, so I just stood in one corner, watching them. Jun's mother was smaller than I remembered her and looked even more birdlike darting around our room than she had flitting through the large Manhattan apartment. I ended up directly across from Mr. Oko, in the farthest corner of the room, though while I was trying my best to be inconspicuous he seemed intent on making a keen impression of the room and everyone in it. Mrs. Oko was the only one speaking, asking Jun hushed, urgent questions, in Japanese, about her belongings. Finally, she zipped the bag, and Mr. Oko stepped forward to pick it up. He looked at Jun and nodded in my direction. "We'll be at the Four Seasons in Boston," Jun said to me before following her mother, now scurrying out the door after her father. When they were out of sight, she turned back quickly. "I'll try to call." She shut the door firmly behind her.

I threw myself down on my bed. The Okos had left a fresh, foreign scent, but the room felt strangely undisturbed, despite the flurry that had been there. It suddenly felt too quiet. I picked up the phone and called home. My father answered.

An hour later, he had driven the twenty minutes to Wellesley and was waiting for me outside the dorm, his headlights casting the only light on the dark circular driveway.

Massachusetts is not well-lit at night. I have thought sometimes it clandestinely resists any complete conversion from its seventeenth-century roots. We passed ghostly, dim Victorians and neatly vacant concrete strip malls, reaching the highway before my father spoke.

"Do you want to tell me what's happening?" A shard of light through the windshield glinted off his glasses. He looked like he'd been getting ready for bed before he picked me up. He had on what he called his reading cardigan, and his face was showing the beginning of a gray shadow where he'd have to shave in the morning. "Are you not doing well at school?" The skin on his face looked slack, almost relaxed.

I looked out the window, watching the trees on the side of the high-way, same after same. "Maybe not as well as we had hoped." Some lovelorn graffiti on the granite above an underpass. I could sense him swallowing the urge to ask more. "I guess, maybe, I won't get to know everything after all."

"Who can know everything?" my father asked, surprised.

I looked back at him, equally surprised.

He took his eyes off the road to look at me. "Oh. That does sound like something I might have said."

"Maybe," I replied. "It's one of my friends," I told him. "Not me."

"Is it Jun?" he asked.

I tried to catch his expression, but he was watching the road again. I nodded, though he couldn't see me. "Yeah," I confirmed.

I didn't know how to explain. What did I have to explain? I felt restricted by Jun's own silence, as if she would sense any word I might say about her.

When it was clear I would say nothing more, my father reached over and cupped my chin in his palm. He had a way of touching my face that made me want to fall into his hand. We were nearly home. The porch lights had been turned on for us. I assumed it was my father who'd turned them on as he left to get me, but my mother was sitting up in the kitchen, wrapped in a ratty brown-and-white velour blanket that had floated around the downstairs of our house for as long as I could remember. It once had the pattern of horses, or lions, but the imperfect creatures were faded now. She led me unsteadily to my room, explaining that it was clean and ready. Perhaps my sudden call had reminded them of a time when I was more in need of them, when my needs were more easily met.

"How long can we expect you to stay?" my mother asked after she'd switched on the small, shaded lamp beside my bed. Her hair had come undone around the sides and I noticed a few streaks of gray at her temples. I told her it would be a few days, thinking I had no idea what would happen until I knew what would happen with Jun, where she would be after the pretrial meeting with the dean. I knew I couldn't be in our dorm room, her absence constantly reminding me of where she was and why.

I brushed my teeth in the small, cold bathroom across the hall from my room and went to bed immediately after. I fell asleep almost at once, then woke up an hour later. The house was quiet, and I suddenly realized that, in a dream, I had seen my mother as well. I wanted to get up and go look at her, but instead I lay in bed, holding on to the illusion until I fell asleep again.

I had class the next morning, a review for an upcoming exam I was not well prepared for, so I hurried out, borrowing my mother's old car and accepting her invitation for lunch. I drove back to campus, wondering how long the dip back in time would last; I was still at home, my mother wasn't so weak, I was always dashing off when my father hoped I would stay a bit longer.

My mother made a soothing if mild fish-and-potato bake for lunch, one of her specialties. She served it with frozen peas, barely cooked, and a tart lemonade from a carton. The kitchen had been rearranged. My mother explained that they were considering further renovations. She had spilled some peas on the counter and was retrieving them, one by one, returning them to the bowl she'd chosen. The kitchen table had been pushed up against one wall, a chair on either end. I pulled out mine so that I could sit beside my mother instead of across from her.

My father was home but had taken his plate into the next room to eat in front of the television my grandmother had set up there for just that purpose and left behind. I realized my mother must have had to buy the fish that morning, not having expected me, but she dismissed my concern over the trouble she must have taken, telling me she was going to use it for their dinner but that it was an easy switch. I wondered how my father would feel about his dinner becoming a leftover; he liked to have his freshest, most complete meal at the end of the day. It occurred to me that this, too, might have changed, that for all I knew they were ordering in every night, eating in front of the television on portable trays. The whole of the house had taken on a hollow, convenient feeling, as if there were a set path within it that my parents stuck to, all of the other rooms growing dusty and shadowed.

My mother and I took our time over our lunch, and she did not ask me to explain why I was there, why I'd come home abruptly in the middle of the week, or what had sent me running. I was grateful for that kind of attention, the way it felt removed from anything else on my mind. The afternoon was clouding over, but my mother rarely turned on the lights during the day, so we sat in the fading sunlight as she made tea and rummaged for a box of cookies. She told me once that one of the few responsibilities she'd had as a girl was to arrange company plates of appetizers or desserts. When she did so, she became almost girlish in her absorption, laying them upon each other like dominoes.

The canned sounds from my grandmother's television drifted in from the hall. I was abruptly absorbed by another memory of an afternoon with my mother. I must have been about seven, and the weather was warm, spring or summer; we were outside together and she was laughing, which made me giddy and I jumped away, challenging her to a race, which made her laugh again. She had her hair down and it blew around her face, and in my memory she looked almost as young as I was. I think most children must have a similar experience of their mothers at this age, when we are young enough to catch her as a girl herself, yet old enough to understand the privilege of what we've glimpsed. I don't think there's been a year in my life when I haven't wondered about my mother at the same age, always looking for signs that I might be the echo of the life just beyond my reach. I wonder if all girls feel this way about their mothers, if we all want nothing more than to internalize them and, in return, are forever frustrated because we cannot, because we are always too young.

She set the plate of cookies in front of us before asking me again how long I expected to stay.

"I have a friend who's in trouble," I said, avoiding her stare.

"So you came home?" she asked.

"She's asked me to stay out of it," I said.

My mother nodded. "I'm glad you're here," she said. "You're looking thin. Have you been sleeping well?"

I told her that I had. There is something awful in being so well in the face of upheaval. She asked what play was on the docket for the next fall; I told her it was *The Tempest*.

"A beautiful play. I like to think of you doing those plays. You seem happier, more like you were when you were very small." She hesitated.

"Before Dad's heart attack, you mean," I filled in. "And Teddy."

"Before all that, yes." She took a deliberate sip of her tea. "Has it been cast yet?"

I told her it had, that I had not auditioned.

"Why is that?" she asked.

I wasn't sure I knew how to answer her. I feared that since my mother had become sick I had been using the stage as a veneer to cover the pain I felt when she'd fallen ill. But it was still there. And with it the tumbling sensation that I was losing ground on who and what I thought I needed to be. I was beginning to feel a desperate pull to walk around in my own life with my eyes uncovered, depending, up until then, on seeing the world by peeking through my fingers. "My schoolwork is slipping," I said. "But that's not why, really." I wanted to be home with her, I suddenly realized. That's what I had wanted all along. I watched her face for signs that she'd just read my mind; the thought had been that clear.

"Mmm." She nodded. "It must take a lot of time from your work." She paused, grappling with some inner conflict over how to talk to me. "You know what I want to know? There are so many sons and fathers in those plays, but where are all the mothers?" It was a good question, but she asked it almost facetiously, almost to prove a point she thought she should make. I felt sure she cared nothing about mothers in plays. She was so without artifice that the question took me by surprise. It could have been that she was, for one of the first times I could remember, attempting to make conversation.

I nodded, catching on. "I guess they're implied," I said, making us both smile.

"Not in *The Tempest*, though, are they? I think one feels the need for a mother in that play. Maybe they wouldn't have all gone rushing out into that storm." She looked distracted. I wondered when she had read it. I wondered if she had read far more than I had ever realized. The veins on her hands as she sipped her tea stood out. "It's strange that you girls would be so excited about plays that have so few mothers," she continued. "It seems like you're so busy looking to lead the sort of lives that men have led, like that's a rare privilege. Sometimes I wonder if you're not locked up in just as tight a frame as we were. Despite all the opportunities you have now." Her mouth had turned down at the edges, pulled by invisible twin weights.

I moved closer to her. "Do you remember, when I was little, how mad you would get at Dad when he'd go off on one of his Rose Kennedy riffs?" She smiled a little. "I don't think I fully understood his obsession, either," I said. "Well, maybe that's not true. But I wasn't always that sure about her." I spoke softly, for fear she might shut me out in an instant. "I remember when you said she'd just about killed her daughter." I took in just enough air to breathe out the next question: "Do you remember?" And then I suddenly felt that I had asked her several other questions, including ones about mothers tiring of the lives of those around them, perhaps even their own.

I knew I'd have to wait a long time for her to respond, and it seemed for a moment that she might not respond at all. So after a while I just began speaking again; I told her about what I found that one day, under the piano, and still had, and she listened, her face fixed in an indecipherable expression. And then, just briefly, she smiled.

"She had an Earhart photograph under there?"

I nodded.

"And you think that proves something?"

My heart caught in my throat. "I do," I said.

"What, exactly?" she asked. Her voice was almost clinical in tone. "When did she have the lobotomy, Naomi? Do you remember?" Her tone was sharp.

"Nineteen forty-three," I answered.

"And the house was restored when?"

"Nineteen sixty-seven," I replied, the stone hitting its mark and sinking into my stomach. "You think she couldn't have put it there?" I said out loud. Then I looked up at my mother, a wave of anger passing through me. "Who did, then? Who else would have taken the trouble to hide it away?"

My mother pressed her lips together. "I'm not sure it matters so much, Naomi." I could see that she was as upset as I was, and I hated that she could fool us both with such thin imitations of herself. She began collecting our dishes.

"It does matter," I said, defensive. "It mattered to her. It mattered to Rosemary."

"How do you know that?"

I tossed my napkin on the table. "I don't. But you don't, either. And who the hell else would have put them there?" The heat rose in my face and suddenly I was a young girl again, feeling sick on a piano bench, playing the game of what my mother might say if she didn't stop speaking for once.

"I don't know," she said. "Maybe her mother did. But you're probably right," she smiled at me too kindly. "Hard to imagine Rose crawling under the piano, isn't it? Harder to imagine than Rosemary herself, no matter how far gone she was." She brought the dishes to the sink and turned the water on, then turned it off a moment later, thinking better of what she had been about to do.

"You know they found Earhart's body, right?" she said after a while. "Long ago, in 1940. The bones of a Caucasian woman of her height, on the Polynesian island where they thought she went down. But people still must insist that she was never found. They don't believe it could have been her."

"You do?" I said.

"Well, as you might say, who else could it be?" She left the sink and sat back down at the table with me. "I guess I believe that when a person becomes heroic, the only thing we don't want to accept from her is her death." She smiled, wryly. "The poor woman has been dead for fifty years and no one will bury her." She began worrying her hands and then her fingers. She was nervous. "I suppose it could have been," she said then, so softly I could barely hear, "Rosemary, as a young child. It was her mother's piano."

"Yes," I said. "It might even have been later. She didn't go away completely. She was just different."

"Naomi. How can you know that?"

"I don't," I said. "I'm just guessing."

"It's a nice guess," my mother admitted after a moment. Her voice when she did was almost inaudible. "You've always had a nice way of seeing things. You learned that from your father." I let her take my hand in hers and work my fingers gently, searching for something with them.

"You know, I used to have a memory like yours," she finally said. "When I was a girl, they called it 'photographic,' though I guess they don't like to use that word anymore. I hated it. I didn't want to remember everything I read or saw. I think that's part of why I left school. Your grandmother couldn't believe 'who she was raising' when she found out I had." She sighed and rubbed her hands over her eyes. "I believe you've hated it, too, Naomi, despite how well it's served you?"

I didn't answer her right away. I took in what she'd told me, wondering if I'd already known. There was suddenly a gentleness between us where a tension had recently been. "I suppose it's been helpful, at times. I wish, sometimes, that there were things I could forget."

"Yes," she whispered. "Of course." For the first time in my life I saw her face break, looking into mine. It was like watching a crack wind down a statue. "Oh, Naomi," she said. "There's so much I've wished you could forget. And I tried to keep the worst things from you, just so you wouldn't have to remember. It was a mistake to think I could do that. Such a mistake." She stood up suddenly. "I have to show you something." She steeled herself, looking at me directly in the eye. "You won't forgive me for it," she said before turning her back to me and walking to the mudroom behind the kitchen. I heard her twisting the dial that locked the safe there.

She came out clutching something close to her chest. "Maybe you're right," she said quietly, trying to compose herself. "Maybe I've kept too much to myself." She put a thin stack of letters down on the table. "But there was so much to protect you from." She gestured to them without saying another word.

The return address on all three was a New Jersey one.

8/10/90

Dear Mrs. Feinstein,
There have been problems with my boy. The doctor say he have
stroke. I do not understand what to do. I know we have not been
friendly, but I have no assistance and I think to write to you. We
will be at the hospital for some time, but I will look for your letter.

Sincerely,
Chava Rosenthal

8/22/90

Dear Mrs. Feinstein,
Thank you for your reply. I do not mean to ask you for anything.
The boy is being sent to mental hospital for good. Thank you for
your time.

Mrs. Avraham Rosenthal

10/1/90

Dear Mrs. Feinstein,
I should not have sent these letters. You are a kind woman.
I am sorry I am not more pleasing. I have returned to live
in Brookline again. The boy is at LEMUEL SHATTUCK
Hospital. He has blood disorder, and strokes. He does not know
me mostly, or anyone else. The doctors say he has brain damage.
My address is:

> *1648 Beacon Street*
> *Apartment 3*
> *Brookline, MA*

Mrs. Chava Rosenthal

"Oh, no, Mom." I put my head down on the table. "Oh, no." I
could find no other words.

I heard the scrape of her chair as she pulled it next to me. I was suddenly sobbing, the shock and grief I thought had dulled suddenly springing from a place I hadn't known was still there. My mother was stroking my hair, tentatively. "I'm so sorry, Naomi. I'm so, so sorry. I thought it was best you didn't know. I thought it wouldn't help to know."

She had made me doubt what I knew was true. I knew then that I had never let go of Teddy. I had only moved forward, dragging him behind me, unseen. Once broken, the heart will always remain able to split along its fault lines.

"Please, Naomi," my mother was saying. "I just couldn't tell you. I couldn't do that to you. And then"—she was stroking my hair, as though I were an animal that might be soothed—"when you came home yesterday, I could see. You had been hurt anyway. And I knew I'd have to tell you. Even if it was so long overdue."

I pulled her arms around me, over me. She leaned in, her body resting on mine. "He was there all along," I said, again and again. She held me. In my mind's eye, I looked back at him, seeing him fade away from me all over again. It was the first time since that night she came to bring me home from the train station that I felt anything like hate for my mother. How could she ever think that keeping so much to herself would be the way to keep me safe. How could I believe that she had wanted to protect me?

TWENTY-EIGHT

I took the letters back to campus with me that afternoon. I didn't know what else to do. The meeting with the dean was the next day. I was just holding everything close, as Mrs. Rosenthal had held her misery, as my mother had held herself.

The moment I got to campus, I retreated to the house. We were planning a particularly expansive production of *Tempest*, and Ruth had already begun the preparation of sets and costumes, despite the fact that most of them would just sit there over the summer. She stationed me at the kitchen table with piles of navy fabric, a sewing needle, and thread. We had no sewing machine, and I knew only one stitch. The work was painstaking and mercifully distracting.

I am sure that at that moment, no students other than Tiney, Jun, Elena, and me knew what had happened. It came as no surprise to me that both Jun and Tiney wouldn't want to speak of it, and Elena was nowhere to be found. But Ruth sat watching me for a few hours as I sewed beads onto the skirt, wrists, and neck of a dense costume. When my neck grew tired, I sat back against Mrs. Rosenthal's letters, tucked into the bag I'd hung on the back of my chair.

Just as we were getting ready to wrap things up, Ruth sat down across from me. When I didn't speak to her, she picked up a swath of fabric and began to work it, settling in to wait me out. After a while, Julie walked in through the back door, the one that led off the kitchen. The rest of the house was empty.

Julie sat down, watching us work. She had come for Ruth, but Ruth was making no move to get ready. I wanted to stand up and get her coat, find her books and bag and hand them to her. She always carried so many things, so that it was a series of movements that took her or left her anywhere. And at that moment she was reclining, ignoring Julie sitting upright, her coat still on, telegraphing her desire to get going.

"Naomi was just about to spill the beans," Ruth announced. She began to recite a record of everything she'd noticed that Jun, and maybe I, had thought would go unnoticed: that Jun hadn't been seen for days; that neither one of us had shown up for auditions; that Elena was sick with a flu in May; that I had stationed myself at the house for the better part of an afternoon to work on costumes when I couldn't sew. Julie nodded, accepting Ruth's case for suspecting that something was up, and looked at me.

I told them. It suddenly became clear to me that it wasn't a secret I was keeping for Jun alone; it was one that Tiney wanted me to keep as well. I became angry at them both for the way they had pinned themselves and me to it, as if we had all agreed that this whole, terrible thing would be done, above all, with discretion. I know now there was more to it than that. But I was more afraid, too, than angry, afraid enough to think if I called for help it might just come. So I told them, as well as I could.

The house, when empty, had a way of creaking and settling so that just when you thought it was most quiet, everything you said would be punctuated by the structure around you. Ruth listened until I was done, but Julie became agitated almost immediately, asking me questions for which I had few answers. A rash of anger grew on her face as she spoke.

"You're the only one who knows, aren't you?" Julie asked me. "And where's Jun?"

When I told her she stood up. Something had clicked in her that made her even angrier.

"Well, it's simple, then," she claimed. "We've got to speak up, get involved. Tiney can be smoked out." Ruth began to shake her head. "What?" Julie snapped, already angry with Ruth for what she would say.

Ruth's posture, in contrast to Julie's, made them both tense; as Julie had grown rigid, Ruth had remained immobile, absorbing what I told them with the same evenness with which she'd been watching me sew.

"Jun didn't want you to tell us, right?" she asked me.

"Yes," I said. "Not you, exactly. No one."

"Doesn't matter," Julie clipped.

"Julie," Ruth said, looking at her. For only a second they exchanged a look, but neither one could stand it for longer. Ruth looked at me when she spoke again. "I think we need to respect Jun's wishes," she said.

"She's going to get kicked out," Julie said. "Tiney knows it and you know it, and I'm sure Naomi does, too."

"Not necessarily," Ruth said. "Think of her parents. She won't be kicked out."

"Every other student at Wellesley has a pedigree, Ruth. The school has plenty of money. I'm not going to watch her hang herself. She's not going to fight it, Ruth. You know Jun."

"That's her choice," Ruth said. "Jun knows what she's doing."

"Naomi saved your life," Julie spat. "The least you could do is show a little backbone, help her out." She started to pace, unable to stay still. Ruth glared at her. I began to feel that I was no longer part of the conversation.

Julie turned to me, her pupils the size of pins. "She doesn't just walk out on the lake because of Grandfather Wiefern," she said. Something shifted in Ruth's expression.

"Julie," she said, but no sound came out.

Julie continued to look at me. When I looked over at Ruth again, she had turned her head away from us. She was sitting near a window, so the reflection of her profile in it looked like a bare sketch; just the most basic, elemental lines of her face.

"Her little sister died when she was four," Julie said quietly and clearly. "She drowned." I saw her swallow, the only qualm I'd seen in her since she'd decided to speak. "Fell through the ice."

I could see from Ruth's face now, the way her skin had turned the palest gray, that she'd been there.

"She won't talk about it," Julie said cruelly. "She'll just stare off."

Ruth was behaving, looking away.

"Julie," I said. "Stop."

"Why?" Julie interrupted me. "It's the truth. I can't just sit on it because she wants me to."

It felt like Julie was trying to drown Ruth, intent on revealing an emotional weight far too great for her cousin to support. I looked away from Julie's stare. "Ruth," I said. She didn't acknowledge me. I felt stuck between the two of them, unable to move. I was convinced that if I stood and interrupted the tension between us, they would have both collapsed, not from the loss of something substantial, but something imperative, some small lynchpin that supported the whole.

I spoke again to Ruth. "You know, when I was young, about nine, my father had a heart attack." She made no move to indicate that she'd heard what I'd said. "I was with him at the time. And I thought, maybe, that there was a way I could have stopped it. That maybe there was a way that I could learn to stop such things." I looked at Ruth's hardened expression, wondering if she could hear me. "But the moment it happened, I think, it was already out of my hands. Even though . . ." I lost my train of thought and Ruth looked up at me. "Well, maybe we just don't get to save other people, especially the ones we think we should." She raised one eyebrow at me, just beginning to consider the intrusion of a doubt.

The front door opened and slammed. It silenced all three of us:

Ruth with her arms at her sides, Julie and me with ours on the table.

Instead of going straight through the hallway to where we were, whoever had come in was walking through the great room. I thought someone must have lost something; I could hear her looking. I think we all hoped she would leave again, not come back through the door from the great room to where we were. Ruth and Julie would not meet each other's eyes; it was an awful moment of waiting to see if what had been started would continue.

And then Mr. Oko was in the kitchen. His face was like stone, finding us there. He was dressed in a suit, and Jun, behind him, was in a dark skirt and sweater. Her expression was a mirror of his.

I stood up quickly and bowed, and Mr. Oko bowed very slightly in return. He took in Julie and Ruth, then walked through the other door of the kitchen. We heard them go up the stairs.

Ruth and Julie both looked at me as though I had an answer. The three of us listened to them walking above us. If they spoke we could not hear it, though we listened for that, too.

When they finished their tour, they walked back down the stairs and paused in the hallway. After a moment they were in the kitchen again. I stood up, making the space between Mr. Oko and me even shorter, though it called for more distance.

"Naomi," Mr. Oko said.

I nodded.

"You will be at this meeting with the Wellesley administrators?" he said. "About Jun?" I nodded again. "I have been banned, as has the rest of the family." His face did something quickly, a centered collapse, then righted itself immediately before he spoke again, "You will represent her, then," he said. "As a friend."

I nodded. There was nothing else to be said. I looked at Jun, behind him, but her face was blank. I wondered how long their tour had lasted, if they'd walked all over the Wellesley campus, her marching behind him in this way, not speaking as they passed the places where she'd been on her own for three years, ending up here.

"Jun has told me she has done nothing wrong," he continued. Again, his face warped, righted itself. He dropped his voice. "Do you believe this to be true?"

I was startled by his question. "Yes," I said. And Ruth or Julie must have made a motion, too, because he took them in, quickly.

He stood there for what seemed a long time, holding us all to our places. The house was as silent as it had ever been. He took in the costumes on the table, the appliances, the low ceilings, the windows with their thin red curtains. Finally, he asked me a question.

"Is this also the house of Amanda Wilcox?"

I nodded.

"The Shakespeare house," he stated. "I do not understand why these plays are so popular in my country. This is English work," he continued, "and does not belong in Japan. They are, as you might say, different beasts." He nodded, as if agreeing with someone about something. "Maybe you do this because you think you will become like Shakespeare?" He tried to laugh a little. "Anything can happen in this country, as I understand it." He paused.

"I am surprised to be here," he said under his breath. Jun flinched. Her father turned to her and spoke to her in Japanese, and then they were gone.

"It's a tour of the school," Julie spoke first. "He's having her walk him through."

"Jun's part of the school, at least," Ruth conceded.

"It's a funeral march," Julie concluded.

I said nothing. Instead I left the kitchen and went to the front door, staring out of it until I could make them out, already far off and down the main road, indistinguishable from one another but connected by the ten feet or so that separated them. I would have known them anywhere, by the simple way that Jun would always walk behind him, by seeing that in the distance they kept between them they carried something vital.

*   *   *

The first May snowstorm in seventy years fell that night. Back at my dorm, I had several brief dreams about Teddy that came together as one chaotic nightmare. Toward morning I woke myself up and tried to think of something else. The storm came in as wind, then cold, then freezing rain, then hail, and, finally, the snow itself, heavy and quiet. By the time the sun rose, the storm had stopped and the entire campus was covered in a glittering, refractive light. The snow melted fairly quickly, but the small buds and leaves on the trees remained encased in ice. The streets were not passable that morning, so the pretrial was postponed until early afternoon.

I was the first to arrive at the dean's office, followed by Jun, then Tiney, and finally Elena. Jun and Tiney were wearing suits under their coats, looking like they might be lawyers for Elena and me. The four of us sat outside on the benches, waiting to be called in. Once she realized Jun wouldn't speak, Tiney began to glance her way. She was staring openly at Jun by the time Dean Silas poked her head out a few minutes later. Seeing that we were all there, she opened the door wider to invite us inside. It made me wonder if she ever fully stepped outside her rooms.

There were separate seats for everyone there: armchairs for each one of us, not unlike the setting of a forum. The office seemed emptier than it had been when I'd visited the dean on my own, and the spaces were filled with natural light. It gave me a sense of relief for the time being, as we took our seats and the dean made civil comments about the weather outside.

Dean Silas was joined by the associate dean of the college, a stocky African-American man named Martin Banks. The only time I'd ever seen him up close before this meeting was during our first week of school, and from then on only at a distance, making his quick, efficient way across campus. They stood for a minute at her desk, going through papers to prepare for the meeting, but then they took their seats and it was clear that the preparation was complete. They both sat, taking us in, each of their expressions a shifting cocktail of strain and disbelief. I studied the dean's expression in particular, waiting to see on what side of the emotional territory it would land. As I waited, she forced a smile and asked us if we had each received a printed copy of the Wellesley College Honor Code and read it.

"You realize, girls," she said, removing her glasses and her smile, "that if these accusations are true, the consequences for the accused are grim." She looked at Tiney, who was nodding. All at once, the solemnity felt like absurdity, and a quick bubble of hilarity rose in my chest. A laugh like a cough broke through as I pictured the most incongruous thing possible: Weingarten in his presidential masks. The dean glared at me. I think she was already predisposed to be rid of someone.

"Given the circumstantial nature of the evidence against you, Miss Oko," she continued, "Dean Banks and I have decided to meet with you girls before determining if this issue will need to be addressed at a formal college trial." She smiled, a reassurance. "This is usually our process in such situations."

Jun was sitting with her hands folded in her lap, not returning any of the dean's expressions. Tiney nodded, smiled, and frowned timidly, but accordingly. On the stage, Jun's integrity had lent her grace; here it looked cold in the face of Tiney's attentive excesses.

"Miss Wilcox," the dean began, checking her papers, "please state the nature of your accusation."

I think this startled Tiney, but she rallied quickly.

"It is my belief," she started, her voice hushed but urgent, "that a final examination under my care was taken from me. Miss Oko"—she would not look at Jun now—"was the only other student who knew of its whereabouts, and I understand that after all other reasonable searches, at my suggestion"—she smiled just slightly, as she might at something clever—"the Chief Justice found the missing examination among Jun's papers."

Dean Banks cleared his throat. We all looked at him. "I am not sure that your own search efforts need to be included in your accusation, Miss Wilcox. Or do they?"

Tiney looked momentarily confused. "No, I guess not," she said.

"I urge you to include in your statements only exactly what you would like to have recorded," he said. He sat with his legs crossed, one hand on each arm of his chair. The posture made him appear at one remove from the discussion. I hadn't expected him to speak.

The dean stopped their exchange. "Miss Oko," she said, looking at Jun, "do you understand the nature of the accusations against you?"

Jun said that she did.

"And you have named Miss Feinstein as a character witness should this go to trial," she continued, taking me in the first time. "Miss Page"—she looked at Elena—"you may be excused. Professor Chang has had the time to correct your examination and has determined that there is little chance you saw, or used, the copy beforehand." She smiled weakly, if generously, at Elena, who took a moment to comprehend what was being said to her, then dashed from the room like a startled rabbit. Her boots left two heavy, wet stains in front of her chair.

Tiney sneezed, and a thin trickle of blood made its way down her nose. This surprised us all, and the dean stood to find a box of tissues, which were located in the far corner of a credenza behind Dean Banks's chair. While Tiney held the reddening tissue to her nose, Dean Silas began again.

"Miss Feinstein," she said, "I don't suppose you can recall where you and Miss Oko were on the night of March 9th?"

Tiney looked at me directly for the first time. I told Dean Silas that I could recall March 9th, and realized as I did that it had been a weekday night and that I could remember nothing remarkable about it. We were all studying at the time. It had been the week before midterms and I hadn't spent much of it with Jun. Most of us had been holed up in one place or another with our private plans and anxieties. My memory had nothing exceptional to offer. I indicated as much to the dean.

She nodded. "Miss Oko has stated that she had no witness to her actions that evening." I felt I had passed some test of honesty for admitting I knew nothing. I almost wish I'd had the right fiction to offer.

The dean continued to confirm information; I think she was hedging a bit. Finally, she addressed Jun. "Have you prepared any sort of explanation, a defense against the accusation?" She looked almost afraid to hear what Jun would say, somehow vulnerable to Jun's own culpability. I suppose she was, though when a student faltered it was kept quiet. "Is what Miss Wilcox says of you true?"

Jun shook her head. "No," she said simply.

Dean Silas did not wait long to see if Jun would elaborate. She nodded and stood up, turning her back to us, to the scene outside her window. "I understand your father is in town," she said quietly. "Both of your parents."

Jun confirmed that this was true. The dean turned back around and studied her. "You'd be surprised at how many women come here to please their fathers," she said conversationally. "I imagine they might even leave to do the same thing."

Jun's expression did not change. The dean returned, again, to her papers. Her mood shifted.

"Miss Feinstein," she said. "You mean to tell me you have no firm recollection of Jun's whereabouts for"—she looked down at her sheet—"nearly twelve hours, even though you were roommates?"

"Jun and I are friends," I said, my tone suddenly petulant. I was uselessly angry that the statement alone couldn't convey what it meant to me. "We're roommates, but I never felt . . ." I paused, fearing that everything I said might be useless, too. "I never felt I needed to know where she was all the time." I looked at the dean. "I didn't think it was my business to know where she was at all times," I said more firmly. I thought of the late night when I first spoke with her, how it had been the fact of her in the rain in the middle of the night, her open displacement, that had drawn me to her. I realized that we had grown to trust each other not because we had been the greatest of confidantes, but because each of us honored in the other what she couldn't even name herself.

By this time Dean Banks had risen and offered Tiney another tissue, seeing that the first was saturated. All eyes were once again on the gruesome display. "It's nothing," she said from behind her hand. "I've had them since I was a kid. When it gets cold quickly."

"Miss Wilcox"—the dean's tension was shifting from one to another of us, like a ball in a maze—"you and Jun were friends before this incident. Am I right?"

Tiney nodded obediently.

"You were even roommates first year, is that correct?"

Another nod.

"And both members of the Shakespeare Society, as are you, Miss Feinstein," she said, looking up at me before turning back to Tiney. "As is Miss Page. Are you sure no one else had access to the bag with the examination in it besides Miss Oko?"

As she answered in the negative, I began to realize that Tiney must have left her study session with Jun and gone directly to the library, waited until no one was near Jun's carrel to hide the exam there, and then returned to her room so as not to disrupt her own roommate. She would have had to have acted with speed and deliberation. She would have had to be unflinching.

Tiney was providing a dutifully false account of her actions. She held up the new tissue to her nose, muffling her voice. "Believe me, I didn't want to believe that my good friend might have done such a thing, but I had no choice. I've tried to imagine how it could have been anyone else but her, Dean Silas, but I can't. To me, it wasn't just a breach of the honor code, it was a personal attack." Jun had gone pale, but showed no other reaction. I felt the room grow quiet in response to her. The full weight of Tiney's accusation had struck, or maybe it was just the composed way in which she'd delivered it. It wasn't clear and it doesn't matter. But at the time I wanted, desperately, to know who else in the room, behind those silent faces, knew what it was that Tiney was doing. Everything she said was crude and transparent, but no one could object to it. It appeared too much like fact.

I think, to this day, that the dean suspected Tiney right until the end, maybe even knew that what she did was driven by some bottomless jealousy of Jun, one that even Tiney might not have known the depth of. But Tiney's status as an exceptional scholar among exceptional scholars had made her almost untouchable: She was the sort of student who lives at the top of the academic food chain, a place where people float, at so many great institutions, virtually undisturbed.

Jun clenched her teeth, stiffening her jaw. It was hard to see the life in her at all. She looked coolly unsympathetic. I had a sudden need to call out, signal her, let her know how she was being seen, that her face revealed nothing that might save her. I had the irrational urge to reach out; I envisioned myself gripping her shoulder, her face turning toward me, the dawn of realization coming over her, a softening in her eyes.

"She's lying," I said. It took a moment for the dean to realize I'd spoken. "She's lying," I repeated.

No one said a word. After a moment, the dean cleared her throat. "Miss Feinstein," she began.

I didn't wait for her to finish. "It can't be true." I stood up. "Think about it. Where is there a smudge on Jun's record, where is there any indication that she'd need or want to cheat? Why isn't something being said for that? Why isn't who she is defense enough?" I was tumbling forward, trying desperately to find a hold, trying to find something to say that would be enough to bring it all to the great, grinding halt that just wouldn't come. I knew, even before I spoke again, that my words would seem empty. "Miss Wilcox is lying," I began again. And then I caught Jun's eye.

She looked indescribably poised yet absolutely alone. Her expression did not change as she returned my stare. She had asked that I respect her decision and instead, I was standing before her and everyone else, insisting that I could save her. She fixed her gaze on me, its directness as clear as any flood of emotion. She had wanted nothing from me but for me to take my seat. I finally did.

The dean spoke. "Miss Feinstein," she said sadly, "please refrain from any more outbursts. Miss Oko," she continued, "have you anything else to add in your defense?" Jun shook her head.

"I have no proof," she said, "if that's what you want."

The dean sat back in her chair, ready to distance herself from us all. "Apparently none of you has anything at all to support any of this, do you?" she asked, though she did not seem to be expecting an answer.

Tiney's nose had stopped bleeding, and the sun was now pouring into the room. She sat with the tissues hidden in her hand, waiting for some kind of cue. I guessed the meeting had come to an end. It was becoming clear that each of us had exhausted what she had to say. Dean Silas and Dean Banks spoke quietly with one another.

"It looks like this will have to go to trial after all," Dean Silas said when she turned around. Her face began to reorder itself. "You'll all be called, of course. You'll be receiving the appropriate papers in the mail. They'll be certified. You'll have to sign for them," she trailed off, her voice disengaged. Then she stood, giving us a thin, practiced smile. "For the time being, Miss Oko, you will have your library and extracurricular privileges suspended. Should you need materials to study for your final exams, you will have to send a friend with an approved list." She looked at me and nodded. She was more comfortable now, making arrangements, sending us away. "Miss Oko," she added, waiting for Jun to look up, "your past performance at the college is meaningful. Miss Feinstein was right to direct us to it." She waited another beat while Jun stared back at her. "I would suggest you not disregard it, either," she finished. Jun thanked her before picking up her bags to leave. Dean Silas remained immobile. Tiney left just after, looking theatrically somber. I watched them go.

The dean's voice startled me. "Miss Feinstein. Did you ever decide what it is you intend to do?" She forced a smile.

"I'm sorry," I said. "What?"

Her smile broadened. It seemed that once Jun and Tiney left the room their concerns went with them. "When we met earlier this year you were struggling a bit. Do you remember?" she asked kindly. "I notice your grades haven't improved." I looked at her, realizing that my grades were the furthest thing from my mind.

"No," I said slowly, "they haven't, have they?" Then I turned around and walked outside, hoping to catch Jun again before she left.

She was retrieved by a black car that had been waiting outside the building. I think I asked her how she was; I'm sure she answered something, but both of us had our eyes on that car. It was a rich, plasticky-looking thing, and it hummed off down the wet road.

I don't know how long Tiney was behind me before I noticed she was there. She had a cigarette in her fingers, and after a while she lifted it to her mouth, the thin line of smoke extending upward. She was taking me in. There was a small trickle of blood just beginning again on one side of her nose. She caught me looking at it and wiped it away quickly with her sleeve. "You know," she said, dropping her cigarette and putting it out with the toe of her boot, "Jun and I used to be close." She shoved her hands into her pockets and scrunched her neck into her coat, making her pale head look as exposed and foreign as a turtle's. "I trusted her." To my surprise, there were tears beginning to stand out in her eyes, and I wondered how she'd brought them there.

"Why?" I whispered. My words caught in my throat.

She blinked but didn't answer, her eyes open wide, innocently, as though capable of reflecting any expression. "She made me trust her. She made me think we could have a friendship. But we didn't, did we?" She smiled ruefully. "It's every man for himself, isn't it?"

A few days later, I returned to our room to find Jun sitting at her desk, working. My first thought was to wonder if, had I moved back in earlier, I would have summoned her earlier, too, brought her back sooner. I smiled, and she grinned back. There were bags beside her bed. When I opened the closet to hang my jacket, it was empty of her things.

"What about the trial?" I said to the vacant hooks and hangers.

She waited until I turned back around. She was dressed in dark pants and a blouse, her hair pulled back against her neck. She looked older and more refreshed than she had at the pretrial. "I've decided to skip it," she said, as if speaking of a party or some other passing event. She clenched something in her hands, maybe it was a pen, maybe some other inconsequential object. "My parents and I have decided it would be best to bow out gracefully. Tokyo University has agreed to my transfer."

I thought back to the beginning, to where we'd come from. I wanted to know, suddenly, everything about her that I didn't already know. I wanted to tell her what I'd learned about Teddy, and my mother, and to find the words to all the other questions I hadn't yet asked her. I gathered my thoughts, ready to spill, but as I looked at her she began to smile, curiously, as though about to ask something herself. And, I've frozen my memory there, on her welcoming, questioning face.

TWENTY-NINE

Mrs. Rosenthal's apartment was on the third floor of a small apartment building, one of a row of them that lines the part of Beacon Street that runs through Brookline. The street spans several towns, including and ending in Boston.

For some reason the sight of her name printed so matter-of-factly on the mailbox surprised me: Chava Rosenthal. I pressed the black call button, and it was several moments before the buzzer unlocking the door responded.

The elevator up to her apartment was ancient, with two doors: a standard, mechanical inner one and a latticework metal one on the outside. The latter needed to be pulled aside and folded in on itself to get to the other one, and the procedure was clunky and laborious. By the time I was finished with it, Mrs. Rosenthal was standing at her open doorway, waiting for me.

She was already an older woman when I knew her as a girl, and she did not look much different. She still wore a dark skirt and a long shirt, but her gray hair was uncovered, tied low in a loose bun. She lifted her hand to it, self-consciously.

"I am not as observant as I once was," she said.

The apartment itself was sparsely furnished. A threadbare couch and easy chair, a foldable dining table, a television with a standing tray beside it. No paintings or photographs on the wall, only two snapshots on a modest bookcase: one of Teddy, one of her husband. I had to stop myself from walking across the room and picking them up to peer into them.

She stood nervously just by the door. "Please, sit," she said, gesturing toward the couch.

She walked into the galley kitchen and retrieved a small plate with stale, store-bought *rugelach*. They had been filled with apricot preserves, which had congealed from sitting out too long. "I don't cook so much anymore, either," she said, apologizing. Her vagueness touched and disarmed me. How long had she been living here alone?

She sat down across from me. "You are prettier than you were as a child," she said. "I see a little of your father in you now. Not so pale."

The light coming in from her window was hot and hit the couch just where I was sitting. She had no curtain, but there was an ancient venetian blind half dangling from it. I stood up and played with it until it hung straight, then lowered it, cooling the room.

"Thank you," she said. She had lost some of her accent.

Several more moments passed. Neither one of us touched the food. The only sound was the large, mechanical clock ticking on the bookcase, beside the photographs.

She was the one to speak first. "Your mother did not tell you?"

I shook my head.

She nodded. "A mother's job is never easy," she said sympathetically. "Were you angry?" she asked curiously.

I nodded, looking at her. I forgot for a moment that she hadn't carried him. I had been searching her face for traces of his.

"It was so strange, how you children went on," she continued. "I thought you both were crazy, for a while. I often thought to myself, children are not supposed to love each other like that." She shook her head.

She looked like she had nothing left to say. I sat back and folded my hands across my eyes.

"It frightened me," she said quietly. "It was not only because you were who you were. It was because of my son. I never made him laugh. He made so many drawings of you. And birds. None of his parents! None even of his home." I fought the urge to reach out to her, to be comforting. But she was still stern, still forbidding, despite her weakened manner. I still felt she saw me as emblematic of what she didn't trust: a questionably Jewish, female intellectual who had stolen her son's affections. I was clearly not someone she would have chosen in any way. But, at that point I'm not sure that I was striving to be chosen any longer.

"Why did you write to her?" I asked.

She looked momentarily confused. "And not to you?"

"Yes."

"You were a child. Even with your old-woman ways. I'm sure your mother felt the same way. It was probably right that we went away."

"Did you never wonder what I'd think? That I wouldn't forget?"

"No," she said. "I never thought you would forget."

"So you thought it was better that I wondered." I clenched my hands beneath my legs, trying to grip the couch, hunching my shoulders. She was upset, too, her hands white at the edges of her chair.

"I have had to bury both a husband and a son," she said. "A father and a mother. You're not the only one who has suffering."

"He's not dead!" I nearly shouted.

"He is as good as dead," she said, slowly and clearly. The old Chava came out to protect her son as viciously as she once had. I suspect it was better, in her mind, to think of him as gone than to think of him as beyond salvation.

I stood up. "I'm going to see him," I told her. She didn't react. I gathered my things and made for the door.

"Is it true?" she asked me. She was still sitting in her chair. "That you are going to be a doctor?"

"Yes," I said. "I think so."

"Vat kind of doctor vill you be?" Her accent returned with her emotions. "A cardiologist? Someone who makes the new hearts?"

"You've spoken with my mother?"

"A little."

I sighed. "I'm not so sure anymore," I admitted. My hand was growing warm on the doorknob. "It will be a while before the technologies are good, if they ever are."

She sat back in a satisfied way, nodding to herself, dismissing me. "Yes. The technologies. They aren't so good, are they? Not good enough to make a heart, at least. Maybe that's how it should be. Why should men be able to make a heart? This work is not what we are meant to be doing." She nodded again, confirming something. I said goodbye and showed myself out.

I learned from my mother that although Teddy was living at Shattuck permanently, he was frequently transferred to McLean Hospital for evaluation by a neurologist who had taken him on as a sort of pet project. Whereas Shattuck is in Jamaica Plain and has the institutionalized look of most places that care for the chronically ill and poor, McLean is in Belmont, a quiet, well-kept suburb west of Boston. It's made up of a few dozen grand buildings, so that it has the feel of a wealthy community. It was established in 1811, and its grounds were designed by Frederick Law Olmsted, the famed landscape architect who also designed Wellesley. But whereas Wellesley's gothic buildings and orderly greens are stately, McLean's are rambling, taking their time.

When I arrived on the grounds, I was directed to Proctor House, one of the largest and most beautiful buildings on the premises. I was greeted at the front door by a pleasant nurse who looked at my visitor's pass approvingly, as though it were a merit badge.

"Teddy!" she exclaimed when I told her who I was there to see. She winked at me. "What a lovely boy. Let's see"—she checked her watch—"two o'clock. He should be in the great room. He does stick to his schedule, that one."

She led me to a set of double doors. They opened just as we approached them and a tall doctor in a white coat stepped out, closing the doors behind him.

"So you're . . . Ms. Feinstein?" he said, holding out his hand after taking the visitors' sheet from the nurse and checking it.

His name tag read Dr. Wilkinson. "Yes," I said.

"I'm Mr. Rosenthal's doctor," he said, grinning broadly. "You're the first friend to visit him here! He will be delighted. Tell me"—he indicated a pair of armchairs by the window, gesturing for me to take one—"how long have you known Teddy?"

I told him we had grown up together. That we had been neighbors.

"Oh no," he said, as he took the other seat. "You must be Naomi." I nodded.

"He remembers very little, my dear," he told me, leaning forward confidentially. "He came into my care nearly catatonic. We suspect there had been several strokes before his mother realized he needed medical care. He has a genetic blood-clotting disorder; it can manifest itself in this way." He squinted at me, wondering how freely he could speak. "I know, it's hard to hear," he said, reading my face and trying to comfort me. I shook my head. It hadn't been the drugs or alcohol, after all; it was just something endemic to the blood he had inherited. A sudden relief flooded through me. Maybe it hadn't mattered at all, what I remembered for so long.

"I know he was adopted," I said.

He nodded, looking relieved. "He has settled in to Shattuck well. I bring him here because I believe that a change of pace is excellent for the synapses. Also, it's closer to my office." He smiled sheepishly at his own admission.

"I must warn you, young lady," he added, his voice suddenly low, "he will probably not remember you."

"I know," I said, stiffening.

"But I should mention it." He looked over at the reception desk, where the nurse was busying herself with papers. She got the hint and gathered a pile of them before leaving through a door at the back of the room. "He came with the usual clothes and suitcases. But also with drawings. Many drawings. I suspect he was particularly prolific in the months leading up to the strokes. I suspect the increased pressure on the brain led to somewhat of a manic state of creativity. The drawings are beautiful, really. He was quite the junior ornithologist; had a real predilection for yellow birds. Still does, actually! And there are many of you, as well, my dear. His mother explained who you were. You were much younger. His visual memory of you stopped when you were both"—he squinted at me—"I suspect, around twelve or thirteen. We haven't yet made sense of that particular curiosity."

"April 26, 1988," I said. "It was the day they moved away," I explained.

"Right. Right!" He took out a pen from his breast pocket and made a note. "See, you're already helpful! So, are you sure you are prepared to see him, Ms. Feinstein?"

I nodded.

"I am sorry to have to explain still one more thing," he went on, his body not yet releasing me to the double doors, "but you must know that he should not be upset."

I got his meaning. "Of course," I said. "No histrionics. Promise." I crossed my heart.

He grinned, taken by surprise. "Well, good, then." He stood up and went to the doors, opening them like a man introducing an act.

The ceiling inside was nearly thirty feet high, and the length of the room stretched impressively from one end of the long building to the next. In some ways it reminded me of Camp Milnah, with its polished wood floors and board games scattered on various tables beside oversized windows. There was a Ping-Pong table, too, and a television hummed away in one corner. There were fewer than ten residents there, and the majority of them were fixed on an episode of *Wheel of Fortune*. A tall young man, well over six feet, sat like a planted reed at one of the tables near the window. I couldn't see his face from where I stood.

The doctor nodded. "That's him," he said. He looked down at his watch. "I'll be back in twenty minutes."

No one paid any attention as I walked across the room, though I felt my footsteps were so loud they were echoing off the walls. Teddy was toying with a checkers set, placing the reds on the white squares and the blacks on the black squares. When he looked up I sucked all my breath in at once, like a reverse collapse.

I quickly took the seat across from him. He had changed very little, his illness keeping him in a permanent expression of immaturity. His skin was pale and smooth and he needed to shave the little bit of hair that sprouted over his upper lip. His lips were fuller and better-shaped than they had been when he was a boy. His eyes had not changed. Looking at me, they were the foggy, dense color they used to be whenever I had upset him. His hair had been cut quite short, and his fingers were incredibly long and thin. He looked like a junior Abraham Lincoln with a buzz cut, pensive and freakishly tall and thin, his sensual features almost grotesquely pronounced.

"Hello," he said. He looked at me with concern. I reached across the table for his hand, and he took mine. I tried to wipe away the tears with the back of my other wrist.

"Are you hurt?" he asked me, anxious.

I shook my head no.

He relaxed a little at this. "What's your name?" he asked.

"Naomi."

"That's a pretty name. I'm Theodore. Or Teddy. Some people call me Teddy."

I dropped my head into my arms, trying to catch my breath.

After a while he leaned forward. "Are you sure you're okay? You're new here, aren't you?" he whispered conspiratorially. "Sometimes some of us don't always know if we're okay."

I turned my head onto my arm and laughed. I laughed until he did, too.

"We have a buddy program here," he said. "I could be your buddy," he added tentatively.

"Okay," I said, wiping my eyes. "That sounds good."

He reached into his pocket and took out a crumpled piece of paper, smoothing it out on the table in front of us. "I was trying to get this one all morning," he said. "But it kept moving." He shook his head. "It's not very good," he announced, staring down at it.

I reached out and turned it toward me. It was a sparrow, the details so small and fine that even the jagged lines of the individual feathers stood out. "It's lovely," I said. "Just like the bird."

"I need some colored pencils. Or a camera. A camera would be great." He sighed. "There are a lot of bird pictures in my room. I don't know if I drew them all. I think if I did I would've written my name on them and then I'd know. I live at Shattuck, mostly. Dr. W lets me visit here. How about you?"

"I'm between places right now," I said. "I'm not a resident here, though. I've just come to visit you."

His smile was crooked and broad. "Wow," he said. "Neat." Then, suddenly, he raised his finger and pointed at me, "Wait, do I know you?"

I nodded my head just slightly, trying to act casual. I busied myself with wiping my eyes again. "We used to be friends," I said.

"I'm sorry," he said. "I don't remember." He looked crestfallen.

"That's all right," I said quickly, taking his hand again. "We're still friends."

"Cool. You seem nice. And you're really pretty." His grin bordered on lecherous. "Most of the people here are not my friends. That lady in the pink thinks she's my mother. I hate that. And that fat guy says he's Richard the Third. There aren't three Richards!" He laughed out loud, enjoying the joke. "Dr. W is cool. Maybe he could help you."

I looked a little confused.

"You were crying," he pointed out. "He helps people who cry."

I stayed with him until Dr. Wilkinson ushered me out. I came every day for the next month of his stay, then began regular weekly visits at Shattuck. Teddy was limited in his conversations, sticking mostly to birds and drawings and Dr. W, and occasionally, much to our mutual amusement, imitations of other residents. He never asked where his mother or father or anyone else was. He was not able to recall anything beyond a few days before or after the present, and his life held a similarly simple pattern: games, drawings, visits from me or his doctor. Some days he had to ask my name several times, but he was always profusely apologetic. Curiously, his degeneration had done little to affect his charm, and I coasted on his warmth, my concerns shelved when I was with him. Before long our junior year had ended and it was summertime. A strange ease began to work its way into my life, and I began to stretch beneath it, realizing that the space it created made new room to breathe.

THIRTY

Jun was back home and enrolled at Tokyo University by the time Ruth, Julie, Calbe, and the rest of the class of 1995 graduated that June. Their graduation day was breezy and bucolic—it couldn't have been more pleasant if it had been ordered by some all-seeing, even-tempered administrator. Ruth and Julie had stayed close until they left, though I rarely saw them speak, just saw that the tension they held between them had been kept taut. It's sometimes hard to believe that it was Ruth's stunt on the lake that led me to Shakes and all that came after. I would always be in some debt to her, though I haven't seen her since her graduation day.

That summer I put in a request for a single room in Pomeroy, a dorm off the main quad, one of four set on a hill a good distance off from the lake. The room I was eventually assigned was on the back of Pom, facing the rear entrance to the college, so that I could hear traffic on the outside street rushing by, particularly at night and in the rain. It was a private, hopeful sound.

My visits to Teddy continued between a lighter class load and more frequent visits to my parents. Sometimes my father even joined me at Shattuck, though it made him uncomfortable to be there. "So much suffering," he would mutter. "Like Mom?" I asked him once. He nodded, his eyes brimming. I took his hand, wondering if either one of us would ever have the courage to look suffering in the face and not think we might break from it. I told him how I had begun to study neurology and psychology, too, that I wasn't as interested in cardiology as I had once been. He nodded again, still collecting himself. "I know, I know," he said, as if conceding something he'd known for a while. "It's good work you'll do. Too much pain for me, but you are different. I used to wonder if anything made you afraid. You were always charging ahead! A funny girl you were, *ketzi*."

"Yes," I said.

"Did you know you couldn't even count past ten until you were almost five?" I laughed, shaking my head. "It's true! You got to ten usually, but you could never quite make it to twenty. I swear to god you were inventing teens. We thought there was something wrong with you."

"Maybe there was," I said, still laughing.

Tiney was awarded the Marshall scholarship, to much fanfare, and planned to do her graduate work at the London School of Economics. At the opening of our senior year, just before her application was due, she offered up the piece of stage left that was buried in the roof, the relic that Jun had shown me more than two years earlier, to the administration.

A man came with a ladder and knocked at the door, asking for the president, a position I had been elected to two weeks earlier. After Jun left, there was such a void for me at Wellesley that I needed something huge to fill it, something that might come close to honoring what she had sacrificed. He asked me if I knew anything about an object in the roof. I told him I didn't, then stood outside on the lawn, watching him scuttle clumsily over the shingles. He was in a yellow coverall, and he stood out like a flag as he became more confident and began to walk upright. There were two huge pockets on either side of the uniform and two more on the back, a misfit shell he had to negotiate as he walked. I wondered how well it protected him. A crowd was gathering outside. A.J. was at my side.

"Did you know about it?" she asked me. I told her I had.

"It was Amanda." She answered the question I hadn't asked.

I took my eyes off the roof and looked at her. "She told them where it was? Just because?" I wasn't as surprised as I sounded, not for long. I could see only the round of his back; he was prying a shingle loose in the wrong area. I wanted to call to him but didn't. It was easier to watch him hit and miss, lend some time to it, approximating ceremony or some other kind of care.

"You're surprised?" A.J. was saying. "Is it less surprising than giving up Jun?"

Jun had left as quietly as she had wanted to: It was rumored, effectively, that she had started working at her father's company prematurely, that this was her reason for finishing at Tokyo University.

"Elena told you," I realized out loud.

"She got drunk after graduation last spring," A.J. said. We were both still watching the work on the roof.

"Who else did she tell?" I asked.

"Ruth," A.J. said.

"She already knew."

A.J. nodded. "Think of it this way," she added conversationally as the man began to pry around the right area. "It's been there less than seventy years. That's really no time at all. Wellesley itself has only been around for about a hundred. Will himself was born only about four hundred years ago. Pocket change as far as years are concerned." A.J. had switched to a geology major, her fingers now frequently stained with mineral dust. "It was barely there at all."

The man had now displaced several shingles, and small pieces of debris were skidding down the roof, getting caught in its grooves. "I thought all this was important to Tiney, too."

"I think she just found herself here, like she was following some kind of homing device." A.J. shoved her hands under her arms, drawing herself inward. "The allure, you know, of Shakespeare." The sun on the man above us made the yellow of his suit nearly glow. He stepped away from it, on to the other side of the roof. "Sometimes I think he was just another man, though, you know? Not so different from everyone else. But people like Tiney would never see it that way. Her appetites are too big to be constrained by reality. Though, you're right, I've never seen her happier than she's been here. She did love it. Does love it. She probably loved Jun, too."

The man stood up, straightening to his full height, even though he was on a slant. The roof was more comfortable to him now. He held the relic in his hand and made his way over to the sunny part of the roof and held it up there, to be sure he'd found what he was looking for. He shook his head, as though disagreeing with someone, then fished a plastic bag from his pocket and dropped it in. He collected his tools and found his ladder again, and a few moments later he was on the ground.

"Found it," he told me in a friendly way. He pulled out some papers from one of the two enormous back pockets on his uniform. "I'll need you to sign." He'd unfolded and handed them to me. I did as I was told.

We received a very nice letter from the president and the library's head archivist, written in a tone that suggested we were all good friends who'd had the same goal in mind all along, and the relic was stored in the special collections area of the library. I went to see it shortly thereafter. I needed a pass to get on the separate elevator at the back of the building. It was a tiny, rickety thing that shook as it lifted me.

Special Collections was on the third floor, designed like a museum with a wide-open space in the middle of the main room and lines of smooth cases around the edges. The relic was on display beside an original folio edition of *Coriolanus*, which I hadn't known was there, and it looked even plainer than usual in comparison. Without the description etched into plastic beside it, it would have looked comical; a warped rag of wood under thick, tempered glass. I laughed, and the heavy walls and thick carpet absorbed the sound.

A few hours later, I came back to my room to find a message from my father.

The acoustic neuroma that had been found on the left side of my mother's brain two years earlier was thought to have been typically finite, though there were always exceptions. This is what Dr. Stern explained to us, using a silver pointer to direct our attention to what looked like a small black beetle resting in the MRI image of the right half of my mother's brain, then a pin-sized black spot on the left side, as though the film had skipped or been punctured and another picture might reveal something different. He drew our attention to the benefits of a standard, annual follow-up examination, and he gave us a new word to chew on: "neurofibromatosis," or, in my mother's case, NF2, followed by the requisite statistics.

I wanted to know if appropriate questions about my mother's genetic history were asked when the first tumor appeared. I waited until he was done talking to bring that up. He stared at me, his glare equal parts outrage and discomfort. I told him I thought it was terribly important for him not to be mistaken, that he should have patience and an open mind. He bristled, and my father elbowed me in the side. I knew how obnoxious I was being, but I didn't care. He asked me if I'd like to examine her case file, to see if I would have proceeded differently. I knew it would only conceal the essential fragments, that even if asked, my mother would have provided little information on her family's genetic predispositions, most probably because she did not have that information herself, or held it incompletely. My father began to sweat, his hairline growing damp. I declined the doctor's offer. He straightened his shoulders and stood taller when I did. The truth is, he had little reason to doubt himself. I wondered after his own mother, picturing only a diminutive version of Dr. Stern himself. I finally asked the question I'd been working up the courage to ask.

"Do you think there's a connection between NF2 and depression? She's been depressed her whole life." I didn't look at my father. "Wouldn't a growth in the brain affect the mind?"

"The mind?" he scoffed at my misplaced question. "No one knows," he added, dismissing me.

"How could you not know that?" I asked, surprised.

He looked back at me, equally surprised. "Who could know such a thing?" he asked.

Sometimes my stomach turns when I remember that I forgot, again, that my mother was sitting there during that particular moment; I can't understand why, on more than one occasion, I have remembered only my father and the doctor and me speaking, only the picture of the two hemispheres on the light box in front of us. And this realization is worse because I would have had to work to blot her from the scene. Of course she was there. It was her diagnosis, her appointment. We were there only to learn, to become better informed, because it was thought that a family that was better informed would lead to greater support for the patient, which could lead to an optimal outcome: a robust life, for several years or more.

I kept my room at Wellesley but went home on the weekends. My parents did not disallow this arrangement, though they went through the motions of dismay. I completed my coursework dutifully and missed the MCAT deadlines that would have placed me in the most competitive pool because I was needed at home. At first the tumors were small enough that my parents decided to take the course of "watchful waiting," a term they plucked from a brochure. Later, after my mother lost her hearing entirely, we reverted to the initial medical obfuscation: neurofibromatosis. It kept questions, most notably our own, at bay.

The tumor on the right began to grow first, pressing on her auralcranial nerve. As she began to lose the hearing in her right ear as well as her balance, being around her was like being on land, admiring the mysterious grace of someone walking through water: every move slow and careful. She needed to watch my lips to understand what I said to her. Oftentimes, as she did, she would move her mouth, too, as mothers will open their own mouths when they feed their children. I returned her bracelet, fastening it to her wrist to remind her that there were some things she had once believed in.

Once her hearing was completely gone, I began to talk freely to her. At first I would only do this when she was reading or watching television, when her eyes weren't on me, but by the time she got to the point of sleeping most of the day, I would speak as the thoughts occurred to me. I told her first every detail I could recall or imagine about what happened with Jun and Tiney, how I'd been involved. Then I began to read to her, pulling out my favorite books, the very ones I'd memorized, just so I could have the comfort of turning those pages once again. I read to her from Psalms, lingering on the thirty-fourth. I recited the prayer for daughters while she slept. I read to her from Einstein when she was awake, returning to Teddy's favorite passage about gravitations and love. In the middle of this I got the idea that I should read the plays to her, and so I pulled *The Riverside Shakespeare* from within the pile of books I'd brought back from Wellesley.

First I read the ones we'd done, lingering on *The Tempest* and *Richard III*, the senior year productions I hadn't taken a role for, then the ones I'd wished we'd done but hadn't, and finally them all, casting my friends in their old roles and new ones, hearing their peculiar voices as I read. I felt I was reciting something that drew them nearer: Ann was a lion-haired Caliban; A.J. a brilliant Iago; I used Phyllis to change Bianca's petulance to sultriness; Tiney as Ophelia; Jun as the Duke of Kent. Then I told my mother about Ruth and Julie and Mr. Oko, about Weingarten and Keigo, and about the adult Teddy. Then I began to tell her everything I could think of that was real and foreign to me about the Wellesley outside of the house, how that realness and foreignness together kept me there, forever trying to solve them both. And then I told her about everything before then, about being her child, how I sometimes thought I'd already spent my life missing her, how I'd marveled at her beauty and poise and wondered how it could be mine, how I finally understood why she hadn't wanted me to be a part of her sickness, a part of the uglier parts of her life. And, finally, I told her how I'd tried to save Teddy, then Jun, and had always been trying to save her, and that by not allowing herself to be saved she had probably saved me.

And when I ran out of things to tell her about myself, I began to tell her the story of her own life, imagining for both of us the parts I didn't know, until I had spun a great and colorful thing for us to consider together. But this came much later, almost two years after I had graduated, after my mother was too ill to make sense of me, after an easier thing was between us and I began to notice the onset of a curious peacefulness.

For the first two years following Jun's departure we wrote to each other regularly. Her letters arrived on tissue-fine paper in hasty, tall handwriting, so that she frequently filled more than a dozen of the narrow, transparent rectangles. I learned that she had done well at Tokyo University and had begun the young-executive program at Oko Industries almost immediately after graduating. She played practical jokes on her coworkers there until they no longer regarded her with reverence, and she rose quickly in the ranks from that point on. I wrote to her of nothing, and then of my mother's illness, and at times, as I read her responses, I remembered how she had crouched down on the track with me, watching me to understand.

The same fall that my mother received her diagnosis, an article had appeared in the *New York Times* entitled "How to Succeed? Go to Wellesley." It detailed the accomplishments of our alumnae in duly impressed prose for all of its erudite readers to absorb. It was framed discreetly behind the main desk in the Career Center of the college, to the left of an enormous hand-drawn map of the college, and to the far left of an enlarged print of the college seal.

To be fair, the counselor assigned me in the months before graduation was new, though not to the world. I guessed her to be in her late fifties, though she behaved as if she were much older. She began by telling me things I already knew about my chances at medical school, how at best I might be admitted to a respectable institution, but that an elite school was most likely beyond my reach.

"It looks like you've spent quite a bit of time at the Shakespeare house." She shot a strained grin at me. "Perhaps another hospital would have been better?" She folded her hands over the file she had been studying, leaning forward in a friendly way. "You know, you could still do something with this English major of yours. Politicians don't care as much about grades. Have you any activist tendencies?" she asked solemnly.

I shook my head.

She looked at me a moment too long, perhaps hoping I might reconsider, then fought against the corners of her mouth as they began to fall into a grimace. She finally achieved a game smile. "You know, if this country ever elects a woman president, I'd be shocked if she weren't a Wellesley alumna." The tree just outside her window was full of tiny green buds. She looked so peaceful in the frame of the shade, so well contained. She glanced again at my papered history, then shook her large, round head, like a stately ox ridding itself of flies.

She could see I was having fun watching her, and bristled. "Your grades are just not competitive with your peers, I'm afraid. We have even more students than usual applying this year, and with no MCAT scores yet, you'll have to wait another year to apply, and then, of course, you'll be competing with a whole new crop of students for available spots." She brightened, closing the folder almost completely over one hand, "You know, many of our English majors also have great success as academics, in graduate school." She looked down again, leafing through. "Though you'd have to take the GRE. Soon." She grinned almost wolfishly at me. "Would you like to become a scholar of Shakespeare?"

"No," I replied. "Not really." I stood up and walked toward the window, wondering what else I could see outside if I got closer. I opened the glass and leaned out, the scent of warm, fragrant air almost overpowering. "This tree is incredible," I said, leaning out farther and calling back over my shoulder. "What kind of tree did you say it was?"

"I didn't. I don't believe we were discussing trees," she called back to me, standing up now, too. She sounded nervous. Maybe she suspected that the only real explanation for my behavior was that I intended to jump and she would have to try to prevent me.

I pulled my head back in dutifully and closed the window with care. The black sash fitted into its apron seamlessly. It was a pleasure to have closed it so neatly for her. I leaned against it. "I think our time here is done," I said meditatively, closing my eyes. I knew I was laying it on thick and I didn't care. I thought about opening the window again and climbing out onto and down the tree, the white buds falling like snow before me as I descended. I opened one eye and smiled at her. "You've really been quite helpful," I said in my best Wellesley voice.

"Of course, dear," she said. Her waist in its suit rolled around her middle, like a life raft. I thought better about throwing my arms around her to see if my hands would meet on either end and gathered my things instead, bowing just slightly as I left. She caught herself, then bowed quickly in return, like a plump soldier.

I walked by the students waiting outside in the hall wearing suits in muted colors, their stiff résumé folders on their laps, the solemnity of promise in their faces. At one point I had hoped to be among their ranks, and I still could not have said what it was that made me walk down the hallway and back outside, dropping my books and standing alone in the doorway of the building, looking up and marveling at the etched marble in the archway before stepping away from it and making my way onto the grass. I passed under the dean's window and gave her a brief salute of appreciation.

I walked straight through the quad and onto Campus Drive, following it to the back entrance. My shoes were not designed for travel and it was almost ten miles to home. I took them off and began to run in my thin socks, feeling the slick way they made contact with the concrete, realizing they'd tear before too long and stopping only to pull them off and throw them into the woods that lined the college. I ran over the streets first, then through backyards and parks, taking surface streets instead of the highway. The cement was hard and warm from the day, the parks rich with grass, the dirt paths dusty and full of small stones; I wove through them, avoiding the roots and rocks, seeking out the softest footfall, though the farther I ran the more the bottoms of my feet began to tear and my shins began to burn, the pain clear and clean, like beauty. I turned onto our street before nightfall. As I ran toward the house I saw that the porch lights were on, as if they had been expecting me.

THIRTY-ONE

Our graduation took place a few short weeks later. I had grown used to Jun not being there anymore, but the pain of missing her took me by surprise on that day, and I left quickly after the ceremony, using the pouring rain as an excuse. Much fuss was made over how we had come and gone in a downpour, which I didn't mind so much. The college began fading into a pleasant, distant memory almost as soon as I left it.

What is it to say that the years that followed were my happiest, my most difficult? As my mother deteriorated even further, I became her primary caretaker, and was able to manage only brief weekly visits to Shattuck or McLean. My father insisted on driving me, though he had stopped going inside, just waited in his car. Sometimes he took a nap with the windows cracked open. He always seemed refreshed when I emerged.

My life took on a rhythm, and I passed the days easily with little time to wonder, meeting what she asked or needed as completely as I could, then sitting down with my father at night to eat dinner. As the care she required became more complete, it also became easier, more of a matter of habit, and it was a gift to offer it. Though I can't say it wasn't astonishing to watch her beauty and body fail, the tumors protruding like symbols on her neck and spine, so that they seemed to translate her body into something we could not hope to recover.

It became more comfortable for her to lie on her side or stomach, her head turned in profile like an ancient cameo, muted and still. She began to fail in the spring, and I took to letting as much fresh air into her room as possible, thinking at the end that it might infuse her with hope because I imagined this was something she might want, but the room was always a bit windy, shaken. Everything about us had begun to move in small, unpredictable ways. My father shied from the weather I was letting in, and stood at the door when he came to her room, watching. I think from where he stood the protrusions on her body were less apparent, so that the distance allowed him to imagine her again as whole. I think it was remarkable to both of us how smooth she had once been.

When we made it clear that we wanted her to die at home, Dr. Stern continued with his monitoring but came to our house to do so. The day before she died he strode into the room, the wind blowing his coat around him like a cape, and pronounced her comatose. After I closed the door behind him, I went through and closed all the windows and doors in the house, and when I was done, my father came back into the room and sat beside her. I took her other side, and the next afternoon we were listening attentively to her as she passed in a full sail of silence.

Her service and burial were in keeping with Jewish tradition, Grandmother Carol standing tight-lipped beside her grave, as though her daughter had only just begun to disappoint her. During the first day of *shivah*, she came and sat in a red chair in our house, one she'd given my mother as a housewarming gift. It had been made to look like velvet, and had scrollwork on the arms. After several hours had passed of her being uncomplaining but displeased, she asked me about my plans now that my caregiver role had ended. I told her I intended to attend the Graduate School of Biomedical Sciences at

UMass with the goal of conducting medical research in neurofibromatosis and she shook her fine head.

"They used to say that girls went to Wellesley to make a difference in the world. It was your motto or something. Have you done that? Made a difference? Do you intend to?" Her face was open and curious, if not harsh. It was the most direct exchange we had ever had.

"No," I answered. "I don't think I have. Or will."

She nodded, accepting my answer. "Your mother was the same way. Could have had an uncommonly good education, but she had other ideas. Perhaps if you had been a boy you would have done more with your potential," she remarked.

"I have had a good education," I said. "And now that I'm doing what I want with it, it's also uncommon."

"I meant uncommonly *good* Naomi," she scolded. "You could have become a doctor, or even have done more with tennis. You didn't even try to join the team, did you? What a waste," she shook her head again, agreeing with herself. "You're a lovely girl, mind you. You'll probably make someone a fine wife. But you could have made something of yourself." She smiled, suddenly, ruminatively. "I'm not sure if your mother ever told you that I played tennis rather well in my day. Of course it helped that I wore the uniform so well." She looked at me approvingly. "You've kept your figure nicely," she commented. I thanked her. My father sat with his head in his hands. The only other guest we had that afternoon was Dr. Stern, who commended me on my sense of filial duty.

"I spend a great deal of time at nursing homes with parents who have no children to look after them," Dr. Stern intoned, "and I am glad to see a break in the pattern." He must have been less than forty years old.

"A young man"—my father nodded his agreement after he had left and we sat in the darkened living room.

"I'll be back," I told him, standing up and kissing him on his bowed head.

It was a warm day, and I walked slowly to the Kennedy Birthplace, the papers warm in my hand. It hadn't changed: still the neat brick path, the yellow door, the heavy flag above it waving its visitors in with majestic confidence. I wondered if Rosemary would be glad to know her things were returning back to the home where she had been a hopeful child, to the piano her mother had played, in the end, only in her company. It suddenly occurred to me that Rosemary, like me, had tried to hold on to the things she most feared losing, had created her own set of objects to cling to as she felt the intangible slipping. But the only thing that ever really gets irredeemably lost is the self, and it can never be held in the hands. Knowing this, with my mother gone, I felt ready to release my captured familiars. The door was unlocked, as usual, but for some reason it surprised me, as if I had expected to find people still living there.

There was no one in the hall. I took a long moment to enjoy the re-membered smells, the small intimacies of the place. Then I unhooked the velvet rope to my right, walked into the music room, and pulled the piano bench gently aside. The papers fit well under the slats, and I stood up, rubbing my hands at a job well done.

"It's about time." A voice said behind me.

I turned around quickly. A much older woman stood there, but her hair was still black, her skin still a striking contrast to it—Mrs. Olsen.

"I'm only here on Tuesdays," she said, answering my unspoken question. "Just as a volunteer. Impossible to be rid of me, I suppose." She must have been near eighty, stooped over, her keen eyes hooded under their lids.

"Didn't you ever wonder why I gave them away to you?" She gestured into the room. "How they ended up in your backpack?"

I shook my head. "I thought I'd stolen them, to be honest."

"Hah! As if I'd ever let such a thing happen. Mind you, I should have been strict with you. You should have been taught a lesson. But when I found them on the floor—you must have been holding them somehow and then dropped them during your father's incident—is he well, by the way?" I nodded. "Anyway, I found them just before you left and decided they should go with you. I figured such a curiosity belonged with a curious girl." She smiled a little. "Actually, I don't know what I figured. A little mischievous myself, I guess. And I had a feeling you would return them when you were ready." With that she turned and walked away. I didn't get the chance to ask her anything more or speak to her again. But there was something about that house, I concluded, that made people want it to live again, maybe even get a little messy. There had been children there, children who believed they might one day learn to fly. I let myself out.

I looked at my father that night and wanted to tell him what had happened with Mrs. Olsen, and with what I'd found all those years back, but it didn't feel like a story he needed to hear. Maybe one day. Instead of speaking, I just studied him, realizing that he was not yet old, despite what he might have thought. I think that for some time he had actually looked forward to aging, to the ease of entering into the expectation of death in a pleasant, open way. Maybe this was because he had always feared he couldn't be the sort of father and husband he demanded of himself, the one who could sally forth and protect when the wolves appeared at the gate. He pulled his dinner into his mouth piece by piece, like a man pulling weeds from a garden without looking up, and I sent him to bed shortly after.

We had a handful of neighbors visit us the next day, and on the third day, more distant family friends, including the rabbi of the temple my father attended now twice a year, during the High Holidays. My father retreated into a back room with him, and I manned the door alone, welcoming some people I didn't know, a few of whom knew me. Sometime after lunch I opened the door to a Mr. and Mrs. Nathanson and saw, out of the corner of my eye, the shape of someone so familiar that my breath caught in my throat before I could put a name to him. Keigo.

The Nathansons turned at my expression with pleasantry and befuddlement on their faces, and I made the introductions instead of throwing my arms around him. Someone else ran up the steps. Art. "I was parking the car"—he grinned. I wanted to hug him, too.

After I'd shepherded them all in and called my father out, I returned to Keigo and his former roommate, the *Troilus and Cressida* fan, Art. They were standing in the hall as the Nathansons and the rabbi and my father took seats in the living room.

"Can you stay?" I asked them.

Art nodded. I brought them into the kitchen, pulling what I could find onto the table for them until Keigo stopped me with one hand on my arm.

"Jun told us," he said. He looked a little embarrassed, "She figured you would keep it to yourself. She had me subscribe to the *Boston Globe* three months ago, with orders to check obituaries every day. Though she was looking herself, too, whenever she could." I laughed and then sat down at the table and began to cry. I had to put my head in my hands to finish. I lifted it and told him to tell her that I was beginning graduate school nearby. I didn't ask what else she had told him, how else she was making her way. Her letters had slowed and become less detailed as she'd become busier with work, but they'd never lost their warmth. I still missed her, and I told him as much. I told him to tell her that her letters shouldn't be so Japanese and British, that she could tell me about something other than the weather. Keigo nodded somberly.

I admitted I hadn't known he was still in the area, and he said that the MBA program at Columbia was on break, that he had returned to New York in order to set up an Oko Industries base in Manhattan. Art told us both that he had stayed because he could never return to Indiana. "I've been singing at bar mitzvahs to pay the rent," he confessed. Keigo and I laughed, and then Art did, too. The rabbi walked in and, seeing the remnants of the laughter, nodded his approval.

Art stayed long after Keigo left, but returned on his own the next day and the day after that. I stopped looking for Keigo to join him. I found myself sorry on the last day of *shivah* that we had no excuse to see him again anytime soon. But he began visiting my father every Sunday after that, soon confessing to him that he hoped I'd be there, too. Almost a year after my mother had died, I found myself in my parents' kitchen with him, sharing a meal. Or at least I thought we were sharing a meal. I looked up to find him not eating.

"Do you mind," he began, "that I fell for you the night I came to see you in the play with Keigo?" I swallowed. His mouth dropped into a frown.

"The one when you fawned over A.J.?" I asked. "When you were following Ann around like a puppy?"

He smiled and nodded. "Ann. Yes. She spent a lot of time around you."

"But your crush on me didn't keep you from sleeping with her, right?" I eyed him, challenging.

He stood up and put his arms around me. "I didn't sleep with her." He kissed me deeply. "She was my only offer that year, too. And I didn't have a crush on you." He kissed me again. "I really did fall for you. I couldn't even figure out how to talk to you. You might remember I was a little awkward. A little effusive, maybe?"

I laughed, remembering, then kissed him back. When he sat down, I refilled his glass, bringing him a napkin, too. I was dumbfounded by the simplicity of our love, as it became that, and let it wash over me slowly, marveling at the ease of it, too. It had become clear to me how rare a gift ease was, and I was relearning to live around it, hoping that I could one day accept it, too.

A few years out of graduate school, I took the weekend off to attend Dr. Orchuk's retirement party in Connecticut. I was planning to take the train from South Station, and sat at a café until it was time to board. I hadn't been there since I had gone to try to find Teddy years before, and it was changed: more people and more vendors. There were a few others sitting in the café, waiting in between their travels. A woman with slick reddish hair and an angular face caught my attention, and it took me a moment to place her as Phyllis. I got up and went over to her, standing at her table until she looked up.

"Naomi Feinstein." Her smile was as broad as I'd remembered it, though there were sets of wrinkles at her eyes and on either side of her nose, the fine skin there already thinning.

She was still teaching classics, now at a private girls' school. I told her that my husband was a music teacher, someone I had met in college. She asked if I had become a doctor, and I forgot that she knew that had been my intention. I told her I was a medical researcher, that we were seeking a cure for neurofibromatosis. That's an odd thing to do, she said; she'd never heard of the disease. Yes, I said, and we'll probably never find a cure for it, either.

"Well, it's admirable, anyway," she patched. "You're a credit to the school. You should present at the alumnae research conference."

"They ask for significant findings," I told her.

"Right," she said, then asked if Jun and I still kept in touch. I told her that we did, occasionally. She frowned into her coffee. "I heard about what happened," she said. "With Jun and Tiney. Julie and I stayed in touch." She shook her head. "It surprised even me," she said softly, "that she offered up the stage."

"Oh," I said to my own surprise, dismissing her, "I don't think anyone really knew it was there. Now at least it can be missed a little." Phyllis stared at me, her face as quickly and startlingly blank as my mother's had been that last year, as though she'd forgotten who I was. I reached forward and touched the side of her head. It was as smooth as I'd imagined it would be. I told her that I'd always thought she was beautiful. Then I told her goodbye.

I have had some very late nights at work this year, when I'm puzzling over something and feel frustrated by what's so near—feels so tangible, but I can't reach it—and I have to force myself to go home when I simply cannot think any longer. I try to sneak into the kitchen to make tea, but Art usually wakes up and comes in after me, turning off the kettle if it hasn't boiled yet and taking me to bed. "There are more things in heaven and earth, Naomi," he likes to say, "than are dreamt of in neurofibromatosis research." I hate the bad joke so much I laugh, as he knows I will.

On weekends I take long runs along the Charles, letting what comes to mind linger. Sometimes I find myself reliving the oddest of conversations with Jun, or my parents, or Teddy. Two years after my mother died, Art walked me around Lake Waban three times. The first time around I showed him where Ruth had walked on the ice, the second time I showed him where Jun and I had run the day I understood she was leaving. The third time around, we made a new important place together, building on a Wellesley tradition and consummating our engagement, forced to navigate a surprising number of thorns.

Art now visits Teddy with me every other Sunday, sometimes even goes on his own when I'm feeling too discouraged to see how far he's deteriorated. If Teddy's alert, they play Go Fish. He's only remembered my name once or twice in the past ten years, but I think he recognizes me otherwise. Art and I live in a different part of Brookline from where I grew up, a busier part closer to Boston. But it doesn't feel that different at night. I think once you spend a certain amount of time ending your day in a particular corner of the world, it becomes difficult to turn the lights off anywhere else. And my father lives in an apartment nearby, with a few pictures of my mother on the walls. He's hung my Wellesley diploma there, too, and we like to joke that he earned it as much as I did. I once asked if he wanted me to build a little shrine to Rose beneath it, and he told me I was "very funny." His heroic crushes have mostly lapsed in the face of my easing away from blind ambition, and he asks me now about my "noble and impossible problems," seeming to find it agreeable that I have found solace in the unknown. I hope that some of my solace has drifted his way, and sometimes, when he laughs at the worst of Art's jokes, I think it has.

I also removed my mother's urn from his mantel, explaining that it was morbid, and placed it in the cedar box I dug up with my father before he moved, now polished and beautiful again, though it still smells like fermented medicines. The other things Teddy and I once hid are in there, too, as is my mother's scarf. I wear her bracelet, though. Sometimes, even, in the lab.

I have often thought of how angry she was with me that night I insisted it was my right to know her better, how her face had shown as much fear as fury. I have wondered why it took me so long to see how frightened she was, how we all lived so full of fear, and why I needed to see that to release both her and myself. Maybe her fear was too close for recognition, too deeply ingrained. Or maybe I felt I would betray both of us by separating from it enough to allow it out into the open. I think those ties must begin at birth, when each of us is born into the same shared tragedy, the preternatural knowledge that we are, from then on, at one irretrievable remove even from those dearest to us. The first touch so many of us feel is the doctor's, pulling us from our mother into ourselves. And so we cry, grieving. And so we breathe.

ACKNOWLEDGMENTS

This book would never have come to be without the support and talent of countless individuals.

Thanks to everyone at Harper, especially my brilliant editor and friend, the extremely talented and wonderful Maya Ziv, whose passion and vision for Naomi sustained me through the considerable challenges of publishing a debut novel. Thanks also to Jonathan Burnham and Kathy Schneider for their early support, endless patience, and gracious attentions. Thanks to Ed Cohen for his meticulous and fearless copyediting; John Jusino for his eagle editorial eye and patience; Nicole Judge for her inspired marketing direction; Mark Ferguson for his patient guidance through the virtual unknown; Tina Andreadis and Katherine Beitner for their wonderful publicity work; Fritz Metsch for his beautiful pages; and Archie Ferguson for his gorgeous cover design.

Thanks to my extraordinary agent, Lisa Grubka, whose integrity and wisdom have guided me steadily through the glories and pitfalls of publishing, as well as everything in between. Thanks also to Stéphanie Abou, who believed in this novel's legs abroad and would have made a great college roommate. Thanks, too, to Michelle Wiener at CAA for her early visions of Naomi in film.

Many thanks to the countless friends and family members who served as early readers and critics of the novel, as well as essential sources of inspiration and support. Special thanks to my father, who not only answered every last medical question I had while I was writing this novel, but taught me how to listen for what people don't say; my mother, who taught me the importance of courage in writing and is never shy with criticism or praise; my sister Shayna for insisting on my best work; my sister Rachel for listening to far more bellyaching than any good friend should; and my brother, Gabriel, who refused to read quickly. Thanks also to Judy Percer for her willing and able surrogate parenting, Elizabeth Percer for the loan of her name, and Tom Percer for having such great taste in women.

I am also deeply indebted to Aurora Serna and Diane and Dick Sands, who didn't just watch my children while I wrote, but loved them, too; Dawn Wells Nadeau for teaching me about the depths of friendship; Malena Watrous for her caustic humor and keen literary insights; Susan Terris for mentoring me in many ways and going to bat to help me learn about "Fundies"; Jacqueline Higgins-Woo for being one of my earliest, bravest readers; Shana Kelly for believing in me from the first; Curtis Sittenfeld for leading me to Shana and so many others; Jim Roberts for his beautiful photos and thorough description of the Kennedy National Historic Site; all the past, current, and future members of the "real" Shakespeare Society, for being the best players I've ever known; and to Wellesley College, for inspiring women to make a difference in the world.

Finally, thanks to my husband and three children, who showed me how to love life more than art.

ABOUT THE AUTHOR

ELIZABETH PERCER is a three-time nominee for the Pushcart Prize and has twice been honored by the Dorothy Sargent Rosenberg Foundation. She received a BA in English from Wellesley and a PhD in arts education from Stanford University, and completed a postdoctoral fellowship for the National Writing Project at UC Berkeley. She lives in California with her family. This is her first novel.

About the author

About the book

Insights,
Interviews
& More . . .

Read on

Meet Elizabeth Percer

Originally published on Linus's Blanket, *www.linussblanket.com*

Would you give us a bit of an introduction and let my readers know who you are, how you got started writing, and what kind of books you like to write?

I grew up in Massachusetts and had never been any farther west than Pennsylvania until I bought a one-way ticket to San Francisco a week after my college graduation. I've lived out here ever since, but I think I will always be a Bostonian at heart. I'm the third of four children, have three children of my own, and have uneasy parenting relationships to a cat, a bearded dragon, and a Betta Splendens (aka a Siamese Fighting Fish) and his reclusive companion, The Yellow Snail.

I wish my answer to how I got started writing was more interesting than it is, but the truth is that I've been writing ever since I could write. My writing has taken several important evolutions, though, such as the evolution from writing for praise to writing for the sake of writing well. This particular evolution took place around fifteen years ago, and I think it represents the point at which I transitioned from being an emotional scribbler to a purposeful writer. There was no major external shift to bring in this transition; rather, I think I just took a turn in a relationship toward writing, one that foregrounded constancy instead of a more romantic, impractical ideal.

And to answer the third of three questions masquerading as a single one, I like to write the kind of book I would want to read.

I am often struck by the different ways writers respond to the process of writing a book. Linus's Blanket *refers to my use of reading and other activities as a means of escape and comfort. Can you share with us any routines, food or recipes, or favorite books or rituals that help you through the writing process?*

I think escape and comfort are definitely good tools to have at one's disposal when engaging in any creative activity. It's frightening to go into the unknown terrains of one's mind. To paraphrase Anne Lamott, "my mind is the bad neighborhood I try never to go into alone." I think, though, that the more I write, the less frightening that bad neighborhood feels, and there's a certain amount of comfort that I gain from knowing I've gone into it again and again and know how to emerge from it (relatively) unscathed.

That said, I love to work around the ritual of tea. There's something to the process of making tea that soothes and relaxes me. Actually, I think I find anything that requires a steady rhythm to be a great companion to the practice of writing. I'm fond of comparing a sustainable writing practice to a seasoned athlete's practice: it's hard to show up every day and face one's ▶

Meet Elizabeth Percer *(continued)*

weaknesses in the name of getting stronger, but the more you do it, the easier it becomes.

I also love to run and walk and listen to the Bach cello suites before and/or after writing, but never while writing (though I do have a challenging tendency to come up with solutions to problems in my work while running).

What was the most interesting thing you found out while researching this book that you ultimately decided not to include?

I began writing the character of Naomi's mother based on the little I gleaned from my own mother about my maternal grandmother, who died before I was born. In early drafts of the novel, I named Naomi's mother Hannah, after this grandmother. Somewhere along the way, though, I tried to fictionalize her further by naming her Theresa instead. After making this choice, I began diving into my mother's family tree to try to learn more about her ancestors, and came across my grandmother's birth certificate: her full name was Hannah Theresa Hayes. I love those weird coincidences, and use them as a sign when I'm writing a book that I'm on the right path. There's no space in the novel to delineate them, but they inform it all the same.

In the past I have visited a blog called Daily Routines, which is all about the

schedules of writers and creative people. What does a typical day look like for you, and how do you manage a busy schedule?

Honestly? By the seat of my pants. I definitely get into rhythms, and it's glorious when I do, but the truth of creative work, I think, is that it always surprises you. So I'll create a structured routine for a while, but it usually demands restructuring after a month or two. This used to make me crazy and distrustful of my own ability to forge a regular practice, but I've learned to recognize it as the peculiar nature of my regular practice. This works well for me, as the mother of three children who are growing and shifting with head-snapping speed. I think the peace I've made with writing—and perhaps mothering—is that it does demand your constancy, but you must be ready to stay with it even when it switches paths on you entirely. This is what draws me to it, too, the sense that my work will never stale if I only allow it free rein with its growing pains and spurts. Again, the idea of a solid relationship to one's writing comes to mind: all good, long-term relationships require compromise and have periods of fallowness as well as fertility. I think that learning to accept these fluctuations is critical to how I navigate my own short-lived routines.

By the same token, I work quite hard to maintain a constant connection to my creative self, so if the writing is not ▶

Meet Elizabeth Percer *(continued)*

flowing or if the flow of life is interfering with the writing, I will be sure to at least check in regularly with the more nebulous, fanciful parts of my mind. I might do this with reading, drawing, running, walking, observing, listening to music, cooking, etc. I find my creative self is not that particular, so long as I feed her regularly. ∽

Notes from the Underground

THE SHAKESPEARE SOCIETY fictionalized in *An Uncommon Education* is based on the actual Wellesley College Shakespeare Society, which was founded in 1877 (two years after the founding of the college itself). It's the oldest continuous society on Wellesley's campus, and was established by William Henry Durant as an honor society for Wellesley's exceptional humanities students.

As is often the case with gifted and imaginative youth, however, what an adult might identify as potential may very well backfire into rebellion. The members of the Shakespeare Society have always embraced the opportunity to study and perform Shakespeare's plays outside the constraints of the classroom, but somewhere along they way they also cultivated a genius for testing the boundaries of female propriety. In 1898, a performance of *A Midsummer Night's Dream* caused the *Chicago World News* to exclaim over the players' performance "in tights, real, genuine tights, the same wicked garments in which the naughty chorus girls do their highkicking in." Several years later, despite the fact that dressing up as men was expressly forbidden at the college, a woman appeared onstage in full drag before an audience that included the college's president. A well-planted faculty member was reputed to have leaned in and declared, "I'm so glad we got ▶

rid of that silly rule about tights, aren't you?" And so the incident blew over.

My own experiences at Shakes were perhaps born out of my latent desire to rebel. After an unexpectedly lonely first year at the college that was quite similar to the one Naomi experiences in the book, I returned as a sophomore with renewed determination to find some of that women's college solidarity I knew must exist even for shy, creative types who wouldn't major in political science or economics. When I first came across the posters advertising "teas at Shakes," I experienced a brief, heart-thumping feeling that I'd found what I was looking for even before I knew what it was.

Shakes wasn't for the faint of heart or for those miraculous Wellesley women who seemed to arrive on campus knowing who they were and where they wanted to go. It was for those of us who recognized that any realization of self was not going to come with a clear professional label or quest for financial security. Perhaps this simultaneous sense of free fall and liberty enabled us to embrace the Bard's ambiguity-rife plays with a no-holds-barred, take-no-prisoners vibrancy that we were probably expected to have devoted to our academic work.

And that, for me, was where so much of the society's magic lay. Yet this was not escapism so much as it was a rebellion, a rebellion against the overwhelming pressure to *become*, to strike our individual mallets against the gong and stake our territories in the adult world. For better or for worse, we were much better at play than planning, at wonder than at knowledge, at youthfulness than at maturity. We decorated that Anne Hathaway house with formal paintings and informal sketches of Will; ancient books and dog-eared scripts; spirit-glued beards and musty Elizabethan dresses that had been used for productions long before we were born—some even before our own mothers were born. It wasn't always a happy place, but on a campus where so many of us were constantly seeking to become, within the Shakespeare House we allowed ourselves permission to just be. ❧

My "Book Diet" While Writing *An Uncommon Education*

IT IS ACTUALLY IMPOSSIBLE for me to identify my favorite books, never mind *a* favorite book, so when people ask me, as a writer, to recommend books, I like to share my book diets with them. Because I can be porous when I read, I have to be very careful to choose appropriate selections when I am writing. My choices during the process of writing *An Uncommon Education* may not be obvious ones, but they all helped me along in one way or another. Here are just a few:

The Great Gatsby by F. Scott Fitzgerald

OK, so maybe this *is* one of my all-time favorites. When I first conceived of a novel about the Shakespeare Society at Wellesley, I did not want to write in the first person. I can imagine few things more boring or dangerous than attempting to fictionalize my own life story, and I worried that I was in danger of doing just that, given my own significant experiences on the same paths my characters travel in the novel. At the same time, however, I wanted to invoke a sense of intimacy between the reader and the narrator, and to give myself the freedom to fully explore the faults of a single individual's perceptions. My initial solution was to borrow Fitzgerald's technique of using the first person to tell another, more central, character's story (as Carraway does for Gatsby). And this is what I did for the first few months with Jun's character, until Naomi began to assert herself in that wonderful way that fictional characters occasionally do once you have lived with them for a while. All my carefully laid plans were tossed to the curb, which is always an excellent sign for me as an artist.

Lolita by Vladimir Nabokov

Really, another favorite (I'm doing a terrible job of upholding my own words!). I read Nabokov again and again for his stunning prose. It literally jolts my own writing awake, and is perfect when I'm in a slump or lacking for linguistic inspiration. I love *Lolita* in particular, though, because of the extraordinary feat Nabokov manages to pull off by allowing a truly reprehensible character to also be vulnerable and complex. One of my main goals as a writer is to encourage understanding—not at the cost of truth but in the service of it, as Nabokov so deftly does in this work. Also, Nabokov taught at Wellesley in the fifties, and he makes these juicily snarky references to female students that titillate and delight me with that squirmy feeling one gets when at the edge of one's own intellectual and creative thresholds.

The Chosen by Chaim Potok

I love the intense vulnerabiliy in this work, the family relationships, and the friendship between Danny and Reuben. Potok does an extraordinary job of

My "Book Diet" While Writing
An Uncommon Education (continued)

portraying the significance and importance of platonic friendship, an undersung source of some of the greatest love stories I know. I wanted to create such a friendship within my own novel, and I birthed Naomi and Jun's dynamic with the tennis scene that occurs just before they both arrive at Wellesley. (Those who are familiar with *The Chosen* might remember a certain baseball game that was the inspiration for this tennis match.) I also relied on Potok to be sure that I maintained an acute awareness of the kaleidoscopic display of belief and interpretation that one finds in American Judaism.

Bel Canto by Ann Patchett

I will always be indebted to Patchett for paving the way for settings in contemporary fiction that rely on strangers being thrown together in unexpected ways. I love the drama this setup creates, and the opportunity it provides a writer to unglue her characters for the benefit of everyone involved. Patchett does this most expertly in *Bel Canto*, but it's a technique she uses to great effect throughout her work.

Say Uncle: Poems by Kay Ryan

Given a certain tendency I have to go on and on and on, I rely on Ryan to bring me back to attention. Her economical, intensely vibrant poems constantly remind me of the potential of language at the most basic level: the word. She's the literary equivalent of that teacher whose scathing incisiveness demoralizes and inspires you. I always make better word choices after reading Ryan, and think about my decisions more reverently. It helps me to stop tossing words about like cheap candy and think of them as nourishment instead.

Wellesley: A History by Arlene Cohen

Cohen does a concise job of capturing the college's history in a relatively slim volume, which is also a rich source for random facts about this fascinating institution. The pictures alone are worth the price of admission. ﹏